Temptress in Training

"*Temptress in Training* ... is fast-paced, fun, and filled with a great romance."

"[The] intricate plot comes to an exciting climax."
—*RT Book Reviews*

"An exciting amateur sleuth espionage thriller ... Terrific romantic suspense as love and danger collide."
—*Genre Go Round Reviews*

"There are surprises in store for readers ... An entertaining story and one that historical romance readers will enjoy."
—*Romance Reviews Today*

Damsel in Disguise

"I loved it! ... For anyone wanting a nice, light tale that pulls you out of the everyday ... I recommend *Damsel in Disguise*."
—*Romancemama*

"Every page turns into a delight from this fantastic author who has an extremely quick wit. Not only is this book a great find for the romance readers out there who simply love historical novels, but it's also filled with the twists and turns that adventure fans crave ... [Heino] definitely has a gift, and readers will be glad that this author has chosen to share that gift with the rest of us."
—*Night Owl Reviews*

continued ...

"Passion, deception, disguises, and mayhem all combine in *Damsel in Disguise*. Susan Gee Heino has penned a story that's almost Shakespearean in its plot, with lords and actors, villains and rogues, mysteries and a heroine who cross-dresses to rescue her hero . . . I like that Ms. Heino's characters are unconventional, and her writing style definitely appealed to me."
—*Joyfully Reviewed*

"A fun comedy of errors." —*Midwest Book Review*

Mistress by Mistake

"A funny, sexy romp! Destined to become a reader favorite."
—Christine Wells, author of *Sweetest Little Sin*

"Sparkling with superbly crafted characters, humor, and deliciously sexy romance, Heino's debut . . . is splendidly entertaining." —*Booklist*

"I loved . . . *Mistress by Mistake*." —*Romancemama*

"An amusing Regency romance . . . A wonderful historical."
—*The Best Reviews*

Berkley Sensation Titles by Susan Gee Heino

MISTRESS BY MISTAKE
DAMSEL IN DISGUISE
TEMPTRESS IN TRAINING
PASSION AND PRETENSE

Passion and Pretense

SUSAN GEE HEINO

BERKLEY SENSATION, NEW YORK

THE BERKLEY PUBLISHING GROUP
Published by the Penguin Group
Penguin Group (USA) Inc.
375 Hudson Street, New York, New York 10014, USA

Penguin Group (Canada), 90 Eglinton Avenue East, Suite 700, Toronto, Ontario M4P 2Y3, Canada (a division of Pearson Penguin Canada Inc.) • Penguin Books Ltd., 80 Strand, London WC2R 0RL, England • Penguin Group Ireland, 25 St. Stephen's Green, Dublin 2, Ireland (a division of Penguin Books Ltd.) • Penguin Group (Australia), 250 Camberwell Road, Camberwell, Victoria 3124, Australia (a division of Pearson Australia Group Pty. Ltd.) • Penguin Books India Pvt. Ltd., 11 Community Centre, Panchsheel Park, New Delhi—110 017, India • Penguin Group (NZ), 67 Apollo Drive, Rosedale, Auckland 0632, New Zealand (a division of Pearson New Zealand Ltd.) • Penguin Books (South Africa) (Pty.) Ltd., 24 Sturdee Avenue, Rosebank, Johannesburg 2196, South Africa

Penguin Books Ltd., Registered Offices: 80 Strand, London WC2R 0RL, England

This is a work of fiction. Names, characters, places, and incidents either are the product of the author's imagination or are used fictitiously, and any resemblance to actual persons, living or dead, business establishments, events, or locales is entirely coincidental. The publisher does not have any control over and does not assume any responsibility for author or third-party websites or their content.

PASSION AND PRETENSE

A Berkley Sensation Book / published by arrangement with the author

PRINTING HISTORY
Berkley Sensation mass-market edition / March 2012

Copyright © 2012 by Susan Gee Heino.
Excerpt from *If I Fall* by Kate Noble copyright © 2012 by Kate Noble.
Cover art by Jim Griffin.
Cover design by George Long.
Cover hand lettering by Ron Zinn.

All rights reserved.
No part of this book may be reproduced, scanned, or distributed in any printed or electronic form without permission. Please do not participate in or encourage piracy of copyrighted materials in violation of the author's rights. Purchase only authorized editions.
For information, address: The Berkley Publishing Group,
a division of Penguin Group (USA) Inc.,
375 Hudson Street, New York, New York 10014.

ISBN: 978-0-425-24698-6

BERKLEY SENSATION®
Berkley Sensation Books are published by The Berkley Publishing Group,
a division of Penguin Group (USA) Inc.,
375 Hudson Street, New York, New York 10014.
BERKLEY SENSATION® is a registered trademark of Penguin Group (USA) Inc.
The "B" design is a trademark of Penguin Group (USA) Inc.

PRINTED IN THE UNITED STATES OF AMERICA

10 9 8 7 6 5 4 3 2 1

If you purchased this book without a cover, you should be aware that this book is stolen property. It was reported as "unsold and destroyed" to the publisher, and neither the author nor the publisher has received any payment for this "stripped book."

ALWAYS LEARNING   PEARSON

*To my sisters, Diane Gee Frasca and Ellen Gee Mangine.
You are beautiful, talented, funny, intelligent women.
But I still tell everyone you're both older than me.*

Chapter One

LONDON, ENGLAND
MAY 1820

The candlelight was lovely and Penelope knew hers was the prettiest gown in the room. She also knew this was not by any accident. Her brother spared no expense in his desperate efforts to get her married off. The only thing good about Anthony's efforts was that this gown he'd paid for was the exact shade of blue to compliment her necklace. Indeed, she did love this necklace.

She put her hand to it, enjoying the feel of the warm gold and the smooth stones set into place to form the stout body of a beetle. Not just any beetle, though. This was a scarab—an amulet fashioned by Egyptian hands many, many centuries ago. Indeed, she'd paid a pretty penny for it and no doubt Anthony would scold when he realized that's where all her pin money had gone, but she could not care. This was the finest piece of her collection.

She'd hoped whatever magic it might still contain would work to ward off the suitors her brother wished for, yet it appeared Anthony's power was far greater than even that of the sacred scarab. Suitors had been hanging on her all night. Pity none of them actually suited her.

Mercy, but it had been nearly impossible to get rid of them.

She'd managed, however. It had required she agree to stand up with Puddleston Blunk for the entire country dance, and there were fourteen couples to work through before she could finally claim exhaustion and send the lout off to procure her a lemonade. Now she was alone. If she didn't dream up a way to disappear soon, though, he'd return and she'd be stuck with Puddleston on her arm until Mamma showed up to pry him off. And Mamma would likely not do that. Mamma said Puddleston Blunk was a good catch.

Heavens, but if there was ever a time to decide on a plan it was now. She had no intention of catching someone like Mr. Blunk, by accident or on purpose. There were other things she wished to do with her life, and all she needed was Mamma's permission and a healthy pile of her brother's money. So far both of those had been elusive.

Oh, it wasn't as if she hadn't come up with a plausible scheme. Indeed she had, just this very afternoon. But it was somewhat outrageous. Risky, even. Did she dare consider it?

She glanced nervously around Lord Burlington's crowded ballroom. Nothing out of the ordinary; no one she did not know. If she did have any hope of carrying out her plan, none of the men present would fit her purposes. Her eye fell on the row of young ladies seated with their chaperones against the far wall. Those were the plain girls, the girls with poor connections or even poorer dowries.

Her quiet friend Maria Bradley was there. She looked miserable. Penelope would have given nearly anything to have joined her there on that wallflower row. Oh, if only she and Maria could trade places. How cruel Fate was to truss Penelope up in a beautiful gown and surround her with suitors when any one of these young ladies might so much rather be in her satin shoes.

Then again, it hadn't been Fate at all who'd done this to her. It had been Anthony. If he could only listen to reason! She did not wish to marry. She wished to travel to Egypt and dig for mummies. Was that so very much for a woman of three and twenty to dream of? Apparently it was, because both her brother and her mother became nearly apoplectic at the very mention of it.

Which was why she had tried to soothe them by announcing her hope to go there and meet the well-known Egyptologist, Professor Oldham. They'd exchanged several letters and she'd found him fascinating. He was mature and respectable, and she'd be in the care of some family friends who were planning a journey there. How could Anthony or Mamma possibly object to such a sensible venture?

But Mother had had to call for her salts and Anthony had declared he'd burn in hell before he allowed his sister to drag the family name through mud—well, more mud, as he put it—and go chasing off to Egypt after some fortune-hunting Lothario. As if her correspondence with Professor Oldham had ever been anything beyond intellectual! Why, she'd not even written to him using her own name. Still, Anthony ordered her to cease all communications with the man and confiscated her letter-writing paper. Honestly, was that even legal?

If Anthony would but listen to her! Couldn't he see that sending her to Egypt would only make her more responsible, more respectable? She would have a purpose, meet educated people, and fill her idle time with noble, scholarly pursuits. The longer she was forced to dance around here in London like a mindless ninny, the more desperate and unpredictable she would become. Surely no mere husband could remedy that.

If only there were some middle ground, something between wasting away in genteel uselessness and being married. Something that could take her out from under Anthony's wing, yet not shackle her to someone else. But what could that be?

She'd come up with the only plausible solution: an engagement. And she'd tried that. Four times now she'd been engaged, hoping that would buy her some leeway, that as an engaged woman she'd finally be allowed to make some of her own choices or pursue her own goals. In each case, however, she found it provided her even *less* freedom. And by now Anthony would recognize another engagement for what it was—a ruse to escape his rule. If she tried that route again, no doubt Anthony would call her bluff and drag her immediately to the altar with whatever sap she'd chosen and make it final. That would not help her at all.

Unless, of course, Anthony might not call her bluff. Ah, that was the scheme that had invaded her mind earlier and would not quite let go, despite its outrageous ridiculousness. Still, she could not help but wonder . . .

If she found a fiancé so unacceptable, so objectionable, wouldn't Anthony's brotherly concern cause him to intervene? And if he truly believed she wanted to marry such an objectionable person, wouldn't it stand to reason he might see fit to put some distance between her and the object of her misplaced affection? Perhaps given the choice between seeing his dearest sister wed to some ogre or gone off to Egypt, Anthony might just choose Egypt. She knew *she* certainly would! All it would take was careful planning on her part, and selecting just the right man to play his part.

This was where her scheme hit a snag. A big one. Where on earth would she find such a fiancé? Someone so dreadful that even Anthony would not want her to keep him, yet at the same time there would have to be something about him, something that Anthony might believe was irresistible to her. The scheme would never work if Anthony did not fully believe she honestly wanted the fellow.

So just what would this wantable yet objectionable man look like? Certainly she'd never seen anyone like that, not in the tight, dull circle Mamma and Anthony kept her in. But perhaps her sister-in-law Julia might know someone who . . .

A blustering shout interrupted her imaginings.

She couldn't quite see over the ballroom crush, but she could certainly hear some sort of racket going on at the far end of the room, near the door. Drat, if only she were just a bit taller! Finally something interesting was occurring and she could not see it.

She pressed through the crowd to get a closer look. There was, after all, no way she was going to miss ogling at what might be her only bit of excitement all Season.

Whispers and scandalized murmurs breezed through the pack around her, but she could not hear enough to get the gist of things. She could, however, begin to pick out a few words here and there from the loud male voice shouting over the hushed din. Indeed, things were getting more than interesting. She ducked under Lady Davenforth's enormous bosom and pressed past Sir Douglas MacClinty's portly abdomen. No one noticed her, so she kept on, moving slowly toward the front of the room. Mamma would surely have a fit, but Mamma hadn't seen her so far. She could gawk as blatantly as she liked.

"It just isn't seemly, sir!" the blustering male voice was saying.

"Yes, it seemed a bit unusual to me, too," another male voice said.

This was a deep voice, a voice with tone and texture that Penelope was certain she'd recognize if she ever heard it again. It was a good voice, warm and amused and certain. She could picture the man it belonged to as smiling while he spoke. She could imagine he had a glint of mischief in his eye.

She could also tell he was more than a little bit drunk.

"But for shame, sir! You had your hand on my wife's, er . . . arm!" the first voice stormed.

"No, sir," the second man corrected. "I had my hand on your wife's, er, bosom."

The crowd gasped. Someone—most likely the blustering gentleman—choked. The man with the warm, amused voice said nothing, despite all the tumult around him. Penelope decided she simply must get a look at this person.

There was a chair against the nearby wall, so she scooted herself to it and hoisted up her skirt. Surely with all the fuss these gentlemen were causing no one would so much as notice a woman with strawberry ringlets standing atop a chair, would they? Of course not. Up she went, steadying herself by grasping onto the nearby fern propped securely—she hoped—on a plaster column.

Ah, now she could see the men. She easily recognized her host, Lord Burlington, and he appeared much as he usually did: red-faced, jowly, and, well, blustering. The other man was a different story. She drew in a surprised breath.

For all his cultured tones and textured warmth, the man appeared very unlike his voice. She expected someone dashing and rakish, someone who lived by his wit and reveled in the stimulation of intelligent conversation, among other things. Someone who appreciated fine spirits and looked down his nose at lesser men. A dandy, even, who was sought after and used to being admired. That was how he had sounded, at least.

What she saw when her eyes fell upon him was something quite different.

By heavens, but the man was a hermit! He was unkempt, with dirt in his hair and whiskers on his face several days old. His clothes were a disaster. If he had been dressed for mucking a stable or plowing a field, he would have been only slightly overdone. The man was a positive horror!

And now he noticed her. She clutched the fern for support when his eyes locked onto hers. When he smiled she thought she felt the chair shift beneath her feet.

"If you'd let me explain, Burlington," he said to the blustering man, although his eyes remained fixed on Penelope. "I was trying to tell you that you have reached a hasty conclusion where your wife is concerned. I was walking into the room as she was walking out of the room and we merely collided. There was nothing more than that."

"But you were alone with her. Your hand was on her . . . Well, don't think I haven't heard of your reputation, sir."

"Yes, yes. I daresay everyone has heard of my reputation and this is hardly going to rectify that, is it? Oh well. I assure you, in this instance, at least, I am innocent."

"I ought to call you out!" the first man blustered on bravely.

"Well, I suppose I could shoot you on a field of honor if you insist, but I really would so much rather not. My head is going to be bloody ringing enough in the morning, as it is."

The crowd laughed at that, and the red-faced man went even more red-faced. He seemed to realize he was running out of practical reasons to continue his blustering, but it was obvious he wished to continue. He glanced around nervously and at last was reduced to giving his disheveled companion a frustrated sneer.

"Since my wife would be very much distressed at the thought of a duel, I shall let you go this time."

"Ah, Burlington, that's terribly kindhearted of you."

"But watch yourself, man. And do what your uncle sent you to Town for in the first place; find yourself a wife and leave everyone else's alone."

The hermit only gave half a smile at this advice. "Isn't it thoughtful of my uncle to keep all of London so well informed of my endeavors."

"If your endeavors did not breed scandal and dishonor at every turn, no one in London would give a fig for them. Watch yourself, Lord Harry, unless you really don't wish to live long enough to make use of that title your unfortunate brother will be forced to leave you one day."

"Leave my brother out of this, Burlington."

"Why? Are you ashamed of having a half-wit in the family, sir? Do you wish his compromised body would just hurry up and die so you can finally make use of that title?"

For a moment it seemed something would explode. The hermit seemed to grow larger, his shoulders tensed, and his expression was harsh and cold. Even from this distance she could see something raging behind his eyes. But then it was gone; he became calm and amused once again.

"Oh, that ruddy title," he said. "I tell you, Burlington, there are plenty of other things I'd very much rather make use of." Again, his eyes fell on Penelope, and for just a moment she felt as if she might have an inkling what the man meant—and she did not mind it.

"But I also tell you," he continued, turning back to his grumbling confronter, "your wife is not one of them."

With that, the man nodded at those around who still observed their altercation, then he gave Penelope a special nod all her own, and departed. He turned on his heel and abandoned the assembly. Penelope clenched the fern so tightly she was left with nothing more than a handful of tiny green leaves. The dratted chair was still moving. She was sure of it.

"Penelope!"

This blustering screech was her mother's. Penelope started and very nearly fell off her precarious roost. Bother. Of course Mamma would appear now and discover her this way.

"Oh, hello, Mamma," she said, as if standing on chairs in someone's decorated ballroom was perfectly normal. "I thought I saw a mouse."

"More like a rat," her mother said, glaring in the direction the hermit had gone. "You pay no attention to that man, Penelope. Harris Chesterton might be heir to the Marquis of Hepton, but he's hardly fit for polite company. And here you are gawking on a chair? Honestly, Penelope, what can you be thinking?"

Honestly? Well, she was thinking she'd just discovered the perfect fiancé.

* * *

Harris Chesterton left Lord Burlington's house empty-handed, but he couldn't help but smile. True, he'd not actually gotten what he'd come for and, yes, he'd been caught prowling about the bowels of Burlington's home when he should not have been there, and of course he'd very nearly gotten dragged into a duel with that blustering fool Burlington—not to mention what he'd had to endure with the prying Lady Burlington—but still the night had not been a total waste. He'd seen something that changed his life.

That girl, the one who stood on a chair. Ah yes, he'd seen her quite clearly. He couldn't actually recall much of what she looked like, but he'd noticed one thing about her. She was wearing the scarab.

The Scarab of Osiris. He knew it instantly, had held it in his hand and felt the smooth gold, the carefully carved insect form, the warm amber orb at its head that fairly glowed like the sun. It was a beautiful piece. And it was stolen.

He knew, because he'd been the one to steal it.

After it was originally stolen from its place in a dead pharaoh's tomb, of course. He'd been merely trying to return the thing, along with several other treasures that had been looted from their rightful place and brought here, to England, where they did not belong.

Oh, certainly, he did not begrudge the legitimate men of science and conservation who worked within the proper authority to responsibly excavate and preserve antiquities to be shared with the world. He simply had a bit of a problem with the wholesale pillaging of one nation's history to fund the luxurious tastes of a few private citizens in another. The young woman on the chair was a perfect example of that.

She was just another of these well-bred simpletons who was hungry for gold and sparkling things without ever stopping to wonder at the meaning, the history, the eternal significance of pieces like that scarab. No doubt she'd lined someone's pocket well, probably with more thought to how the lapis lazuli of the scarab's wings matched her blue eyes quite remarkably than to any concept of the hopes and dreams of its ancient creators.

Damn. Harris could do little but kick himself. What an idiot he was to fail so miserably at keeping these articles safe. And just a matter of days before he'd needed to give his reclaimed collection back to the people who asked—no, demanded—it returned.

But now that he knew where at least one piece was, perhaps he could track down the rest. Perhaps he could save these priceless treasures after all. And perhaps that would save his friend, Oldham. Indeed, far more than a friend.

First, though, he'd have to find a way to locate that woman. It wouldn't be an entirely unpleasant task, he had to admit. The scarab did bring out the blue of her eyes quite remarkably, now that he thought about it.

"WE WILL HAVE NO MORE OF THIS EGYPT NONSENSE," Anthony, Lord Rastmoor, declared, silencing his sister when she tried to protest. "It's all I can do to keep you under control here in London. I can't even imagine the havoc you might wreak traveling off to some foreign land on your own."

"But I wouldn't be alone," Penelope protested. "I would be traveling with Mr. and Mrs. Tollerson. They've been friends of the family for ages. They'd keep close watch over me."

"Mr. and Mrs. Tollerson can't even keep close watch over their own teeth. They are far too old to keep you on a leash, Penelope. You'd run all over them. Look what happened when I left you alone with mother and you nearly became prey to that loathsome Fitzgelder."

Oh, he just loved to bring that up, didn't he? And he never seemed to have the facts right about it. Totally unfair.

"That was five years ago, Anthony," she reminded. "And as you recall, I was quite in control of things where Fitzgelder was concerned."

He merely snorted at her for that. "Just as you had been with the dozens of fiancés since then, I suppose."

"Three, and I never really intended to get engaged to any of them, Anthony. The first one was a misunderstanding. The second one tricked me, and the third . . . well, I'm not entirely certain what happened there."

"It is always one disaster after another with you, isn't it?"

"But it's never my fault! Anthony, if you'd simply give me a chance—"

"No. If you want to go to Egypt, little sister, then find a husband. Let *him* take you there. Let *him* try to keep you from knocking over the Sphinx, or whatever ruddy mess you might make of the place."

He was serious, she knew. But where on earth in all this sea of London foppery and English propriety did he expect her to find a husband who might have the slightest inclination to go to Egypt? She did not run with an especially adventurous crowd. He and Mamma had seen to it the young men she met were all properly dull and impossibly proper.

Very well, then. If a husband was what it would take to get to Egypt, then a husband she was going to find. Well, a fiancé, anyway.

She would implement her plan. She'd thought to give begging and pleading one last try this morning, but since that had clearly failed, she had no other recourse. Anthony had pushed her into it.

Now, all she had to do was find that dreadful gentleman from last night. And really, the morning post had already helped her along in that. The man's uncle, Lord Nedley Chesterton, as it turned out, was hosting a ball in honor of his own birthday. She and Mamma had received an invitation. They would accept, of course.

Surely the man's nephew—the very hairy Lord Harry she had seen last night—would wish to help his uncle celebrate the occasion, even if he was a hermit. She only hoped he would not be forced to shave. True, he had seemed to be hiding rather nice features beneath that scruff, but Anthony would surely hate him more if he remained wooly.

Penelope smiled for her brother over her breakfast. "Very well, Anthony. Your word is law. I suppose there's nothing more to be said on the matter."

"There isn't."

Silly Anthony. He actually believed he was correct.

Chapter Two

Drat, but it seemed Penelope had gone to all the trouble of having a new gown made, her hair done in an especially elaborate fashion, and excessive pinching of her cheeks to give them the proper glow all for nothing. Lord Nedley's ball was well under way and there was not a sign of his hirsute nephew. What an annoyance. How was she going to get engaged to the man if he didn't bother to show up to meet her?

"Can you not for one moment look at me, Penelope?" her friend, Maria, asked as they stood against the far wall where a low dais of two steps put them in excellent position for viewing the crowd.

"No, I'm afraid I cannot," Penelope answered, quite honestly.

"Then you should either tell me who you are looking for and I can help you, or I'm afraid I would like to go sit down. The way your head keeps going back and forth like that is making me dizzy."

"Bother," Penelope said, stamping her foot and turning to look at her friend. "I am wasting my time. Clearly he's not here."

One of Maria's eyebrows rose and she smiled. "He?"

"Of course it is 'he.' I could not very well become engaged to a 'she,' could I?"

"You?" Maria said, and kept that eyebrow raised while her mouth took on a pensive quirk. "To be honest, I would not be surprised by anything you might do when it comes to getting engaged, Penelope. But seriously, you haven't found some gentleman you truly do fancy, have you? How could I not know about this?"

"Because it's quite recent." She went back to scanning the crowd again. "Botheration. I very much hoped he would be here."

"Who? For goodness' sake, you simply must tell me!"

Penelope studied her friend for a moment. Could she trust her? Of course she knew she could trust her, but should she? Was it fair to put this on Maria and expect her to go along with such an outrageous plan?

Then again, what were friends for?

"Lord Nedley's nephew, Lord Harry."

Aha, so Penelope had managed to surprise her friend, after all. Maria's mouth hung open.

"You wish to marry Harris Chesterton?!"

Penelope shushed her. She reached out and held on to her arm, too, since it appeared by Maria's sudden pallor and blank expression she might be about to fall over.

"Of course not. You know I don't wish to marry anyone just now. But I do wish to become engaged to him."

"Oh, well that's a relief," Maria said, her frown revealing that she just might be a bit facetious.

"Listen. It makes perfect sense. Anthony will think Lord Harry completely unsuitable for me, and I will profess an undying affection. So, Anthony will do his brotherly duty and ship me off somewhere to keep us apart."

"Yes, of course I see how this is an excellent plan." Maria was still frowning.

"Well, what better place to ship me than off to Egypt with the Tollersons, of course! They are leaving in just a few weeks time. Anthony has declared he will not *let* me go with them, so I intend to make him *force* me to go with them."

"And Harris Chesterton is willing to be party to such a scheme?"

"I'm sure he will once I explain it to him."

"Good heavens, Penelope! Do you even know Harris Chesterton?"

"I've seen him."

"But do you know anything about him? Haven't you heard what sort of person he is?"

"Mamma indicated he was completely unsuitable."

"Which is precisely why you will not be seeing him here, or at any other polite gathering."

"I saw him at Lady Burlington's ball last week."

Maria actually smacked her arm with her fan. "You did not!"

"Indeed I did. He was horrible, all hairy and dirty looking. And there was quite a row over him, too. It seems Lord Burlington caught the man in a rather compromising position with his wife. Burlington's wife, I mean."

"So I assumed, and it's not surprising. From what people say, Harris Chesterton is a positive rake. The worst kind, because he is so very mysterious about it."

Now Penelope felt her own eyebrows go up a bit. "Oh? Do tell."

One of the very many things she loved about Maria was that the woman was such a good listener. For some reason, most people seemed to think the poor girl rather thick and a bit slow, even. But Penelope had known Maria practically all their lives and she knew better. Maria was not slow. She was simply quiet. She did not much like to talk. True, this was something Penelope had a hard time comprehending, but she'd learned long ago that while Maria might keep her lips closed on most occasions, her ears were always open.

If anyone knew the dirty details of gossip on Lord Harry Chesterton, it would be Maria. Penelope did her very best to keep her own lips shut tight as her friend spilled what she knew. And it seemed, happily so, that Maria knew a lot.

"His uncle is the trustee for Lord Harry's older brother, the Marquis of Hepton. Hepton, sadly, is not well and has never been quite competent. It's common knowledge he will never marry or have his own heir, so we can all expect Lord Harry to inherit from him as well as their ancient grandfather, the Duke of Kingsdere."

"How fascinating," Penelope said.

And indeed, it was. Surely Anthony would believe she might be interested in such a man. Although, she hoped Anthony did not determine the man's expected inheritance was more attractive than his more obvious flaws. It would defeat her purpose if Anthony did not have enough reason to reject this man as husband material.

"His uncle despises him," Maria went on, much to Penelope's satisfaction. "The two of them have a long-standing dispute."

"Over what?"

She hoped it was something sordid. Indeed, Anthony would hate that.

"No one knows. Some say it was a woman, some say Lord Harry wishes to do away with his brother and inherit sooner."

"Ah, but that's perfect!"

Maria frowned. "What? Did you not hear what I said?"

"Oh, no . . . I meant how dreadful that he hates his brother so."

"I'm more inclined to believe it is likely some of his amorous exploits have caused the rift," Maria said. "Lord Harry is known as rather a rogue. In fact, they say his senses are so jaded that he's forced to travel all over the world to strange lands to find women sordid enough to tempt him. As Lord Harry is dependent on his brother and as Lord Nedley is trustee, I've no doubt they have frequent disagreements over the financial aspects of such a lifestyle."

Well, the bit about the man's love of travel was good. All the more reason for her to claim interest in him. Anthony would be more likely to believe it. And hate it.

Maria went on. "He's very rarely in England, and when he is, he is so debauched and degenerate that he goes about unkempt and is unfit for society with anyone aside from his equally dissipated friends. They say Lord Nedley would rather see his nephew die of his unwholesome lifestyle than to live and inherit the title."

"But I thought Lord Harry's uncle had sent him to London to find a wife?"

"Wherever did you get that idea?"

"Lord Burlington said so, and Lord Harry seemed surprised that he should know such detail. I assumed it was the case."

Maria simply shrugged. "Well, if Lord Harry married and produced an heir, that would push Lord Nedley further from the title. Still, he's probably hoping the man will take a wealthy wife. That would make sense. Everyone says it is just a matter of time before the duns will be at his door."

Hmm, well this was promising. She needed a horrible fiancé, and the most horrible man possible was out looking for a wealthy wife. A match made in heaven!

"Though who'd be desperate enough to marry someone like that, I can't imagine," Maria finished. "Hardly the perfect husband."

"Well, he's absolutely perfect for my purposes. All we need is an introduction."

"Good luck with that. I certainly don't know anyone who actually knows the man, and I doubt your brother would be much help."

"No, he and Mother seem to be content to bury me under the likes of Puddleston Blu . . ."

But her mouth could not continue to form the syllables. Across the room, a figure moved. He was tall, elegant, finely dressed, and the crowd seemed to part for him as he proceeded along. As well they should. He had an air about him of authority, and Penelope simply could not take her eyes from him.

His wealth of chestnut hair was cut fashionably long and hung about his face in a carefully carefree manner. His shoulders were broad, and his limbs were long and muscular; there was delightfully no need for padding underneath. His skin was darkened by the sun, as if he had just been scooped up from some exotic location and dropped here in the center of London. But his clothes and his bearing were every bit the gentleman. An exciting gentleman. A dangerous gentleman.

He paused where he was, and his head turned slowly, deliberately. His eyes met hers, and it was as if he'd expected to find her there. Perhaps he had. He smiled.

"Penelope?" Maria said from someplace far away beside her.

"It's him."

"Him who?"

"Him!"

"Good heavens. You mean *him*?"

Penelope nodded.

"Er, are you certain?" Maria asked.

Penelope nodded again. Dear Lord, but he was still looking at her. His eyes were so cold she felt a shiver run through her.

"He doesn't look quite so horrible as you made him sound," Maria stated.

No, he most certainly did not. He was breathtakingly not horrible. Not at all. And to think, she'd hoped the man would not shave. Good gracious, what had she been thinking?

"I'm not so sure you want to go through with this plan," Maria said.

Oh yes she did! No, wait. She needed to be reasonable. This was no awkward hermit. This was a worldly and experienced rogue. If even half the things Maria had heard about him were true, Penelope could be getting herself into very hot water by so much as contemplating having anything to do with this person.

Yet, how could she not? He was so obviously perfect in every way. Perfect for her plan, that was. He was exactly the sort of person Anthony would be desperate to keep her away from. One look at him and everyone would want to keep their sisters away from him! Egypt would not seem far enough.

"Penelope, you're not honestly thinking of . . ."

"No, certainly not," Penelope said quickly, knowing it was what she ought to say. "I see my initial estimation of him was a bit hasty."

"Indeed! Heavens, but he looks as if he could eat you alive."

Yes, didn't he, though? She never thought she'd find herself so eager to become someone's meal. And he still had his eye on her! She couldn't look away even if she had tried.

"I think we should go find your mother," Maria advised.

Penelope wasn't certain she remembered what a mother was. Oh yes. Mamma was the woman who would take one look at Lord Harry's expression and whisk Penelope home to be locked up with chains. No, if this plan was going to have any hope of succeeding, she must avoid her mother at all costs.

But Lord Harry, it seemed, decided not to cooperate. Without so much as a nod in her direction, he took his gaze from her and continued on through the crowd. Well, that was a fine way to treat his future fiancée! She had half a mind to go stalking after him.

"We should go sit down," Maria said, taking Penelope's arm and leading her off the dais toward a nearby row of chairs.

Penelope had to admit sitting might be a good idea just now. She'd suddenly realized she'd forgotten to breathe. How odd.

She followed Maria—who did not let go of her—but spared one last glance after Lord Harry. He also spared one glance her way. She caught his cold gray eyes one last time, just before he stepped out through a rear doorway. This time his smile was accompanied by an approving nod.

She had to remember to breathe again as Maria deposited her in a chair.

"That is not someone you need introduction to," Maria announced.

"No, of course you are right."

After all, it seemed as if Lord Harry saw no need for introduction, either. His gaze had been as familiar as if they'd been well acquainted for years. If he'd spoken one word to her while staring the way he had, Anthony would have gladly called the man out.

"Stay here. I see your mother, and I'm going to get us something to drink," Maria said and scurried off toward the long table at the other side of the room where liveried servants poured weak lemonade.

Yes, Penelope saw her mother, too. The woman was barely twenty feet away, chatting with some other matrons, their feathers and turbans bouncing merrily. The woman hadn't seen her daughter yet.

Penelope chewed her lip. What should she do? It would only be a moment before Maria came back or before Mamma noticed her. Lord Harry was gone from the assembly. He had not spoken to anyone, and it seemed they had no friends or acquaintances in common. It would appear she had lost any chance to gain that introduction.

Unless, of course, they truly did not need one.

HER EYES WERE EVERY BIT AS BLUE AS HE'D REMEMbered them. The rest of her was rather easy to look at, as well. And she was wearing that scarab again, as if to taunt him with it. Perhaps she was. He knew she'd been looking for him, hoping to catch a glimpse of him here at his uncle's ball.

He'd been hoping to find her, too. Certainly there was no other reason he'd bothered to show up. If he really wished to give his uncle a happy birthday, he'd have stayed away.

But he hadn't had any luck finding the girl through any other means, so he decided to try his luck here tonight. And he'd succeeded. He'd found her, and she'd found him.

He'd seen the expression on her face when she saw him. Hell, he didn't entirely expect her to recognize him, but she had. He'd seen her lips, watched her speak to her companion. *It's him.* Oh yes, she'd been looking for him, indeed.

Why, he could not be sure. Should he be flattered? Judging from her expression, she'd expected him to appear in the same condition he had last week.

Well, that had been a mistake. He'd not at all meant to be seen that night.

Tonight, however, was different. He fully expected to be seen. He was glad that not only was he seen, the seer had approved of what she saw. Indeed, she approved very much, and he rather liked that.

It would make it all that much easier to take back the scarab. He'd become rather well versed in removing jewelry—among other apparel—from ladies. Getting that little amulet back into his possession, and learning how she came by it, would be child's play. Simple and quite enjoyable.

Of course, first he had to meet the girl. He still did not know who she was, but the fact that she was here indicated she was someone. She would have good connections, at least. And that might pose a difficulty. Good connections did not often approve of him.

Usually, he enjoyed that. Let the old man suffer shame for his actions; let him cringe with embarrassment at the very mention of his name. It was nothing less than the pompous hypocrite deserved. Still, in this particular instance, it was proving a nuisance. Harris needed to find out about that woman. He needed a way to her.

Unless, of course, she would simply come to him.

Good God, but was she doing just that? He'd gone out of doors to clear his head, to avoid his uncle, and to plan his attack.

It never dawned on him the chit might be so dramatically smitten she'd actually follow him out here. Yet here she was, stealing out through the doorway, peering over her shoulder for fear of being caught. He ducked into the shadows.

She hadn't seen him, but she was clearly looking for him. She could have no other excuse for being here just now, so close on his heels. And she'd left her companion behind, he noticed. He waited and watched.

She glanced nervously around, the moonlight playing off the shimmering silk of her gown. It was the same amber color as the orb carried by the scarab she wore at her neck. That enviable beetle hung from a golden chain, resting snugly just above the creamy white mounds of taut female flesh. Harris itched to get his hands on all of it.

When at last she had crept safely away from the door to be hidden from those within, Harris made his move. He stepped up close behind her, dropping his voice low and hoping she did not start and run away.

"You are looking for someone, miss?"

She did jump a bit, but she did not bolt. She took a quick step back and turned to face him. Ah, but that scarab did look happy positioned as it was against her satin smooth skin.

"You!"

"You were looking for me?"

"Er, yes, actually I was, Mr. Chesterton. I mean . . . Lord Harry."

So, she knew who he was. Not surprising, since anyone she asked would have taken great joy in expounding on his many vices and disagreeable qualities. What was surprising was that she must have heard all this and still had come out here after him. She was taking quite a risk, being alone with him here. He could hardly wait to learn why.

"Then I am the most fortunate man in all London, Miss . . . er, Miss . . ."

"Penelope Rastmoor."

Blast it, this was Rastmoor's sister? He hadn't seen the man in years, but he'd always thought well of him from the few friendly dealings they'd had over the years. Damn, but he didn't much enjoy the idea of toying with a decent cove's sister. After all, if he'd have been fortunate enough to have a sister, he suspected he'd not play nicely with anyone fool enough to toy with her. He doubted Rastmoor would be any more charitable.

Still, the chit had come out here of her own free will . . .

"Perhaps you know my brother?" she asked.

Had his expression been so obvious? "I do."

"Well, he isn't here tonight," she announced.

And that was an invitation if he'd ever heard one. He took a step toward her.

Very well, Miss Rastmoor. You have set the course for this evening. Let us see where it takes us.

"What a striking amulet," he said, reaching for it and brushing her skin with his fingers.

It was a bold move. He was entirely too close to her; he could feel her quickened breath against his hand as he picked up the warmed scarab and bent in to study it. His face was mere inches from hers. He could see the pulse pound at her neck, feel the heated tension radiate from her. She was terrified.

Yet she did not move an inch.

"It is Egyptian," she said. Her voice was tight and it wavered. "A scarab, pushing an amber orb that represents the sun."

"You need no such amulet, Miss Rastmoor," he said, replacing the scarab and letting his fingers trail along the golden chain, over the gentle slope of her collarbone and up to the sensitive nape of her graceful neck. "Your smile itself is brighter than any sun."

She had to take a deep breath before she could answer. "You're very good with words, sir."

"I'm very good with other things as well, my dear."

"Yes, er, I see that."

But no, she did not see, because her eyes were falling shut as he buried his fingers in her tumbling curls and pulled her face toward his. He gave her ample time to pull away, but she did not. By the time his lips touched hers, he was as eager for the taste of her as she appeared to be for him. Her lips parted easily, and he found himself enjoying not the chaste, teasing kiss he had planned, but something far deeper.

He held her tightly, pressing her against him to feel every inch of her tantalizing curves. His mouth took possession of hers, her sweetness and willingness fueling a desire that was wholly unexpected. He knew, of course, kissing Miss Rastmoor would be pleasurable. He never dreamed it would be so overwhelming.

Best to cut things short, considering that his hand had just skimmed down her silky back and was now exploring the wonderful roundness of her shapely bottom. And she was allowing it.

"It would appear Miss Rastmoor is good at a few things, as well," he said, coming up for air.

She, too, was catching her breath. Her huge blue eyes blinked up at him. "Heavens, but you're even more wicked than everyone says you are!"

"Now, don't act quite so righteous, my dear." He brushed a strand of hair from her face and traced her flushed lips with his thumb. "You seem to be someone who rather likes wicked."

"But my brother doesn't," she said. "He is absolutely going to hate you."

Now he didn't much care for the sound of that. "I thought you said he wasn't here?"

"He's not, but once he finds out we've become engaged he'll boil over like a scalded pot. Oh, he'll be furious."

Harris shoved her away as if she'd suddenly become scalding herself. "Now wait one little minute here!"

"No, no, it's no reason to panic," she said, suddenly shushing him as if she expected him to stand here and discuss this with her. "I'm not trying to trap you, or anything."

"It sure as hell seems that way," he said, scanning for the quickest, darkest way out of the garden. "Damn it, woman, did you think by luring me into a few stolen kisses I'd feel compelled to drop down on my knee and offer for you?"

She stood up very straight and jabbed her pointy little chin into the air. "I don't recall luring you at all, sir. To be more accurate, you swooped down on me like a vulture."

"Oh, don't play all missish. You knew exactly what you wanted when you followed me out here. And I know for a fact you liked what you got."

She was at least honest enough not to deny it. She did, however, point out the obvious.

"As did you."

"It was a blasted kiss! That's no reason I should be expected to pay the ultimate price. You're lucky I didn't insist on more from you. Hell, if you knew anything at all about me you would know I don't give a fig for your honor, or mine either, for that matter. Haven't you heard? I'm a hopeless case; a bounder and an unscrupulous scoundrel."

"Oh yes, I've heard," she acknowledged, but still did not run for the hills. "And I've also heard your uncle has pulled the rug out from under your finances until you get a proper wife."

"And you think you'd like to apply for the job?"

"Heavens, no! It's just that I'm in somewhat the same situation, you see."

He really had no idea where this was going, but damned if he wasn't intrigued. What the hell was this minx up to?

"You need a proper wife?" he asked.

"No. I need a proper fiancé," she replied. "Or rather, a very improper one."

"Well, forgive me, Miss Rastmoor, but as I have no desire whatsoever to end up someone's husband—"

"Shut up, will you? Listen. You want your uncle to ease up on your resources, don't you?"

He carefully did not answer. Just how much did the girl truly know about his resources? She had the scarab; could she have also learned certain things about his dealings? Was she aware just how desperate he truly was for his uncle to turn loose some funds?

"My brother thinks I need a husband to keep me in line," she continued.

"If tonight represents your usual behavior, I must say I'm rather inclined to agree with him, Miss Rastmoor."

"Well, he'd never agree with you," she said curtly. "In fact, he would likely give me anything I wished rather than see me married to you. No offense, sir."

"None taken."

"Good. So you see how convenient this is for us, don't you? You need a respectable fiancée, while I need a very *dis*respectful fiancé."

"Ho there; let me see if I comprehend this. You would propose an engagement as a way of blackmailing our troublesome relatives?"

She smiled brightly, and he was positively stunned to discover he was already thinking up what he could say next that might reproduce such a thrilling effect.

"Yes! That's it exactly. You are cleverer than you look, sir."

"Thank you, I suppose."

"Now, I would probably only need about two weeks engaged to you before I could sway my brother to my wishes," she said, mentally calculating. "How long do you think it would take you to convince your uncle you are deserving of his support once again?"

Considering he was nearly thirty years old already and the man despised him more as each day went by...

"It would take a good deal more than two weeks, I'm afraid."

Now she pouted. "Really? Oh drat. You've dreadfully mucked it up with him, haven't you?"

Good God, but she was lovely when she pouted. Thank heavens she was not interested in anything more than a false engagement just now. Whatever poor sap she set her sights on for the permanent situation would have little hope of escape.

For himself, however, he had to admit her outlandish plan held some merit. It would put him in position to get to know the cheeky tart—and the circumstances surrounding that pretty little scarab—rather more intimately. Indeed, this might actually work out very well for him.

Unless, of course, her brother was not quite the slow-wit she seemed to think him. He might jump at the chance to get her married off and call for the parson tomorrow. Well, it wouldn't be the first time Harris had ignored duty and done whatever the hell he pleased. If the girl was willing to take this sort of risk, she'd have to live with the consequences when he abandoned her.

And by that time, he'd have the scarab and whatever helpful information he could pry out from her. And just maybe he'd take a few other liberties along the way, as well. It was not as if Miss Rastmoor seemed unwilling. Lord knew he wouldn't be.

Very well; he'd do it. He'd find out more about her ridiculous plan and use her for whatever he could. Indeed, an engagement to a respectable female might just garner some little trickle of favor from his damned uncle, after all.

"My uncle might have much against me, Miss Rastmoor,"

he said, moving closer to her again, "but he's always had a soft spot for beautiful women. Perhaps if he thought I was sensible enough to attach you, he might be inclined to overlook some of my past, er, iniquities."

"Really? You mean, you would consider it?"

That lock of unruly hair was back down in her face again, so he gently pushed it away. "It does seem an opportunity for both of us to benefit."

"Yes, that's exactly what I thought," she said, but he could hear the little catch in her voice.

His touch, his nearness was having an effect on her. Good. That would be useful. As long as he could make certain this effect only ran one way.

"I am taking a great risk, though," he said, trailing one finger over her earlobe.

"Er, you are?"

"Once our engagement is broken, my uncle will not be very happy. Any goodwill I've gained will possibly be lost."

"Yes, I see that."

She did have quite attractive earlobes. The glittering gems she wore there were small and tasteful, just enough to add to the sparkle of her eyes. Those eyes were sparkling more than ever as he watched the ember of desire flame to life behind them. Damn it, but he would enjoy this little game.

"You would not ask me to involve myself in this somewhat risky endeavor without some form of recompense, would you?"

"Er, what?"

"Payment, Miss Rastmoor. I'm afraid I'll have to ask for payment."

"Payment? But Anthony only gives me pin money. How much would you need?"

"Hmm, that's a good question."

He dragged his touch down along the golden chain, brushing the scarab then continuing down farther, until his fingers caught on the smooth bodice of her gown. She drew a quick breath, and for the first time it appeared she was not able to make herself meet his eyes. So she was not quite as brazen as she pretended.

"Perhaps we should see how things go before we agree to terms," he suggested.

She was hesitant in her answer. "Er, but what if I cannot afford it?"

"Rest assured, Miss Rastmoor. Before this is done, I will require payment. But I promise, it will be something you already possess. In abundance."

Obviously she was not ignorant of his meaning. He would give her credit for that; she was not stupid. But she cleared her throat, brought her gaze up to meet his, and forced a convincing smile.

"So how do we proceed, then?" she asked. "A handshake between conspirators?"

"A handshake? No, my dear, that is for honest gentlemen. Our agreement is something altogether different."

As if he would settle for a handshake when he had the tasty Miss Rastmoor close at hand. He moved quickly before she could refuse, and once again his lips took ownership of hers. He expected resistance, now that she'd accomplished her business, but found none. Instead she was as pliant and accommodating as he could have hoped for. Indeed, as he pressed his hand into the small of her back and fairly crushed her to him, she gave a slight moan that was nothing short of raw desire. The sound of it reverberated in his core, and he felt an answering passion rise up within him.

No, a handshake would never do for his dealings with Miss Rastmoor. This kiss was not nearly enough, either. But it would have to suffice for now.

He heard the voices from the doorway. Someone was coming, calling for her. They would be discovered this way if he did not gain some control over himself very, very soon.

She gave a little murmur of pain when he pushed himself away from her. Her eyes grew huge when she, too, heard the voices. He read the myriad questions that raced through her mind.

"I'll take care of everything," he said quickly.

He spared just one heartbeat to lay two fingers on her lips. She stared at him without moving, but he knew exactly what she was thinking. He could see it plainly, written in fear on her face. If they had been left undisturbed, she would have been helpless to resist him. The idea both frightened and thrilled her.

That, he knew, would be her downfall. With one last glance

for good measure, he ducked into the shadows. Oh yes, he'd require payment from Miss Rastmoor, that much was certain. The only question was, would he be satisfied with the scarab, or would he demand the lovely body it hung on, as well?

"PENELOPE? ARE YOU OUT HERE?"

It was Maria's voice. And it was louder than needed. She was calling from the doorway; Penelope knew a warning when she heard it. She tried desperately to collect her composure as Lord Harry disappeared into the darkness of the garden behind her.

Her lips still burned from his touch. Dear heavens, but the rest of her burned, as well. What on earth had that man done to her? Worse, would she be able to *undo* it quickly enough that her mother might not notice?

"Penelope!" the woman nearly shrieked, pushing past Maria in the doorway and scurrying out into the garden. "Who was that? Who was with you?"

"What? Who was what, Mamma?" Penelope asked, not having to work very hard to sound surprised and a bit confused.

"Your mother was worried when we could not find you," Maria said, trailing behind the fuming matron and scowling at Penelope. "I suppose you were weary from the crush inside and needed fresh air."

"Er, yes," Penelope said, recognizing a helpful suggestion when it came her way. "I needed some air."

"I don't see how you could get very much of it with that man draped all over you," Mamma said. "Who was he, Penelope?"

"A man? I don't know what you're talking about, Mamma."

"I saw him, Penelope. He was right here just before we came out."

Mamma turned to Maria for corroboration, but thankfully the girl simply shrugged and shook her head. "I'm sorry. I didn't see anyone, Lady Rastmoor."

Indeed, Penelope owed her friend for that.

Mamma stalked around the garden, but the place was dark and there were plantings everywhere. Lord Harry was well gone by now, thankfully. Claiming an engagement with a man was one thing; being caught making love to him in a darkened garden was quite another!

"Well, he was here," her mother said when it was clear there'd be no finding him now. "You have a lot to answer for, Penelope. Come along. I believe our evening is over."

They followed Mamma back into the glowing din of the ballroom. Penelope had to admit, she was not looking forward to whatever inquisition Mamma would have planned for her. No doubt she'd tell Anthony all about her suspicions, as well. Drat. She'd best come up with some plausible story right away.

Fortunately, she was given a slight reprieve. Their exit from the ball—and the subsequent question-filled carriage ride home—was delayed. A group of nattering matrons beset Mamma as they made their way through the room, and a boisterous Mrs. Babb-Winkle went on quite exuberantly to ask Mamma's opinion of the new hat Lady Castlethwait had been seen wearing in the park this week. Well, of course the hat had been an absolute horror, so Mamma was forced to give a few words on the topic.

"Thank you," Penelope whispered to her friend as they waited quietly for the hat conversation to exhaust itself.

Maria frowned. "I cannot believe you went out there!"

"Well, however else was I to meet him?"

"And did you?"

"I did. We had quite a pleasant, er, conversation."

"Yes, I can see by the way your hair is mussed and your gown all askew. Very pleasant conversation indeed."

Good heavens, Maria was right! Penelope hadn't noticed what a mess she was. Hoping not to draw attention, she tugged at her clothes and patted her hair. My, but what that man could accomplish in so little time . . .

"So," Maria asked through a false smile, "are you completely ruined now or just slightly tarnished?"

Penelope opened her mouth to reply, then thought better of it. In truth, she really did not know the answer to that.

"Ask me again in a day or two."

Maria rolled her eyes and uttered something that sounded rather like a prayer. How odd. She'd never known her friend to be particularly religious.

Chapter Three

Well, this would be an uncomfortable meeting. Harris stood outside the large, fashionable Mayfair home of Lord Rastmoor and wondered why his feet refused to move. Not one step. It was as if walking up to that door and announcing his presence was physically impossible for him.

The morning was pleasant, as far as London mornings went in May, yet Harris felt a distinctly cold chill in his bones. Particularly in his feet. He tried to swallow but his mouth went dry.

Good God, but he never expected an offer of marriage would be this difficult. Hell, especially considering he had no intention of actually ending up married. He hoped that chit appreciated what he was doing for her.

It had been obvious by her actions—or perhaps he meant reactions—last night that getting what he wanted—er, needed—from her would hardly take the effort of playing along with her ridiculous false engagement. However, upon reflection this morning, he'd decided to humor her. The end result would be the same, but paying this particular call today would simply make things neater. Perhaps in the end it might even serve to protect her. Somewhat.

Very well. He'd best get this over with. He'd faced sandstorms, grave robbers, curses, kidnappers, and his hateful uncle over the years. Surely one protective brother couldn't be as bad as all that.

The butler answered the door almost immediately. Perhaps the servants had taken note of him during the fifteen minutes it had cost him to dredge up the courage to knock. Damn, but this was distasteful.

"Lord Harris Chesterton here to see Lord Rastmoor," he announced.

The butler seemed unimpressed, but ushered him in. He was left cooling his heels in a rather comfortable drawing room, but not for long. Rastmoor appeared quickly, wearing a slightly confused smile.

"Chesterton," he said, extending his hand. "It's been some time, hasn't it?"

Harris took his hand. So far, so good. "Indeed. Since before your marriage, I believe. Er, congrats on that, by the way."

"Thank you. Have you breakfasted yet? Care for anything?"

"No. Thank you."

"Very well, then. What can I do for you?"

Rastmoor offered a chair, so Harris took that, as well. He probably ought to be sitting for this. They both should. It would make things harder for Rastmoor to get his hands on a weapon before Harris got back out to the front door. If things should come to that, of course. Not that he expected they should. He hadn't taken *that* many liberties with Miss Rastmoor last night, after all. Still, there was that little matter of his lack of finances and his sad reputation . . .

"Uh, Rastmoor . . . I know we haven't been much in company of late, but you know I've always considered you a decent fellow . . . my friend, even."

Rastmoor seemed to get the idea this was not a simple invitation to the races. "That's good news, Chesterton. But what brings you here today?"

"I come about . . . well . . . that is . . ."

"Yes?"

"It's about your sister, Rastmoor."

There. He'd spit it out. Now he waited for the explosion.

"Oh no," Rastmoor said, but it wasn't much of an explosion. "What did she do now? If it's cost you anything, Chesterton, I'll make remuneration, of course."

"Er, what?"

"Did she break something? Insult someone? Steal anything? Go ahead, and don't spare the details."

This was not exactly the response he'd prepared for. Harris cleared his throat. "No, er, it's nothing like that."

"Oh? Then what did she do?"

"Actually, well . . . she agreed to marry me."

Ah, now things seemed to be going a bit more predictably. Rastmoor's face went blank. Then his eyes grew large. Then his hands clenched and his knuckles went white. Then he rose to his feet. Harris reminded himself he truly had no reason to fear this man. He was quite capable of defending himself, should the need arise.

At last Rastmoor lunged at him. But instead of the blow Harris half expected to receive, the man grasped him by the hand and pulled him up into a back-slapping embrace. Indeed, this was going far better than he'd anticipated.

"By God, how did you do it, man?" Rastmoor asked when he stepped back and eyed Harris with something akin to glowing admiration.

"I beg your pardon?"

"How did you get her to agree? She did agree to the marriage part, right? This isn't just another engagement, is it?"

"Another?"

"Three of them, Chesterton! Three times I've had some poor cove come here and announce her acceptance, babbling on about his great esteem for her many virtues—and that's not even counting the disaster five years ago with our damn cousin, Fitzgelder."

Harris swallowed back the dread that was suddenly creeping over him. "Miss Rastmoor has been engaged already? Four times?"

"But you're the first one I can actually believe she might be honestly interested in. Congratulations, old boy!"

Damn, but this did not bode well. The chit routinely engaged in, well, engagements? And she'd been involved with *Fitzgelder*? For Jupiter's sake, Harris had heard about that blackguard. Not fit company for anyone, let alone for Miss Rastmoor. And that seemed to be saying a lot.

But to think, he'd been touched by a plague of guilt that his own brief connection to her might leave her damaged in society's eye. He'd put himself through this sham interview with Rastmoor purely for the sake of the girl's honor. How ridiculous, since quite clearly she'd given that up long ago. What was he getting himself into here?

Perhaps he'd best get himself out of it right away.

"I was concerned, sir," Harris said when he could come up with coherent sentences again, "that perhaps you might have qualms about my, er, history."

"Oh, I know what people say about you, Chesterton. I also know only half of the rumors about any man are ever true—and I don't really care which half that is. If Penelope has developed a fondness for you, that's good enough for me."

"But there's the matter of my finances, as well. I'm afraid I'm rather dependent on my uncle, and he's not particularly generously disposed toward me."

"No worries there. My sister's well provided for. The settlement our father left for her ought to do nicely. Besides, you can expect a healthy wedding gift from my wife and I. Anything to see my sister happy."

Damn, this was not at all going according to plan. Yes, he expected to convince Rastmoor his engagement to Penelope was real, but he thought he'd have to put forth some effort to do that. He certainly did not expect to be welcomed into the family with open arms and an open purse! Blast, but if he were not careful this man would have him married to the little schemer in a fortnight. And that was the last thing he wanted.

That open purse, however, did make for a tempting offer. He wondered just how nicely that settlement from her father would do. He'd never considered getting himself a wealthy wife as a way to solve the desperate situation he'd recently found himself in, but he couldn't say at this moment he wasn't just the slightest bit tempted.

Could it be that Penelope Rastmoor might not simply be the key to finding his missing artifacts, but she might unwittingly take a more active role in saving Professor Oldham's life along the way? It was a completely new way of thinking. He'd have to take some time to contemplate, to consider his options. Just how far would he be willing to go for the only man who'd ever treated him like, well, family?

"Right, then," he began, deciding to play cautiously for now. "I'm sure your generosity would be appreciated, Rastmoor. We both do want dear Penelope to be happy, don't we?"

Penelope and her mother looked up as Anthony returned to the breakfast room. He was smiling. That was odd. Anthony rarely smiled in the morning unless he was home at Gaberdell with Julia and the children. And he never looked directly at Penelope and smiled at her, especially when just a few minutes ago he'd been fuming over the stories Mamma was telling him of seeing her alone in the garden with a strange man last night.

"What is it?" she asked, nervous.

"Who was here to see you?" Mamma asked.

"I believe I've found your mystery gentleman, Mother," he said, still smiling.

"My what?"

"The gentleman you said you saw in the garden with Penelope, of course."

Mamma sniffed. "He was no gentleman. He was all over her! Simply dreadful. Penelope, you will not be leaving this house again. Ever!"

"Nonsense, Mother," Anthony said, helping himself to another plateful of, well, everything. "She'll be out driving today."

"Driving? I should say not," Mamma declared. "Anthony, if anyone else had seen her last night, the gossip would be unbearable. Honestly, Penelope, I can't imagine what you were thinking."

Penelope could well recall what she'd been thinking. She recalled it a little too well, actually. In truth, even last night during the drive home, subjected to Mamma's lectures and threats, she hardly thought of anything aside from Lord Harry and his too-wonderful kisses. Well, except his equally too-wonderful hands. And perhaps his strong shoulders and that mischievous gleam in his silvery gray eyes. Oh bother! Just how was she supposed to think of anything but Lord Harry if Mamma refused to drop the subject?

"I'm sure she was thinking of what a beautiful bride she'll make—finally—and how happy you will be to see her future secure—finally," Anthony said.

Penelope stopped chewing. Wait a moment... Anthony was speaking of brides and futures and he was smiling... She choked on a sausage.

"You did indeed see her with someone last night, Mother," he went on. "She was giving her consent to his marriage proposal."

Now Mamma stopped chewing. She choked on her tea. Quite a feat, to choke on tea, really.

"She was *what*?!"

"I just spoke with the gentleman and everything is arranged. He seems quite eager to make it official, as a matter of fact."

Mamma was still sputtering. "A gentleman? You mean... she actually accepted someone?"

"Indeed she did, and I have a good feeling about this one, Mother."

"And just who is this unwitting gentleman?" Mamma asked.

Penelope cringed.

"He's from an old and respected family," Anthony said, slathering jam on his bread.

"Who is he?"

"He's in line for not one but two titles someday, Mother," he went on.

"Who is he?"

"Got along well in school, I recall hearing," he said.

"Who is he?"

"Well traveled, so they say."

"You're avoiding the question, Anthony. Now who is this so-called gentleman I'm supposed to let marry my only daughter?"

"Herlish Jestershun, Mother," Anthony replied.

Penelope knew what he'd been trying to say, but his mouth was so full of strawberried bread that the sound came out a bit muddled. Oh heavens! Lord Harry had come and officially asked for her? He'd spoken with Anthony as any proper suitor would and Anthony had approved? My, but she suddenly wasn't quite sure how she felt about this.

"What was that, Anthony?" Mamma demanded.

He swallowed but ignored her question. "I'm sure you and Penelope will have a marvelous time selecting fabrics for her new wardrobe, and there will be preparations to make . . ."

"What was that name, Anthony?"

Penelope bit her lip. So Lord Harry came and talked to Anthony, just as if this were a real engagement. How very thoughtful of the man. He came to press his case with her older brother and even managed to win him over. How wonderful.

No, wait. It was not wonderful. Anthony approved it! He was ready to send her off to buy wedding clothes! He was supposed to be cautioning her, warning her that this course of action might lead to ruin. He was supposed to be against such an alliance! Oh, this was not wonderful at all. This was dreadful!

"Now I've got to be off," Anthony said, pushing his plate away and rising. "I have settlements to draw up and announcements to be making . . ."

"Oh no you don't!" Mamma said, holding up her hand to stay him. "The gentleman's name?"

Anthony swallowed and glanced toward the door, clearly wishing for escape. But then he smiled. Again.

"I think Penelope should give you the excellent news."

Ooo, the coward. She would have certainly scowled at him, but thought it best not to give Mamma any further reason to be unhappy with her just now. Perhaps it was just as well that Anthony expected Mamma to oppose the match. It showed he was not as entirely enthralled with the idea as he was purporting.

Penelope cleared her throat then replied evenly, "He is Lord Harris Chesterton, Mamma."

"What?!" Mamma burst from her chair, rattling dishes and sending tea slopping about. "That was Harris Chesterton with his hands all over you in the garden last night?!"

Now Anthony raised one eyebrow at her. "*All* over you?"

"Only the appropriate parts," she replied, feeling rather small as they loomed over her.

"There are no appropriate parts!" Mamma exclaimed. "Good heavens, but I should have known there would be trouble when I saw the way you were looking at him last week."

"Oh, so it was love at first sight, was it?" Anthony asked.

"I don't know that love could possibly have anything to do with it." Mamma sighed. "The man has barely been back in the country a fortnight after some of his wild travels, and yet you think you know him well enough to agree to marry him, Penelope?"

She thought it a bit early in the game to say something like, "Perhaps if you had let me go to Egypt I could have found someone more acceptable," although it was tempting. After all, it was the truth. Still, she ought to play along with this until Anthony was as convinced as Mamma that an engagement with Lord Harry was completely the wrong thing. Then she would lay her cards on the table. Then she would have something to bargain with.

"He seems genuinely to care for me," she said, batting her eyes and hoping they believed her. "Is it so very wrong for me to want to be loved?"

"There, she's completely happy with him and so am I," Anthony said. "Now I'm off."

And he was. Without any further question or concern over what she'd just done, he left. Mamma, however, stayed.

"This is not settled," she said. "Not by a far cry."

Well, that was good to know. To hear Anthony, one might think she'd end up married to Lord Harry in no time. At least Mamma still showed some sense about these things. Although, she could ill afford to let the woman know it.

She tucked up her lip as if she were trying not to pout. Really she was trying not to smile.

"Mamma, don't you want me to be happy?"

Mamma was used to these dramatics, so she merely rolled her eyes. "You'd best think long and hard about this, Penelope Rastmoor. You play at this marriage game as if it means nothing. But it does mean something—it means your whole life, my dear. It would be a shame to see you end up with someone despicable just for the sake of getting yourself some attention."

Penelope rose to excuse herself. Breakfast had gone on far

too long already. "Thank you, Mamma, but I assure you this means far more to me than simply getting attention."

HARRIS WISHED HE'D HAD FUNDS FOR A BETTER CARriage. Usually that thought would never enter his head; caring what others thought of him was usually the last thing he'd do. Today, however, it would have been nice to arrive for Penelope in something a bit more showy than the clattering gig he'd managed to secure. Surely she was used to the finer things. It would not take her long to realize practically every carriage in London was finer than this one.

Not that he cared what Penelope thought, either. She was merely a means to an end. Rastmoor had suggested he take her driving today, so he would take her driving today. Hell, he never expected the man to be so accommodating! It was practically too good to be true, but who was he to complain? If Rastmoor wanted to throw away his sister and his money, Harris knew exactly what to do with both of them.

She came dashing out of the house the moment he pulled up. What, was he not expected to go inside to collect her, perhaps make uncomfortable small talk with her mother or be scrutinized by the servants? Well, this was a pleasant relief. He jumped out of his seat to help her into hers.

"Anthony is out and I thought we might spare the discomfort of meeting Mamma," she said.

Her gown was yellow, as bright as a daffodil. It made the blue of her eyes even more blue. Her bonnet matched to perfection—he supposed, not really being a bonnet expert—and he flattered himself to think she had gone to some extra effort to appear particularly fetching. And she did. She appeared quite as fetching as any woman he'd come across here in London. He couldn't deny a moment of pride as he realized passersby would notice that he was the one handing her into his shabby carriage, and not some other lucky man.

"So, your mother is not overjoyed at your good news?" he asked when she was situated and he had climbed up next to her.

"She thinks I've decided hastily and . . ."

She didn't continue, so he knew of course there was more

to her mother's disapproval. Well, he could only credit that to the woman. It would be an odd mother, indeed, who might actually wish her daughter to make a match with the infamous Harris Chesterton.

"And your mother does not approve of me," he finished for her, slapping the tired horse into motion.

"No, not really."

"Well, that's good, isn't it? Doesn't that fit with your plan?"

"Yes, but I would not want you to feel . . . well, insulted, or anything."

He had to laugh at that. "Miss Rastmoor, I assure you it would take a good deal more than your mother's lack of approval to give me insult. In fact, I would be rather concerned for you both if she did approve me. I am, after all, quite the monster."

"No, you aren't," she said lightly.

He glanced at her and discovered she was serious. "Not a monster? Well, then, I am evil, at least."

"Certainly not evil!"

Hell, was the chit rethinking her initial estimation of him? That could be a bother when it was time to end this charade. He needed to put her more in mind of his true character. Just as he needed to overlook those huge blue eyes and the swell of her hearty young bosom.

"You will allow I am wicked, though, will you not?"

She laughed, and it was a sound he very much enjoyed, despite the fact it made it nearly impossible for him to overlook the dancing blue eyes or the, er, other bits.

"Yes, I will allow you are wicked." She giggled.

He eyed her. "You will allow me to *be* wicked? Or you will simply allow that I *am*?"

"According to my mother I already did allow you to be wicked last night."

Memory of how she felt in his arms ran like electricity through his body. He itched to touch her, though of course that would be folly. Rastmoor's generosity would surely disappear the moment he suspected Harris did not treat Penelope with the utmost respect. If Harris felt the urge to manhandle his new fiancée, he'd best wait until they were alone and there would be no one around to carry the tale.

"And just what exactly did you let your mother believe we did last night, Miss Rastmoor?" he asked. "I think I would have remembered it this morning if we'd done anything truly wicked." Now he smiled at her. "And I'm certain *you* would have."

Her cheeks went a lovely shade of pink. Even after four fiancés and a turn with Fitzgelder the girl could still play the innocent. And perhaps she was; he had no way of knowing. Yet.

"It's discourse like this that makes you the perfect pretend-fiancé, Lord Harry," she said. "If you speak that way around my mother, in no time she will insist Anthony sways me against you."

"I thought you expected it to take two full weeks to bend him to your will?" he asked.

Two weeks seemed adequate. Harris would do well to be in the man's favor a short while. Hell, Rastmoor's unknowing generosity might save Professor Oldham's life. And if Harris could use his pretty little companion to lead him to her source for that stolen necklace, then perhaps all this deceit might be justified in the end. Of course, it wouldn't hurt to give the girl some additional motivation to encourage her brother in his generosity, would it?

"It may be more difficult than first expected," Penelope was saying as she clutched at the side of their carriage when he intentionally guided them through a gaping hole in the roadway. "Heavens, if we hit any more of those, this poor gig will likely fall to pieces around us!"

And then perhaps Rastmoor might feel compelled to procure them a better one—which might be sold for a proper penny when all this was finally over, of course. It was going to take a good many proper pennies to rescue Oldham.

"Terribly sorry," he said. "I'm afraid I'm not made of money as your brother seems to be. If you are unhappy to be seen around town in such a sad rig as this, I don't know what's to be done about it."

"I don't mind being seen in it," she said, righting her jostled bonnet. "I would simply prefer not to be seen tumbling out of it. Pity we couldn't borrow Anthony's lovely new curricle."

"Yes, pity, but of course he has frequent need of it for himself.

But tell me, my dear, what makes your estimation of our scheme assume that things are now more difficult?" he asked.

"Well, because Anthony likes you, of course."

"He likes me?" *Excellent. For now.*

"Unimaginable, isn't it? So we'll simply have to think up ways to make him not like you."

Without disrupting the flow of funds, of course. Hmm, yes, this was becoming more difficult. Quite a dance he and Miss Rastmoor had committed to here. It was going to be exhilarating to follow it through from step to step.

"Perhaps, Miss Rastmoor, we should continue our drive through the park. I'm sure as opportunity arises we can find ways to assure that your brother might not be altogether pleased with certain aspects of my behavior."

She laughed again. "Gracious, Lord Harry. Are you suggesting I should allow you more opportunity for being wicked?"

By God, he most certainly would like to suggest that. He knew of two or three places where a couple could go to be all manner of wicked right in the middle of London. But no, that was actually not what he'd been suggesting. He would have to be far more subtle than that.

"Sorry to disappoint, my dear, but I was merely thinking perhaps we could find a family friend or Rastmoor acquaintance for me to insult or otherwise verbally injure."

"Oh yes. That would probably work," she replied.

And damned if she didn't sound disappointed.

Chapter Four

The park was full on this pleasant afternoon. Penelope was glad she'd gone to so much effort to look her best. The moment Lord Harry guided his rattle-clap gig onto the carriage drive, she knew they were the center of attention.

It was exactly the sort of attention they needed, too. Oh, but she could practically see the juicy gossip dripping from the lips of London's fashionable matrons. Men were watching with a combination of perplexed curiosity and knowing conjecture. No doubt rumor and innuendo would circulate like wildfire and soon Anthony would be hearing things he would not very much care for. He would realize what a mistake he'd made by allowing her to accept Lord Harry.

And then she could begin her campaign. She would pretend to be hopelessly infatuated. She would claim life was not worth living without her dearest Harry. Eventually she would announce that the only way to mend her broken heart would be to sail away to Egypt.

Then Anthony would pack her bags and send her off. Ah, but things were working exactly as planned. Even better, actually. She found Lord Harry's company to be quite agreeable. Considering what a horrible person he was, of course.

"Are you warm enough?" he asked, seemingly oblivious to the gazes and gawking around them.

She'd brought a light wrap but left it draped low so as not to hide the expensive lace trimming her gown. There was a slight chill to the air, but the day was remarkably clear and the sunlight warmed her. She smiled at her companion and made sure everyone knew he was expressing a very fiancé-like concern for her comfort.

"How sweet of you to worry, Lord Harry," she said, just a bit louder than needed. "I'm quite comfortable. As long as I'm with you."

Hold on, did he just roll his eyes at her? Silly man. Could he not realize their watchers would notice? When it was safe she might have to remind him what was properly expected.

"Your esteem warms me, Miss Rastmoor," he said, though since it had been accompanied by that eye roll, his words did not have the romantic effect she assumed he had intended.

Oh well, she supposed she could not expect more. Likely he was doing his best, and she should be glad for that. It did not seem his careless eye roll had let too many people in on their ruse. From the looks on the faces of passersby, they were indeed giving every impression of being a very smitten couple.

Certainly, they were not easy to overlook in this forlorn conveyance. Penelope was very nearly jostled right out of her seat as their poorly sprung wheels clattered over a series of deceptively deep ruts. Honestly, it was almost as if Lord Harry were hitting them on purpose.

Of course he wasn't, however. It was simply that she was used to traveling Rotten Row in a much finer carriage, one that did not bump and list and jar her teeth so dreadfully. How Lord Harry could sit there so seemingly proud and confident when she knew they must look quite ridiculous in this dilapidated rig, she had no idea. She rather was impressed by his demeanor in the face of such indignity, as a matter of fact.

She would see to it that Anthony found them something a little bit better to travel in. It just would not do to be seen about like this day after day, and she did intend to be out and about with Lord Harry as frequently as possible. What better way to assure Anthony's feeling that he must do something drastic to separate them?

Of course, it seemed nearly everyone was in the park today to see them in this pitiful carriage. What would they think if tomorrow they showed up in something shiny and new? Hmm, what would they think, indeed? Perhaps Lord Harry would be branded a fortune hunter! My, but wouldn't that simply be wonderful. Anthony would hate it.

"What are you smiling about?" Lord Harry asked, giving Penelope a sideways glance.

"What? Oh, I was just thinking that we will very likely be the talk of the town after simply driving through the park."

"You do seem to love attention, don't you?"

"Why do you say that?" It was as if he'd been talking to Mamma.

"Because you carry yourself so well. People cannot help but pay attention to you, and you, my dear, give every impression of enjoying it."

"When it is attention that suits my purposes, yes, I suppose I do enjoy it."

"Heaven pity the thing that doesn't suit your purposes, Miss Rastmoor."

She supposed she could have been offended at his words, since they did seem to imply he thought her just a bit self-centered, but he was smiling good-naturedly so she decided he'd meant nothing by it. He had a good laugh. It was confident and free and just loud enough to secure a few glances from the one or two people who had not already taken note of them. Penelope laughed along with him.

Ah, but then she noticed a gleaming barouche coming their way. The hood was folded down, and she had no doubt who was inside. Her laughter faded and she felt her muscles go tense. Drat, but she was not quite ready for this meeting.

Lord Harry seemed to notice. "Who is that?" he asked.

"Lady Whorton."

"That tells me little."

"She is the mother of my most recent fiancé."

"Ah. The ancestor of my predecessor."

Penelope slid a glance at him and frowned. "Don't ancestors have to be dead?"

"Is that what you wish for Lady Whorton?"

Hmm, tempting thought. And Lord Harry seemed the sort

of person who might possibly be able to make such a thing happen. But no, she was not quite as desperate as that. She shook her head.

"No, but I would very happily settle for blind right at this moment."

"What? And miss such an excellent opportunity? I'm disappointed in you, Miss Rastmoor."

She struggled to relax her tense body and melt the ice from her artificial smile. If Lady Whorton was going to see her with Lord Harry, she was not going to see her looking nervous and self-conscious. By heavens, if anyone would be disappointed in her today, it would be Lady Whorton. Not Lord Harry.

"Of course you're right, sir," she said, feeling brighter already. "It is a lovely day and I am having a most wonderful time."

"Of course you are. After all, you are with me."

Oh, but the man's vanity was delightful. She couldn't help but laugh in earnest. How many people wasted so many hours in false modesty and such outrageous self-deprecation that the hearer was forced to dole out endlessly contrived flattery and exhausting encouragements? Certainly Lord Harry needed none of that. He did not demand her praise, nor, she suspected, would he much value it should she volunteer. It was quite refreshing, as a matter of fact.

The barouche was drawing nearer, and she could see it the moment Lady Whorton's eye caught on them. First there was that familiar look of scorn when the lady recognized Penelope, then there was an expression of sheer delight as the woman took note of their pitiful carriage, and then came the final stage. The woman's face contorted in a wave of horror at seeing Lord Harry.

Odd. Penelope would have expected her connection to someone the likes of Lord Harry to provide limitless amusement for Lady Whorton. It seemed, however, that it took the matron several heartbeats before the realization of what she was seeing—what Penelope's proximity to Lord Harry—must mean. Finally the facial contortions softened and her lips tipped into a sly, evil smirk. Ah, now this was the Lady Whorton Penelope had come to know.

"Why look, Amelda," the lady chirped loudly to the woman seated next to her. "I do believe it's Miss Rastmoor."

Penelope smiled sweetly and tucked her fingers into the crook of Lord Harry's arm. He didn't bat an eye and simply smiled, touching his hat in deference to the ladies in the approaching carriage. The barouche slowed at the matron's command.

"Lovely day, isn't it, Miss Rastmoor?" Lady Whorton called.

Penelope smiled as if greeting her own dear grandmother. "Oh, indeed it is, my Lady Whorton." In her mind she adjusted the spelling to *Wart-on*. Just for the fun of it.

Lord Harry slowed their carriage, and now both sets of passengers were stuck having to make conversation. Penelope decided she was up to the task and snuggled yet closer to Lord Harry. He still smiled.

"I wonder that your brother should allow you to go driving alone with no one but a household footman?" Lady Whorton said after a slightly uncomfortable pause.

Ah, so she was ready to get right into it, was she? Most excellent.

"Such a pity that your eyes must be failing in your advanced years, my lady," Penelope said as if syrup veritably dripped from her words. "You must not recognize Lord Harris Chesterton. You know, heir to the Marquis of Hepton?"

The lady noticeably sneered at Penelope's remark but pretended to suddenly recognize Lord Harry.

"Why yes, so it is Lord Harry. I could hardly recognize you, sir, driving such a . . . cart."

"And I almost did not recognize you, Lady Whorton, in your lovely barouche," Lord Harry said in his rich, cultured tones. He very nearly brought Penelope to giggles when he added, "I should have rather expected to find you pulling it. I hope this does not mean you've come up lame?"

Lady Whorton glared at him as if he were something rather foul. "I should have expected Miss Rastmoor to end up associating with the likes of you, Chesterton. We all know the sort of woman you prefer."

"Oh, you mean the sort who doesn't hurl insults at me on the street?" he asked.

"I mean the sort who would hurl herself into your bed, Lord Harry," Lady Whorton said.

It was brazen enough that even Penelope was shocked. Indeed, she knew the woman still held a grudge over the way Penelope had jilted her son, but to speak this way about her on a public road was entirely beyond the pale. What must Lord Harry think!

A quick glance his way did not indicate that he thought very much. He was, however, not smiling nearly so broadly as he had been. And his hand reached up to pat hers where it still rested on his arm.

"I'm going to assume you did not mean to give offense by that, Lady Whorton," he said, and all trace of warmth was now gone from his voice. "And as it is my fervent hope Miss Rastmoor will indeed be hurling herself into my bed very soon, my fiancée and I will simply thank you for wishing us happy."

Now Lady Whorton appeared to be shocked. "Fiancée? You cannot mean you are to be wed!"

"Indeed, that's exactly what I mean," Lord Harry said. "Don't we make a beautiful couple?"

Lady Whorton exchanged appalled glances with her companion. Penelope had no doubt the news of their engagement—with a somewhat embellished depiction of the unpleasantries passed between their carriages here today—would soon be spread like wildfire throughout society. It was better than a newspaper, even though she could still feel her face burn from the lady's bold insults.

"Well, I don't know about a beautiful couple," Lady Whorton said with a disdaining sniff. "But I will say the two of you certainly deserve one another."

Lord Harry still kept his hand on hers. "Thank you. We do get along famously."

With that he nodded politely at the ladies and touched the reins, setting his horse into motion again. The carriage rattled and lurched. Penelope held on to his arm, partly to keep from spilling out onto the ground, and partly because she was suddenly dizzy.

What had they done? They'd both publicly insulted Lady Whorton, right here in Hyde Park in the fashionable hour! Heavens, if she was not already damaged in the eyes of society by her silly engagements and her erratic behaviors, she certainly would be damaged now. By this time tomorrow there was no telling what London would think of her.

After all, Lord Harry had claimed he fervently hoped she'd be hurling herself into his bed! Oh, but this was quite dreadful. There was no way Lady Whorton wouldn't delight in telling everyone all about it. Tongues would be wagging! Then again, this was what they wanted, wasn't it?

"What a charming mother-in-law you almost had, Miss Rastmoor," Lord Harry said when they were at a safe distance. "I hope your intended took a bit more after his father."

"He didn't."

"Ugh."

"Yes, that's what I thought. That's why I had to tell him I could not marry him."

"But whatever convinced you to accept him in the first place?"

She had to think about that for a moment. "Er, I don't believe I did."

"No? Then how on earth did you become engaged to the man?"

"Well, I was engaged to someone else and when that ended . . ."

"By your choice or his?"

"Mine, of course."

"Of course."

"When that ended, Buttleigh just seemed to appear at my side everywhere I went."

Lord Harry turned to her. "Buttleigh?"

"Yes. Buttleigh Whorton."

"Good God."

She couldn't help but laugh. "Oh, and you have room to talk, Harry Chesterton?"

"Harris. My name is Harris."

"And everyone calls you Harry. Chesterton."

He could hardly fault her for giggling, so she giggled.

"Very well," he said. "I will allow that a man's name is hardly his sole measure. Apparently this Buttleigh had some redeeming qualities for you to consider marrying him."

"But I didn't. He was there, and the next thing I knew his

mother was announcing our engagement. I put up with it since it seemed to make my own mother fairly happy and it was nice to attend balls and the like without constantly fending off suitors, but of course eventually I had to break it off."

"Break his heart, you mean."

"I did no such thing! Less than one week after I'd thrown him over, Buttleigh ran off and married the daughter of the local butcher from the town where he grew up."

"What? He lost you so he ran off with the butcher's daughter instead? That's a bit unexpected."

"No, not really. He talked incessantly of the girl right from the start, but of course his mother would never allow that match. It would seem being engaged to me showed him it was better to follow his heart than follow his mother."

"That's not quite something you should be bragging over, I think."

"I don't care if it makes me seem an inferior fiancée. I'm happy that Buttleigh is happy. Although, I'm sure he'd be more happy if his parents hadn't gotten furious and cut him off completely, but that can hardly be called my fault."

Lord Harry shook his head. "You realize, of course, little Buttleigh's mother is going to take great pleasure in vivisecting your reputation after our conversation today."

"Of course. That's what we want, isn't it?"

"Is it?"

"She'll say terrible things, Anthony will hear them, and he'll begin to realize just how dangerous you truly are. He'll drive you away and give in to my demands in no time!"

"Really. As quick as all that?"

"I would certainly expect so."

"Because I am so very dangerous?"

"I thought we had already established that?"

"No, I believe we determined I was entirely wicked."

"Oh, that's true. Well then, you are wicked *and* dangerous."

"I see."

"Surely it cannot come as a surprise to you, Lord Harry!"

"No, but what does surprise me is the fact that you can be so convinced of my depravity, yet here you sit, Miss Rastmoor, quite conspicuously alone and helpless with such a wicked, dangerous man."

Lord Harry slowed the carriage again, and now he was leaning toward her. His tone was light, but the fire in his eyes was anything but that. She glanced around them, suddenly seeking security in the sight of so many passersby swarming around, parading on horseback or in carriages, all desperate to be seen in all their finery on this lovely London day. They all seemed very far away, though, compared to Lord Harry's heat-inducing nearness.

"I am hardly alone, sir," she said and was appalled when she noted a slight tremor in her own voice.

He smiled. "Oh? As far as I'm concerned, Miss Rastmoor, you are very much alone just now."

Suddenly she realized this was true. She was alone. Anthony was not here, her mother was not here, not even Maria was nearby to let out a squeal should anything untoward happen. From the way Lord Harry was looking at her, eyeing her as a hungry dog might eye the butcher's shop, she felt very much alone, indeed. And Mamma had warned her what happened to ladies who end up alone with disreputable gentlemen.

"Er, shouldn't we be moving along, Lord Harry?" she asked, and there was that dratted tremor again.

"Indeed we are, Miss Rastmoor," he said, leaning in even closer. "I think we are moving along quite nicely."

With that he brought his hand up to touch her face. Drat it all, but she felt her eyelids droop. Was he going to kiss her again? Of course she hoped not. It would be terribly improper. And she really would not like him to get the wrong idea about her. Despite what she'd done in his company thus far, she did have a very high moral code. Kissing here on the street would be very, very wrong.

Still, he smelled so fresh and so manly and his hand was impossibly warm, his worn glove soft against her skin . . .

She nearly melted right there into the cracked leather of the seat as his arms encircled her. He brought her close, and it felt like eternity before his lips finally contacted hers. She couldn't help but sigh in relief. His kiss was gentle, but secure. He was not some tentative boy, fearful she might cry out in horror or run to her mamma. Lord Harry kissed like a full-grown man.

Like a man who knew what he was about. She did not have to pretend to enjoy it as she had when any of her past suitors had stolen a kiss. No, Lord Harry's kiss was like heaven itself. She simply gave in to the sensation and let his lips explore hers, his tongue playing a game she'd long imagined yet still could not name. She held on to him for fear he might pull away long before she had what she needed from him.

Whatever on earth that might be.

He was pressing her into the hard seat, his body solid against hers, and so delightfully masculine. His hands moved over her, and she felt as if sparks of energy emanated from his touch. She wanted more of him, deepening the kiss and arching her body to give those roaming hands better access to places to roam.

He didn't roam far enough, though. Long before she was ready, he pushed himself away from her and smiled.

"I think that should give our audience more than enough to whisper about today, don't you think?"

For half a heartbeat she was confused by his words, then the meaning sank in. Ah yes, their kiss was merely a performance. Of course she knew that. He'd simply been playing his part, posing as the infatuated suitor. Surely that was all she had been doing, as well.

She cleared her throat and sat primly upright, adjusting her clothes. "Yes. Yes, that should do nicely."

Drat. She sounded as if half her voice had been gobbled up by that kiss and all she had left was a weak, breathy whisper.

Lord Harry had the nerve to actually laugh at her, taking up the reins again and slapping the horse into motion. He seemed to have already forgotten what his hands had been doing just seconds ago. She wished to heaven that did not annoy her so.

They rode the rest of the way in silence, nodding to the few people who stared at them with something less than animosity, ignoring the rest, but arriving back at home without further incident. Penelope felt her blood had finally stopped pounding in her veins, but one quick glance at Lord Harry as he pulled the brake and hopped out to run around and assist her set it to pounding again. She was quite frustrated with herself, affected so much by one simple kiss.

Then again, it had not been one simple kiss. It had been three simple kisses, and none of them had actually been simple. They had all set her off-balance.

Well, after such a public display, there would hardly be need for any additional kisses. Indeed, she should definitely avoid them if at all possible. It seemed kissing Lord Harry was quite unsettling to her system. She would have to recall that in the future, should the man feel the urge to ever attempt such a thing again, which she had no reason to believe he might. After all, he was simply playing a part. His kisses were hardly meant for anything more than that.

Which, of course, unsettled her even more than the actual kiss.

HARRIS WATCHED AS PENELOPE DASHED UP THE STEPS and into her home. He tried not to admire her figure, the light fabric of her gown swishing temptingly around it as she moved, but it was impossible. Penelope Rastmoor was more than just an attractive female. She was inspiring.

And damned if that kiss they'd shared in the park hadn't been just a tad bit *too* inspiring for him. He'd very nearly gotten carried away. He'd almost forgotten what this was all about.

It was about obligation—his obligation. He needed to get his mind back to business and concentrate on finding those artifacts. It was not simply a matter of choice; it was life and death. For someone quite dear to him. Miss Rastmoor was not simply a delicious tart he could toy with for his own entertainment; she was his means to salvation.

Or rather, Professor Charles Harris Oldham's salvation. It would not do to forget that. Even when his body told him it would very much like to.

Leaving Miss Rastmoor behind her closed door, Harris climbed back into his shabby carriage and guided the horse from one fashionable street to the next. He'd not done anything to secure the scarab or any information on how it was obtained, but he decided the afternoon did not need to be an entire waste. He would drive past Lord Burlington's house and determine if there might be yet another way into it.

He knew the man kept antiquities; he had reason to believe not all of them were gotten legitimately. He'd spent the better half of an hour scouring the man's cellar and storeroom last week, only to be discovered by Lady Burlington and forced to play the part of a drunken—and randy—sot to give excuse to his curious wanderings in another man's house. Unfortunately for him, the lady had been rather taken by his performance and had demanded performance of another kind. Harris had been only too happy when her husband interrupted and threatened murder.

Still, though, he knew Burlington was connected to the stolen artifacts. There must be a way to find them, to get into that house and see for himself just how many the man had collected and how difficult it would be to get his hands on them. Again. Time was running out.

He slowed his horse to get a good look at the house, larger than most around it. It had likely been built before the others on this street and was once even grander than it appeared today. As it was, Harris would have quite a job searching the place. It would be far easier if he had someone who knew the house, someone who could give him an idea where to look for things. But how was he to do that? Certainly he was no friend to Lord Burlington or any of his cronies.

Ah, but an opportunity presented itself just as Harris was about to give up for the day. He smiled. A young woman—a servant, from the looks of her—left the house by a discreet door set off to the side and clearly meant for only the unimportant to use. She was small and trim and glanced up at him with the appreciation he often saw in women's eyes when they took note of him. Until they realized who he was, of course.

But this servant girl simply blushed at the nod he gave her and let her smile grow even more appreciative. She did not mind that the notorious Lord Harry was staring at her. Ah, but this was most excellent. He believed he had just found his entrée to Burlington's home.

It did cross his mind, however, that his new fiancée might not at all approve.

Chapter Five

It was a bit dreary outside. Not the best day for going out shopping with Maria, but Penelope wasn't about to complain. Everything was working out splendidly for her, even if she did have to dodge a puddle or two.

The gossips had been merciless. Indeed, from what she'd heard about herself already today, she and Lord Harry had acted as absolute heathens in the park yesterday. They'd been accused of everything from threatening Lady Whorton's very life to stripping themselves naked and cavorting in the Serpentine. Really, she ought to be very upset about it, but the more she thought on it, the more she could merely smile.

Anthony would be livid. This gossip was all she could have hoped for, and more. Once it reached her brother, he'd explode with anger and decide drastic measures must be taken at once.

She could practically feel the Egyptian sand between her toes. Ah, but making Lord Harry her fiancé had been nothing short of genius. In fact, she rather hoped she might bump into him today as she and Maria strolled along, pausing before shops and admiring a bonnet here or an assortment of fans there.

"I had quite a difficult time convincing her, as a matter of fact," Maria was saying, although Penelope had to admit she hadn't been paying close attention and really had no idea who Maria was talking about.

Her mind kept wandering back to her time with Lord Harry and that scandalous kiss he'd given her. Oh, but that was a stroke of genius, too. She hoped the heat that was rising to her cheeks at the memory of it did not show. Aiming for distraction, she studied a rather tidy pair of gloves and wondered if they would go with the new gown she was having made. It was not quite enough of a distraction to get her mind back on the conversation at hand, but she nodded and made sounds of encouragement for Maria to continue.

"Aunt Clara is certain that you are quite the fallen woman and I will come to no good if I continue to devote my time to you," Maria said. "She was quite against my accompanying you today."

This managed to catch Penelope's attention. "What? Your aunt did not wish you to come out with me today?"

"Can you truly blame her, with everything people are saying about you and Lord Harry?"

"Surely you know rumor is only ever half true."

"Indeed, but even at that you would still be guilty of quite a bit, Penelope. Truly, aren't you the least bit concerned?"

"Of course not. I told you, Lord Harry understands completely that this is merely a sham."

"It doesn't sound as if he understands that at all, taking such liberties with you as he has."

"We have to be convincing, Maria. Anthony simply must believe Lord Harry is a bad influence on me, but at the same time he must also believe I truly wish to marry him. It's all there is to it if he is to believe there's no recourse but to send me away."

"It would seem you are leaving him no recourse but to rush you to the altar. Honestly, Penelope, did you really let that man kiss you in public, in full view of everyone?"

"I did."

Maria shook her head. "Well, I suppose I must give you high marks for bravery. Still, some of the bravest souls are the ones who perished for their cause."

"And now you are being dramatic. I promise, I have no desire to perish for my cause."

"It's not exactly your desire I worry about," Maria said with a sigh. "I'm worried your new friend might be approaching this arrangement more for his own benefit than for yours."

"Of course he'll benefit. He's building goodwill with his uncle."

"That isn't the sort of benefit I was referencing, and you know it. Besides, how on earth can his stuffy old uncle feel any goodwill toward him if all he hears is how shamefully the two of you have been behaving? Is it true your so-called fiancé referred to Lady Whorton as, er, a cow?"

"Certainly not! He inferred the woman is a draft horse. That is something entirely different."

Maria cringed. "Oh, Penelope. I cannot see how this will possibly turn out for good."

"That is because you have no vision. If you would simply trust that Lord Harry is . . ."

She didn't finish her statement. For one reason, she realized she simply did not know enough of Lord Harry's good qualities to adequately defend him. Considering Maria's position on the matter, Penelope doubted a recounting of the man's skill at doling out insults or using his tongue for other more pleasurable pursuits would do much to win him any favor.

Secondly, she could not finish her statement because she realized the two of them were no longer alone at the shop window where they had paused. A tall, elegantly dressed gentleman with an exquisite woman on his arm was approaching them. Noticing the way his gaze digested Penelope's person and the too-friendly smirk on his face, it seemed safe to assume he was not here to gawk at silk-covered fans.

She had no idea at all who this gentleman was, but she did immediately recognize the woman. An actress. She recognized her from the theater. She'd heard a few things about her, too.

It was shocking enough that these persons were blatantly staring at her this way, but then the man had the audacity to speak.

"But I do believe this is Miss Rastmoor. Good day to you, miss. My warmest wishes on your upcoming nuptials," the man said.

Penelope frowned at him. His tone was warm enough, but she could not at all condone him approaching her this way and speaking to her as if they were, in fact, acquainted. They were not. Nor did she wish to be.

"I'm sorry, sir," she said, making her voice just as cold as she possibly could. "I'm afraid we've not been introduced. Should I know you?"

She decided the sound he made could very well be called sniggering.

"You should," he said. "But since I truly doubt Harris has wasted much of his time with you talking about me, I suppose I'll have to simply introduce myself. I am Ferrel Chesterton, cousin to your dearest intended."

His cousin, was he? No, Lord Harry had not mentioned him. Not that he would have had any reason. Since they were not truly to be married, it was rather unnecessary to discuss each other's connections. And this particular connection, at least, did not appear at all to be the sort of person she'd like to discuss, let alone become acquainted with.

Maria seemed to feel the same way. Already concerned over Penelope's proximity to scandal, the arrival of this gentleman caused her to blush noticeably. The way the man's gaze shifted from Penelope to Maria, it seemed he was looking for an introduction there, as well. She did not give him one.

So, he proceeded to announce his companion. "And this is the lovely Mrs. Gladding," he said, presenting the woman as if it were the most proper thing to do.

The woman actually held out her hand to Penelope. Well, this was beyond the pale. Was she honestly expected to take it? To be seen here on the street greeting a married actress who was strolling about with a gentleman who was clearly not *Mr.* Gladding? Good heavens, but this would create even more gossip than her carriage ride with Lord Harry.

She glanced quickly at Maria, but the poor girl seemed too shocked by all of it to even so much as look in her direction. Indeed, Maria appeared rather ill. Oh bother, that was all she needed just now; to have her friend toss up lunch all over Mrs. Gladding's fine footwear.

Hoping to at least distract from that, should it happen, she reluctantly took the actress's hand and smiled at her. "How unexpected to meet you, Mrs. Gladding. I've seen you on stage."

The woman actually appeared flattered. "Thank you, Miss

Rastmoor. And please do give my regards to your sister-in-law. She and I worked together on occasion several years ago."

Penelope nodded. Indeed, if Mrs. Gladding had worked with Julia it must have been quite some time past. Julia left the stage five years ago when she and Anthony married. Still, though her own brother had seen fit to marry an actress, surely Anthony could not approve of Penelope being introduced to one on a street corner. And since this awkward encounter was directly a result of her connection to Lord Harry, it stood to reason this might be yet another reason for Anthony to send her off to Egypt. Perhaps befriending an uncouth gentleman and his actress friend would not be such a bad thing, after all.

"I was quite surprised to hear my cousin had at last found himself a worthy bride," Mr. Chesterton said. "But upon meeting you, I see I should not have been surprised at all. How could Harris possibly *not* become slave to such beauty?"

Ugh, and how could she possibly *not* become nauseated by such obvious flattery? Indeed, Mr. Chesterton—though he was certainly handsome enough—was not very much to her liking. He was far too friendly, and far too eager to gawk at Maria, who seemed even less impressed with the gentleman than she was. Lord Harry's relatives certainly had much to be desired if this man's manners were any indication of the rest of the clan.

"I would like to think Lord Harry is very much a willing participant and not some sort of slave to anything, sir," Penelope said sharply.

"Oh, I'm certain willingness is the least of his troubles, Miss Rastmoor. I can't wait to see him again and congratulate his good fortune. I know all too well how difficult it is to secure a good wife."

"Unless, of course, you don't mind securing someone else's," Penelope said, smiling sweetly at Mrs. Gladding.

Mr. Chesterton frowned, but then Mrs. Gladding laughed.

"Mr. Chesterton is most kind to help me with an errand for Mr. Gladding," the woman said with far too much sparkle for it to be believable. "I have had a new coat made for him as a surprise, and as Mr. Gladding is very nearly identical in size to Mr. Chesterton, I've prevailed upon Mr. Chesterton to come for a fitting."

Oh certainly. As if anyone could believe that silly tale.

But Mr. Chesterton seemed to think they likely would. He nodded his head briskly.

"That is indeed what I am here for today," he chirped. "The Gladdings have been friends of mine for years. Naturally I'm only too eager to help with this surprise."

"Of course you are," Penelope said with just as much sparkle as Mrs. Gladding. "How very kind of you. Don't you think, Maria? Isn't Mr. Chesterton the very picture of kindness?"

"It would seem so," Maria said. Her expression would seem to indicate she felt exactly the opposite.

Before Penelope had opportunity to find out any more about this Mr. Chesterton and his married companion, they were interrupted again. This time by Maria's own Aunt Clara. Aunt Clara appeared even less happy to see Mr. Chesterton than Penelope had been.

"Maria! Come away right now!" the woman said, appearing at their side with her maid bearing a healthy assortment of parcels.

Maria complied instantly and Penelope did, too. For some reason this seemed to surprise Aunt Clara.

"Oh. Well, Miss Rastmoor, I suppose as we did bring you here, we ought to convey you home. Hurry along, please."

Aunt Clara did not give one minute's hesitation but turned on her heel and marched toward their waiting carriage. Maria and the maid scurried after her. Penelope could only nod weakly toward their new acquaintances, then bustle after her companions. It was a most uncomfortable meeting that ended with an even more uncomfortable exit.

Penelope followed Maria up into the carriage, and little was said between the ladies. Aunt Clara stared fixedly beyond them, and Maria stared at her hands folded in her lap. So much for pleasant conversation. Penelope stared out the window and wondered just what exactly had happened in the space between her engagement yesterday and this unhappy moment. Had her scandalous day in the park truly been enough even to offend her closest friends?

And why on earth should Mr. Chesterton think he had any right to approach her that way on the street? With a known actress by his side, of all things? Granted, Penelope had actors in her own family thanks to Anthony, but that was different.

Certainly when Penelope saw Lord Harry again she would tell him exactly what she thought of his overly forward cousin. That is, if she were to actually see Lord Harry again. It dawned on her he had said nothing of it, made no arrangements for meeting her anywhere or taking her driving again. Perhaps their little jaunt yesterday had been all he felt was needed to establish the situation. Heavens, but she supposed he could very well think just such a thing.

He'd done more than his part to make them appear a couple. He'd smiled, laughed, and doted on her as a real suitor. Also, he'd done more than his part to make himself appear horrid, just as they planned. He'd driven an embarrassingly shabby cart, he'd insulted one of society's prime matrons, and . . . well, he'd kissed her before God and all the world.

He'd kissed her nearly senseless, as a matter of fact. And she'd let him. Yes indeed, she could certainly see that he might feel he had done enough. Certainly society seemed to agree.

Perhaps Penelope had gone just a bit too far, after all. In her efforts to manipulate Anthony, she'd forgotten to worry for the rest of the world. Clearly society's attitude toward her was going to be altered by all this. Drat. Now she would have to concoct a solution for that, as well. It was most exhausting to have to be in charge of so very many schemes.

Perhaps Lord Harry could help her decide what needed to be done. Yes, he was quite clever. He would know how to advise. She certainly did not wish to jeopardize Anthony's poor impression of him, but certainly Lord Harry could think of some way to make their betrothal just a bit more acceptable to the rest of the town. She would ask him the next time she . . .

Oh. But that was right—she had no idea when there would be a next time. That thought was less than pleasant, in fact. Drat it all.

She stared out the window and thought the day suddenly even more dismal than it had been. Clearly Maria was upset, Aunt Clara was fuming, and now Penelope had become someone whom strange men and disreputable women thought they could glibly approach on a public street. Worse, she realized she was quite distraught at the possibility of never seeing Lord Harry again. Indeed, this was turning out to be a most disagreeable day for her.

And it got worse. As they passed by, her eye fell on a familiar cart waiting at the side of the street. For one split second her mood lightened and she scanned the nearby walkway for Lord Harry. Any lightness went away the moment she found him.

He was there, indeed, quite near his pitiful cart, looking just as dashing and enticing as he had yesterday. But she appeared not to be the only one who noticed this about him. Lord Harry, she noted, was not alone.

A young woman was there; a small, curvy, giggling creature who had her hand on his arm and flashed doe eyes at him as he led her toward his cart. Oh, but it was disgusting the way he smiled at her and fawned over her so. She'd been carrying a large parcel, but he took it from her and added it to the one he already carried under his arm. Indeed, it appeared he'd been rather generous in his purchases for the girl.

Well, that was odd, considering he'd told her his uncle left him with rather empty pockets. How nice that he'd managed to scrape together a few pennies for this dear girl. Oh, but Penelope could have nearly flown right out of Maria's aunt's carriage to wipe the smile off the young woman's sweet face and remind Lord Harry that he had a fiancée now and could no longer dash about with giggling women on his arm. Nor was he to buy them things, even if they were things from Mr. Tilly's Grand Notions, where she and Maria had spent a good five minutes laughing earlier at the most hideous shawl ever.

No, a man with a perfectly good fiancée like Penelope should certainly not do that. Except that Penelope was not really his fiancée. Drat, but it had never dawned on Penelope that Lord Harry might indeed already have some particular lady friend he would not wish to dislodge from his affections for something as silly as a faux engagement. For all she knew, this giggling creature could be his real fiancée, one that his uncle disliked and the very reason Lord Harry might have agreed to her scheme in the first place. He would gain his uncle's favor, pry loose some funds, and be able to afford marrying the woman of his choice. He could buy her every hideous shawl in London.

But for heaven's sake, he could not do that now. Whether he had a real fiancée or not, as long as he was pretending to be promised to her, he owed her at least the appearance of fidelity. And that did not include the giggling miss and her parcels.

By God, she would find a way to see him again and she would tell him exactly what she thought of his little tart there on the street. Then perhaps she would suggest they work just a bit harder to assure this false engagement was believable. That could mean another ride through the park, perhaps. And just to make certain he was willing, she'd see what she could do about improving his conveyance situation.

Although, she had to admit as she watched him tenderly assist his pretty companion up into the seat, he seemed to be doing just fine with the dilapidated conveyance he already had.

THIS MAID FROM BURLINGTON'S HOUSE HAD NOT BEEN exactly the first thing on his mind today, but when Harris ran into her coming out of a shop he decided not to ignore a golden opportunity. He'd initially come out here in the hopes of finding Penelope. He'd called at her home, as any dutiful suitor might, only to be told by the butler she was out shopping.

That came as good news. It seemed fortuitous, as this would put her securely in the polite company of respectable chaperones, yet he could happen along and run into her, furthering their acquaintance and further gaining her trust but not leading him into a position where he might become, er, distracted again. That scarab would be in his hands very soon.

Yet he'd not taken into consideration how many places there were for a respectable lady of means to shop.

By God, but he was weary of looking in shop windows at bonnets and trimmings and buttons and buckles and heaven only knew what other sundries these women needed to hunt for out here. He'd had no luck whatsoever finding Penelope, though in one shop he decided to take a chance and announce to the shopkeeper that he was hunting a silk shawl for his fiancée, Miss Penelope Rastmoor. The shopkeeper seemed surprised at that.

He announced Penelope had been there only minutes before, in fact. He then pointed out a particularly expensive shawl he claimed she'd been admiring, and Harris felt bound, at that point, to purchase said shawl since he claimed that's what he'd been after in the first place. The shopkeeper wrapped it in paper for him, and Harris was rather glad to have it out of view.

It did not really look like something he would expect Penelope to admire, and he couldn't quite see how the variety of red stripes and garish orange fringes would really compliment her coloring or—truthfully—anything on the planet. In fact, there was no way of knowing whether Penelope had been there and even seen the shawl, or whether the shopkeeper had neatly swindled Harris out of several coins he could ill afford to throw away today. No wonder most normal men hated shopping.

It was while he'd been grumbling to himself over his bad fortune that he'd nearly walked into the maid on the street. He recognized her from Burlington's house yesterday and was quite pleased to have come across her so easily. He'd thought there might be some actual effort needed to locate the girl again, yet here she was right in front of him. And blushing quite prettily, too. Indeed, this would work nicely.

He tucked Penelope's neatly packaged shawl up under his arm and greeted the young woman.

"Pardon me, I'm afraid I very nearly walked right into you, miss," he said.

She giggled, blushing deeper. "No matter, sir, you didn't hurt me none."

"Say, don't I recognize you from Lord Burlington's house?"

She seemed inordinately pleased to be recognized and giggled even more. "You do, sir! I work in his upstairs. Today Mrs. Bostwig needed me to come out and pick up these new linens she'd ordered."

"What a pity it isn't a nicer day for you to be out walking like this," he commented.

"If it was a nicer day, sir, Mrs. Bostwig would have come out herself. But I don't mind. At least I ain't been rained on yet."

"Ah, but sadly that appears as if it might be about to change. Clouds are rolling in and it is quite a ways to your destination."

She frowned up at the sky, and it was all he could do not to laugh at such an easy little target. Trying to appear just a bit awkward—that seemed to usually take young ladies off their guard—he cleared his throat and spoke.

"If it isn't too forward of me, miss, I'd gladly offer the use of my conveyance to get you home before the rain."

He pointed to it, and realized the fact it was not some grand, gleaming chariot was likely a good thing in this maid's eyes. She seemed to feel quite comfortable with him, indeed.

"Oh, would you do that for me, sir?"

"But of course. I am heading that direction myself and it would be my duty as a gentleman to share my conveyance in such a situation as this."

She giggled some more and gushed her many thanks as he hoisted her up. She was not nearly so well-formed and graceful as Miss Rastmoor when he'd been privileged to help her into his carriage yesterday, but the maid was attractive enough, and he would have no trouble at all convincing her she had charms enough to catch his attention. She would likely tell him all he needed to know about her master's house and where any certain artifacts might be. Perhaps she dusted them every day and could even count them for him.

Yes, finding her here was fortuitous indeed. And now he had that shawl, an excuse to visit Miss Rastmoor once his interrogation of this little morsel was complete. Surprisingly, he was having quite a pleasant day, after all.

"So tell me," he began with his most disarming smile, and his carriage jolted into motion. "How long have you been employed with Lord Burlington, Miss . . . er . . ."

"Milly, sir," she said, grinning so that he might take note of adorable dimples. "Milly Cooper."

"Well, Milly Cooper, I'm very glad to meet you." And now he gave her a glimpse of his own adorable dimples. "I am Lord Harris Chesterton. But please, do call me Harry."

And she did. Quite readily.

AUNT CLARA'S CARRIAGE DROPPED HER OFF RATHER unceremoniously, and there was nothing Penelope could do but give a quick good-bye to her friend and dash indoors. It was just as well, since the dreary clouds now seemed to be threatening rain. Good. Perhaps Lord Harry and his dimpling little friend would get doused. And all their packages with them.

She was in a decidedly foul mood as she trotted up to her

bedroom, ignoring her mother who called a greeting from the drawing room as she passed. At least, she hoped it was a greeting, although on further reflection she wondered if perhaps it hadn't sounded just a bit more like a summons. As if she'd done anything today to earn more of Mamma's lectures.

She must have, because no sooner was she in her room with the door slammed shut behind her than Mamma had appeared, opening it and waltzing inside without so much as a knock. Drat. Another lecture was on the way.

"Did you have a pleasant time with Maria and her aunt?" Mamma asked. The tone was sweet, but Penelope knew that could be deceptive.

"Yes, I suppose so." She waited to see where this was going.

"Find anything interesting?"

"To buy? No, but I did see the most hideous shawl at Tilly's. Orange fringe with red stripes, if you can imagine that atrocity, and Maria said . . ."

"Did you see your fiancé?"

". . . it was the worst thing ever and even a color-blind chimpanzee would have sense enough not to buy such a . . . er, what?"

"Did you see your fiancé? He was here, you know, looking for you. Our efficient butler didn't have the good sense to lie, however, and told the man where you'd gone."

"He was here? Looking for me?"

"If you met up with him, Penelope, I should like to know about it. From what I hear went on in the park yesterday it would appear we need to keep a much tighter tether on you."

"Keep in mind that everything you hear about what happened in the park yesterday might not be completely true, Mamma. You know how people love to invent gossip."

Mamma was understandably not convinced.

"Oh? Did someone invent your future husband's public declaration that you will soon be, er, throwing yourself into his bed?"

Penelope felt her cheeks go warm. And not simply because it was more than a little awkward to hear her own mother speak those words.

"I believe the actual phrase was 'hurling' myself, Mamma, but it was only after Lady Whorton implied that—"

"And did you let him take liberties with your person?"

"Well, that depends on what you mean by liberties, I suppose."

"Penelope, did you allow that man to kiss you on the carriage drive?"

She tried to hide a reminiscent smile as her cheeks went even more warm. "No, actually he kissed me on the lips, Mamma."

She held her breath while Mamma was silent. It seemed perhaps this had not been the proper moment to inject a bit of humor. Drat.

"So," Mamma said at last. "This time you really do intend to marry."

Shock of all shocks, Mamma's stern face now broke into a smile. Granted, it was not the most joyous of smiles, but it was a smile nonetheless. Not sure what to make of it, Penelope thought it best to hold her peace. For now.

"I have to admit," Mamma went on, "I suspected this was just another of your false starts, my dear. I worried that perhaps you'd even chosen this man as a way to needle your poor brother."

"What? You think I might do that?" *Gulp.*

"Yes. Frequently. But I believe this time, perhaps, you may actually be serious. Just possibly you've finally met your match."

Mamma was still smiling, and now she sat down beside her on the bed, taking Penelope's hands in hers.

"I cannot pretend this is the man I would have chosen for you," she went on slowly. "But I've learned from your brother that there are occasionally some areas where a mother might not always know best. If you've given your heart to this Chesterton fellow, and if he cares equally for you, as he claims to, then who am I to disapprove? You have my blessing, Penelope."

Penelope found it decidedly hard to swallow around the big lump that involuntarily formed in the back of her throat. Mamma was being so kind, so understanding, so wonderfully maternal and sweet . . . Penelope felt just awful. What sort of horrible game was she playing at here, anyway? To deceive her own mother this way, she never expected it to feel so, well . . . wrong.

"Thank you, Mamma," she said. "But I—"

Fate had a knock at the door, preventing her from spilling out whatever words of confession might have been ready to bubble over in her heart just then. She clamped her lips shut as Mamma's maid poked her head in through the doorway.

"Shall I bring your tea, ma'am, before it is time to dress for this evening?"

"Yes, Nancy, that's just what we need right now," Mamma replied, patting Penelope's hand and then standing.

"Dress for this evening?" Penelope asked, finally daring to make eye contact. "What is this evening?"

"Did you forget?" Mamma said. "We are invited to a musicale at Lord Burlington's house."

Oh drat. She *had* forgotten that. Patrice and Lettice Burlington were forever inviting them over for the most miserable musical entertainments imaginable. Penelope was certain she was not at all up for this tonight. How ever was she going to get out of it?

"And perhaps we shall see a certain someone there?" Mamma hinted, still smiling at her. "After all, he was there for Lady Burlington's ball, was he not?"

Oh, but this was correct! Lady Burlington's ball was where she'd first seen Lord Harry more than a week ago. Would he be there again? Perhaps Patrice's deplorable viola and Lettice's dismal pianoforte wouldn't be quite so horrible if he were there. She hoped he would be, actually, as she had something to say to him about his behavior with that girl on the street. Yes, she most certainly had something to say about that.

"See? You're looking more lively already," Mamma said. "Now, Nancy will bring some tea and you can get cleaned up and dressed nicely for this evening. Let's hope your fiancé does the same. As I recall, his last appearance at the Burlington's seemed a bit, er, impromptu."

Yes, and she half wished that unkempt hermit had never bothered to clean up. It was far too easy for every shop-going hussy in London to notice for herself what a dashing man Lord Harry turned out to be under all that hermit-ness. And he, it seemed, enjoyed the notice. Indeed, Penelope would definitely have something to say about that.

Chapter Six

There was no sign of Lord Harry, hermit-ish, unkempt, or otherwise. It would seem, despite his recently announced engagement to a popular member of society, the man had not been added to Burlington's guest list. Penelope could only think the man most fortunate for it. The music was, as expected, excruciating.

She did note, however, that the elder Miss Burlington's gown was particularly attractive, and it seemed as if Miss Lettice was trying a new hairstyle, to rounding success. At least Penelope would have something nice to say to the ladies after suffering through the murder of Mozart and this hashing of Haydn. She could only pray the torture was nearing an end.

Ugh, but all the false smiles and pretend applause had given her a headache. On top of it all, no matter how hard she tried to rid her mind of the very absent Lord Harry, she just could not. More specifically, she could not rid her mind of the image of the elegant man escorting that young trollop with the parcels. It was completely unfair that Penelope was trapped here, subjected to the night's musical misery, while Lord Harry was off doing who knew what with that woman. And her parcels.

Having had all she could take, Penelope quietly excused herself. She needed air. She needed to stretch her limbs. She needed anything that would distract her from that dashed vision of Lord Harry's handsome face and the tender way he escorted that female.

Just outside the music room, a young maid popped up from the bench where she'd been positioned to wait upon her master's guests. She asked if Penelope would like to be shown to the retiring room. How thoughtful. Actually, Penelope would have much rather been shown to the front door, but she decided to settle for the retiring room.

"Yes, thank you. I . . ."

But her words strangled in her throat and nothing but a garbled little wheeze came out. Penelope had looked directly into the young maid's face and was stunned speechless. It was that selfsame little miss who had offered Lord Harry her parcels! She'd recognize those huge, dewy blue eyes anywhere.

Oh yes, she'd been the one to offer up her parcels. And probably whatever else she'd had to offer up, as well. Heavens, but this was most uncomfortable!

"Miss? Are you well?" the dewy eyes asked.

"Well? Er, yes . . . of course. I just, er . . . retiring room?"

"This way, miss."

Now Penelope found herself actually following the girl, trying desperately not to wonder how the perky sway of the young maid measured up to her own. Did Lord Harry find this girl more attractive? Did he miss those dewy eyes when she was not around? Did Penelope really care one way or the other?

No, of course she did not. Her relationship with Lord Harry was purely business. It was simply a means to an end, and she couldn't care less where he placed his affection. Or his parcels. She simply required that in all public situations he give the impression of being properly infatuated with her. Not this little maid, no matter how enticing her sway or her blue eyes.

The girl led them to a door, which she opened to reveal a sitting room. It appeared the other guests were more polite than Penelope and had all remained in the music room. This room was empty.

Penelope was about to thank the girl and dismiss her—after all, there was no sense to being rude or cold toward her. It was certainly not this poor girl's fault that Lord Harry was a dismal fiancé. But then her eyes caught on the interior of the room.

"Oh my!"

"Yes, Miss?"

"This is not the room the Burlingtons usually use for ladies' retiring during their musical performances."

"No, miss. I'm afraid Miss Lettice's prized pug done something rather nasty to the carpet in the usual room. They've had to send it out for cleaning. The carpet, that is. Not the pug. He's upstairs on a pillow in Miss Lettice's room, same as ever."

Lucky Pug. And how lucky for Penelope! She'd never seen this room before, or its breathtaking contents. My heavens, but how had she never known Lord Burlington was such a collector of Egyptian antiquities?

"Is there anything I can do for you, miss?" the girl asked.

"No. Er . . . yes, perhaps you can. What can you tell me about these artifacts? Do they all belong to your master?"

"Oh yes! He quite fancies the old things, as a matter of fact. I overheard him going on and on to one of his gentlemen about how valuable they is and what an effort it was for him to get them."

Truly? She herself did not recall hearing Lord Burlington going on and on about these items. Not that she'd ever had much conversation with the man, being more a friend to his nonmusical daughters than to him. Still, she might have expected to catch a word or two about such a collection as this. In fact, she might have expected to read something in the papers or hear other people talking about something so impressive. How odd that she hadn't.

"I had no idea Lord Burlington has been such a longtime collector."

The maid shrugged. "I don't know how long he's been at it, miss, but he surely has gone wholeheated into it now. Ever since these bits and pieces arrived last week, it seems all that matters to him."

"Last week? *All* this arrived just last week?"

The dewy eyes fluttered and the maid nodded. "Yes, I think so. Don't recall seeing none of it before then. Looks like just a lot of heathen dust catching, if you ask me, but they must be quite the thing! Gentlemen come at all hours to look at them with his lordship."

"Oh, is that so?"

Penelope sauntered deeper into the room, glancing about at the various artifacts. There were gold figurines, carvings in ivory and lapis lazuli, wooden relics of furnishings, even what appeared to be the tiny sarcophagus of an egret. She was in awe. She was a bit confused, as well. How could she not have known Lord Burlington was such a lover of Egyptology?

And some of these items, as she studied them, appeared to be quite amazing. In fact, one article in particular caught her attention. She hesitated only slightly, then reached to touch it.

It was a small alabaster jar, probably once used for holding cosmetics. She knew that because Professor Oldham had written extensively on his discovery of one such piece in some of his recent correspondence. He'd been delighted with the condition of the object, describing in detail the fine carvings of interlaced fish on the jar, and the lovely carved spoon that had been found with it. Apparently Egyptian women had used cosmetics in such quantities that they needed spoons to ladle them. Penelope had not been quite certain how the spoon and the cosmetics jar should work together, but she did know that what she was looking at right now fit Professor Oldham's description perfectly. The alabaster jar did indeed have little fish carved into it in a ring, as if the creatures were swimming circles around the lip of it, and there was indeed a spoon resting just beside the jar. It was carved into the shape of a girl carrying a water pitcher on top of her head.

What were the chances these two items were so common that they should turn up in multiples? Professor Oldham seemed to indicate the style and condition of the items he had unearthed made them quite unique. Yet, here were two others that appeared, at least to her eye, nearly identical. How very odd.

Professor Oldham specifically had mentioned that his discoveries would be placed in a museum there, in Egypt, kept for the people whose legacy it was. The man was quite adamant about that, as a matter of fact. Everyone knew Professor Oldham was not a pillager. That was one of the reasons she first chose to contact him, to try to increase her knowledge of the subject from someone not merely qualified, but noble, too. Professor Oldham did not ravage graves of the dead for his own personal gain, but he studied the ways of the past so that all mankind today and tomorrow might benefit from the beauty of it. She appreciated such forward thinking.

So what was this cosmetic set doing here in Lord Burlington's retiring room? It simply couldn't be the same set Professor Oldham had found. Surely he'd be very interested to hear of this one, though. A forgery, perhaps? True, she hadn't yet received a reply to the last letter she'd sent, but of course he wouldn't mind her pestering him with something as amazing as this. She'd have to get a very good look at this set so she could describe it properly to her distant friend.

"I don't think the master would like you to be touching that, miss," the maid said behind her.

Drat. She'd forgotten about the girl. She wondered how likely it was Lord Harry could say the same. She wondered what he'd say when she told him that she'd met the girl this way. In fact, she wondered what he'd say if he thought she'd managed to get the girl talking of him.

"It's awfully pretty, isn't it?" Penelope said, keeping her voice sweet and breathless. "I can imagine it might have been a gift for a lady, from her lover, perhaps."

"I don't know, miss. These things come all the way from Egypt, you know. Dug up from under the sand in some ancient mummy's tomb. Who knows what heathen purpose they were for."

"I'm sure the ancient Egyptians gave gifts to the living, just like we do. Don't you have anyone special who might give you a trinket now and then?"

"Nobody ever gave me nothing like any of this, miss. Like I said, this ain't just ordinary trinkets. His lordship don't let just anyone in to see them, as a matter of fact. Seems like only gentlemen with plenty of bob."

"Oh? But he's opened the room for ladies tonight."

"And it was only after much bellowing at poor Miss Lettice, let me tell you! Scared her little dog, too. Poor thing. It wasn't his fault he got locked in that other room all day and no one could find him. He couldn't help but make the nasty. The master said at first there would be no ladies' retiring room. Her ladyship was quite appalled, I can tell you. But in the end, Pug went up to his pillow and the master said ladies could use this room tonight if they had need of it. And do you need it, miss? If you're feeling faint, there are salts here, on the table. If you have difficulties with your gown, I can assist you and—"

"No, thank you. I merely needed a bit of air, that's all. Such a crowd in the music room tonight. It was feeling a bit close."

"Yes, Miss Burlington and Miss Lettice do have very many friends. And what lovely music they make, don't you think, miss?"

"Er, it's like none other."

The maid laughed. "Yes, that's exactly what his lordship said about it!"

"Then their father is more aware of his daughters' talents than I knew."

"Oh, I don't mean Lord Burlington. No, he never says nothing kindly about their music. I meant a different lord."

"You often discuss your mistresses' musical abilities with gentlemen?"

"Of course not, but that's why it is so funny. Here I am discussing it with you, and you have said the very same thing Lord Harry said when I discussed it with him just today."

"Lord Harry? Are you in service to him, as well?"

She hoped her words didn't imply quite enough to be vulgar, but she simply couldn't keep herself from asking. The maid's response would no doubt reveal all.

Really, though, the maid's dimpling titter revealed very little. "Oh no! We were riding in his carriage."

Bother. That much Penelope already knew, didn't she? What she longed to know was *why* was this maid riding in Lord Harry's carriage.

"I asked if he would be here tonight for the musicale, and he said he'd been rather undecided." She giggled again. "That's how he said it, too, in his very fine way; 'raw-ther undecided.' He's such a gentleman, Lord Harry."

Well, then clearly the girl did not know him so very well after all.

"I take it you were unable to persuade him," Penelope noted. "I don't see him here tonight."

"No, I suppose not. I thought perhaps I had persuaded him, as he seemed more than eager to have me tell him all about the master's collection here. Quite amazed by it, he seemed."

"Oh? Lord Harry is interested in Egyptian antiquities?"

"I don't know about that. He simply said the way I described it all made it sound 'raw-ther enchawn-ting.' He said I have a natural way with words."

"Did he? How nice." She wondered what other "enchawn-ting" things Lord Harry claimed the girl had a natural way with.

"He said he'd love to come to the musicale and get a look at the collection for himself, but I had to explain Lord Burlington always keeps this room locked up."

"It's not locked now," Penelope pointed out.

"No, but only because poor Puggy got locked in the other room and made shame-shame on the carpets. I didn't know that was going to happen when I talked to Lord Harry."

"Ah, so he did not know there would be access to this room."

"Pity. Perhaps if he knew he could see the collection he would have come tonight."

"I'm sure he had very good reason not to be here tonight," Penelope said.

After all, he would have surely known she herself would be here, yet he stayed away. Clearly the man had some pressing business elsewhere tonight. Probably he knew this little maid would be busy working so he found himself someone else to provide entertainment. After all, Lord Harry was hardly the type to go out of his way to gaze at some long-buried bric-a-brac.

"Well, miss, if you don't be needing me I'd best get back out to my bench. Her ladyship was awfully concerned someone might go the wrong way and wander into the other room and catch sight of the wretched floor conditions. She made me promise I'd keep watch and direct guests the right way."

"That's fine, yes. Thank you."

The maid stepped toward the door to make her exit, but seemed to remember something at the last minute.

"One thing more, miss," she said, somewhat tentative. "My mistress was all a'worry for her floors, but my master cares only for his collection here. If you don't mind, he made me promise to ask anyone who entered here to please not touch anything."

"Very well. I'll keep my hands to myself. I'm only here for the air, after all."

The girl curtsied before leaving. "Thank you, miss."

Finally Penelope was alone with the treasures. What beauty!

But that delicate jar and its exquisite spoon had left her confused. Could all of this be authentic? Or had Lord Burlington fallen prey to the many forgers she heard were out there looking to take advantage of the uneducated with heavy pockets? From what she knew of him, Lord Burlington was certainly that.

Surely if any of these items were illegitimate someone would want to know about it. If only she'd brought some paper with her she might take down some notes of what she saw here; she might record pertinent details that could possibly help to bring the forgers to justice. My, but wouldn't that be quite a tale to tell Professor Oldham? And perhaps even Anthony might take her interest in Egyptology a bit more seriously if she could in some way prevent other gentlemen from being duped.

Well, there was a desk in the far corner of the room. Perhaps she could find writing implements and make some quick observations. She darted over to the desk and hurried through its drawers, finding what she needed right away. And to think, she'd been ready to consider this evening a sad waste of time!

She sat at the desk—wishing someone had thought to put a light at this end of the room—and was just about to make her first mark on the paper when a sound caught her attention. She glanced up, but the room was still empty and the door was still closed, just the way the tittering maid had left it. It almost seemed she had imagined the noise, until she heard it again.

It came from the window, on the other side of the room. Not quite a tapping, Penelope could only determine it was more of a scraping sound. And now the curtains began to move, rustled by a sudden brush of air from outside. The sound continued and it was all too obvious exactly what it was.

A burglar was breaking into Lord Burlington's treasure room!

Damn. Burlington's blasted windowsill snagged his trousers and gave him a rather uncomfortable splinter in a decidedly uncomfortable place. Harris hoisted himself into the room and was careful not to utter any of his mental profanity out loud.

He failed miserably when something heavy wacked him on the back of the head.

"Bloody hell! What the devil . . ."

And then he saw the wielder of this something heavy. *Penelope.*

"Penelope?"

"Lord Harry?"

The deceptively delicate female looked quite as stunned as he felt. She did not seem quite as dizzy as he felt, however, which he counted a good thing since at the moment he was doing well to keep himself upright. If he'd had to nobly dash out an arm to save a wobbly Penelope, he was quite certain they'd have both tumbled to the floor.

"What on earth are you doing climbing in through Lord Burlington's window?" she asked.

"Ah, Miss Rastmoor," he said, cleverly avoiding an answer to her question. "How very pleasant to see you. And how nice that you've decided to strike me only once with that, er, object."

She blinked once at him, then twice, then her gaze shifted to the item in her hands. It was Egyptian. It was made of ornately carved wood. It was easily recognizable as being from a tomb he and Oldham had excavated together. More importantly, it was an overlarge phallus.

Miss Rastmoor, of course, could have no idea what she'd just clubbed him with. She did, however, seem instantly remorseful. As was he. Blast it, but the throbbing bump she'd given him at the back of his head pounded dreadfully.

"I'm so sorry!" she exclaimed. "Did I hurt you?"

"What, with that tiny thing? No, no. Of course not."

"Yes . . . it is rather heavy, isn't it? Are you certain I didn't hurt you?"

Thank God the pain in his head was extreme enough to keep him from fully enjoying the complexity of this delicate situation. Miss Rastmoor waving that thing around was almost too much to take without succumbing to laughter. Laughter, though, might draw unwanted attention, and that would not be good. His presence here tonight was not exactly requested.

"I'm fine," he said. "But what the devil . . . Put that thing down, will you?"

She did. Sort of. She placed it on a nearby table, on its base.

The blasted thing stood ramrod straight, pointing directly up at the ceiling. It was positively indecent.

Miss Rastmoor, however, paid it little mind. "What are you doing, climbing in the window like that?"

"I might ask you the same thing," he replied.

"I wasn't climbing in the window."

"Well, you're in here. What were you doing in here, Miss Rastmoor?"

"I was here for the Burlington ladies' musicale. And I was allowed to use the front door."

"Yes, but what are you doing in *here*? In this room?"

"This, Lord Harry, is the ladies' retiring room. I was retiring."

He cocked an eyebrow and glanced toward the phallus. "With that?"

Perhaps she did have a clue what it was, after all. Her face went a charming shade of scarlet. She was still standing rather near to it, and after just the briefest pause she reached out and casually laid it on its side. Now it was pointing directly toward her. Harris wasn't certain which was more disconcerting, its previous position or this. Or the idea that Miss Rastmoor might wish to, er, retire with it.

"I'm quite certain Lord Burlington would not approve of you entering his home this way," the lady said, stepping away from the phallus and moving to casually peruse an assortment of smaller artifacts that appeared to have been placed in no apparent order along the mantel over the unlit fire.

Damn, but he'd gotten distracted watching the girl's filmy gown float against her delicious curves as she moved. He should have been formulating an excuse. Just why had he been climbing in through Burlington's window, anyway?

"I was coming in here to . . . that is . . ."

"Don't bother inventing a lie. I know exactly why you are here, Lord Harry," she said, whirling to face him.

Her gown whirled with her, and he was treated to another view of those curves, not to mention a hint of ankle. He thought perhaps the phallus twitched, but he could have been wrong. He needed to keep his mind on more important matters and make sense of her words. Could it really be she knew why he was here?

"You do?"

"Yes," she assured him. "And you cannot expect me to approve."

"No, actually, I didn't expect you to even know about it."

She smiled, smug. "Well. I do know about it."

"And just what do you intend to do about it?"

Now she chewed her lip and seemed to consider. He watched her, hoping she was not determined to cry out and turn him over to Burlington. That would be most uncomfortable, and certainly the man would go to greater trouble to hide his collection after finding Harris lurking here. It would be damned difficult to track it down again, giving the old blighter ample time to sell it off piece by piece to his anonymous customers.

"Well, I would like to order you to stop, but I don't suppose you will agree to that, will you?" she said.

"Uh, probably not."

She frowned. "No, being a man, I didn't think you would."

"Perhaps if you understood the urgent nature of things . . ."

Now she appeared actually horrified. "Lord Harry! I assure you, I do not wish to understand anything more about this than I already do."

"But it's a very complex matter," he tried to explain. "It's not nearly as sordid as you might think, Miss Rastmoor."

"Oh?"

"It's become a matter of life and death."

It was clear she was unconvinced. She rolled her eyes.

"Honestly, Lord Harry. I'm quite certain no one has ever died from, er, lack of completing your goal."

"You'd be surprised the level of desperation, Miss Rastmoor. A man in my position would go to great lengths."

"Please, sir! I don't want to hear anything about your great lengths. But how on earth can you expect me to condone this? And with everyone just in the next room! It's . . . it's indecent."

"If you'd let me explain, you'd understand it's being done with the noblest intentions."

This certainly gave her pause. Her fair brows arched up and her blue eyes went round.

"Noble intentions?"

"Of course! You don't think I do this simply on a lark, do you?"

"Actually, I had rather thought so."

"Well, I don't. I abhor being reduced to creeping about like this, but there is no other way. Now if you don't mind, my time is rather limited, so you may either leave quietly, or stay and watch."

"Watch? Good heavens, sir!"

"You're right. That might implicate you, as well. Then I suggest you should leave, Miss Rastmoor."

"Of course I will, but . . ."

"But?"

"Have you told her about me?"

"What?"

"Your little maid."

"My little *what*?"

"Your maid! The one you were sneaking in here to meet, no doubt. I saw you with her earlier today, you know, and I have to say it's rather unfair of you to be pretending to be engaged to me all the while you're planning assignations with her."

"Planning assig—? Miss Rastmoor, you misunderstand. I wasn't—"

"I suppose I am glad to hear you have noble intentions—at least you *claim* to have them—but what can possibly be noble about climbing through a window to engage in . . . well, in what you claim to be desperate to engage in!"

"Oh, for Hades' sake."

The blasted girl thought he was here to shag a servant! By God, he'd set her straight right away. He'd inform her that, in fact, he was here to . . . no, that was no good. He couldn't very well tell her he was here to take inventory of Lord Burlington's antiquities collection so he might plot a return trip to rob it all, could he? No, actually, he couldn't. She'd likely rush off and warn the man.

Hellfire. He'd just have to pretend to be shagging a servant.

"You found out my secret," he said, producing a rather dramatic sigh.

"You can't truly be serious about your so-called noble intentions, can you? I'm a very modern thinker, of course, but surely you aren't serious about marrying a . . . a . . ."

"A servant?"

"She seems quite a pleasant girl, and she does seem completely taken with you, but—"

"You've spoken to her?"

"I have, and I suppose I should have suspected your motives when she told me how interested you were in learning which rooms in his lordship's household would be locked tonight," she said, knitting her brows to contemplate things.

Clearly it was a complex matter for her, as she wandered the room while she spoke.

"I take it you assumed this was all the better for you to plan an illicit rendezvous, meeting her here in a locked room. Pity she didn't get a chance to notify you that Miss Lettice's pug soiled the carpet in the other room causing Lord Burlington to have to make this the ladies' retiring room, instead."

"You discussed Miss Lettice's pug with her?"

"She mentioned it, yes. Now I see why it was of such interest to her."

Botheration. So Miss Rastmoor had been making friends with that silly little maid he'd met yesterday, had she? Why the devil would she feel compelled to do that?

Because he was supposed to be her fiancé, of course. She'd be understandably miffed to find he was about to botch the performance by gallivanting around town with another female. Yes, he could see it in her eyes. She *was* miffed. He supposed he was fortunate she truly hadn't known who he was when she'd struck him with that phallus. No doubt she would have swung the thing quite a bit harder.

"Then I suppose my plans for the evening are spoiled, aren't they?" he asked, pretending to be very downcast.

"Absolutely. I can't have you dallying with someone right here under the noses of half the people I know. Heavens, Lord Harry, what would they think?"

"It would certainly help motivate your brother to wish our engagement ended."

"Yes, it might, but it would also make me look a dreadful fool," she said, stopping by the table with the phallus and absently adjusting its angle so that now the bloody thing pointed straight toward Harris.

"We certainly can't have you looking the fool, Miss Rastmoor."

He'd been sauntering along after her, so he was near enough

to touch the phallus just enough to shift it away from him. She noticed and frowned at him. Like a rebellious child, she shifted it back. He, in turn, re-shifted it again.

"Do you have some special prejudice toward this item, sir?" she asked, moving it back into place.

"No, I just would prefer not to have it staring at me," he said, putting it where he'd had it.

"It's a piece of carved wood. It isn't staring at you."

"It certainly seemed to be staring at *you*."

"Well, now it's going to roll off the table."

She was right. With all the repeated shifting, the item had been left too close to the edge and was just about to totter off onto the floor. Instinctively, they both reached out to save it. Harris was fastest, grabbing it and pulling it away from her as if he'd won some kind of prize.

"Ha!"

"Oh, don't be a child. Put that down before you break it," she said, reaching to take it from him.

"It won't break. It's solid wood."

But she had her hands on it and was giving a good tug. "It's ancient! It shouldn't be handled like that!"

"Then perhaps you should let go and let me do the handling."

"You wouldn't know what to do with it."

"I'll wager I know a fair bit more than you do!"

"Is that an insult to my education or my ability, sir?"

"You may trust *my* education, Miss Rastmoor, and I promise that you are handling it far too roughly."

"If you would just give it to me, then—"

Her demands were cut off by a loud clearing of the throat. Harris gritted his teeth and turned his head to see they were not alone. Lady Burlington had apparently entered the room to retire. And now she found them thrusting a giant phallus back and forth.

Miss Rastmoor must have realized the oddity of the situation. She squeaked and immediately took her hands off the object. Unfortunately, so did Harris. Without the squeak.

The phallus clattered to the floor between them.

"Aha," he said, giving Miss Rastmoor a triumphant grin. "I told you it would not break."

* * *

PENELOPE COULD HAVE POSITIVELY DIED. WHAT HAD she been thinking, to let herself get sucked into Lord Harry's juvenile behavior? Arguing over the artifact as if it were a child's toy. Ridiculous! Thank heavens she had no reason to suspect the man might have even the slightest clue what the object in question actually was. Likely he thought it was some sort of crude animal carving, accusing it of staring at him, of all things. Honestly, the man must be half-blind.

But Lady Burlington did not seem to be. She, in fact, seemed to see quite well.

"Apparently I'm interrupting. You've dropped something, Lord Harry."

"Why Lady Burlington, how nice to see you. Dressed."

That last word was uttered rather softly under Lord Harry's breath. Penelope assumed she'd heard incorrectly.

"So the rumors I've heard are true," the woman fairly purred, stepping into the room and smiling first at Lord Harry and then at Penelope. "I suppose I should be wishing you happy, although it appears you hardly need my wishes."

"Oh, but you misjudge the situation, Lady Burlington," Lord Harry began.

Penelope was more than a bit interested to hear what excuse he might invent to explain what the woman had just walked in on, but she knew she could hardly allow him to continue. Of course he would try to protect her reputation and claim there was nothing untoward happening here, but it could only do him damage if people were to learn he'd been breaking into Lord Burlington's house to meet with a mere servant girl. Indeed, that news would damage him as well as any credibility they'd built for their own supposed union.

No, she'd best not let the man do anything noble at this point. Besides, she really didn't want anyone questioning why she'd been lingering over these artifacts so long, either. If there were underhanded dealings with forgers, she hated to risk alerting them to her suspicions.

"Thank you for your well wishes, Lady Burlington," Penelope said quickly. "And I'm sure this must look very awkward, the two of us here together, all alone, in such close proximity... but we are to be married, after all. Surely Lord Harry's noble intentions can be trusted."

Even Lord Harry snorted at that one. Indeed, as she'd expected, the man had no noble intentions. It was just as well she'd found him here before he'd had further opportunity to take advantage of that poor maid who clearly had no idea of his character. Penelope would be sure to warn the girl.

"Usually young ladies take more care not to be found alone with their gentleman, Miss Rastmoor," Lady Burlington said with a smirk. "I fear Lord Harry has led you astray."

"Of course not. Lord Harry is the very model of propriety. But come, sir, perhaps we should allow Lady Burlington some privacy. You and I will simply have to find a quiet corner elsewhere to continue our... conversation."

She knew, of course, the woman would not for one minute believe they'd been deep in conversation or that there was any part of Lord Harry that so much as resembled propriety, let alone be the model for it. Indeed, this brief encounter would likely be more than enough to get Lady Burlington's tongue wagging quite fluently. The gossips would be convinced Penelope was fully enamored with the disreputable man, and Anthony would begin to change his mind about things.

She laid her hand on Lord Harry's arm for him to lead her from the room. True, she hadn't gotten the full description of that alabaster jar or any of the other artifacts, but she supposed she could remember enough of them to send a fair report to Professor Oldham. It was time she and her fiancé took their leave.

Lord Harry seemed to agree. He laid his hand over Penelope's and gave Lady Burlington a very pretty bow.

"Good evening, Lady Burlington. I hope we run into you again sometime," he said.

"Oh, I have no doubt you will, Lord Harry. It seems you and I have been rather stumbling over one another of late."

"Yes, it does seem so, now that you mention it."

The lady laughed. "How unexpected, too, since our motivations are so dramatically different." She sent a quick, disapproving glance over Penelope.

"Yes, they are," Lord Harry agreed. "So perhaps I can expect there will be no additional stumbling."

With this nonsensical phrase he gave one more little bow

and led Penelope to the door. She was quite pleased to be leaving Lady Burlington behind. She did not at all approve of the dismissive way the woman had looked at her.

They didn't quite make it out the door, however. The young maid suddenly popped up in front of them, apparently fresh from her post in the corridor and smiling far too brightly. Penelope borrowed one of Lady Burlington's dismissive glances and gave it to the girl. She didn't notice.

"Lord Harry! I had no idea you were here, sir," she said, blushing and dropping curtsies as if they might save her life.

"Hello, Milly," he said, sounding disgustingly pleased to see the girl. "I must have missed you in the hallway when I came through."

For a moment the girl appeared to wonder how on earth that could have been possible, but Lady Burlington was doing more of her throat clearing and got the maid's attention.

"Oh!" the girl said, jolted to attention and turning her focus on the lady. "Here is your reticule that you left in the music room."

She held up a little silk bag that perfectly matched Lady Burlington's burgundy-colored gown. Lord Harry stepped aside—practically shoving Penelope out of his way—so the girl could hold it up for her ladyship. Curtsying and blushing again, the maid brushed past Lord Harry and scurried into the room, carrying the bag to its owner.

"Thank you," Lady Burlington said, taking the bag, but hardly bothering to take her eyes from Lord Harry.

"And you'll be happy to know that Miss Lettice's pug is still safely upstairs," the servant said as if she were pronouncing something grand.

Penelope noticed Lord Harry's left eyebrow arch upward. "Miss Lettice's pug?"

She girl turned her smile on him again. "Yes, sir. The little thing was quite persistent in trailing her ladyship around the house earlier, before he somehow got locked in the other room. He would not leave her side. It was as if she carried kidneys in her pockets, or something."

"It was most disturbing," Lady Burlington said. "Kidneys in my pockets, indeed. I'm glad Lettice has locked that little pest away so he doesn't come to bother our guests."

"As you've recovered your reticule and now have Milly here to keep you company, Lady Burlington, perhaps Miss Rastmoor and I should take our leave. I would hate to think that we've replaced that pug and become a bother to you."

Lord Harry nodded politely toward her ladyship and took Penelope's arm to guide her from the room. This time there was no additional maid to pop up and stop them. They made it safely from the room and out into the grand hallway, pulling the door shut behind them. Thankfully, they were alone again. So-called music still emanated from the music room, and apparently the rest of the guests were still in there pretending to enjoy it. No one was out here to notice them.

Lord Harry removed his hand from her arm. "It was a pleasure to see you, Miss Rastmoor, but I daresay it might be a good idea if you did not mention to anyone how we met tonight. In fact, you might not want to mention I was here at all."

Indeed, she was inclined to agree with him. "But what of Lady Burlington? Surely she will take great joy in mentioning it."

His dark brows knitted together. "Perhaps not. Either way, you can simply deny. If I leave here without anyone else seeing me, then it's merely her word against yours."

"And of course, your little friend Milly."

"Don't worry about her. I'll see that she's discreet."

Penelope wasn't entirely successful at keeping the snippy tone from her voice. "Yes, you do seem to have a way with her."

He seemed about to speak to that, but polite applause from the nearby music room indicated the performance was finally at an end. If Lord Harry didn't move quickly, Milly's discretion would no longer make one bit of difference. Penelope decided to let the subject drop. She had far too much on her mind after discovering that room full of artifacts to worry about having to explain Lord Harry's presence just now. Besides, the sooner he left this house the less chance he'd have of running into smiling little Milly again.

"Go," she said. "And by the way, that large rectangular item across from us is the front door. You should use that next time you wish to enter or leave a fashionable home."

"That will entirely depend upon the circumstances, Miss

Rastmoor," he said, giving her a very wicked smile and just the hint of a bow.

She found it a bit worrisome that her heart fluttered at the smoldering look he gave her. Then his usual air of mischief took over and he laughed, nodding at her and turning away to exit quickly and silently through the large rectangular door. No one saw. Not even a footman seemed to be on duty just then. Lord Harry was gone, and just as he said, should Lady Burlington choose to mention what she saw in the retiring room, it would simply be her word against Penelope's.

Not that Penelope's word held much weight these days. She slipped into the back of the music room and quickly joined in with the applause and the milling crowd. She found her way to Mamma's side and was all smiles and politeness as they flattered and congratulated the Burlington ladies on their delightful entertainment. Penelope had to admire her mother's acting abilities. One would actually believe the woman had enjoyed the evening. Mamma's usual friends stopped her to catch up on the current state of Lady Castlethwait's headdress, and it seemed no one had noticed Penelope's disappearance at all.

This seemed to present her with a most excellent opportunity. Did she dare? Surely there could be no harm in it. Perhaps it might actually be considered a good deed. She chewed her lip and pondered.

What would Lord Harry say about it? Well, she hardly gave a fig what he might say. She would do it, and there was little he could say about it. Yes, she would do it, indeed.

Smiling at those milling around her, she wandered back out toward the entrance hall. With luck Milly would have resumed her position on the bench by now. And perhaps she would be receptive to taking a new position, as well.

She would be a lovely addition to the staff at Rastmoor House. Yes, Penelope would appreciate having another maid to assist in certain duties. And really, the girl was clearly not appreciated here. Nor was she watched carefully if she was able to plan a clandestine tryst with the likes of Lord Harry.

Why yes, Penelope would be doing a good turn to rescue the girl from this house. And from Lord Harry.

Chapter Seven

Harris loitered in the shadows outside Lord Burlington's house. The Rastmoor ladies seemed to be some of the first to depart the evening's musicale, but nothing in their actions gave him reason to suspect Lady Burlington had caused trouble for Penelope by announcing what she'd interrupted. Or rather, what she'd thought she'd interrupted. He supposed he owed the girl quite a debt for playing her part so enthusiastically.

At first he'd wondered why she'd been so willing to implicate herself in what that matron obviously suspected, but then of course he realized it would play remarkably well into Penelope's plans. If her brother were to get word of a secret assignation right under the noses of their very best friends, he would certainly have cause to question Harris's value as husband material. Indeed, not only did Penelope's playacting protect him from being caught in his real goal, but it seemed to suit her purpose quite well. He could count on her to keep up appearances.

He wasn't so certain he could count on Lady Burlington for as much, however. It might only be a coincidence, of course, but how strange that he'd encountered her twice now while prowling around the home. He'd have to take care that it did not happen again. She was just the sort who might start to question why. If she'd come in and he'd not had Penelope there with him to concoct a plausible explanation, things might have gotten a bit uncomfortable.

As if things hadn't begun uncomfortably enough with that blasted chit hitting him over the head with an ancient phallus. What could the girl possibly have been thinking? If he'd been an honest burglar she'd have merely succeeded in making him angry. She'd have been an easy mark, all alone as she'd been in that room full of antiquities. Lucky for her it had been him and not any of the dozens of other sorry criminals who might want to get their hands on Burlington's collection.

As if any of it truly was Burlington's. Damn the man, but he'd clearly been far more involved in this whole business than Harris had suspected. Oh, certainly he'd followed the trail and knew Burlington had received some of the stolen goods, but obviously it was more than just *some*. It was practically *all*. And that meant Burlington was not merely an unsuspecting collector, but was involved in marketing these stolen goods. If Harris did not act quickly, Burlington would sell off those items one piece at a time and they'd be scattered all over the kingdom. There would be little hope of getting them back after that. The law favored those in possession and gave little credit to the origin of antiquities.

The Egyptian government was hardly a solid entity capable of preserving its treasures for its people. No, antiquities went to the first man who dug them up and claimed them for himself. Professor Oldham was considered a fool by many for his outlandish notions of preserving his discoveries for the people of that foreign land, only sending a few of his finds home to England to be enjoyed and studied here. No wonder certain factions of Egyptian people found him so hard to believe. Their distrust of an honorable man now meant Harris was forced to resort to thievery.

He hated it, but he'd do it to save the man. All he needed to do was figure out a way to get back into Burlington's house and spirit away several cartloads of fragile antiquities. Then he simply needed to find the rest of them. The jewels.

He still had no idea where those items had gone. He'd seen no trace in that room tonight of the breathtaking ornaments that had once been a part of this collection. Did Burlington have them? Or had they been distributed separately? The fact that Penelope proudly wore that pretty little scarab seemed to indicate that might indeed be the case.

It was a bit shameful that he'd been in company with the girl so many times now and still was not one step closer to learning anything about how she she'd come by her scarab. Clearly he'd let himself become distracted from the goal, and he simply could not allow that to continue. Indeed, Penelope was a bit of a distraction. But he was not some desperate schoolboy. He knew what he was about.

Time was wasting and he could ill afford dawdling. Professor Oldham's life depended on him. No matter what he had to do, he would not let the good man down. Penelope, on the other hand, would surely regret what had to be.

THE LETTER WAS A BIT MORE DIFFICULT TO WRITE than she'd expected. Surely Professor Oldham would want accurate descriptions, but Penelope was finding these rather hard to come by. It seemed no sooner would she begin picturing one of the objects from last night than images of Lord Harry would flood her mind and she'd find herself hopelessly distracted. What a bother that gentleman was!

And why had he come through the window that way? Surely if he and the empty-headed maid were set on conducting an affair, the girl could have found an easier way to smuggle her lover into the house than to expect him to climb through the window into a supposedly locked room. And if that room had been locked, how did Lord Harry expect his little tart to come meet him in there? Clearly the man's head was in a muddle over the girl.

That left Penelope in quite a prickly mood. She'd been far too lenient with the man last night. Hadn't she meant to tell him just how displeased she was that he would be conducting himself so shamelessly where that maid was concerned, when in public he was supposed to be engaged to her? How had he managed to avoid the sharp words she'd been preparing for him?

Because he'd startled her, crawling in through the window

like that. And then, of course, she'd felt so bad for having hit him. Well, she'd thought him a burglar. What else could she have done? But heavens, what she'd hit him with!

She doubted he could've had much understanding of the ancient Egyptian practice of burying the dead with all the items they might find useful in the afterlife, but surely even a novice could look at that phallus and get some vague idea what it was carved to represent. In generous proportions. She'd been mortified.

Indeed, it was small wonder she found herself distracted as she tried to craft the letter to Professor Oldham. She'd had quite a lot going on of late. Besides, she couldn't help but be just a tiny bit worried. Professor Oldham had always been very prompt in his replies to her various queries and letters of discussion. This recent lull in his correspondence was not like him.

Could it be that he'd discovered her secret? She'd tried so very hard to be careful, but perhaps something she'd written had given him a clue. Perhaps she'd gone and ruined everything by letting the learned man realize who she was. She knew what would happen then. She'd never hear another word from the man. What serious scholar would bother corresponding with an uneducated female? Even if she had read and reread everything the man ever wrote and had eagerly studied every book on the topic of Egyptian antiquity she could get her hands on.

She knew he'd never forgive her for misrepresenting herself. Men were funny that way. His pride would never let him take her seriously. That was why she'd been so careful to give no hint to her true identity and always signed her letters from P. Anthonys. She never came out and declared herself male, but she'd made sure it was implied. Perhaps he'd seen through her deception.

Well, so what if he did? Wasn't she proof that a mere female could be quite astute? She'd make her careful description of that alabaster cosmetics jar fit so perfectly he'd virtually see the object before him as he read. He'd realize that she was someone to be taken seriously. Even if she was just a female. She rubbed the familiar wings of her dear scarab for luck and pulled out another fresh piece of paper.

After three more false starts, she was finally pleased with her description. She'd managed to include detailed reports on at least six of the objects she'd seen last night that seemed to correspond with some of the finds written of by Professor Oldham. He would realize that not only was she quite concise in her explanations, but clearly she was well versed in his work. Surely he'd be impressed by such close attention to detail.

She was just putting the finishing touches on these details when she heard someone at the front door. Mamma had gone out for some errand already, but Anthony was still at home. Perhaps he was expecting someone. She was not; it was still too early in the day to expect friends. She felt no need to trot over to the window to look down and see whose carriage might be waiting out in the street.

Unless of course it might be Lord Harry's rackety little gig. It could possibly be him, couldn't it? Not that he'd said anything about coming around today, but he might, mightn't he? She abandoned her letter and trotted to the window.

It was Lord Harry! He had come to see her. How lovely. How very sweet of him. She dashed to the mirror and tidied her hair. Her morning dress was not the best she owned, but it was new this Season and would certainly do for an unexpected visitor. The light green color went well with her complexion, she thought. It would do, indeed.

She would not keep Lord Harry waiting to change into something better. Certainly she had no wish to let the man think she was eager to impress him. She wasn't. It was only polite to make sure she was at least presentable when the butler announced the gentleman had called for her.

She pinched her cheeks—merely out of habit—and straightened the wrinkles from her gown. True, she didn't wish to keep Lord Harry waiting, but perhaps it would not be good to go racing down to the drawing room the moment official word of his arrival reached her. Still, if she didn't hurry, how was Lord Harry to know she was not going to any effort to enhance her appearance for him? He might assume that was the reason for her delay. He might assume that implied an eagerness on her part to look good for him.

Bother. If only she had known he was coming she would not have this dilemma. She would have to mention that to him.

As well as instructing him on his responsibility to avoid crawling through respectable windows in pursuit of feminine game, she would insist he notify her before he simply showed up at the door. Apparently Lord Harry needed a lesson or two in properly conducting a sham engagement.

But why hadn't the butler or someone come up to tell her the man was below? There was nothing more she could do to improve her appearance without actually going to some real effort. What was the man doing downstairs without her?

She slid open her door and peeked into the corridor. No sign of any household staff come to announce her caller. Odd. She left her room and crept toward the staircase that led down to the front entryway. Yes, now she could hear voices. Lord Harry's for certain. And Anthony's.

"Are you sure you wish to do this, Rastmoor?" Lord Harry was saying.

"I am," Anthony replied. "Chesterton, considering the situation and my sister's possible discomfort from it, I feel I'm honor bound to address it right away."

Well, that didn't sound very good. What could Anthony have heard that should make him suddenly summon Lord Harry without bothering to tell her about it? Heavens, it could be practically anything! There was no telling what rumors Lady Burlington might be spreading this morning.

What was Anthony going to do about it, though? Had he called Lord Harry here to inform him the engagement was off? Surely Anthony would have mentioned that to Penelope if it were his intent. Then she could have begged and pleaded and he would have had to soothe her by promising anything. Even Egypt. That had not happened.

Then what else could he be planning? Perhaps he meant to give Lord Harry a firm talking-to. Anthony was very good at lectures. Generally, though, he preferred to take action. The frequent lectures Penelope received from her brother generally came with some sort of alteration to her allowance or a curtailment of activities. Rarely did Anthony just talk. If he called Lord Harry in today over some rumors he might have heard, she could be fairly certain he intended to take action.

And an action that required him meeting privately—he'd just ushered Lord Harry into the drawing room and pulled the door shut—with the gentleman in question seemed to imply one action in specific. He was going to force them to marry! He was in there now, demanding Lord Harry come up to snuff, and she'd actually end up married to the blackguard!

Drat. That did not fit in with her plans. No, not at all. She'd best get herself down there and take care of this immediately.

The men were both standing when she let herself into the room. They turned to look at her as she rushed in. If Anthony was angry with her, he hid it well. He was good at that, though, so she was careful not to let down her guard. Lord Harry's expression was even harder to gauge.

"Ah, here she is now," Anthony was saying. "She's the one you have to thank for my decision, you know."

"I rather suspected that," Lord Harry replied.

"It wasn't me!" she protested. "It was Lady Burlington, I'll wager. Anthony, whatever she told you, honestly you can't believe it, can you?"

Anthony frowned. "I don't really care what Lady Burlington has been saying about it, Penelope. I've seen it with my own eyes and, to tell the truth, I'd be a pretty sad excuse for a brother if I didn't do something to protect you."

"Anthony, you don't need to do this," she said.

"But if it's what he feels he must do, I see no reason to argue," Lord Harry said quickly.

She glared at him. "But if he understood how mistaken Lady Burlington was about what she saw last night, then perhaps he would not feel he must do this."

Now Lord Harry was glaring at her. "As your brother said, Lady Burlington has nothing to do with this, Miss Rastmoor. If he feels this is something he must do, then perhaps you ought to let him."

"I thought you assured me you did not wish to let him."

"It would be quite rude of me not to let him, in this instance."

"I think I should have some say in the matter, sir."

"I don't see why on earth you would. Your brother is a competent adult; he can decide where to bestow his possessions."

"His possessions? What, as if that's all I am—"

"Wait just one moment," Anthony interrupted. "Penelope, what are you talking about?"

She glanced from Lord Harry's expression of frustration to Anthony's of suspicion. Drat. Perhaps she'd been a bit hasty in assuming she knew what they were discussing here.

"Er, what exactly are *you* talking about, Anthony?" she asked slowly.

"Your brother was most graciously offering me a new carriage," Lord Harry answered. "At your suggestion, I was led to believe," he added.

Ah, yes. She had spoken to Anthony about that. Well, how nice to see he'd considered her request and was prepared to rescue her from having to be seen about town in Lord Harry's rattle-clap rig. Too bad she'd forgotten all about that.

So then, did this mean the gentlemen were not discussing marriage terms? Oh bother. She hoped she hadn't put her foot into it too deep this time.

"So just exactly what did Lady Burlington see last night that she's so very mistaken about?" Anthony asked.

"Nothing," Penelope said quickly.

Lord Harry shrugged in blissful ignorance, and his angelic expression was the very paragon of virtue. Anthony was hardly appeased.

"But then why did you seem so eager to race in here and proclaim that—"

The sound of a carriage arriving outside the window provided a blessed interruption.

"Oh look!" Lord Harry exclaimed. "Could this be the very thing? I say, Rastmoor, you've completely outdone yourself."

Penelope glanced past him out the window. Indeed, the shiny new phaeton was quite eye-catching. This was his offering to Lord Harry? Heavens, but she had no idea her brother thought quite this highly of her unsuitable fiancé. Surely he wouldn't give the man such a prize if he did not welcome him into the family. Goodness, very worrisome indeed!

"I hope you find it adequate, Chesterton," Anthony said, confirming that this was exactly the carriage he'd been expecting. "I know it's a bit extravagant, but consider it an early wedding present."

"I'm quite indebted to you," Lord Harry said.

"Indeed you are," Anthony agreed. "I'm letting you have

my sister, after all. See that you continue to deserve her. Just what was all that about Lady Burlington, anyway?"

Drat it all, but if Anthony was feeling so very graciously disposed toward Lord Harry, any mention of last night might completely work against her. The very last thing he'd do would be to allow her to run off to Egypt. Likely the very first thing he'd do would be to drag them both off to the parson. Not at all what she wished for. Oh, but she had to get Lord Harry out of here before he ingratiated himself even further or she'd never be rid of the man.

"What a lovely carriage, Anthony! You are simply the best brother ever. Please, Lord Harry, you must take me driving in it straightaway!"

Lord Harry seemed to think that a rather prudent idea, as well. He smoothly ignored Anthony's question and seemed to suddenly become as enthralled with the carriage as she was.

"Excellent notion, Miss Rastmoor. Surely your brother can have no objection. Such a fine carriage demands to be shown off, especially if it is conveying the loveliest young woman in all of England. Will you give us your leave, sir?"

Penelope pretended to be flattered, and she was quite certain she detected a slight eye roll from her brother, but Anthony put up no objection to them taking a ride in the beautiful carriage he'd provided. Good. Perhaps this Lady Burlington business would be soon forgotten.

"I'll get my things right away!" she said, flitting about as if this were the most exciting thing ever.

"Perhaps this will be useful on our outing," Lord Harry said, suddenly producing a small parcel, carefully wrapped in tissue.

She frowned at it. Had she seen this before? Yesterday, perhaps? She grabbed it from him and ripped it open. Her reaction was, most likely, not quite as refined as she might have wished.

"Good God! It's that shawl from Tilly's!"

Lord Harry seemed pleased that she should recognize it. "Indeed, the shopkeeper told me you'd been admiring it. So I bought it for you."

Oh. Oh dear! Somehow he'd been horribly misinformed. Heavens, but he'd meant to make her happy by presenting her with this monstrosity. Well, she supposed she ought to work harder to pretend. It was, after all, the least she could do after nearly slipping up in her ravings about Lady Burlington's gossip.

"Er, thank you ever so much," she managed with a mostly convincing smile.

She gushed as much as she could stomach, hoping it would prevent her brother from pursuing additional questions about what might have happened. Lord Harry did his own gushing on and on about Anthony's kindness and generosity and the many fine qualities of the carriage he'd just received, and finally Anthony seemed eager to escort them out the door. They were in the phaeton and down the road without further difficulties.

"What the devil were you thinking, barging in there and rambling on about Lady Burlington, of all things?" Lord Harry asked when they were alone and safely some distance from the house.

"I thought Anthony had heard rumors and perhaps he had called you here to demand we marry right away!" she replied, not altogether pleased that he would go from flattering fiancé to insolent business partner so quickly.

"Well, it appears we've been lucky and Lady Burlington has kept her thoughts to herself this time."

"That hardly sounds like Lady Burlington."

"Agreed. I'll have to admit, I myself was a bit concerned when I got your brother's note that he needed to meet with me this morning."

"You were worried he might order me to cry off and then your uncle would be less inclined to think more favorably toward you?"

"No, I was worried he might order me to set a date and strap a Miss Rastmoon–shaped noose around my neck."

"Well! How dreadful that would be for you, no doubt."

"Oh, don't take on. You thought the same thing and came running down the bloody stairs blathering on and on and just about made your brother seal the deal! For a truth, Miss Rastmoor, I began to worry perhaps you'd decided not to honor your promise that this engagement is only in pretense."

"Oh, I have full intent to honor that, sir. As if I'd ever consider actually marrying you!"

"Then I'm happy we are in agreement."

"Yes, we are."

"Odd, though."

"What?"

"I don't know that I've ever met a truly happily engaged couple who are fully in agreement on anything."

"That is because they have nothing to look forward to but a lifetime with each other. We can be safely assured of a lifetime without each other."

She laughed as she spoke, but somehow the words didn't sound nearly as cheerful as they were meant to.

"Then perhaps we should enjoy what time we do have with each other, Miss Rastmoor. Are you finding your brother's carriage to be everything it should be?"

"And then some, sir. Anthony did very well, did he not?"

"He did indeed."

She sat back in the comfortable seat and had to admit she was enjoying the ride. Even if Lord Harry had many moments of insufferableness, he could also be quite charming. It was a shame his uncle could not see any good in him and kept the poor man so desperately poor. Lord Harry looked good driving this phaeton. It suited him.

He glanced over at her, and she realized she'd been staring. She looked away quickly. Bother, but she had no time for staring at Lord Harry. She should be planning her journey to Egypt, plotting exactly what balance of tears and arguing it would take to convince Anthony when the time came.

Lord, but that time had best come soon. Too many more of these pleasant rides with Lord Harry and she was likely to miss them when it was over. That did not at all suit her purposes.

DAMN. PENELOPE RASTMOOR LOOKED ESPECIALLY FRESH and glowing and lovely today. Harris was finding it difficult to keep his mind on the more important matters at hand, such as tooling his beautiful new phaeton around the nastiest piles of unpleasantness in the roadway or thinking up ways to get his hands on the treasures he so desperately needed to rescue Oldham. Even the appreciative and covetous glances of passersby did little to distract his mind from the young lady seated next to him.

The brilliant scarab glinted enticingly, and he was practically itching to get his hands on it. And all the rest of her. What on earth was wrong with him? Penelope Rastmoor was the very last woman he should find himself interested in. She was shallow, self-centered, uneducated in anything important, and she very clearly was not at all interested in him.

Perhaps that was the crux of his problem. He was used to attracting females, used to being the object of desire. With Penelope, it was very clear she desired only to get what she wanted out of him then be rid of him.

It was almost embarrassing how terrified the girl had appeared when she'd come rushing in on them, fearing that he was about to set a wedding date. He could hardly blame her, of course. If Rastmoor had heard some vile rumors from Lady Burlington it would have been only natural for him to expect the lovebirds to begin setting dates and sending out invitations. That, of course, is what people did when they were engaged. He should have been prepared for such a thing.

"You know," he said, careful to keep his eyes on the street ahead of them despite how much he'd rather have turned to admire his companion. "It would not be a bad idea for us to concoct some ready answer should Lady Burlington decide to start spreading rumors of finding us together last night."

She thought about this for a moment, and nodded. "I suppose you're right. But perhaps simply denying her charges would be best, after all. Unless of course someone other than Lady Burlington saw you there and might corroborate her story. Were you seen? Did you, er, go back there once I was gone?"

"No. I did not. No one else saw me."

"Well, no one else but Milly, the housemaid. Are you saying she is not of significance enough for us to worry over her word?"

"A housemaid? No. We may simply deny."

He could feel her eyeing him. What did she expect him to say? It seemed she was waiting for something.

"And should your brother wonder why we are in no hurry to set the date," he went on, deciding this was perhaps the direction of her thoughts, "we'll tell him, uh, we wish to wait a bit."

"For your uncle."

"What?"

"We'll tell him we're waiting for your uncle to finish arranging for your finances."

"Indeed, that sounds plausible."

"Of course it is! Isn't that what this is about, after all? You are willing to go along with this so that your uncle will look on you favorably and will arrange for you to have a better living? See, it's the perfect excuse because it's partially true."

He acknowledged her point. "Yes, I see. And every habitual liar knows that the best falsehood is one that employs a great deal of truth."

"Exactly."

"I worry for you, Miss Rastmoor. You appear far too good at this sort of thing."

"I've lived under my brother since Papa died years ago, sir. I'm afraid I've had to learn a few things to survive."

"To survive? Rastmoor doesn't strike me as an ogre, my dear."

"No, he's not an ogre. I love my brother, I do. It's just that, well, his goals for me are very much different from mine. If it were up to Anthony, I'd never do anything, go anywhere, meet anyone, or learn anything at all."

"Sounds like a very safe existence."

She actually snorted at that. "Yes, doesn't it? But what fun is it to be safe all the time?"

He had to admit the prospect didn't exactly sound like much fun, but he could truthfully say the idea of being safe certainly had its merits. The girl had no idea just how lucky she was to have family who looked out for her well-being and actually wished to keep her around them. He could barely recall the last time any of his so-called family truly wished for his company, no matter how many times over the years he had craved theirs.

"I'm sure Rastmoor has your best interests at heart."

"I know, I know. He believes he does, but really he has no idea what my interests are."

"From what I've seen of your interests, my dear, your brother may, in fact, be quite wise in holding you on such a tight leash."

"Oh bother. Not you, too!"

He had to laugh. "No, not me, too, Miss Rastmoor. If you may recall, I am currently playing the role of villain in one of your schemes, so you can hardly accuse me of being party to your boredom."

"Well, you certainly don't seem to be playing the villain with much conviction, Lord Harry. My brother is quite in love with you, it would seem. I fear things are going far better for you in this plot than they are for me."

He twitched the reins and the finely bred horses eagerly increased their steps. The phaeton was well sprung and did not lurch or jolt in the least. They rolled along in perfect comfort and admirable style.

It was not the fashionable hour, so Harris had not bothered to steer them toward the park. Instead, they were traveling roads lined with homes of the well fed and highly regarded. The traffic was light and the sunshine filtered through the leafy overhang where a row of ash trees had grown full and mature along one side of the street. Indeed, his companion was correct. Things certainly were going well for him.

He'd found most of the stolen collection, the scarab was nearly in his possession, and now he'd gotten a brilliant new phaeton out of the bargain. Indeed, all he needed was to put it all together and Professor Oldham was as good as rescued. It would be up to Rastmoor to rescue his sister. Harris hoped to be a continent away by the time Penelope was left to face society's censure alone.

He did regret that. True, Penelope had run headlong into this sham engagement knowing it could not possibly end without at least some damage to her reputation, but still he couldn't really pretend to take pride in his involvement in her ruin. Enjoyment, perhaps, but certainly not pride. Likely that was what pricked his conscience the most, the fact that he truly was enjoying himself.

He enjoyed the pretense of respectability, the easy acceptance he'd received from Rastmoor, the glorious sensation of driving and being seen in this remarkable new carriage, and of course he enjoyed Penelope. If he had his way, likely he'd enjoy a good deal more of her, too. That would, of course, be reprehensible, but he was hardly one to worry over such foolishness as honor and morality. His uncle reminded him at every possible moment that there was no honor in him—not from the start. Why should he deny himself what Miss Rastmoor was making so very easy?

At least, he thought she would make it rather easy, should he ever get around to asking. He'd simply have to ask the right questions.

"I've noticed you wear a rather striking pendant. Egyptian, I believe?"

"Oh, you mean my scarab. Yes, it is striking, isn't it?"

"A gift from someone?"

"No, actually, I purchased it for myself."

"Really? Er, rather an unusual purchase, I should think."

"Should you? I don't think so in the least."

"But it's not exactly something one sees around every corner."

"Which of course merely adds to its allure."

"Is that what the shopkeeper who sold it to you said?"

"Shopkeeper? Honestly, you cannot come by something like this in a simple shop, Lord Harry."

"Oh? You came by it through some other means?"

"Well, I . . . Oh look. There is someone waving toward you, just ahead."

He glanced in the direction she pointed to discover there was indeed someone waving toward him. Bother. Just when he was getting into conversation that would prove most enlightening, now they were distracted. Miss Rastmoor would likely wonder at his interest in her jewelry when he tried to bring up the subject again. The last thing he wanted was for her to become curious and discover just how valuable her little bauble truly was.

But there was nothing he could do. Approaching were two young men on horseback. Harris recognized both of them. He was only barely tolerant of running into one of them. The other he would rather wish to hades than suffer the interruption.

"Hello, cousin!" the tolerated one called, smiling.

Ferrel. What the devil was he doing here? And with such annoying company. Harris eyed his younger cousin and the gentleman who rode along beside him.

"Hello, Ferrel. Markland."

"Good day to you," Ferrel said, cheerful as always. "And to Miss Rastmoor, as well."

He could not say he liked the warm smile Ferrel had ready for the young lady. "So you and my fiancée are acquainted?"

"Only just," Ferrel replied. "We met yesterday. It's most pleasant to see you again, Miss Rastmoor."

"Thank you, sir," Miss Rastmoor said with a polite nod.

Harris approved of the cool tone she used. He would have approved even more if her gaze had not shifted to Markland and lingered over his elegant form.

"May I present my friend George Markland?" Ferrel said. "He is just arrived in Town."

Ah, pity he'd chosen now to arrive. Another few weeks and Harris would have been gone and missed this happy reunion.

"Yes, Markland and I have met," Harris said, carefully ignoring the fact that the introduction had most likely been for Miss Rastmoor's sake. "I hope your family is not missing you too much while you are in Town, Markland." *And how soon before you leave?*

"My grandfather's health continues to be poor, but he assures me I can be spared from his bedside to attend to business here. How surprised I was to arrive and hear of your engagement, Chesterton. May I extend my good wishes?"

No, actually, you may not. He didn't say that out loud, of course. No reason to make things unpleasant at this point. With luck, they'd never so much as lay eyes on Markland again during his stay in Town and there'd be no reason to inform Miss Rastmoor of the unpleasantness between them. The sooner Harris could make polite small talk and then be rid of the men, the better.

"I am indeed a most fortunate man," he said. "I find being engaged is quite a comfortable circumstance. I encourage everyone to try it at some point."

Markland did not reply. Ferrel, however, thought it was great fun.

"Listen to him, Markland! My cousin is natting on like some silly schoolgirl in love! Oh, but this is rich. I never would have thought to see the day, Harry."

"Obviously Miss Rastmoor is a true Incomparable, to reduce our Lord Harry to this condition. I tip my hat to you, miss."

Miss Rastmoor seemed to find the gentlemen quite amusing, and she laughed easily for them. Her smile for Markland's flattery was warming inordinately, and Harris could not like that one bit. Fortunately, as they had paused in the street to pass these pleasantries, they were now blocking traffic and it was time to move on. Harris could not have been happier for it.

"And now the incomparable Miss Rastmoor and I must be off on our way, gentlemen," Harris announced. "I bid you well, Cousin."

"Indeed, Harry. Perhaps we'll meet up soon."

"Perhaps," Harris conceded, considering it would be rather difficult to avoid him now that they'd run across each other again.

Ferrel would likely seek to trot after his heels as he'd often done before. Harris could only hope he would not bring along his smug and superior new friend. Perhaps, in fact, Harris would be forced to fabricate some good reason for Ferrel to avoid Markland. True, he'd likely not find any real issues to score against the man, but that was a part of the problem. George Markland was too damn perfect, and Harris would make well certain that as few people as possible ever figured that out.

Miss Rastmoor especially.

Chapter Eight

She wasn't certain, but it seemed Lord Harry had not been very pleased to see his cousin or his friend Mr. Markland. Penelope had no idea why that should be the case. True, Ferrel Chesterton had been abominably forward yesterday when he'd approached her in public, but he'd seemed earnestly pleased to run into his cousin. And Mr. Markland seemed quite cordial. Perhaps she had imagined any ill humor in Lord Harry at meeting them.

No matter. Lord Harry's connections were the least of her concern right now. She'd do well to worry more for the pressing matters at hand. Such as Anthony's growing fondness for a future brother-in-law he was supposed to despise.

"I'm getting a bit concerned about Anthony's attitude toward you," she began. "I fear you are not nearly as disgusting to him as I had first expected."

"I'm not sure if I should be flattered or not, Miss Rastmoor."

"Not, I should think, since disgusting Anthony is our top priority."

"Yes, that and impressing my uncle."

"Yes, that, too." She had to think about this for a moment.

"It does seem quite a conflict, doesn't it, to accomplish both tasks at the same time?"

"It does, I admit."

"I suppose we may have to concentrate on one at a time, and since once we've managed to turn Anthony completely against you your uncle is hardly likely to be pleased, then perhaps we should work toward gaining his favor before we increase our efforts to lose Anthony's."

"It would seem logical to approach things that way."

"Very well. I'll allow Anthony to continue to like you just a bit longer."

"You are kindness embodied, Miss Rastmoor."

His smirk assured her he was mocking now. "I'm so glad you are finding this whole thing amusing, Lord Harry."

"And I am, my dear, I assure you. Would that all my engagements were to prove this entertaining."

"All of them? And how many have you had, sir?"

"I'm pleased to say you are my first, Miss Rastmoor," he said, then glanced at her with lowered brows and flashing eyes. "Pity you cannot say the same for me."

His tone made her blush. Her cheeks grew warm and she found herself staring at her lap. The man's eyes, his words, the deep warmth in his voice . . . It was impossible for her not to recognize his implication.

She supposed, in fact, she ought to be somewhat insulted by it. Why, obviously he implied by his tone and flashing eyes that she'd behaved badly with her previous fiancés. Insulting, indeed. Yet she wasn't insulted. He was teasing her, of course. Far from being insulted, she found herself oddly flattered by such warm attentions.

How ridiculous of her, to blush at his teasing. As if she welcomed it! Very well, perhaps she did. What female could not? Lord Harry was, after all, impossible to ignore from a feminine viewpoint. She simply must get hold of her silly emotions and recall that theirs was a relationship of convenience and nothing more.

He was still eyeing her, though, and drat it all if he didn't appear to be considering her most convenient indeed. The blushing continued. Botheration! This was most decidedly *in*convenient.

"I believe I explained to you the situation regarding my various fiancés, sir," she said, aiming for pert and a bit chilly.

"You babbled something about them, but it was nothing like an explanation. I rather assumed you had something to hide."

"Well, I do not. I simply do not wish to spend hours discussing ancient history."

"No, you prefer to grab ancient history up from a table and bludgeon me with it as I enter the room."

"You entered the room through the window, sir! Honestly, you cannot continue to blame me for doing what every sane human would."

He laughed at her again. Extra drat; she found she enjoyed that, too. She enjoyed seeing the sparkle in his eye, the hinted dimple in his cheek, and knowing somehow she'd been the one to put it there.

"London can rest well at night as long as Miss Rastmoor has her funerary phallus close at hand."

"However did you know what that was?" she said, then realized she was rather indicting herself. A decent and proper young lady would certainly have no inkling what that item had been. "I mean, is that truly what I grabbed up last night?"

"I regret to inform you, my dear, that indeed it was. In all its wooden glory."

So he had recognized it for what it was. Well, of course he had. What else could it have been? Even if the man had no knowledge whatsoever of Egyptian antiquities, he'd certainly have recognized that object. And, dear Lord, she'd been wielding it around like her weapon of choice! She was blushing again now; she could feel it.

"I should have thought you might have known what it was yourself," he said.

"What? No, of course not. I'm shocked you should think so!"

"Well, you wear that Egyptian pendant around your neck. I merely thought perhaps you had a certain propensity for antiquities."

"Oh. Yes, well, I do enjoy some of the more aesthetic items. They are quite lovely, aren't they?"

"Indeed," he said, and was eyeing her scarab again. "This one in particular, because it is adorned by you, my dear."

"I believe you are teasing me again."

"What? No, in this case I am perfectly serious. Your little scarab would not look half so pretty on anyone else. You were wise to purchase it for yourself. Where did you say that you got it?"

Now she knew he'd been teasing her. No man who flattered in earnest would have been so quick to change the topic and pursue mindless small talk this way. She tried not to be disappointed.

"From a friend, sir."

"A friend who collects antiquities?"

"Er, not that I know of. My friend had come by it and did not wish to keep it, so I purchased it with my pin money."

"Pin money, you say? Your brother must be very generous indeed."

"I believe he's rather proven that point today, don't you agree?"

He nodded. "Indeed I do. Anthony Rastmoor has proven himself a generous and benevolent man, even if he has insisted that you never do anything, go anywhere, meet anyone, or learn anything at all."

"Perhaps I did exaggerate a bit about Anthony's rules."

"And perhaps your brother has relaxed his rules now that you are a respectably betrothed woman."

"Perhaps. Now if we can only see such an effect on your uncle!"

"I'm afraid that might be a lost cause. Come, why don't you tell me more about your scarab and how your friend came to possess it?"

"Oh no, don't think you can change the subject so easily. It's not fair that I should be getting all the benefit of this engagement. We should think up some way to convince your uncle that you are worthy of his high esteem, after all. Why, certainly if he believed you reformed, he'd reverse your financial difficulties immediately. Somehow we must show him that you are every bit respectable now. Yes, that is what we must do."

"Clearly. But how, exactly, do you propose we do that, my dear?"

"Well, perhaps you could introduce me to him. If I pretend

to fawn on you and drivel on and on to him over your many virtues, that might have some effect."

"Oh, I don't doubt your ability to drivel and fawn, Miss Rastmoor, but I'm afraid an introduction would be rather difficult. I'm told my uncle has left London for Kent, the family seat, and I've certainly not been issued an invitation. In fact, I doubt he even knows I've become engaged."

"What? He doesn't know? Well, then I must send him a letter. Yes, that is what I'll do."

"A letter? You make it a habit of sending unsolicited letters to men you've never met, Miss Rastmoor?"

"No! Of course not. Don't be silly. I just . . . I was thinking aloud, that's all. You should be the one to send him a letter, of course. Then you could tell him of our engagement and you could give him my good wishes."

"And like magic his heart will melt and he will clutch me to his bosom?"

"Surely he would at least wish you happy. It's a start."

"A start. Yes, I suppose it would be."

"Excellent. The sooner we win him, the quicker we can alienate Anthony."

"Indeed, we have such fun to look forward to."

"Actually, I hate to say it, but it would appear we have rain to look forward to just now, Lord Harry. Heavens, look how dark the sky has gotten."

It was true. Clouds had rolled in where the sun had been shining but minutes ago. She should have been paying closer attention. Now if they did not get home quickly, Lord Harry's beautiful new carriage was soon to be a wet new carriage. And them along with it.

"Here, let me put up the hood," he said, pulling the carriage off to the side of the street and drawing to a halt.

He pulled up the brake and dropped the reins. Penelope remained comfortably in her seat while he climbed down and began working at the elegant hood, pulling it up first on one side, then going around to the other to adjust it when it appeared it had gotten stuck. She tried to be patient, but really all she could think was that someone she knew might come by and see her in the dreadful shawl. The air had begun to chill, though, so she had little choice but to hug it around herself.

Lord Harry seemed to be having some difficulty managing the hood. She tried to help him, pulling on it from where she sat. It was stuck. She gave an extra tug and finally it loosened. Rather unexpectedly, in fact. She nearly fell off her seat. Groping to catch herself, she fell against the lever and released the brake.

Ordinarily that would have done no harm besides a bit of bruising. However, just at that moment a coach clattered by at a rapid pace. The driver's whip went wild and snapped in the air a hair's breadth away from Lord Harry's horses. They flinched. Then they jolted.

Penelope was tossed completely out of her seat and fell onto the footboard as the beautiful phaeton lurched into sudden motion. Discovering their reins slack and the brake released, the horses surged forward and lunged into the street. Lord Harry called after them, but of course that did little but add to the chaos of the moment. Penelope fumbled to regain her seat, but she was tumbled to and fro, unable to do much more than fall about, ending up wedged into the narrow space and completely unable to so much as see the terrified horses, let alone control them.

Dear heavens, but she was trapped here as the carriage sped up and careened forward! There was no telling what might happen. She'd be upset for certain, likely thrown under the galloping hooves or knocked senseless against the pavement. She couldn't even find her breath to cry out for Lord Harry to save her.

But then the carriage was slowing. Voices shouted around her and she was finally able to grab onto something to regain her balance and pull herself up out of the veritable hole she was in. She righted herself with as much grace as was possible, which of course meant none at all, and finally plunked her backside securely into the seat, clutching the leather around her for dear life.

The carriage rocked, but it did not overturn. Instead, it came to a stop and she brushed her disheveled bonnet back to look around. Lord Harry had saved her after all.

No, wait . . . she was wrong. It was not Lord Harry. A gentleman on horseback was there beside her, sitting with cultured elegance as if rescuing wayward carriages was an everyday occurrence for him. He held his own horse in check with one hand, while with the other he gripped the halter of one of her horses. His hat sat perfectly erect on his fashionable head and he gave her the kindest of smiles as he turned to assess her damage.

"Are you well, Miss Rastmoor?" he asked.

She had to catch her breath before she could answer. "Yes, thank you, Mr. Markland."

"That could have been quite a nasty accident there," he said. "Are you certain you are not injured?"

"Yes, I'm quite well, thank you," she said, feeling all sorts of self-conscious in her mussed condition. "But how did you come to be here? Didn't we pass you going in the other direction?"

"We were, but the party we'd been going to meet was not at home. Ferrel went on to another engagement, and I returned this way." He smiled a remarkably perfect smile at her. "And I'm rather glad that I did, I must say."

"Yes, as am I," she agreed. "The horses bolted and I was all jostled about, and—"

"And just where was Chesterton while all this was occurring?" Markland asked.

"I'm right here."

His voice indicated he was jogging up beside the carriage. She turned to see him, and met his eyes for one brief moment. Then his full attention was turned toward Markland. She supposed it was a good thing she hadn't been truly injured. No words of worried compassion came to ask after her.

"Ah, there you are, Chesterton. It would appear you lost something," Markland said.

"But of course you are only too happy to return it to me now, aren't you?" Lord Harry said, holding out his hand to take the reins from the other man.

"If you're certain you can take care of it."

Lord Harry glared daggers at that. Penelope sank back into her seat, feeling the tension between the men as if it were a living creature on its own. The fact that she could have very nearly just been killed seemed to have escaped both of them as they stared and postured. How vexing!

"I will take care to get Miss Rastmoor safely indoors before the rain," Lord Harry said, fairly ripping the reins from Markland. "If you don't mind, Markland, we'll take our leave."

Markland nodded with perfect politeness, nudging his mount to take a few steps backward as Lord Harry easily swung himself up into the seat beside Penelope. His warm, solid body brushed against hers, and she couldn't help but notice that every muscle in his arm and shoulder was taut. She wished she hadn't noticed that detail quite so thoroughly, in fact. It sent a most unmaidenly flush over her body, and she was suddenly warm despite the chill wind picking up around them.

"By all means," Markland said. "Miss Rastmoor's well-being is vital. I should be only too happy to see it assured."

Markland smiled toward her again, and his words were flattering, but Lord Harry's response was less than courteous. He didn't even bother with a polite nod or any other parting pleasantry, but simply snapped the reins and began to guide the horses back into the roadway. Taut muscular shoulders aside, she could only think the man very rude. Especially considering a doting fiancé should certainly have been more grateful to the man who saved his beloved's life.

"Good day to you, Mr. Markland," she called back, ignoring Lord Harry's sullen looks. "And thank you so very, very much."

"It was a pleasure to assist you, miss," Markland said, touching his hat. "I hope we might meet again soon, but in much less dramatic circumstances."

Yes, she could heartily agree with that. Her brief ride in a runaway carriage was more than enough to convince her she did not need to experience anything like that again. She would have expressed her agreement, but Lord Harry turned the carriage sharply and she was forced to sit quite properly, unable to lean forward and so much as wave at Mr. Markland as they left him there in the roadway. She frowned at her companion.

"My, but anyone would think you disliked that man, Lord Harry," she said.

"I do."

"And from the way you are slapping the horses there one might think you dislike them, as well."

His aggressive hold on the reins went immediately more slack.

"I'm concerned about the rain. The clouds seem to be rolling in much quicker than before."

"Should we stop to put the hood up?"

Now he glared at her with something like the look he'd given Markland.

"I am teasing you," she said, though it appeared the man was in no mood for humor.

"I'm sorry for what happened, Miss Rastmoor. I will never let you be endangered again."

"It wasn't your fault," she assured him. "The horses were spooked. They don't know you and you don't know them; you could not have guessed they would behave that way."

"I should not have let it happen. I'm sorry."

"Well, no harm done. Your lovely new carriage was not harmed, and Mr. Markland came along in time to rescue me."

"Yes, he did."

"So we are all very fortunate. You should have at least been civil to the man, though. He seemed affable enough."

"Did he? I have made it a practice never to trust anything that Markland might seem."

"Ah, so there is a story there. Tell me, what is it between you?"

For just half a moment she thought he appeared as if he might consider telling her. But then the moment was gone and his jaw clenched and his eyes went cold.

"Nothing. We have a very long-standing difference of opinion, that is all."

"Clearly it is not, but I suppose whatever it is, it is not my business."

"No, it isn't."

She shrugged and pulled her hideous wrap more tightly around herself. "Very well. Perhaps I might run across Mr. Markland somewhere, now that we've been introduced. He might be more forthcoming."

"I don't doubt that he would," Lord Harry said, more cold than ever. "In fact, he'd very likely tell you anything you wanted to hear. Just realize, my dear, that you would have little way of knowing which bits of it are true, and which are his own fabrication."

"I'll remember that, Lord Harry," she said. "But you realize, of course, exactly the same might easily be said of you."

Harris was not at all happy to hear Miss Rastmoor compare him in any way to George Markland. He wished he were free to inform her just how mistaken she was. He and George Markland were nothing alike.

At least, not in any of the ways that honestly mattered. He refused to contemplate the similarities that had become so painfully obvious to him over the years. All that mattered, truly, were the differences. And those were plentiful.

"At least it appears we made it to your home before the rain started up," he said, pulling the phaeton to a halt in front of the grand Rastmoor town house.

"Thank you," Miss Rastmoor said.

He rather hoped she might say more, but she didn't. There was nothing more for him to do but hop out and help her down. Once again, he'd surrounded himself with the girl and still he was no closer to learning what he needed to know about the scarab. All he'd done was allow her to be practically killed by his own carelessness. Clearly this false engagement was not turning out entirely as planned.

If he did not do something soon to get what he needed, he was going to begin seriously doubting his abilities. And he was quite certain that where Miss Rastmoor was concerned, he would be more than able. All he needed was to concentrate on his goal and not let himself be distracted by minor inconveniences like George Markland.

He reached to lift her from the carriage, and it was a very simple thing to let his hands linger just a heartbeat too long as they slid across her body. It took very little effort at all to hold her just the slightest bit too close as her feet hovered above the pavement and she was completely at his mercy. It was pure pleasure itself to gaze into her large blue eyes, made even larger by the surprise of this sudden physical intimacy. Indeed, he was more than able to accomplish his goal.

"When will I see you again, Miss Rastmoor?"

She seemed momentarily at a loss, but found her voice soon enough. "Will you be at Lady Burlington's ball tonight?"

"Lady Burlington is giving another ball?" This was news to him.

"She has had some friends arrive from the Continent and now she's hosting a ball in their honor, I believe. Mamma says we ought to go, so I suppose we will go. I hope you . . . that is, perhaps you will be there, too."

"If you will promise to dance with me, Miss Rastmoor, I will most certainly be there."

She smiled and her eyes became even more blue than he could have imagined. "Then you will most certainly see me, Lord Harry."

"I am looking forward to it already," he said, finding the words felt as sincere as he hoped to make them sound.

He was looking forward to seeing her. What warm-blooded male would not? He would simply have to make sure his anticipation centered more on what he could get from Miss Rastmoor rather than what he could do to her. There was much to look forward to on both counts, but he was determined to keep his mind on business.

However, since playing this little charade with her was a part of his business, there could surely be no harm in enjoying himself along the way. Instead of releasing her once he'd set her securely on the ground, he pulled her closer and leaned in. A simple, tender kiss was certainly not out of character for a smitten fiancé, after all.

Perhaps he should have kept it simpler and not given in to the temptation of her scent, her taste. Perhaps he should have focused more on tenderness and less on the feel of her very feminine curves pressed against him, the delectable roundness of her backside as his hand strayed there. Certainly he should have kept his tongue in his own mouth. All those realizations hit him after the fact, once a loud, forced cough interrupted from the nearby doorway.

Hellfire. He released Miss Rastmoor's heavenly lips to find her brother glaring fury at him. Clearly Anthony Rastmoor felt Harris's action went far beyond acceptable. Indeed, as his brain began to function after momentarily losing control to Miss Rastmoor's many charms, Harris was inclined to agree.

"Penelope, come in at once," Rastmoor said, holding the door wide and giving no invitation to Harris.

But Miss Rastmoor was seemingly unfazed by it all. She appeared cheerfully in control of her full faculties and ignored her brother long enough to give Harris a friendly smile.

"Will you come in for some tea, Lord Harry?"

"Er, no thank you," he replied with a quick glance back in Rastmoor's direction. "Perhaps I should get the carriage under roof before the rain begins."

She nodded, seeing the wisdom in this. "Yes, it would be a shame to get such a pretty thing all spattered with mud or ruin the padding. Well, then I suppose I'll see you this evening at the ball."

He took a nice, respectable step away from her and bowed politely. "I'll look for you there."

Rastmoor had not budged from his spot, so Harris didn't attempt to detain the girl. Indeed, he'd wished to ask her to wear the scarab again, planning to flatter her with comparisons of its brilliance to the celestial blue of her eyes, but perhaps he'd forgo that. She seemed to favor the piece, and with luck she'd choose to wear it on her own. If not, surely he could still find some way to bring it into conversation again. He'd been so very, very close to discovering how she'd come by it.

Miss Rastmoor gave him another smile, curtsied sweetly, then trotted up the steps to meet her brother at the door. He stood still as a sentinel and allowed her to pass. His eyes never left Harris, conveying warning and threat, both at the same time.

It was almost humorous how the man's demeanor had changed. Rastmoor had been all kindness and generosity this morning as he informed Harris of his gift. Odd that one little glimpse of his sister in a warm embrace could change him so dramatically. In the man's favor, however, Harris did have to concede that embrace had gone a good deal beyond merely *warm*. Plus, there had been a good deal of oral activity involved, and they had been standing on the street in broad daylight, after all. Yes, he could understand that most brothers might take exception to a man behaving that way with their sister.

Hell, he took exception to himself for behaving that way with Miss Rastmoor. What had come over him? Was he so desperate that he couldn't manage just a sweet little kiss to pique the girl's interest so she'd be more pliable, giving him information when he saw her again? All he needed from her was the scarab, and a bit of information so he could track down the rest of the stolen artifacts. He did not need more from her.

Yet he'd never been particularly good at keeping the separation clear in his head regarding *need* and *want*. It seemed too often he mistook one for the other. He'd do very well tonight to keep firmly in mind what he *needed*, and not become preoccupied with what he *wanted*.

"I'll just take this down to the mews," he said to Rastmoor, who still stood at the doorway and glared.

"Yes. You should do that," the man replied.

With a simple nod, Harris climbed back into the carriage. Losing his head with Miss Rastmoor was quite careless of him. Indeed, if he wasn't more careful, he'd risk losing far more than self-control.

BREATHE, PENELOPE TOLD HERSELF AS SHE SAUNTERED as casually as she could past Anthony into their home and toward the stairs that would carry her up to the safety of her bedroom. *Now, move my left foot forward . . . now the right . . . Exhale and breathe again . . . now the right foot, er, make that left foot . . . Very good, now the right . . .*

Oh bother. She stumbled on the stairway. It was all so very confusing. Did she really do this whole breathing and walking thing every day without so much as a thought? Heavens, but Lord Harry's simple little kisses unhinged her.

How could that be? She knew he was doing it merely as a part of their charade. But this time it had come completely out of the blue! Perhaps that's what had caused such mental confusion; the man had given her no chance to prepare herself.

Indeed, one really ought to be prepared for a kiss from Lord Harris Chesterton. Just the merest brush of his skin was enough to set the blood racing, the heart pounding. How lucky she was that it so happened to be *her* blood and *her* heart! But heavens, she really needed to get control of herself.

"Penelope!" Anthony called behind her.

She stumbled again, practically falling back down the four or five steps up she'd already managed to take. Drat. Now she was going to be subject to a lecture about what was or was not proper behavior. As if she wasn't just now very painfully aware of her very improper behavior!

"If you don't mind, Anthony," she said, "the wind was getting rather chilly out there and I'd very much like to go refresh myself and warm up a bit before you regale me with another sermon."

"I'm not planning to waste any more of my breath on sermons for you, sister dear. You know very well you were behaving like a hoyden out there, but to be honest, I couldn't care less. Before long you'll be Lord Harry's problem, not mine. I feel quite justified in maintaining my silence regarding that shameless display. I would, however, like to inform you that you have a visitor."

Oh. Well, now. That was unexpected.

"A visitor? Who?"

"I believe you'll find Miss Bradley waiting for you upstairs."

"Maria is here?"

"She arrived some minutes ago and said it was quite important that she see you. I told her you were out, and that our mother is out, as well, but she practically begged me to allow her to wait. So, I did."

"Her aunt is not with her?"

"No, it seems she's come alone."

Oh my! Whatever could be so important that Maria would choose to sit here alone when she would have had no idea how long it might be? Goodness, she'd best hurry to find out.

"Thank you, Anthony. I'd best run up to her."

"Yes, you'd best."

She started back up the steps, thankful for a variety of reasons for her dearest friend. Mostly for the fact that her presence likely had something to do with Anthony's willingness to forgo the sermon. She'd have to do something very, very nice for Maria in return.

"And Penelope," he called after her.

She paused and turned, only slightly hesitant.

"I know I'm hardly the one to make comment," he said. "My own courtship was certainly unconventional, but please, Penelope, for our mother's sake, will you refrain from allowing

Chesterton to veritably devour you right out in public that way? You may not care what people say, but our mother does."

She nodded. Indeed, unconventional was the mildest word possible to describe what passed between Anthony and his wife, Julia, before they were wed. Mamma had gone through all sorts of agonies as she worried for Anthony's well-being and was forced to hear the rumors whispered all through society until things were finally sorted out. Surely she was putting their mother through something much the same.

The only difference in that case, however, was that Anthony and Julia were madly in love with each other. In the end they made it all work out and had been happy ever since. This time things would end differently. There would be no happy ending for her and Lord Harry. Poor Mamma would have to endure all the rumors only to see her daughter run off to Egypt in the end, still unmarried and very likely quite damaged by gossip and innuendo.

"Very well, Anthony. I'll be more careful."

"Thank you," he said and turned to go about his business.

She was glad he didn't prolong the conversation. It was a subject she would have much rather not thought about. This plan was beginning to feel less and less like the brilliant idea she'd initially thought it.

Chapter Nine

"Thank heavens you're back before the rain," Maria said, leaping up from her seat near the window when Penelope entered her room.

"Yes, and I'm lucky to be back at all. You would not believe what happened to me today!"

Maria seemed far less concerned by Penelope's pronouncement than a best friend ought to be. In fact, Penelope thought she distinctly detected a frown.

"I could believe just about anything, I'm afraid," Maria said. "I saw you down there in the street, letting that man take all manner of liberties with your person."

"Oh bother. Must you be such a prude, Maria? I explained to you that Lord Harry must pretend to be my doting fiancé so that—"

"Oh, I know how you explain it, Penelope. But *pretending* would mean public flattery or an overeagerness to open doors for you and pull out your chair at dinner. No, what I saw that man doing just now went far, far beyond *pretending*."

Penelope felt her cheeks burning. She busied herself removing her bonnet and gloves, hanging her wrapper on the peg behind the door. No way would she let Maria see her blushing on Lord Harry's account. That would as much as admit she was guilty of enjoying the man's *pretending*.

Thankfully, the ugly wrapper seemed to finally be worth something, after all. It distracted Maria from whatever rant she had been going to make.

"Good gracious! You bought that hideous thing!"

"No, I did not," Penelope was pleased to inform. "Lord Harry bought it for me as a part of his effort to play fiancé. Apparently the shopkeeper told him I had *admired* it."

She expected that the sweet irony of it all would be more than enough to wipe all thoughts of sermonizing out of Maria's usually tolerant head. It didn't.

"So now he is buying you things?"

"It is part of the act, Maria. Fiancés often buy things for their lovers, I'm told."

"Take care, Penelope. Lord Harry may have already forgotten he is merely supposed to be playacting the part of lover."

"Don't be silly. Lord Harry is not in love with me."

"Of course he's not in love with you, ninny. No one would ever imagine that he is! That's what makes it all the more dreadful. Can't you see?"

"I see that you are overreacting."

"Am I? It appears to me that Lord Harry thinks you've given him free license to use you for all manner of sordid things. One might expect you to overreact a bit."

"Lord Harry has a perfectly good grasp of our arrangement."

"Yes, I believe I just witnessed him grasping your arrangement. He seemed quite pleased with it, too."

She purposely pretended not to comprehend Maria's meaning. "It's a perfectly useful arrangement and you have no reason to be so out of sorts over this."

But Maria was out of sorts. That much was obvious. "Useful indeed, Penelope. He's using you and you're doing nothing to deter him!"

"Is this the great emergency that brought you over here all alone today, Maria? You came without your aunt just so you could scold me about my personal affairs?"

"Not entirely, but I can see it is well needed."

"Very well, you've done your duty and expressed your concern. Consider me scolded. Now, what is it you really came to see me about?"

Finally Maria was at a loss for words. Penelope waited as concern, doubt, frustration, and finally confusion flitted across her friend's face. She couldn't begin to understand what Maria was preparing to say, but it certainly did appear to require much effort. Hopefully it was something other than more scolding.

"Er, will you be attending Lady Burlington's ball?" Maria asked at long last.

Well, that was certainly not worth all the facial expressions. What a bit of a letdown, decidedly.

"Yes, I plan to attend."

"Oh," Maria said, nodding. "Good. Yes, we will have an enjoyable evening then."

"Yes, I should expect we will."

"Assuredly."

"Positively."

There was another pause before Maria continued. "And do you know what you will be wearing?"

"I do."

"Oh," Maria said, with more nodding and another pause.

"Would you like me to tell you about it?" Penelope asked.

"Indeed! Yes, do tell me about it."

"I'll be wearing my new gown, the white one shot through and bordered with gold threads."

"Ah, yes, that should be lovely," Maria said, but Penelope wasn't entirely certain her friend was paying attention.

"And I thought I'd wear my gold silk slippers, even though they are truly from last Season."

"Oh, indeed, that will be lovely," Maria remarked, idly picking at lint on her sleeve.

"And Mamma said I could borrow her turban, the one she wore last week to the theater."

"Yes, perfect for you."

"And I thought I should put bright feathers in it, seven feet high."

"So you should; yes, indeed."

"In fact, I've decided to put a whole live peacock on my head and stroll through Hyde Park dressed as Napoleon."

"Hmm, yes, that would be just the thing . . ."

"Maria, you are not even listening to me! For heaven's sake, what on earth is wrong with you today?"

"What? Nothing! Why should you accuse me of having anything wrong today?"

"I'm not accusing you, I'm worrying for you. The scolding, yes, I suppose I should expect some of that from you—you'd hardly be a friend if you did not worry at least a tiny bit—but now you will not tell me what brought you here. I know it was not merely to hear me describe my planned attire."

At last Maria was paying attention. She sighed and twisted her hands together. "Truthfully, it is partially about that. I did wish to hear about your clothing."

"Then why weren't you listening? Clearly there is something more."

"It's just that you always look so pretty when you are out. You go to everyone's ball and you are always the prettiest lady in attendance. I was simply . . . well, I was hoping perhaps you could give me some notion how to improve my looks. A bit."

Whatever Penelope had been expecting to hear, it was not this. Especially not from Maria! Her friend had never given half a thought to such trivial things as appearance and who was prettier than whom, or any such female nonsense. At least, not in any specific way. Certainly they'd discussed other ladies' appearances, but this was the first time Penelope could sense Maria's opinions being of such a personal nature.

Usually Maria was pragmatic about her appearance. Clothing, she pronounced, was for keeping a body warm and promoting public decency in a socially acceptable fashion. In the years since they had grown up together, Penelope had never known Maria to put any effort into her attire beyond suiting those purposes. Her dearest friend was faultlessly demure, intentionally reserved, and always socially acceptable. She was never truly pretty. Now today the woman wanted to shine?

Surely there must be a reason for this sudden—and drastic—personality change.

"You always look quite nice," Penelope began. Tact was certainly required in this sort of conversation. "But if you are interested in making improvements, I'm sure we can find some areas for, er, refining."

"Yes, I should like that. How shall we go about it, then? Would you come to my house and go through my wardrobe with me?"

"Yes, we could do that..."

Or we could throw those frumpish old rags out to the gutter and head for the dressmaker! But no, she could not suggest that, of course. It might hurt dear Maria's feelings. Besides, the ball was tonight. There was simply no time.

"Why don't you have a look through my gowns, Maria? I have some that have hardly been worn. You might see one you like. We could trim it and have my maid let out the hem. Surely no one would recognize it as mine."

"Truly? Do you think we could do that? Your gowns are ever so lovely."

By heavens, she thought her friend was about to become giddy. Over gowns! It was the oddest thing ever. Who could have imagined Maria had this vein of female vanity running through her like this?

"Of course we could do that," she said, and trotted over to open the clothes press. Lace and muslin and flounces and color of every sort spilled out.

She smiled at her friend as a beautiful—truly pretty—pink blush crept into the young woman's cheeks. She could honestly never recall seeing that before. My, but it was most becoming, as a matter of fact.

"Just one question, if I may," Penelope said, knowing it would make the pink blush go even deeper. "Who is the fortunate fellow you've set your eye upon?"

POCKETS ONLY SLIGHTLY HEAVIER AFTER SELLING HIS old, battered gig, Harris walked along the streets of Mayfair toward the far less fashionable area where his own bachelor quarters were. He'd left Rastmoor's grand gift back in the mews near Rastmoor House, mostly because his benefactor had already paid for the phaeton's keeping there and Harris was damned if he could figure out how to pay to keep the bloody thing in any of the ramshackle mews nearer to his petty lodgings. Likely the carriage would be a far sight safer where it was.

But since he'd already found a buyer for his old conveyance, this meant Harris would be forced to dodge raindrops. He appeared to lack talent for it. Already he was soaked through.

An awning over a nearby doorway provided temporary respite, so he ducked under it. He nodded to the other soggy gentleman who was already there for the same apparent reason. Then he realized he knew the soggy gentleman.

"Ferrel?"

His cousin glanced up at him through bedraggled hair and gave half a smile. "Oh, I see you got caught in this, too."

"But what are you doing? Where did you leave your horse?"

"Hmm? Oh, my horse." Ferrel didn't bother to answer the question but merely shrugged. "Wet stuff, this rain."

"Yes, that's generally the way of it."

"I suppose my coat is ruined."

"It does appear so."

"Damn."

"Markland said you were off to some other engagement. What are you doing out here?" Harris asked, unable to dredge up much sympathy for the man's coat when he could have easily been out of the elements.

The young fool had no reason to be dripping just now. He had not been cut off by everyone who shared his name. He, presumably, could afford to live in a convenient location and not be forced into walking all over the bloody town when rain clouds threatened.

"I'm trying to get pneumonia," Ferrel said.

"Oh. Well, in that case, you seem to be doing well. Another fifteen minutes of this chill and you'll end up fully miserable."

"Good. With luck I'll die."

"Luck? There's no good luck in it for me. I don't stand to inherit a penny should you knock off, Ferrel. You might as well just go on living."

But Ferrel didn't seem to see any humor in this. Apparently he'd been in earnest about trying to catch something deadly. Stupid pup.

"Bah. What point is there in living? Nothing in it for me."

"You've got a couple thousand a year and no one dunning you," Harris reminded. "That's something."

"That's easy for you to say when you've got a beautiful woman set to marry you and her family singing your praises."

Harris could barely believe it, but from all appearances the man was again serious. He had to put forth real effort to keep from laughing at him. Oh, but if his cousin had any idea how things really stood!

"Ah, yes. I'm a lucky man," he managed to choke out fairly convincingly.

"You are. Miss Rastmoor is an attractive and good-natured person. You will be very happy with her."

Now he did laugh. "Not if I can't come up with some way to get myself invited to Lady Burlington's ball tonight."

"What? Why should you want to go to that dull flap?"

"I don't. But Miss Rastmoor fully expects me to be there and to dance with her."

"She'll be there?"

"So she declares."

For the first time a hint of life came back into Ferrel's downcast eyes. "I had no idea there would be so many young people at the event."

"I don't know about that, but she's quite looking forward to attending. Yes, I suppose that would mean there will be others of her set there."

"Well, I have an invite to the ball," Ferrel said. "Surely you could come along with me. If Lady Burlington has invited your cousin as well as your fiancé, surely she could have no objection to you attending, could she?"

Oh, she quite certainly could. But it would be crowded, and her friends would all be there as well as a good number of influential people she had, no doubt, invited to impress. Would the woman really create a scene if he were to walk through the door? No, he suspected not.

"That would be excellent, Ferrel. I would love to attend with you."

"Well, I wasn't fully planning to go, but if you wish to attend . . . and if your lovely Miss Rastmoor will be there . . . yes, I should do it. We will arrive together."

Yes, they would. It would make it just that much harder for the lady to cast Harris back out into the street. He would show a good face for the very generous Rastmoor, as well as do a bit of investigating Lady Burlington's home. And of course he'd be keeping his end of the bargain with Miss Rastmoor. At least, that is what he'd lead her to believe.

"I HAVEN'T THE SLIGHTEST IDEA WHAT YOU'RE TALKING about," Maria said.

Nothing Penelope did seemed to sway the girl from holding to that line, either.

"Honestly, Maria," Penelope finally said in frustration. "There's no shame in it. For heaven's sake, it's about time you started noticing men. They are all around us, you know."

"Generally they are all around *you*," Maria replied. "I simply thought perhaps I ought to take greater pains to look, er, less plain."

"Which leads me—again—to ask why? There must be someone you're hoping will see you appearing less plain, someone particular."

"No! Why must there be someone particular? Have I ever given indication there is?"

Penelope thought about that a moment, then had to shake her head. "No, you have not, which makes this all that much more of a puzzle to me."

Maria had been sitting quietly but now she made as if to rise. "If my wish to be less plain is causing hardship for your small brain, Penelope, then I will be only too happy to leave."

"Ah, so now I have a small brain, do I?"

"Sorry. You know I do not mean that. I'm afraid my aunt has gotten me all worked up today."

"So there is more to it!" She left the assortment of gowns she had laid out on her bed and went to sit beside her friend. "Tell me. What has she done?"

"It's what she's said."

"Which was . . . ?"

Maria twisted her fingers until Penelope feared they would break. Finally, with a sigh, her friend went on.

"She told me I was hopeless."

"What? That's ridiculous. What on earth could she have meant?"

"She meant that I really am hopeless. That she has spent a

good deal of money over the years, securing a fashionable home, keeping us in gowns, entertaining people of the highest quality so we will be welcome in fine drawing rooms, yet here I am, a spinster."

Penelope literally gasped. "Dear gracious! Do not ever use that word around me!"

"But it is true. You must see that, Penelope."

"I see nothing of the sort. You and I are the same age, if you recall. I certainly do not consider myself even close to spinsterhood."

"*You* are engaged to be married."

"You know that's only in pretense."

"But my aunt does not. She's quite disappointed in me, I'm afraid. Here you are, already on your fifth fiancé—"

"Fourth. You know that mess with Fitzgelder does not count."

"Very well, *fourth* fiancé, yet I've not even secured half a one."

Penelope frowned. "What would you do with half a fiancé?"

"That's hardly the point, is it? The fact is my aunt feels it's been her duty to get me well married, and she sees my unmarried state as failure. For both of us."

"For her, perhaps, but certainly not you. You can hardly consider it failure if you've never done much to actually try. And I've always gotten the idea you were not interested in trying, that's all."

"To my aunt, that's the same thing as failing. She's decided we will leave London at the end of next week and not come back again."

"Until next Season?"

"No, I mean we will not come back again. Ever."

"What?! You cannot be serious!"

It was very nearly too much for Penelope to grasp. Maria would be leaving London? Yes, of course they would all be leaving once the Season was over—certainly no one with any good sense wished to remain in Town during the summer—but for Maria never to return! Why, that was inconceivable. How on earth could her aunt expect the girl to finally meet the gentleman she might eventually fall in love with if she did not return to London?

Maria was a woman of reason, of good breeding, of a very specific constitution. How was she going to find a suitable match out in the country, with so very few of her equals? And worse, however would Penelope enjoy next year's Season if she did not have Maria? Indeed, her aunt's mad notion would simply not do.

"Well, we will simply have to figure a way to convince your aunt to let you finish this Season, then bring you back for the next."

But Maria shook her head. "No, I've thought it through, Penelope. It's unfair for me to be such a drain on my poor aunt. I'm afraid she's right; I've spent five Seasons in London and I just did not take. I have no right to put her through this any longer."

"But this is why you are going to let me alter your usual mode of dress, why we are going to make you up to be quite a diamond of the first water tonight! Your aunt will see. More importantly, the gentlemen will see. By this time next week, you'll be turning down proposals left and right."

It wasn't hearty, but Maria finally laughed. A bit. "Now I fear you are mistaking me for you."

"It will be no mistake when your aunt realizes what great potential you have to make a brilliant match. She will let you finish out this Season, and begin planning your return for next. Then I will rest easy at night, knowing my dearest friend will be nearby to protect me."

"Oh, honestly. Protect you from what?"

"From absolute boredom, of course! Without you, I wouldn't dare engage in even remotely interesting conversation. After all, who else could I possibly trust with the truth about such things as false engagements and my terrifying brush with death today?"

"Your brush with death?" Maria's noticeably cocked eyebrow said she was rather dubious as to the validity of this statement.

"Oh, but indeed that's precisely what it was! If you hadn't been so quick to start scolding me the instant I walked through the door, I would have surely told you all about it."

"Very well, I apologize. Now do tell me about this terrifying ordeal."

"I went driving today with Lord Harry."

Now Maria's cocked eyebrow was accompanied by a scowl. "Yes, that is terrifying. Did he think to impress you by driving like a madman in that ostentatious new carriage he's taken?"

"He did not take that carriage. Anthony bought it for him!"

"What? But I thought your brother hated the man?"

"Yes, that was the plan, wasn't it? It turns out, though, my brother is so eager to see me married off to any old lout who will have me that he's quite infatuated with Lord Harry."

"Oh, how dreadful!"

"Yes, isn't it? You understand my difficulty, Maria. This is why I simply can't abide talk of you not being here in Town."

"Surely when your brother hears that Lord Harry was recklessly endangering you while driving today, he will change his mind about the man and begin actively opposing the match."

"Perhaps, although in Lord Harry's defense he did not purposely endanger me. He had gotten out of the carriage to put the hood up to protect us from the rain, and the horses—the horses Anthony acquired for him—got spooked. They bolted and I was knocked about inside the carriage something awful! I'm sure I will be bruised head to foot, and I did quite fully expect to be overturned and trampled right there."

"Oh my! How dreadful for you. I had no idea. Then I suppose it is no wonder you were inclined to let Lord Harry kiss you that way, after he managed to save your life, and all."

"Er, it wasn't exactly Lord Harry who saved me."

"It wasn't? Then how on earth did you stop the horses?"

"I didn't. Another gentleman came along."

"*Another* gentleman? Who on earth was he and why were you not kissing him, instead?"

Penelope smacked her cheeky friend on the arm. "Because I only barely know the man, of course!"

"It was not so long ago you only barely knew Lord Harry, too."

"Well, I was only just introduced to Mr. Markland this morning, just half an hour before he showed up to rescue me."

"And how fortunate that he did, since Lord Harry obviously could not be bothered."

"He was bothered," Penelope said, oddly compelled to defend

the man. "He was very bothered, indeed. It's just that he was on foot and Mr. Markland astride. That is the only reason that gentleman managed to get my carriage stopped before Lord Harry did."

"Mr. Markland?"

"Yes, that is his name. We ran across him earlier while he was riding by with his friend, Mr. Ferrel Chesterton."

"Mr. Chesterton?"

"You recall him. We met yesterday when he so boldly introduced himself to me as Lord Harry's cousin."

"Oh, er, yes, I recall that."

"And he was with an actress, and introduced her to us, as well! I was quite amazed by such presumption, I assure you. But we saw him today and Lord Harry must be polite, so we exchanged pleasantries and Mr. Markland was introduced."

"I see. And . . . was the actress with them today?"

"No, thankfully. We spoke with only the two men."

"And this Mr. Markland, did he appear to be of good character?"

"He saved my life, so I would hardly describe him in derogatory tones," Penelope said, laughing at her friend's very obvious concern for decorum. "But yes, he did seem to be of good character. Good enough, at least, to not be on excellent terms with Lord Harry, I gathered."

"Oh?"

"Yes, but it hardly signifies. He is of an age with Lord Harry and surely they've met here and there. Perhaps Mr. Chesterton has informed him of Lord Harry's unflattering reputation; I cannot say what is between the men."

"So you did not like Mr. Markland?"

"I can't say one way or another. He did cut quite a dashing figure out there, though."

"Quite as dashing as Mr. Chesterton?"

"As Ferrel Chesterton? Heavens, I did not realize I should have taken my watercolors out there to capture the event in such careful detail for you, Maria!"

"I am merely concerned for you," Maria said. "I'm worried what sort of people you are surrounded with these days, that is all."

"Well, fear not. Once my dealings with Lord Harry are over,

I doubt I'll see anything of this Mr. Markland or that rude Mr. Chesterton. Certainly neither gentleman is worthy of being in our fine circle, Maria. You just wait; once I have gotten what I need out of Lord Harry, Messrs. Markland and Chesterton will not even linger in our memories."

Maria seemed to doubt this, too. "I can only hope you are right, Penelope."

"Of course I'm right. Now, let's see if I'm right about this gown for you. Shall I call in the maid and we will see if it flatters your figure as I suspect it will?"

"If you believe there is anything that might flatter my gangly figure, you are most welcome to try," Maria said, sounding at last slightly more herself and less like her aunt.

Penelope rang the bell eagerly. How wonderful it would be to finally do what she'd long wished: to make Maria sparkle. Now that the girl was at last willing, Penelope would see that Maria Bradley arrived at Lady Burlington's ball tonight looking like a new woman.

Oh, but what fun this would be.

Chapter Ten

He'd been right. Lady Burlington was, indeed, up to something. What it was, he still had no clue. Every fiber of his instinct told him she knew more about the stolen artifacts her husband had "collected" than the usual uninvolved wife.

He'd tried to be subtle, but since his arrival with Ferrel half an hour ago, he'd watched Lady Burlington like a hawk. True, she'd been an adequately attentive hostess and made a grand show of enjoying her guests, but Harris had noticed a certain distraction about her. More than once he'd caught her glancing at the clock, watching time as if she expected someone. Or some*thing*. And the secret way she kept her eye on the now-locked door of the treasure room spoke volumes, as far as Harris was concerned.

If he wanted to get those items back into his possession, he was going to have to figure out what was going on and figure it out quickly. Once that collection was broken down and sold off in pieces, his hope of ever ransoming Professor Oldham would be slim, if not nonexistent altogether. But how was he going to catch her up in her schemes?

Indeed, he knew the easiest course. Lady Burlington had made it plain enough she'd be more than agreeable to any advances he might make. Hell, he'd been very nearly forced to make more than advances with her the other night when she'd found him lurking about. At the time it had seemed the best way to cover for himself—pretend he'd been drunk and gone off looking for that sort of entertainment.

But tonight he simply did not think he had it in him. The woman was attractive enough, but still . . . he could not seem to dredge up any desire for her. Not even in pretense. What a sorry scoundrel he was turning out to be! Of course he must do what needed to be done. Even if the thought of it sent shudders of disgust wracking through him.

He was caught off guard midshudder when his eyes fixed on a figure entering the ballroom. Miss Rastmoor had arrived. She looked stunning.

He had no trouble drumming up interest for her, unfortunately.

She was radiant in a white gown that showed off her milky skin in a way that made Harris wish perhaps it did not. And did the girl really need to show off quite so much of that skin? Those youthful bonbons that nearly spilled from her gown would be impossible for any man not to notice, let alone imagine what he might rather be doing beyond simply noticing. Miss Rastmoor had a bosom to be envied. And there, just above those rounded treasures, was the scarab. He wished he could claim his lustful stare had fixed on that object, but knew he'd be lying.

Miss Rastmoor was dazzling, and he was far from immune to it. To make matters worse, her gaze caught on him and she broke into a smile that very nearly lit the room on fire. At least, he sensed there was a fire somewhere.

She'd arrived with her mother. Harris had not had the pleasure of meeting the woman, so of course he would be required to do so now. He knew from the way she was eyeing him, even from across the room, an introduction would be impossible to avoid. He made his way through the crowd toward them.

"Here he is, Mamma," she was saying when he drew near. "This is my darling fiancé. See? He's not nearly so objectionable as you keep implying."

Harris bowed. "It is truly my honor to meet you, Lady Rastmoor."

"I had always assumed I would be introduced to my future son-in-law before he actually went and affianced himself to my daughter," she said.

He held back any number of things he had to say regarding his own wishes for a mother-in-law who might not leave him wondering when the snakes would suddenly sprout from her head. Instead he gave her a charming smile.

"And I had always assumed the Lady Rastmoor I've heard so many wonderful things about would be a woman of more advanced years. Surely I would have taken you for my future sister-in-law."

He wasn't quite certain if he'd hit the mark, but the lady held off from any further outward insults. The cold dislike in her eye did not much fade, however, and left him oddly off-balance. What did he care, after all, if this woman approved of him?

Penelope broke the tension between them. "Oh, I just know you two are going to become the best of friends. Now Mamma, can you please spare me? I know we only just arrived, but I have the feeling Lord Harry would like to ask me to dance."

He would? Well, given that his other option at this point was to stand here being examined—and no doubt found lacking—by this very formidable parent, he supposed he would. Yes, indeed. A dance with Miss Rastmoor was infinitely more appealing than maternal scrutiny.

The gorgon gave her begrudging approval, and Harris led Miss Rastmoor off to the dance floor. Couples were just gathering for another set; his fiancée's timing had been perfect. As they took their place opposite one another for a rousing country dance, Harris realized he'd rather been hoping it might be time for a waltz. Miss Rastmoor truly would have made quite a pleasing armful tonight.

"You appear little harmed by your ordeal this morning, Miss Rastmoor," he said as they waited for the music to begin.

"I am quite fine, thank you," she said, scanning the crowd around them. "I was very lucky it did not turn out to be as bad as it could have. But fortunately Mr. Markland came along and all was well."

Bloody hell. If anyone had to come along and rescue her, why did it have to be Markland? And why did she have to look so bloody thrilled about it as she spoke the man's bloody name?

The music started up just at that moment, which was probably a very good thing. Harris couldn't be entirely certain the bit of harsh profanity that ran through his mind at that point was entirely confined to his mind. He may have actually spoken the words aloud.

"What was that?" Miss Rastmoor said, leaning in toward him.

"Er, nothing," he said, hoping the next string of words that ran through his mind truly did stay in there. Not surprising, they were less harsh yet every bit as profane, as he found himself—once again—helpless to pry his gaze from the expanse of gently rolling femininity surrounding that scarab. The fact that Miss Rastmoor was leaning provocatively toward him did not help redirect these wayward thoughts.

But now it was time to drag his attention back to the matter at hand. They were announcing the dance, preparing to begin. He was finding it unbearably difficult to concentrate, though. It seemed there were other, more enticing, matters he'd much rather have at hand.

"You were never in any great danger, my dear," he said, following suit with all the other gentlemen and bowing to his partner. "I was close behind. The horses would not have run far."

She gave a very pretty curtsy, but laughed at him. "They very nearly spilled me over in the short distance they did run, sir. I realize that for some reason Mr. Markland is not in your good graces, but please allow me to be quite obliged to the man."

More internal profanity.

"Of course I am grateful you were not harmed," he said, deciding it best to leave the conversation at that. "And I see you are wearing your lovely scarab again tonight."

"I don't care that everyone sees me in it again and again," she said, as if he'd accused her of some enormous breach of fashion. "I rather like it."

"And so you should. It is very nearly as lovely as you are."

She smiled again, moving forward and brushing past him in the first steps of the dance. He wasn't quite certain where the sudden rush of warm air he felt came from, but had to admit he rather enjoyed it.

"Ah, you do know how to flatter, sir."

"I know how to do a good number of things, Miss Rastmoor."

She eyed him with one arched eyebrow. "I don't doubt that at all. Pity dancing isn't one of them. You should have turned to the left, Lord Harry."

And so he should have. Quickly he corrected his error, but not before it was obvious to everyone around them. Damn, but he'd best find some way to keep his mind on what he was doing and not on what he'd rather be doing. If he was to be making a fool of himself with mental wanderings tonight, he ought to at least be wandering through his plans to get that scarab into his possession.

"I suppose I should have warned you that I'm an abominable dancer," he said.

"It makes no difference to me," she said. "But perhaps you should have warned the lady whose gown you just trod on."

He had already begun to curse himself again when he realized she'd been funning. "I believe you are determined to make me look bad, Miss Rastmoor."

"But of course, sir. That is the goal, is it not? You look bad, my brother loses his fondness for you, and then I get what I want."

"Your brother is watching us? I hadn't realized he was here tonight."

"He's not, drat him, which means you will have to behave exceptionally badly so that he will hear the reports."

"Exceptional badness is one thing I am very good at, my dear."

She gave a smile that said she had a hint of his meaning and wasn't for one minute worried about it. She took his words in jest, of course. If she knew how serious he was, he wondered if she'd have run away in terror. Any decent woman would.

"Tell me, Miss Rastmoor," he said when the dance brought them near enough for private conversation again. "If your brother is not here, who then are you continually looking for?"

"What? Oh, my friend Miss Bradley. Have you seen her here?"

"I'm afraid I wouldn't know it if I had. I don't believe I've had the pleasure of meeting Miss Bradley."

"Oh, you've seen her. You recall, she was with my mother that first evening when we . . . er, when we met."

He felt he could allow himself to be quite flattered by the lovely pink that stole over her fair complexion. Yes, he recalled that first evening. It was rather reassuring to know that she did, as well. He could not, however, recall this Miss Bradley.

"Oh look! There she is!"

He missed a step as he turned to let his gaze follow in the direction of Miss Rastmoor's. "That is your Miss Bentley?"

"Miss *Bradley*. And yes. She looks quite lovely, does she not?"

"Indeed she does."

Odd that he might not have remembered this vision.

"I helped select her gown for this evening," Miss Rastmoor said with unmistakable pride.

"Clearly you are a true friend."

Now she was practically beaming. "Promise me you will dance with her tonight."

"What?"

"At least once. Please?"

"Well, I don't know . . ."

"Please? It would mean the world to her. And to me."

It would mean he was not getting any closer to obtaining his goal, that's what wasting time dancing with this Miss Bradley would mean. As much as Miss Rastmoor would like it, as much as she might bat her enormous, glittering eyes at him, as much as she might slide her body against his as they passed in the movement of the dance, he simply would not do it. Not even if he wanted to, and he did not want to.

"Please, Lord Harry?"

"Oh, very well." Damn, those mesmerizing blue eyes and her tremulous pink lips.

"Wonderful! I can hardly wait to introduce you two."

She spent the rest of the dance singing the many praises of her partnerless friend. He spent the time grumbling at his own petty weakness. He should be working to get Miss Rastmoor off on her own, to find out what he could about that scarab and do what he needed to do to get it from her. She should be succumbing to his pleas and entreaties, not vice versa.

Well, if it would put him in Miss Rastmoor's good graces, he supposed he could spare one dance for her friend. But only one. Then he would put his full energy into the task at hand. Tonight, Miss Rastmoor would give up her greatest treasure for him. He would sweep her off her feet. He would make himself so irresistible she would not be able to think of anything but . . .

Hell. Her thoughts had already been captured elsewhere, if the look that suddenly came over her face was any indication. Her eyes were fixed on a spot far across the room, and now a slow, meaningful smile pulled up at one corner of her delicate lips. And she was not studying Miss Bradley.

Markland. Damn, why must it be Markland? His beautiful fiancée was gazing off with a smile, pining for Markland while she was supposed to be smitten with him. This was going to make what he'd had planned for later just that much more difficult.

And sweeter.

MR. MARKLAND LOOKED EVEN MORE HANDSOME THAN Penelope recalled. Indeed, he was a fine-looking man. The fact that he was here likely meant he came from a proper family, too. Although, she supposed she couldn't put much stock in that. After all, Lord Harry was here and he certainly was less than perfect. Well, it was unlikely Maria would fall in love with Markland after just one evening. She could investigate him on her friend's behalf later.

For now, though, she would get the two of them together. Oh, but what a lovely couple they'd make! Surely Maria could not object. And the more gentlemen who danced with her tonight, the more other gentlemen would notice. They were positively like dogs with a bone in that regard; if one gentleman appeared interested in a lady, she suddenly became more interesting to all the others.

How kind of Lord Harry to agree to dance with her. The way everyone had been watching them tonight—newly engaged and seemingly mismatched—Maria would surely draw attention to herself if she stood up with Lord Harry. And now that Penelope had good reason to consider herself on friendly terms with such an attractive gentleman as Mr. Markland, it would be a simple matter of assuring that he noticed Maria and became aware of her many good qualities.

She'd never fancied herself a matchmaker, but this was building up to be quite a bit of fun for her tonight. More importantly, once Maria's aunt realized she was suddenly so highly regarded by eligible gentlemen, she would stop her disturbing talk of taking Maria away from London. Penelope's plan tonight seemed foolproof, and would help more than just herself. And to think, Mamma often accused her of being selfish.

"Thank you, sir," she said, curtsying to Lord Harry when their dance was over. "You are an excellent partner."

"No, Miss Rastmoor, it is you who made the dance enjoyable. But come, surely you are in need of something to drink, and perhaps a bit of fresh air?"

"Some lemonade, I think, but I've no need of any change of air. Besides, I see Miss Bradley is making her way over here and I'm more than impatient to introduce you. And don't forget, you agreed to favor her with one dance."

"Yes, so I did."

He wasn't nearly as enthusiastic about it as she might have liked, but she allowed him to be just a bit apprehensive when it came to dancing with a young lady he'd never before met. Perhaps he feared that she had not confided the details of their charade to her friend. Indeed, that would make things a bit uncomfortable for him, wouldn't it? She could almost laugh to picture him stuck on the dance floor with a giddy young woman who expected him to be deep in the throes of true love with her best friend.

Perhaps she might find a way to assure him that Maria knew the details and could hardly be called giddy. Ever.

"Maria!" she called when her friend was near enough. "You look simply stunning! I love what you've done with your hair."

"Thank you. I was half inclined not to come tonight, but knew you'd be terribly disappointed in me if I . . ."

Her voice trailed off when her eyes fell on Lord Harry.

Penelope stepped into the silence. "Miss Maria Bradley, may I please present Lord Harris Chesterton?"

She got the idea Maria would rather she did not present the gentleman, but her friend was too well-bred to let the sentiment show plainly on her face. For long. After a pained moment with just the hint of a dark look, Maria finally nodded. Slightly.

He bowed with consummate grace. "It is a great pleasure to meet you, Miss Bradley. Your friend has told me a great many fine things about you."

"I wasn't aware that Miss Rastmoor spent so much time discussing me with her imaginary fiancé," Maria said with a sugary-sweet smile.

Well, at least now Penelope didn't have to worry about how to inform Lord Harry just how much Maria knew about them. Getting the girl to agree to stand up with him might be a bit dicey, however.

"I see Miss Rastmoor trusts you implicitly, Miss Bradley," Lord Harry said. "She's a fortunate young lady to have such a friend as you to confide in."

"She'd be even more fortunate if she saw fit to take my advice when I warned her this silly plan of hers would lead her straight to ruin, Lord Harry."

"Now, Maria," Penelope said, keeping her voice light and hoping no one around them was near enough to hear. "Lord Harry is everything kind and generous. Why, he would like nothing better than to invite you to dance, isn't that so, Lord Harry?"

Even the people across the room from them could have seen the glare in Lord Harry's eyes. Still, he collected himself and bowed again for Maria, his tone as cultured and polished as royalty.

"It would be my great honor if you would have this dance with me, Miss Bradley."

Penelope fully expected she would have to do some cajoling to get Maria to agree, but she found herself quite surprised when, after only a brief hesitation, Maria nodded to the gentleman and took the arm he offered her.

"Very well, sir. I should enjoy a dance with you, I believe."

Lord Harry nodded acceptance, but he did manage to shoot Penelope one brief, glowering look over his shoulder as the pair left to go join the next set. Knowing Maria as she did, Penelope could almost feel sorry for the man. No doubt he'd be in for a barrage of questions and perhaps one or two accusations. Still, he could handle it.

Lord Harry was nothing if not durable.

Now, she needed to move on to the next portion of her plan. She needed to find Mr. Markland. And she needed a reasonable excuse for strolling up to him and initiating a conversation without drawing too much attention to herself. It would not do to have everyone here doubting her devotion to her very unsuitable fiancé. She would have to be very cautious not to give any appearance of interest in Mr. Markland outside of that which might promote her friend.

The gentleman, however, made it easy. He walked right up to her and smiled.

"Miss Rastmoor, how good to see you so well and unaffected by your earlier disaster."

"Why Mr. Markland, did you expect to see me all frazzled and drawn?"

"Good heavens, no. I doubt even the direst mishap could leave you looking anything but perfectly lovely."

She busied herself with her fan. My, but this gentleman was nearly as adept at flattery as Lord Harry. This of course made her quite warm toward him.

"I thank you, sir, both for your service to me earlier today as well as for your undeserved praises now."

"Hardly undeserved, Miss Rastmoor, as I'm sure your devoted fiancé must tell you again and again. Odd, I should have expected to find him here, latched onto your side and keeping watch over you."

"He is there." She pointed. "I allow him occasional freedom, sir. He is dancing with my very dear friend, Miss Bradley. Does she not seem enthralled by whatever he is telling her?"

"Indeed, she seems to be listening attentively."

"Oh, she is an excellent listener, sir. I have often found that to be a quality greatly to be desired in one's companion. Haven't you?"

"It has its merit, although I have never thought of Chesterton as much of a conversationalist."

"You and he are well acquainted?"

"Somewhat. He seems rather to be enjoying his time with your Miss Bradley, though."

Ah, he'd rather discuss Maria than Lord Harry? That seemed a good sign. Penelope was only too happy to indulge him.

"As they are both quite dear to me, I am hoping they will get along well in company."

"I doubt you have anything to fear on that account," he said, his eyes carefully following the pair through the intricate moves of the country dance. "Chesterton seems to excel in getting along well in company, especially when the company is an attractive female."

Oh, so he thought Maria attractive! This was progressing quite beyond even what she had hoped. Truly, the addition of a fashionable gown, some colorful ribbon, and a few curls had done something remarkable. Maria had been transformed into a beauty.

"She is attractive, isn't she?" Penelope couldn't help but smile. "Although she is one of those dear girls who truly has no idea how lovely she is. Modesty and humility are her nature, Mr. Markland."

He took his eyes off the dancers, and Penelope found him studying her. Likely he was trying to determine if her many praises for Miss Bradley were in earnest.

"You seem to have very high standards for your acquaintances, Miss Rastmoor," he said after a moment's pause.

"Oh no, I try to be quite tolerant of my acquaintances, sir. It is only my friends who must have proven themselves exceptional."

He nodded, and slid his gaze back toward Maria. "Well spoken, Miss Rastmoor. I had determined you to be quite discerning in your tastes. Clearly you are a young lady who appreciates the extraordinary."

How lovely! He was giving her opportunity upon opportunity to recite the many wonderful qualities of her friend. "Indeed, sir, I surround myself with it. For instance—"

"Your necklace."

"Pardon?"

"Your necklace is quite extraordinary."

"Er, yes, I suppose it is. In fact, I was just telling Miss Bradley how—"

"It is Egyptian, is it not?"

"It is, sir. How perceptive of you."

"I have rather a passing interest in antiquities with Egyptian origin."

"Do you? How fascinating."

"Are you aware that this amulet is called a scarab, a type of beetle common to that area of the world?"

"Yes, actually, I had heard that."

"It represents the constant battle of life and death, morning and night, darkness and light."

"Er, yes, so I had heard. The scarab pushes the orb that represents—"

"May I ask where you got it?"

"What?"

"Where you got that beautiful necklace, Miss Rastmoor. Was it a gift from someone, perhaps?"

"No, it wasn't, actually. Why do you ask?"

"No reason. I merely thought perhaps your fiancé might have taken a fancy to it and presented it as a token of his affection."

Really? How very odd. True, now that she thought of it, Lord Harry had asked after the scarab and commented on it a time or two, but she thought it far more likely that he did so merely as a part of their charade rather than any interest he actually might have had in the item. Lord Harry did not strike her as a man who gave much thought to aesthetics. She wondered why Mr. Markland should think him otherwise.

"I purchased the scarab myself, Mr. Markland," she informed him. "I have quite a passion for Egyptian antiquities."

"Do you now? You must tell me about it, Miss Rastmoor. Have you other items you've collected?"

"I'm hardly a collector, Mr. Markland. Not like some I've met with veritable museums in their homes."

"Oh? And who would these fortunate souls be?"

As much as she would have enjoyed discussing artifacts and her passion for the history connected to them, she couldn't help but note the exchange had a distinctly awkward feel. Of course Mr. Markland was just making conversation. She should be pleased to run across someone who shared at least a bit of her interest in Egyptian antiquities. She was silly to feel uncomfortable answering his many questions this way.

Or perhaps it was her guilty conscience that pricked and disrupted her ease. Indeed, her whole purpose in engaging Mr. Markland this way was not to find enjoyable discourse for herself, but to promote Maria's cause. Likely that was the reason for her discomfort. She was going on and on about her own interests when she really ought to be giving Mr. Markland motive to ask for an introduction to her friend.

"You know, Miss Bradley also shares a great love for antiquities," she said, proud of the graceful way she manipulated the discussion.

He seemed honestly impressed with this knowledge. "Does she now?"

"Oh yes. In fact, her knowledge and appreciation far exceed my own."

This wasn't exactly true, but Maria was a clever woman. She was very well read and could easily keep up with Penelope's ravings about the various intricacies of Egyptian history as she learned more and more from Professor Oldham's letters. Penelope had no doubt that her friend could certainly hold her own in a discussion of the topic with Mr. Markland or any other casually interested party.

"Then it is no small wonder that Lord Harry is so fascinated by your friend," he remarked.

Penelope watched the couple still circulating through the steps of the country dance. Indeed, Maria seemed to be having a much better time than Penelope might have expected. And Lord Harry also seemed quite content with his partner. He was not glaring or glancing back over this way with anger as he had right at first.

"Miss Bradley is quite a fascinating person, Mr. Markland," Penelope said, allowing a moment of pride for her protégée. "If you'd like, I would be happy to present you when she and Lord Harry return."

"Yes, I believe I'd like that very much, Miss Rastmoor."

"If you are lucky, sir, she might even be persuaded to join you in a dance."

He didn't speak to that, but he inclined his head in a manner that assured her he found that notion more than a little agreeable. Yes, she was being a bit presumptuous to suggest such a thing when the two of them had not so much as met one another, but this situation called for extra measures. Surely Maria's future happiness was worth bending the rules of propriety just the smallest little bit.

She'd recognized Maria's interest when she'd mentioned meeting Mr. Markland and his subsequent rescue. Her friend seemed to have been quite taken with the romantic notion of being rescued from certain death by a dashing young man. Of course she'd be thrilled to actually meet the hero of Penelope's adventure and would, no doubt, find him to be just as dashing and attractive as one might hope. Maria would likely fall desperately in love straightaway.

And now that Penelope had discovered they shared a common interest in antiquities—even though Maria's interest was really only secondhand—she would have an easier time of drawing them into conversation together. Everything was working out so perfectly! She could not help but smile at her own success. Ah, but perhaps there would soon be a *real* engagement to announce.

That thought made her smile even broader.

HARRIS WAS FURIOUS. MARKLAND WAS STILL HOVERing over Miss Rastmoor, fawning as if he'd never seen a female before. Miss Rastmoor was grinning ear to ear, as if she'd never received hollow flattery from a man before. Damn, but why did she have to look so blasted lovely tonight? Had she expected to run across the man here?

It was all he could do to keep his mind on the dance. He forced himself to pay attention to Miss Bradley and her thinly veiled inquisition as they danced up and down the row of happy revelers. His smile was far from sincere, but he hoped it was enough to fool anyone around them who might be noticing.

"So, Lord Harry, I've heard nothing of a wedding date yet," Miss Bradley was saying. "Can we expect this to be a long engagement?"

He'd give her credit for choosing her words carefully, yet he wished she'd rather chosen none at all. They were hardly the only couple out here on the dance floor, despite the fact that he felt very alone. What if someone should hear her and realize the engagement was a sham? He was not prepared for that; not yet. Miss Rastmoor would be damaged by the scandal that would result, and he would lose his tenuous connection there.

Although, he had to admit playing along with this charade had not exactly been helpful to him so far. Aside from Rastmoor's extravagant gift, Harris had gotten little out of it. That, however, was mostly due to his own lack of action. He'd been too cautious thus far. All that would change tonight. Just as soon as he could escape this interrogation and get Miss Rastmoor alone.

If he *could* get her alone. Another quick glance in her direction showed her laughing with that damned Markland, enjoying his company as if they'd been old friends. Perhaps that was her motive for sending Harris out here to be closely examined by her best inquisitor. And just where was the little hussy's mother during all this? By God, he needed to get away from his promenading auditor and get back to Penelope simply to keep the chit out of trouble.

But trouble seemed a welcome delight for Miss Rastmoor. What was she doing now? Leaning in toward Markland to allow the man a more careful look at her scarab! And everything in its general vicinity. Good God, she might as well be disrobing and throwing herself at the man's feet.

Harris practically tripped over the woman to his left and got a stern warning to watch himself from the lady's thick-browed partner. He mumbled an apology and made a halfhearted attempt to keep up with the steps, but his attention was still fully on Miss Rastmoor and her shocking display.

"Who is that gentleman with Miss Rastmoor?" Miss Bradley asked, noticing it herself.

"Markland. George Markland." At least that would be the man's name until Harris deposited his body in the Thames.

"Ah, so that is Miss Rastmoor's rescuer," Miss Bradley said with a too-knowing smile. "He is even more dashing than her earlier description of him."

"She described him as dashing?"

Miss Bradley wrinkled her nose and considered this. "Or was it attractive? I cannot be quite sure. Perhaps she used both words."

"Dashing *and* attractive?"

"And she would be right on both counts, of course. Mr. Markland is quite dashing *and* attractive. How fortunate that he was nearby to assist her while you were . . . now, let's see. What is it you were doing while she was very nearly killed today?"

The final steps of the dance were completed as the musicians finished the song with a rousing chord. Harris missed all of it, fumbling over his own feet and trying not to let his anger show. How dare this Miss Nobody-Bradley accuse him of endangering Miss Rastmoor!

"Although the ordeal might have been frightening for Miss Rastmoor," he said sharply when he should have been bowing politely and complimenting his partner, "I can assure you, at no time was she truly in any grave danger."

"Because Mr. Markland was there," Miss Bradley finished for him, then had the nerve to continue without allowing him chance for rebuttal. "Come, Lord Harry. I should very much like to meet this Mr. Markland. Is he here alone, do you suppose, or does he attend with friends?"

"How do I know who he bloody travels with?" Harris grumbled.

Miss Bradley actually tsk-tsked at his bad language.

But at least the dance was over. He offered his snippy partner his arm and led her through the throng—he could have sworn people were standing in his way on purpose—toward where Miss Rastmoor still entertained a very smiling Markland. Harris had hopes of remedying that quickly.

He was not encouraged when his fiancée gave a bright smile as he and Miss Bradley joined her and the rotted Markland. Harris recognized feigned innocence when he saw it. Miss Rastmoor pretended to smile and be happy to see them, but he knew she was not. She was covering her guilt, hiding the fact that she'd rather have been left alone with her dashing *and* attractive new hero.

"Why, Lord Harry, look who it is," she said, as if he did not have eyes in his head to notice the blackguard standing—no, leering—over her.

"Markland. How pleasant."

"Good evening, Chesterton,"

It was obvious Markland was as glad to see him as he was. The would-be rescuer glared daggers at him, so Harris glared right back. One tiny hint of instigation was all he needed and he'd plant that scoundrel a facer that would rearrange his nose. His own mother wouldn't recognize him afterward.

Oh yes, he'd forgotten. Being motherless was just one of the things he and Markland had in common.

Chapter Eleven

"Your dancing was divine," Miss Rastmoor was saying, gushing over her friend in some big show for Markland.

Harris found it more than distasteful. Had the girl completely forgotten she was supposed to be his fiancée? She'd not had one word of encouragement for his own dancing abilities, yet now she went on and on about her friend's. True, Harris hadn't exactly set the pattern for all other dancers to aspire to; still the girl ought to realize how ignoring him might appear. It might make it appear her devotion to him was not complete; that she might still be interested in attentions from other gentlemen. From Markland, for instance.

Well, he would not have that. As long as he was supposed to be her fiancé, she would not be allowed to continue this way. It was high time he stop lounging about and take control of things. He had a task to complete and he was determined to do it. Now.

"Miss Bradley is indeed a most excellent dancer," he said, interrupting Miss Rastmoor's gushing. "In fact, now that you've done such a fine job of introducing her to Mr. Markland—and informing her of the man's many admirable points—perhaps she would very much like to dance with him?"

Markland did a fair job of hiding his disinclination for this. Miss Bradley blushed, and the gentleman made her a courtly bow. The ass.

"Miss Bradley, that is a marvelous notion. Would you please step up to dance with me?" Markland asked. His cultured and gracious tone was clearly due to years of training by his stiff-rumped family and certainly not to his willingness to leave Miss Rastmoor.

Miss Bradley, it seemed, was of a mind to accept, and soon they were off to the dance. At last Harris was left alone with Miss Rastmoor. He, however, was not of a mind to enjoy it.

"What was all that about, dangling after the man like a moonstruck puppy?" he asked.

She blinked those huge eyes at him. "What?"

"Don't play innocent for me. I saw you letting Markland paw all over you."

"He was looking at my scarab," she said, a defiant little tilt to her jaw and her eyes suddenly blazing.

"He was looking at more than just your scarab, and you liked it!"

"How dare you! He was asking after my necklace so I was showing it to him. Apparently the man is a lover of Egyptology."

"Oh, he'd like to be a lover, I'm sure."

"He was a perfect gentleman; there's no need for you to go pretending to be jealous. Besides, as you can see, he's rather interested in Miss Bradley."

He glanced out at the dancers taking their positions. Markland was looking directly back at them. Harris saw nothing at all that might convince him the man was in any way interested in Miss Bradley outside of simply being polite. His interest, as far as Harris could tell, was firmly on Miss Rastmoor.

Which meant, of course, that Harris had best be careful to keep his own apparent interest in Miss Rastmoor quite visible. He carefully adopted a more pleasant expression and took a step closer to her. She wrinkled her brow at him.

"We should not be seen quarreling, my dear," he reminded her. "Smile. Pretend you find me fascinating."

She did smile. A bit too much to be quite believable. "I'm not certain I am capable of that much pretending, sir."

"You seem to be capable of anything you wish. I wonder why you wished Mr. Markland to inspect your scarab so very closely?"

"I told you, he asked after it. He seems to have a good understanding of such things."

Likely the man simply had a good understanding of ways to flatter and impress gullible young ladies. "I happen to know for a fact Markland has only the barest knowledge of antiquities. If he told you he had an interest, it was merely to keep you engaged in conversation."

"Because he was hoping to be casually presented to Miss Bradley. Just look at her out there; does she not seem quite happy?"

"I daresay she's a sight happier with Markland than she was with me, yes. But come, let us take a turn in the garden. I believe we have things to discuss."

"In the garden? Do you think that is wise?"

"I thought you were interested in giving your brother reason to regret our betrothal."

"But being found alone in the garden . . . I don't know if that would accomplish that goal. I'm tempted to think it might be more likely to cause Anthony to insist on a hasty wedding."

Damn, how was he going to get the chit alone? He had to get that scarab, and learn where she had come by it.

"Very well, we shall remain here, safely on public display. And I suppose pleasant conversation is required, as well."

"If you are capable of that."

"I'm at least as capable as Markland. So why don't you tell me about your lovely scarab, Miss Rastmoor? You seemed to enjoy the topic when *he* brought it up."

"Because *he* was interested in it."

"As am I, of course. Where did you get it?"

"Haven't you asked me that before?"

"Perhaps, but as I don't believe you answered, then it's hardly a redundant conversation for us, is it?"

"It's hardly a relevant conversation for us, but if you insist on pursuing it, then I see no reason not to—"

Damn damn damn. She broke off her sentence just when he was about to get that all-important piece of information. His bloody cousin had slid up beside them.

"Good evening, Harry," Ferrel said sweetly. "Miss Rastmoor."

"How nice to see you, Mr. Chesterton," she replied, nodding pleasantly.

"Yes, so very nice," Harris said, not as pleasantly.

"Say, have either of you seen my friend Markland? I had hoped to drag him off into the card room with me for—"

His eyes seemed to catch on Markland even as he was asking after the man. He paused in midspeech and seemed quite perplexed to find the man dancing. Why he should be so confused to find his friend dancing at a ball, Harris could have no clue.

"Indeed, Mr. Markland is dancing just now," Miss Rastmoor informed him. "He was so kind to stand up with my friend, Miss Bradley. You recall Miss Bradley, don't you?"

"Er, yes, I believe I recall her," Ferrel said. "I didn't know Markland was acquainted with her. Well, it would seem his time is quite thoroughly spoken for just now."

"Yes, Miss Bradley was pleased when he invited her to dance," Miss Rastmoor said, obviously quite pleased with herself for facilitating that arrangement, for some reason.

"It appears they are one couple short, Ferrel," Harris pointed out, grabbing at this opportunity to get rid of their unwanted third party. "Perhaps you should go find yourself a partner and join in."

Ferrel appeared to be going to reject this suggestion, but then he cocked his head to one side. "Not a bad idea, Chesterton. That is exactly what I should do. I'll stand up with the prettiest lady in the room."

"Excellent notion," Harris said. "You just go on and find her."

"But the prettiest lady in the room is right here, Cousin. Miss Rastmoor, as your lazy fiancé seems to be reticent in his endeavors to entertain you, may I prevail upon you to join me in this dance?"

Harris could scarce believe his ears. His simpering little cousin had the nerve to try and steal away his companion? And one look at Miss Rastmoor showed she was quite flattered by the offer. What the devil . . . Was she actually going to accept the man?

"How kind of you, Mr. Chesterton. Very well, I'd love to dance with you." She smiled brightly at him, then turned to Harris. "I'm sure Lord Harry won't mind, will you, my dear?"

His jaw clenched so tightly his teeth ground. "No. Of course not."

"Good. I would hate to think you might be jealous, or cause a scene," she said, batting her eyes at him. "You know how my brother would hate such a thing."

"By all means, go have your dance. Enjoy. Kick up your heels. I'll simply wait here," he said, hoping she recognized his lack of sincerity.

"Indeed I shall," she said simply, taking Ferrel's arm and letting him lead her to the dance floor.

Hellfire. It was as if the very universe were against him lately. When was he going to get his chance to take what he needed from Miss Rastmoor?

"Left you for another already, did she?" a voice purred at his side.

He turned to find Lady Burlington there, smiling coyly and toying with her fan. Dear God, this was all he needed right now.

"She's a silly little flirt, that one is," the lady continued. "I can't imagine what you see in her. A man like you, Chesterton, should be more discerning. Don't waste your time on little girls when you can have a grown woman."

"Oh? A grown woman is what I need? I don't suppose you might have one in mind for me?"

"I think you felt the same thing I did that night at our previous ball."

Hell. He'd been trying to forget that night.

"I know your uncle expects you to find a wife," she went on, "but surely that has nothing to do with what you want. I can help you with that."

"You know, your husband seemed to feel something that night, too. He felt like murdering me."

"That was unfortunate. In the future I will be more discreet."

"I think it requires a bit more than mere discretion. Why don't we agree not to tempt fate and simply forget we ever had that brief interaction? And this conversation."

"Oh, but this conversation is not over yet. Perhaps I might end up saying something to entice you into tempting fate again."

"Hmm, I doubt that will happen."

"Pity. I thought surely you would be interested in what I have to show you, Lord Harry."

"Perhaps some things are better left to the imagination."

"Even if they might, shall we say, help out a friend?"

He was trying desperately to think up a way to discourage her obvious interest in him when he suddenly realized she was making a rather awkward show of her hand in front of his face. He could not help but notice the ring she wore. *The Pharaoh's Seal.*

Oldham had unearthed that ring last year and so named it due to the cryptic glyphs carved into the heavy gold and surrounded by soapstone and tiny glass beads. It had been among some of the first articles that had been stolen from their collection. Now, it seemed, it had found its way onto Lady Burlington's finger.

She knew something.

"You have exquisite taste in jewelry, Lady Burlington," he said calmly.

"What, this little bauble? Oh, it's just something I picked up for my collection. Perhaps you would like to see what I have to show you, after all?"

"Indeed, my lady, perhaps I would."

She smiled, pleased with herself. He was not at all happy with this turn of events. What had the shifty matron meant about helping a friend? She could only have been referring to Professor Oldham and his situation. What did she know about that? Better yet, how many of the missing pieces did she hold in her so-called collection? Damn, but he was going to have to play things her way, wasn't he?

"That's what I was hoping to hear. I knew my, er, charms were not lost on you, Chesterton. Indeed, I have some magnificent pieces you've not yet seen."

"I've seen quite a bit of your, uh, collection, if you recall, madame."

"Not everything in my possession has been on display for you, Lord Harry," she said with a smile that brought back more of the shuddering. "Perhaps I might have something to rival your lady's pretty little scarab."

"What do you know of her scarab?"

"I know where she got it. Do you?"

"That's hardly any concern of mine."

"Oh, don't lie. I know exactly what you are doing, hunting all over London for some certain articles to ransom a certain person."

"How do you know about—"

"Meet me tonight, after the ball."

"What, tonight?"

"You have other plans already?"

"No," he said, recognizing as well as she did that he could afford to give no other answer.

"Come to me later and I'll see that your dear Miss Rastmoor hears nothing of it."

"And Lord Burlington?"

"He will be otherwise occupied with things I pretend to know nothing about."

"What a delightful recipe for domestic bliss."

"Use the servants' door, Harry," she said, flicking her fan open and licking her painted lips. "I'll be waiting."

"I'll be counting the moments." *And dreading every one.*

Thankfully, she turned away to leave him. He breathed a sigh of relief, but she turned back with one last smile and whispered over her fan.

"Who gave her that scarab? She's flirting with him right under your nose."

"YOUR FRIEND MISS BRADLEY SEEMS TO BE ENJOYING herself tonight," Ferrel Chesterton said as he led them through the first series of dance steps.

"I believe she is. Mr. Markland is being most attentive to her."

"Yes, he is."

"She was most eager to see him here tonight."

"I did not realize he and Miss Bradley were acquainted."

"Oh, they weren't before tonight. But after I told her how

Mr. Markland rescued me today, she became quite enthralled with the man. They make a lovely couple, don't they?"

"I'm hardly an expert on the topic."

"Well I am, and I believe they look lovely. See? She's glancing over here now to make certain I've noticed how he smiles at her."

"He's got a bit of a lopsided smile, don't you think?"

"He's perfectly symmetrical and quite dashing, actually. At least, it would appear Miss Bradley thinks him so. Watch how she lays her hand on his arm."

"Perhaps she is trying to push him away. He does seem to be looming over her excessively."

"He's being attentive."

"Yes, so you mentioned."

"And they look lovely together."

He didn't reply instantly. Instead, he seemed to be studying them to consider Penelope's declaration. She knew, of course, there was no way he could contradict her. Maria did look lovely, and her tall, elegant form was the perfect complement to Mr. Markland's manly appearance. Indeed, Aunt Clara would change her mind about leaving London quite directly.

"They are lovely together," she repeated.

"I will defer to your wisdom in this matter, Miss Rastmoor," Mr. Chesterton said at last. "After all, of every lady here it is very clear you are, indeed, the foremost authority on loveliness."

"How you flatter, Mr. Chesterton!"

"By no means! I speak only the truth."

"Well, I would never wish to call any man a liar, sir. So I suppose I have no choice but to graciously accept your kind, if unmerited, praise."

"Excellent. Then I will not only praise your appearance, but your graciousness, too."

"Heavens, but I'm to become a bit full of myself if I linger in your presence much longer!"

"You've little choice, I fear. Once you marry my cousin, you will be doomed to hear and accept my praises whenever our family gathers for special occasions. Let George Markland try to come up with that many sweet tenders to say about his partner."

"There are a great many sweet things to be said for Miss

Bradley," she assured him, "though it hardly matters that you see them. Mr. Markland seems to have noticed, and that is all that matters right now."

"So it would appear."

"Yes, so it does. I'm quite encouraged for my friend."

"Indeed, Mr. Markland has much to recommend him, I suppose."

"Does he? Other than rescuing me and being decidedly *not* a favorite of my dear fiancé, I must admit I don't actually know much about the man."

"And Miss Bradley knows even less."

"True," she acknowledged. "But you are his friend. What do you know about him?"

"I know that he has an annoying way of making otherwise perfectly sensible ladies swoon like idiots in his presence."

"So he is quite the Casanova, is he?"

"No, he's nothing like that, Miss Rastmoor."

It almost seemed to pain the man to admit his friend was not a scoundrel.

"He is quite preoccupied with propriety and a gentleman's duty, and all that," the man continued. "His fortune is large, you see, and his grandfather is some haughty duke. He takes his position as a member of that family very seriously and would never dream of dirtying himself or his family name with anything so low as even a hint of scandal."

"Mr. Markland is heir to a duke?"

Well, this was far more than she could have ever expected for her friend. Heavens, but Maria had attracted such a man? Penelope had known she'd done well in helping re-dress her dear friend, but she'd not realized she might do *this* well. A duke!

"No, he is not heir to a dukedom. Not the title, anyway. The old duke is his maternal grandfather. Markland simply carries the family name since his grandfather raised him after his mother's death."

"But what of his father?"

"No one of significance, apparently. Markland never mentions him. Oh, I'm convinced that the man is a gentleman and that his parents were properly wed, but once his mother died, it seems the father had little use for a toddling son. He left him with the duke, so Markland's loyalty is to that family. Be assured, he is determined never to disgrace them by marrying beneath himself as his mother did."

"Ah, I see. Was that a subtle warning, sir? You fear my good friend is overreaching herself?"

"Your friend is attractive and gently bred. She cannot be faulted for reaching as high as she might."

"Well said, sir. I see I have convinced you of both her good breeding and her numerous fine attributes."

"Indeed, Miss Rastmoor. I will concede to being convinced on both counts."

"Then I have accomplished my goal and must immediately begin putting my efforts to another task. Let's see . . . what of you, Mr. Chesterton? Clearly you are not as duty bound as your friend."

"I may not have the fortune of Markland, but I assure you I am every bit as duty bound. More so, in fact."

He tried to laugh as if she amused him, but she found the sound not nearly as appealing as it ought to have been. True, Mr. Chesterton had the good sense to acknowledge Maria's high value, but he lacked the grace to entertain with his light conversation for more than minutes at a time. She was quite convinced her first impression of the man still held firm. He had been in the presence of an actress, he'd initially approached her overboldly, and he was even now darting his eyes around the room rather than focusing on her. Not to mention the fact that clearly he had never interceded with his father on Lord Harry's behalf. Indeed, this Mr. Chesterton was not nearly so fine a gentleman as his friend Markland. No, not even so fine as Lord Harry, and that was saying quite a lot, considering the first impression she'd had of that man.

Oddly enough, she could not deny it. She truly preferred Lord Harry's company to that of either of her other partners tonight. She'd much rather be dancing with Lord Harry than with his well-dressed young cousin, here, or even with the elegant Mr. Markland. With luck the set would end quickly and she could return to her faux fiancé. Where was he, anyhow?

She ignored the small talk Mr. Chesterton was attempting and let her eyes scan the room for a moment. At last she found him. Lord Harry was very near where she'd left him, tucked into a corner with . . . with a female!

Drat the man. He was right here in this very crowded room, ignoring his dear fiancée while he cloistered himself for a tête-à-tête with some woman! Who was it? She craned to see.

Ah, Lady Burlington. Well, perhaps she should take relief in that. Surely the woman was simply being a polite hostess and personally greeting her guests. Very personally, it appeared. She was practically hanging on the man. For his part, Lord Harry appeared nothing short of enthralled with her conversation. Why, was he complimenting her on her jewelry? Indeed, it appeared he was.

The man was flattering her! And Lady Burlington gobbled it up, fluttering her fan and leaning toward him, whispering something into his ear. Lord Harry nodded, agreeing to whatever the woman suggested. He was flirting with her!

Ooo, this burned. How dare the man behave this way! First it was dallying with a household servant, and now it was flirting with a married woman in her own home! What was he thinking in that dratted, handsome head of his?

Of course he most likely wasn't thinking with his head at all. Clearly Lord Harry was ruled by other body parts. That blackguard. This was simply too much. She would *not* let him continue this way, not while he was supposed to be her fiancé.

She fairly stomped her way through the rest of the dance. Mr. Chesterton droned on about nothing in particular, and it was more than a relief when at last it all ended and she could let the man lead her back to Lord Harry. If Lord Harry might be kind enough to rip his attention from Lady Burlington and give at least some semblance of interest toward her.

If the poor man had difficulty with that, she'd be happy to rip something for him.

But Lady Burlington was gone by the time they reached Lord Harry. He smiled pleasantly as if nothing at all untoward had happened in her absence. Very well, she could play along. At least until she had her faithful fiancé alone.

"You seemed to be enjoying yourselves," he said as innocently as a babe.

"Mr. Chesterton is delightful company," she said, wasting a glowing smile on the man who had, actually, been rather dull once they'd exhausted the topic of Maria. "But now I'm quite fatigued, I fear."

Lord Harry became all concern and consideration. "Perhaps I should fetch you something to drink, Miss Rastmoor?"

"Yes, and fresh air, I believe. Let us go into the other room, if you don't mind."

Lord Harry gladly accepted her hand as she left Mr. Chesterton's side and moved to his. She would have loved to trample his foot along the way, but decided not to. No sense alerting his cousin to the fact that all was not sunshine and happiness between them.

Mr. Chesterton was at least perceptive enough not to invite himself to join them. He wisely thanked Penelope for the dance, complimented her abilities again, then took himself off to the side. As she and Lord Harry moved away, she found her former partner had already forgotten about her and was back to solemnly searching the crowd. Perhaps all the talk of Markland's good luck at securing Maria's attentions so easily had inspired him to hunt for his own admirer. He'd have to settle for someone less remarkable than Maria, of course, but at least the man was likely to find a more respectable companion here than that actress he'd been with.

For now, it was time to deal with her fiancé.

"LEMONADE, MY DEAR?" HARRIS ASKED WHEN HE LED Miss Rastmoor to a rather lonely corner of the dining room.

He handed her the glass he'd picked up along the way. She eyed it dubiously, but took it and sipped. Yes, she probably had gotten rather parched with all the exertion from batting her eyelashes and smiling so sweetly for Ferrel. Damn, but didn't she realize people were watching?

What was society to think if she went around acting as if she were still the same unengaged little flirt she'd always been? He thought the whole idea had been to convince the world they were ragingly eager to wed. How else was she going to trick her poor brother into meeting whatever silly demands she had?

"You know," she said slowly, "this whole plan of ours is only going to work if we convince everyone around us that we are quite content as a couple."

"Indeed. But after your display with my cousin tonight, I

should expect the only way to do that would be for me to call him out."

"What? *My* display tonight? I danced one simple country dance with the man."

"You flitted about him as if he were the only man in the building. And what were you discussing that had you smiling as if you were made of sugar?"

"We were talking about . . . well, it is really none of your business what we were talking about. *You* should be telling *me* what you were about slinking off into corners with Lady Burlington."

"I did not slink anywhere with anyone."

"I saw you huddled there, fawning over her, giving flattery and devious glances."

"Now you're being ridiculous. I spoke a few words to the lady, yes, but there was no slinking and certainly no fawning."

Devious glances, perhaps, but he was determined to deny all.

"I saw it with my own eyes."

"Your eyes were too busy gazing in worship at every other man in the room, including my scrawny cousin."

"Oh honestly. Mr. Chesterton is nothing at all like scrawny."

"Sizing him up, were you?"

"At least I wasn't remarking on items of his apparel as you were doing with Lady Burlington."

"She is a vain, arrogant matron who waves her apparel in front of everyone demanding their praise. You honestly worry that the casual onlooker would believe I might find myself favoring the likes of her over *you*?"

"Well, you did seem rather cozy."

"I assure you," he said, exasperated with her accusations and glancing around to make sure he would not be overheard, "not a soul here tonight would ever imagine I was at all smitten with anyone who was not my beautiful fiancée."

He hadn't actually meant to sound quite so passionate about this, nor did he intend to come right out and declare her beautiful. She was, of course, but she was by no means the sort of female who needed to hear it. She was already well aware of the fact, and it could only go badly for him if she thought he knew it, as well. Which he did. Damn.

"You think I am beautiful?" she asked.

"I think you are generally regarded as such, as well you know. You were happy enough to let Ferrel go on and on about it."

"So what if I did?"

"So my uncle might hear of it and become suspicious of my ability to maintain this engagement." *That sounded a plausible argument, didn't it?* "And what of your brother? If he hears you are dangling after other men, won't he assume your devotion to dreadful, terrible me is not complete? How then will you sway him to do your bidding in exchange for throwing me over? He'll realize you never truly wanted me in the first place."

He could see this last statement struck a chord. For both of them, this engagement must be perceived as unbreakable. If certain parties were not convinced of a deep *tendre* between them, they stood to gain nothing.

"Yes, you're right. I simply didn't realize that by participating in one innocent country dance I was declaring myself in love with your scrawny cousin."

"I thought you said he was not scrawny."

"It is a figure of speech."

"But is it a true statement or not?"

"It would depend on whom one was comparing him to."

"Compare him to me."

"Well . . . that's hardly the point."

"Isn't it? Go ahead, Miss Rastmoor, defend your position. How does my fine young cousin stand up compared to me? Is he a better dancer?"

"No, but—"

"Then I suppose you found his conversation more stimulating than mine."

"No, not really, but—"

"It is his person, then. You prefer his sandy-colored hair to mine, or the way his coat hangs limp off his narrow shoulders."

"Heavens no! Er, that is—"

"Perhaps you prefer his kisses?"

"No! Of course not."

"So you prefer *my* kisses?"

"Of course. Wait, that's not what I mean."

"You prefer his kisses."

"You know very well I've not kissed your cousin, sir," she said, stamping her foot and glaring up at him.

He'd allowed himself to get very close to her, happy to take advantage of the fact that he was, in fact, anything but scrawny. He felt as if he towered over her delicate form. It forced her to tilt her chin skyward to keep facing him. She was not the type to be intimidated, however, and kept her angry eyes fixed on his. He liked that about her. Also, he was aware of her scent, and he liked that, too. Unfortunately, it made him realize how very much he liked other things about her, as well.

"I don't know that, Miss Rastmoor," he said, praying his hand would stay safely at his side and not reach out to brush the carefree strawberry curls that framed her pretty face. "You seemed so comfortable in his presence tonight."

"That hardly indicates that I've kissed him," she said. "Perhaps I ought to, though, if you insist I provide a detailed comparison."

"Like hell you will."

He lost the battle against his hands and grabbed her by the shoulders. Her eyes got slightly wider in surprise, but she did not pull away, so he dragged her up against his body. Anyone noticing them could simply go to hell as he proceeded to kiss her in a way that would ensure she never bothered to attempt a comparison between him and any other man on the planet.

Chapter Twelve

He was kissing her again. Heavens, but she did like it when he did that.

Of course, it was highly improper for him to kiss her here, tucked into the corner in Lady Burlington's dining room, but what did it matter if they were found this way? He was kissing her! She couldn't think of anything beyond that just now.

She let his mouth have its way with her, gave her arms permission to wrap tightly around him and her fingers free reign to find their way into his thick, dark, heavenly hair. Indeed, there was nothing scrawny about this man. She could feel the strong layers of muscle in his shoulders, as she basked under the engulfing heat that came off him and drank in the sweet delight of wine on his lips. The very idea of ever comparing him—any part of him—to another man was laughable.

He kissed her lips, her chin, the soft spot beneath her earlobe, her neck. She tiptoed up for him so he could continue his kisses on any other part he might so choose, and fortunately he did choose. He also chose to drag her off to the side, behind a screen that had been placed in the room to hide one of the servants' corridors.

They were now blissfully alone, out of sight. The air in this dim corridor seemed suddenly cool compared to the brightly lit dining area, but the heat generated between them more than made up for it. The man's touch, the feel of him pressed against her quite made her head swim, and it was easy to ignore the fact that he was practically carrying her now, taking her farther from the safety of the dining room. The only safety she needed just now was the security of knowing his kiss would continue and his embrace would grow tighter.

"You're too young for a gown this revealing," he murmured as his head dipped to rain kisses over her neck, shoulders, and the glowing area just above her bosom.

"I'm three and twenty and I was hoping others might find this gown rather fetching on me."

"Too fetching," he said, and surprised her by running his hands all the way up from her waist and over her breasts to toy with the gold trim at the bodice.

She drew in a deep breath and let herself lean into him, urging him to continue doing whatever it was he was doing to her. Something a bit like icy fire raced all up and down her body. She craved more of it.

One gentle hand still played over her breast while Lord Harry pulled her closer for another kiss. She obeyed without hesitation. Oh, but he tasted sweet.

"In here," he said, pulling her around a corner and into a small, darkened room.

It must have been some sort of storage area. There were various items cluttering the place, including a narrow serving table stashed against the wall. He swooped her up and deposited her on it. Now she was nearly at eye level with him. All the better to lean in for more kisses, which of course she did.

It was hard to know just which glorious sensations to concentrate on most, the prickly excitement of his mouth ravaging hers, or the searing flames of his hands as they worked over her breasts. Oh! Heavens! The searing flames won out as suddenly her breasts were exposed and Lord Harry was pushing her gown low and bringing his lips down to trail kisses of the most amazingly sensitive sort, first over one breast, then over the other.

She arched up toward him, practically clawing at his coat to bring him closer. The only way possible to do that was to hold her legs wide as she sat there on that wooden table and press herself against him. He did not seem to mind this awkward pose one bit.

In fact, it appeared he was rather pleased with it as he continued to torment her with little nibbles over her responsive peaks. His hands, now, were free to move down to lower areas. She was only halfway aware of the feel of fabric slipping across her thighs as her gown rose higher and higher over her legs.

"Oh . . . my!" she stammered when she felt his skin against hers.

His hands were there, touching her thighs and fanning those flames until she now felt as if a raging inferno burned inside her body. She was fairly begging him to quench it, yet words were positively out of the question. All she could do was utter sounds of animal pleasure when he touched her there, at the hot juncture of her legs. She pressed against him.

He pressed back, holding her tightly, kissing her and brushing one finger over the very area that sent her practically into oblivion. Heavens above! This was something very new, very amazing. She prayed he would never, never stop.

"I could take you here and you'd let me," Lord Harry breathed into her ear.

She nodded for him, but really had no idea what he'd been saying. Oh, but what he was *doing* to her, *that* she was completely aware of! His touch, the gentle pressure he was applying, was something she felt she could never live without. Her body responded willingly, and she was rocking against him as he held her there, enthralled.

His breath was hot and moist as he whispered into her ear, but the meaning of his words was lost. She'd become a slave to sensation, to his kisses and caresses. A wall of heat and pleasure was building up within her, and she was helpless to do anything but respond and beg him for more.

She held him tight, grasping him with hands, arms, and legs. He was still touching her, rubbing her, now coming inside her. One finger, then two. He was searching the inmost part of her, and she was bursting with emotion, with sensation. Giving up any hope of control, she pressed against him again and again, as if it would save her life.

Perhaps it would. That wall that had been building around her seemed to be bearing down on her, threatening to crush her under its size and its beauty. She struggled for air, holding on to Lord Harry and rocking with the motion of his hands.

Suddenly a light exploded behind her eyes. The fire she'd been sensing flashed through her body and the wall collapsed around her, covering her and burying her with heat and pleasure. She gripped Lord Harry, wanting to drag him down into this joyous crush with her. He was the only thing keeping her alive, she was convinced of it.

"Oh my!" she murmured when at last she could draw air again.

"No one has ever touched you this way?" he asked, his fingers still caressing in the most awe-inspiring fashion.

"No, I'm certain I would recall."

She leaned in for more of his intoxicating kisses, and he gladly gave them. She responded, pulling him closer to her and wrapping her legs around him. She was not even shocked when she realized that it was no longer his fingers caressing her. Oh, but his manhood was hard and ready inside his trousers! He truly was going to take her here and she truly was going to let him.

All he needed to do was loosen his trousers. Yes, he was shifting now, moving his hands . . . but no, he was not undoing the trousers. He was . . . how disappointing! He was pulling her gown back over her knees and pushing himself away from her.

"By God, Penelope, we've got to stop this."

"Why?" It seemed a perfectly reasonable question.

"Because we're not really getting married!"

Somehow that didn't seem to matter just now.

"We are at least pretending, aren't we?"

"This was *not* pretending, Penelope. This was very real. Damn it, no wonder you've been engaged so many times already, if you go around behaving this way with every man you meet."

"I do *not* behave this way with every man I meet."

No, that was an understatement. She'd never behaved this way with *anyone*! Oh, but her heart was racing and she found it difficult to speak. All she wanted to do was throw herself against Lord Harry's warm, solid chest and drag his lips down to hers again. It was as if something very awful would happen if she did not feel his skin against hers, his arms around her. Dear gracious, it was the most unsettling feeling, to want his touch so badly.

"Well, you cannot behave this way with me, Miss Rastmoor," he said, his skin practically sizzling where he touched her as his fingers tugged at the fabric of her gown, pulling it back into place over her bosom. "For your own sake, you cannot."

It was still awfully difficult for her to make sense of his words. Any words, actually. Her heart was still racing and she felt strangely weak all over. She leaned into him and stared into his face, hoping to comprehend what he said.

"How shall I behave, then?"

"By putting yourself together. Here, straighten your clothes."

"My clothes?"

He helped her with them, her mind slowly clearing and bits of reality seeping in. But good heavens, what had she been doing? Oh, it was wonderful, and so very, very wrong to let him touch her that way. At any minute now she expected to feel quite ashamed of herself.

However, even as the heat inside her body began to dissipate and the chill of their darkened room began to creep in, shame was not what she was feeling. Anticipation was more the word for it, and that was probably a bad sign. Whatever had gone on between her and Lord Harry tonight, she simply could not allow herself to wish for it again!

"I think we'd best get back out to the dining room," Lord Harry said, trying in vain to tuck a strand of her hair back into place. "Before our absence is noticed."

"It's a bit late for that, Chesterton."

The voice broke into the darkness and wiped away any lingering bits of dazed ecstasy that still hung around Penelope's brain. *Anthony.* Good heavens, that was Anthony's voice! When had he arrived? She glanced up to find him bearing down on them, stalking into the tiny room with Mamma close at his heels. Even in the very low light, she could tell neither of them looked precisely pleased.

Oh dear. This was not going to go well.

"Damn," Lord Harry muttered.

"Quite," she agreed wholeheartedly.

"Chesterton, I'm afraid I'm going to have to ask you to peel yourself off my sister this instant," Anthony demanded.

Lord Harry wisely complied.

"Penelope, go with your mother," Anthony continued.

She knew she really ought to do as he said, but she felt if she tried to so much as move a muscle she might crumble into a helpless little pile. Wherever did the bones go that usually supported her frame? Why were her legs just hanging limp over the side of the table where she was still comfortably propped?

"Now, Penelope," Anthony demanded.

"Here," Lord Harry said to her, helping her down. "Do as he says. All will be well."

She couldn't really imagine how he might think that, but supposed there was no harm in trusting him. Skirting carefully around her brother, she darted over to Mamma's side. She didn't meet Mamma's eyes, but she could certainly feel the scowl. It was not going to be a quiet carriage ride home, was it?

"Come along, Penelope," Mamma said. "I believe you've ruined yourself quite enough for one night."

It was pointless to argue. After all, Mamma was absolutely correct. Penelope glanced at Lord Harry and he simply nodded to her. Mamma took her arm to lead her away. Anthony, however, showed no sign of preparing to leave.

"You and I will be discussing this, Chesterton," he said.

"Naturally," Lord Harry acquiesced. "Perhaps I should come round to your house in the morning?"

"Now."

"Oh. Well, er, that might be a bit inconvenient for me."

"Oh, forgive me. You have plans?"

"Yes, actually, I—"

"Change them. You and I have business to cover."

Penelope tried to give Lord Harry a comforting smile. It seemed a little unfair to abandon the man to face her furious brother just now, but it appeared there was little choice. Mamma was nearly dragging her away. One look at her granite expression and Penelope knew it was pointless to argue. Perhaps she had indeed gone just a bit too far this time. She wondered how on earth Lord Harry was going to make it all well.

And she also couldn't help but wonder—not that it was truly any of her business—what plans the man had for tonight that Anthony insisted he cancel. If they were plans for meeting some other woman, she couldn't help but be a bit smug that Anthony would break them. Although she did rather hope Lord Harry's plans were the only part of him that Anthony might break tonight.

"ARE YOU INSANE?"

Harris didn't much care for the implication, but he assumed Lord Rastmoor's question was merely rhetorical. However, when it appeared the gentleman was going to stand there glowering at him and wait for an answer, he realized perhaps he was wrong. Rastmoor was asking in earnest.

"Not that I am aware of, sir," he replied. "However, I suppose when one is insane, one is likely the last person to know."

"Don't be smart with me. What can possibly be going on in your head, Chesterton, to treat my sister this way, right under the noses of all our friends and some of the ton's most influential people?"

"I'm sorry, of course. I know it shows a great lapse in judgment."

Indeed, a lapse in just about everything. What had he been thinking, to get carried away like that? Damn, but the woman had been so temptingly available for him . . . so tantalizingly in reach, he'd fallen apart. He hadn't needed to go quite so far with things, yet he'd given in to her temptation and behaved like a rutting animal. And what was so damn frustrating, he couldn't very well be assured it would never happen again, given half a chance. It seemed Miss Rastmoor was like some sort of confection he would just keep craving.

"Damn it, Chesterton," Rastmoor began, understandably gruff. "I do understand what it is to be an engaged man. I've not been old and married so very long that I forget what it's like. But, good God, this is my sister!"

"I understand that you are naturally upset, but—"

"And as you claim to care for her, I would expect you to treat her with a bit more concern."

"You're completely correct, Rastmoor," Harris said, hanging his head in a great show of remorse. "My behavior is not at all fitting a gentleman worthy of such a prize."

And now it was time for Rastmoor to agree with him. He would, no doubt, and then would take great pleasure in demanding that Harris abandon all hope of ever so much as seeing Penelope again, let alone marrying her. Yes, that is what would happen now, and he was glad for it. Mostly.

"She may be a bit untamed, I'll grant that, but she deserves to be treated as a lady," Rastmoor ranted. "Damn it, Chesterton, she gets herself into enough trouble on her own; she doesn't need you leading her into it."

"I quite understand."

"Good. Then we both know what must be done."

Indeed he did. The engagement would be dissolved. Harris realized he was already gritting his teeth, as if he dreaded this pronouncement as much as any honest suitor would.

Rastmoor cleared his throat, then continued. "We've got to set that wedding date."

It was almost a shame that . . . wait. What was that?

Harris was expecting to hear something like, "never come near my sister again" or "pistols at dawn, vile seducer." But this was not that. This was very different. In fact, it took a moment for the words to arrange themselves in his head. *Wedding date?* A foreign concept that needed healthy pause to internally translate.

"You mean, you are not going to offer to separate my head from my torso? To have me conscripted to a ship bound for Asia?"

"Hell no!" Rastmoor said. "I can't approve your behavior, but it's very obvious my sister is a willing participant. I don't envy you the handful you are taking on yourself there, Chesterton, but it seems to be what she wants, and I see it is not altogether unacceptable to you. Far be it from me to question the workings of love."

Love? Good God, what was the man rambling about?

"Neither will I stand in the way of it," Rastmoor went on.

"So, if you think you can possibly refrain from ravishing one another in public places for the next fortnight, I think we can manage to arrange for the wedding sooner rather than later."

"Sooner, sir?"

"Sooner? Damn it, Chesterton, have you no self-control at all? Very well, then. We will see about a special license and you can be married within the week."

Within the week? Married? Harris very nearly choked on his own panic.

"How will your uncle take that? I hear he's been quite impatient for you to marry and make a proper man of yourself. You've got that title to think of, after all."

"Er, yes . . . my uncle would be pleased to hear of it, but . . ."

"Good. Then it's settled. You're much more reasonable than I expected, actually."

"I am?"

"I guess that should teach me to put any credit to rumors, eh?"

"Well, I don't know. If you're not entirely convinced I'm the right man for your sister, Rastmoor, I would understand if you wanted to hold off a while on the—"

"Nonsense. You and Penelope have made it plain what you want. Our mother might balk at such a hurried pace, but I'm sure once she has the opportunity to brag to all her friends about how her daughter married by special license, she'll be quite content with things. As for what you and my sister choose to do to celebrate at that point, I do not want to hear about it. All I ask is that you keep things respectable between now and then. Do I have your agreement?"

Hell. So *this* is what his moment of weakness had won him? Rastmoor was slapping him on the back and welcoming him to the family. How was he going to get out of this? More important, how was he going to avoid an angry, scheming Penelope once she realized what he'd done?

He slipped his hand into his pocket. The scarab sat quite safely there, hidden and in his possession at last. He'd had it off her in the first two minutes. Everything that transpired after that had been completely unnecessary toward accomplishing his goals. Hell, but he really was a blackguard, wasn't he?

* * *

"Mamma, honestly now, what exactly do you think Lord Harry and I were doing? We'd been out of the dining room only a minute or two."

Her mother had been railing on and on about "scandalous behavior" since the moment they left the ball and climbed into their carriage. To tell the truth, Penelope had been hard-pressed to really listen to her. She'd been a bit preoccupied worrying about what Anthony might be saying to poor Lord Harry. No doubt he had some rather colorful words for him.

And what would Lord Harry do in return? It would be a shame that their wonderful ruse might be ruined so quickly, before it had been allowed to accomplish anything for either of them. She was no closer to Egypt, and Lord Harry's uncle was likely to be even more disagreeable toward his nephew if he heard Anthony had declared him unfit for marriage. It was quite a pickle, really.

Had it been worth it, though? For that brief, wonderful moment in his arms when he made her . . . Oh yes, it was worth it. That, she realized, was somewhat disconcerting.

When they arrived home Mamma followed her directly up to her room, sending the servants away. Penelope tried to remain calm, removing the decorations from her elaborate coiffure and wondering if Mamma's rant would go on all night long.

"I know exactly what you and Lord Harry were doing, and I'm certain everyone else has a fair idea, too," Mamma said. "Lady Burlington herself is the one who told us she'd seen the two of you sneak off together. For *more* than a minute or two."

"Very well. I will admit I kissed him, Mamma," she said. "That's all it was. A simple kiss." *More or less.*

"And now your brother is likely going to have to call him out over it."

"What? No, surely Anthony has no intention of—"

"No matter what happened tonight—or didn't—you've damaged your reputation, Penelope. Beyond repair, unless Chesterton marries you."

"We're already engaged, Mamma," she reminded, though it quickly began to dawn on her that marriage and engagement were two entirely different things when it came to slinking off alone with a very capable gentleman.

"You say you're engaged, but why has nothing been said about a wedding date, Penelope? It's what I've feared all along. That man is not to be trusted. He's been using you, toying with you and impressing your brother with empty promises and talk of engagements. He's not marriage material, I'm sorry to say. You've been duped, Penelope. He only wants what he can get and, apparently, you gave it to him."

"Mamma!"

"It's the truth; we might as well face it. Sad to say, but I'm quite convinced we've already seen the last of your fiancé."

"I assure you Lord Harry is not nearly as bad as you seem to believe, Mamma. He has some very fine qualities."

"Yes, and you seem to be intimately aware of too many of them."

"Honestly, Mamma! What must you think of me?"

"I think you are a very silly girl to trust that man. After your brother confronts him tonight, just see if he agrees to set the wedding date. I'll bet he won't."

"Er, do you suppose that is what Anthony is discussing with him?" *Not seeking to drag the man out to some quiet field and shoot at him?*

"Of course! The way you two have been acting, it's imperative we get you to the altar as quickly as possible."

"But Lord Harry and I do not wish to marry so quickly! We had thought to wait until, er, at least the end of the Season."

"Then you should have waited, shouldn't you?"

"But we . . . It isn't really as if we . . ."

"Don't insult me with empty denial, Penelope. It makes no difference precisely what you and your dear Chesterton have done or have left undone. As far as society is concerned, you've done more than enough to make yourselves quite scandalized. Sadly, a quick wedding is all that is left to salvage your reputation, and I am quite convinced Chesterton will refuse."

And rightly so, of course. Heavens, but this was spinning quite out of control. How had she let things come to this? She hadn't meant to, surely. If she'd thought for one moment that . . . but she hadn't. She simply hadn't been thinking at all, had she?

She had been quite lost in the moment. How did Lord Harry do this to her? Just being with him, being near him, seemed enough to drive all good sense out of her. She had practically thrown herself at him tonight. Lord, but what she had let him do . . . and how she had responded! Truly she deserved her mother's scorn. But poor Harry.

Of course he would refuse Anthony's demands, that was to be expected. Anthony would be furious, that also was to be expected. What dreadful consequences might then arise she could not fully guess. Perhaps there would be a duel, or Lord Harry would be forced to flee London—flee the country, even! His uncle would cut him off completely. Oh, but it was simply awful, and all because she could not control those dratted animal impulses she hadn't even known she possessed!

"I'm sorry, Mamma," she said, although it was pitifully too little.

"Fine time to realize your folly, Penelope," Mamma replied.

Footsteps and voices sounded below. It was a welcome distraction, until she realized what they meant. Gracious, Anthony was home already! Indeed, it hadn't taken Lord Harry long to deny any wish to truly marry, had it? Oh, but she hoped he hadn't confessed their entire plan.

"Let's hope your brother has not already killed the man," Mamma said as Anthony's footsteps came nearer.

Penelope's heart thudded in her chest as if it would pound its way to freedom.

"Ah, here you are," Anthony said, poking his head through the doorway.

"Well?" Mamma asked. "What happened?"

"Everything is settled," Anthony replied.

Penelope couldn't quite choke back a nervous little yelp. "You mean . . . you shot him already?"

"What? No, of course not. You don't really want me to go out and shoot your fiancé, do you?"

"No, but I was afraid that after . . . well, since everyone seems to think we . . . er . . ."

"Oh, rest assured I'd have been tempted to call the blackguard out if he'd given me any hesitation, but there was no need. As expected, you've snagged your lord but good, little sister. Chesterton couldn't settle the wedding date soon enough."

"He what?"

"I suggested a fortnight, but he insisted it be sooner. So, provided we can get the office of the archbishop to agree, you and your dearest will be wed by special license as early as next week."

Next week? This was unexpected! How on earth were they to get out of this now?

"Did he really agree so easily?" Mamma asked.

"Of course. I told you, Mother, Chesterton isn't nearly as disagreeable as he seems," Anthony said with a smug grin. "After all, he's good enough for our pernickety Penelope, isn't that so?"

"Then there truly will be a wedding? You're certain he's willing?" Mamma questioned.

"Quite enthusiastic, in fact. I think it's safe to say, Mother, that Penelope's reputation, as well as her future, will be happily assured."

Mamma seemed unable—or unwilling—to fully comprehend this at first. Then slowly the lines of worry and anger seemed to fade from her expression and she eyed Penelope with something more akin to maternal affection.

"So it truly is a love match, is it?" she asked.

Penelope wasn't quite able to answer. Fortunately, her optimistic brother covered for her.

"Leave her be, Mother," he said. "We're embarrassing the girl. It's obvious she's completely taken with the fellow, and he with her. Of course I reminded him that, mad for love or not, we insisted on some measure of public decorum, and he assured me he will behave himself in the future. So, Penelope, if I can have your assurance, as well, that you will refrain from any further displays, then I say we all forget this evening's misstep and simply move forward. Agreed?"

Mamma was hesitant. "I cannot approve of such behavior as you exhibited tonight, Penelope. I'm quite disappointed, you know."

"Yes, Mamma, I know."

"And there will, no doubt, be an abundance of talk because of it. People are likely to say dreadful things about you."

"Yes, Mamma, I know that, too."

"But I suppose a marriage will silence most of it. Our true friends will still welcome us, I hope."

"I'm sure they will," Anthony soothed. "Now, Penelope, do I have your word that you will mind your manners? No more creeping about, meeting Chesterton in secret places in order to . . . well, there's simply to be no more of that, do you understand?"

"Yes, I understand."

"Good. Then let us all get to bed. Tomorrow will bring us one day closer to the happy union, and after that, thank God, you will be Chesterton's and I can return to my home."

So he would pawn her off so easily, would he? Yes, of course he would. And it seemed Mamma would, too. The woman considered Anthony's words, then gave a tired smile and patted Penelope on the arm.

"Yes, it is getting late. You will be a married woman soon, so there is no use in my droning on about my concerns."

Penelope felt oddly abandoned as they took their leave of her. The door shut behind them and she was left alone. She sat down on the side of her bed to try to make sense of this whole evening.

So it was all planned out now, was it? She had let Lord Harry take great liberties with her person—great, wonderful liberties that had quite altered her, as a matter of fact—and now he had agreed to marry her. Within the week, even!

Could it be he was serious? Surely not. Still, he was a gentleman and he must have realized what their actions tonight would do to her reputation. Perhaps he had enough of a conscience that he felt he was obligated to give in to Anthony's demands.

Was it possible he'd be willing to go through with it? To actually marry her? Her insides fluttered like trapped mice desperately racing about for escape. There was just the slightest possibility that this engagement of pretense had suddenly become real!

The mice were getting more desperate now. Lord Harry agreed to marry her! Perhaps he did not find her altogether disagreeable, then. Perhaps he found the idea of a lifetime joined to her not nearly as unpleasant as she might have expected. Perhaps, in fact, he was even looking forward to it.

Heavens, but the desperate fluttering inside her was not mice at all. It was her heart, pounding nervously at the realization that she herself did not find the idea as disagreeable as expected. In fact, the mere thought of being fully authorized and allowed to let Lord Harry take more of those wonderful liberties—over and over again!—was not disagreeable at all. It was quite appealing. Good gracious, but she might actually fancy herself just the tiniest bit in love with the man!

This was the very last thing she had expected to come of any of this. Could it be true? She'd purposely selected the most unsuitable man in all of England and now she was falling in love with him? The very notion left her quite breathless.

She put her hand to her throat, looking for the familiar scarab to calm her. Odd, it was not there. She didn't recall taking it off tonight.

Moving to her dressing table she saw the hairpins she had removed and placed there, but found no sign of her scarab. Quickly, she pulled open the drawer and flipped up the lid on the little box she usually kept it in. Empty.

No, she had not removed her scarab. But it was gone! Where could she have lost it? In the carriage? She didn't recall noticing it on the ride home. Perhaps she'd lost it before then. Perhaps when she'd arrived at the ball and removed her wrap it had fallen off.

No, she'd been wearing it at the ball. She'd noticed Lord Harry eyeing it, as a matter of fact. He'd asked after it, too, as had Mr. Markland. Yes, she'd been wearing it during the ball, up until she and Lord Harry . . .

Heavens! It must have fallen off when they, er, during their time alone in that back room. Yes, Lord Harry's hands had been all over her. He must have inadvertently unclasped her scarab and caused it to fall.

But where had it fallen? She had to admit, there hadn't been much open space between their heated bodies tonight. And the clasp she'd had put on her necklace was quite sturdy. She was certain it couldn't have been merely brushed aside accidentally. No, someone would have had to specifically try to undo it to remove that chain.

Those irritating mice in her chest returned, only this time they weren't fighting for escape so much as they were inciting a riot. Her heart thumped furiously and her lungs didn't quite want to work. Too many disturbing thoughts were suddenly bombarding her brain.

Lord Harry had asked repeatedly about that scarab, hadn't he? He'd been particularly interested that Mr. Markland had noticed it, as well. Could it be he took it? *Stole* it?

She hated to think such a thing, but the idea just wouldn't quite leave her. He'd been asking about the scarab, then he took her off to a place where he knew he'd be able to get her in a position to take it from her. Goodness, but he might've taken a good deal more from her tonight if he'd wanted!

But he hadn't wanted, had he? She'd been lost in whatever it was he'd been doing to her; she was clearly at his disposal. He could have done heaven knew what to her and she'd have done little more than thank him for it, given the state she'd been in. Yet he'd stopped; he'd refrained from continuing.

Yes, even before Anthony appeared with Mamma, Lord Harry had been done with her. It hadn't dawned on her to wonder why, until now. Now it all made sense. Now she understood.

He'd seduced her only enough to get what he'd wanted, which infuriatingly was not her, but her scarab. Once he'd had that, he was done. Oh, but now she wished Anthony *had* called the blackguard out tonight. And won.

He took advantage of her not because he cared for her, or even because he was particularly attracted to her, but because he wanted her jewelry! He'd been eyeing Lady Burlington's jewelry, too, hadn't he? That evil, vile creature! And to think for one stupid minute there she'd actually begun to rethink her desire to remain unmarried and go to Egypt. What a fool she was!

But Anthony said Lord Harry had agreed to the wedding. What would that gain him? Did he think she had scarabs aplenty for him to steal day after day? Well, he'd be sadly disappointed.

But no, it would make more sense to assume he truly had no intention of marrying her. He'd likely just agreed to Anthony's terms as a way of avoiding any annoying conflict tonight. For all she knew, he had gone off to the pawnshop and sold her precious scarab first thing. Likely he'd take the money he got and disappear now. Didn't Maria say his senses were so jaded that he craved strange lands and exotic women? Well, surely she was far from exotic enough for him.

So Mamma had been right all along. The man wasn't marriage material. He was a thief. He took Anthony's lovely carriage and her beautiful scarab.

Thank God she'd only fancied herself falling in love with him. How devastating if she'd actually lost her heart to a man like that. Why, if she'd truly been in love with him there was no telling how miserable she'd feel now, or how long she'd stay awake through the night, weeping over him.

As it was, she was quite proud of herself. Once the maid came to help her change and she finally snuffed out her lamp and snuggled down under her covers, it could have been little more than an hour or two that she shed foolish tears. But she comforted herself by attributing them to her lost scarab.

Harris Chesterton was not worthy of her grieving. Even if he had done things to her no man ever had. Or likely ever would.

Chapter Thirteen

✤

Dread hung over him in several layers now. Kidnapping, robbery, betrayal, marriage... His life was full of far too much impending doom. And now on top of it, his watch told him it was nearly time to meet Lady Burlington. He dreaded this most of all.

Which probably explained why he was willing to risk discovery and possible incarceration by wasting time breaking into Lord Burlington's house. The lady had left the servants' door open for him, yet he hunted another entry. Well, he had to know if all those artifacts were still there, didn't he? Little good it would do to subject himself to her ladyship's torture only to find they'd already been removed. Indeed, now was the perfect time to assure himself hope was not lost.

If it was, then at least he would spare himself a night with his shrewish hostess. By Lucifer, he could only imagine what the woman had planned for him. He was revolted at the mere thought.

Placating Lady Burlington's demands—whatever they might be—was the very last thing he'd rather be doing this evening. Especially since he'd so recently been quite busy at the very first thing he'd rather be doing.

He knew, however, he'd do well not to think so fondly of his moments with Miss Rastmoor. Pleasurable, yes. Productive, too. But a wise man would put little stock in it. Could he truly believe he was the first to venture into that blissful land with the woman? She'd been so eager for him, come so easily at his touch. Would an innocent react that way? He'd not made it a practice of seducing innocents, but he somehow expected an untried miss would put up a bit more resistance.

Why should he be surprised, though? He was fiancé number four, after all. Plus Fitzgelder had somehow figured into that mix, and no one could doubt what that must mean. And of course he'd seen the hussy tonight, fluttering her eyes and fawning over her dance partners.

"She's flirting with right under your nose."

He'd not forgotten Lady Burlington's revelation about the scarab's origin, either. He could only wonder what else Miss Rastmoor had gotten from her dancing admirer. But which andmirer?

Clearly there was some measure of familiarity between her and Ferrel. Could he have been her source for the scarab? He didn't see how. It was far more likely to be someone else.

Markland. Markland was involved in it all, he was certain. Who else had reason for it? And certainly Miss Rastmoor had been eyeing the man in a special way tonight. He'd seen it from the start. Had they lied to him about their acquaintance with one another? Perhaps.

George Markland was engaged to the daughter of an influential nobleman. He had been for years. His grandfather approved it and couldn't dote on his favorite descendant enough. Clearly it was in Markland's best interest not to do anything to upset the old man, which admitting to a liaison with Penelope Rastmoor would do.

And as for his access to the scarab . . . damn the man. Was Markland's animosity toward Oldham so great that he'd come to this? Apparently it was. He'd participated in stealing those artifacts and endangering the man's life. Harris would make him pay.

First, though, he'd have to get the items back and have them returned by the kidnapper's deadline. If he could have garnered some favor with his uncle and gotten his hands on money that was rightfully his, things would have been so much easier. But it seemed it was pointless to hope in that direction. His uncle was a heartless bastard who hated him on principle.

His fury was nearly blinding. Damn, but he had to get control of himself. Indeed, despite all the raging emotions, he simply must keep focus. Getting those artifacts and returning them to the dangerous people who held Professor Oldham had to be his first priority.

Taking revenge on Markland would have to wait, as would any of the plans he had for Penelope. And indeed he did have plans for her. He'd find out just how much she knew of Markland's activities and he'd decide from there how much more of his time he'd waste on her.

He hoped it would be considerable.

But before he could do any of that, he needed to ascertain the artifacts' whereabouts. Nothing could be done if he'd lost them. Again.

Damn it, but Burlington had locked the window. Harris had to go around to the rear of the house where he hoped to find access to the servants' area in the lower level. It was late, but not so late that he could expect the entire house to be sleeping. He would have to move cautiously.

He did find entrance, through a narrow door that led directly down to the kitchen area. He could smell the cooking fires, still hot. Most of the lights had been put out, but a few noises in the distance assured him some in the household were still awake. He hung close to the wall, taking advantage of shadows as he moved toward the stairway that would take him up to the family's level.

His boots were far noisier than he wished as he hurried up the steps. Still, he had not run across anyone. He estimated the stairway would deposit him somewhere near the room that had held the dreadful musicale last night. It was then just a short distance through the entrance hall and to the room where the artifacts had been. A simple door lock was no trouble.

He made it to the narrow corridor that would lead him in one direction toward the back of the house, and in the other toward the front. As stealthily as possible, knowing he was in dangerous territory here, he crept along, feeling his way in the near darkness. A weak lamp lit up the entrance hall, and he paused before leaving the safety of the dim corridor. All seemed clear, and he heard no sound of habitation on this level. Giving a final glance, he darted out.

A large form suddenly loomed in front of him. Damn! One of Burlington's footmen. Young. Big. No neck.

"I know what you're up to," the liveried ogre said.

Hell and damnation. This was going to be dicey. Harris wondered which would be the best tack at this point, to come to outright fisticuffs or to simply offer the man money. Which he didn't have. That left him with fisticuffs, which didn't seem such a wise choice.

He opted for diplomacy.

"Of course you do. You're a good man, doing your job. His lordship will be glad to hear it."

"Er, what?"

"That's why he asked me to sneak in here this way, to find out if his staff could be trusted to stay alert. It appears that you can. Well done."

"Lord Burlington asked you to sneak in here?"

"Of course he did! I'm a gentleman, sir. You don't think I go breaking into people's houses uninvited, do you?"

"Well . . . that is . . ."

"No, of course not."

"But why would, I mean . . ."

"Because of the antiquities, of course. You are supposed to be watching over them, aren't you?"

Lord, he hoped he was playing this right. An adept footman would likely see right through him, especially if his master had already disposed of said antiquities.

"Indeed I am, sir," the footman replied. "I been at my post here since after supper."

"Very well, then. And I take it the treasures are locked up tight, just where his lordship had them?"

"Yes, sir, just where they've been the last two days, and one of us is placed here to watch over them day and night. Her ladyship says someone tried to get in the window after them yesterday."

"What? Well, it's good to know that's not likely to happen again." *Damn it.*

"No, sir. We'll be watching like a hawk the next two days."

"Two days?"

"Well, that's when the master says they'll be sent out. Found someone to buy them off him, he did. Seems these treasures turned out to be more trouble than they're worth, always needing guarding and such. And her ladyship making such a fuss over it all, not to mention Miss Lettice's pug has been a bundle of nerves. Seems we'll all be better off to get rid of these old relics."

"Indeed, so it does."

Two days, was it? That meant they were safe for now. Good. He still had time to think. Perhaps things would work out, after all.

"And forgive me for thinking you was here to . . . uh, sorry, sir."

"Forgiven, lad. Rather humorous, actually. To think you almost mistook me for a cat burglar."

"Oh no, sir! I never mistook you for that. I thought you were here to . . . well . . ."

"Well what? What did you think I was doing here, creeping about in the middle of the night if not to steal that treasure?"

The man positively reddened. "I thought you was here to steal my girl, sir."

"Steal your . . . ?"

"Milly, sir. Milly Cooper, what used to work upstairs. I seen you with her a time or two, and she's been going on and on about what a fine gent you are, and all. I been a bit jealous, you know."

"Ah, the little housemaid. Well, I'm happy to assure you, sir, you've no need for jealousy. I'll not be . . . wait, did you say she *used to* work here?"

Now the footman smiled. "Some young lady met her here last night and gave her a fine wage to come work at her house. Milly's all tickled over it."

"A young lady, you say?"

He had a fair idea which young lady that might be. Ah, but Miss Rastmoor was too obvious, stealing a housemaid from Burlington who just happened to have detailed knowledge of the treasure. So Penelope was more involved in this than she indicated!

Of course he gave the neckless footman no inkling of his thoughts. He wished the man well and commended him for his attention to duty. He even dug into his pocket and pulled out the last coins he had in there.

"Here's for your trouble," he said grandly. "Now, would you like to let me out the front door, or should I tiptoe back down the way I came?"

"You should stay right where you are, Lord Harry," a sickeningly sweet female voice called from above.

Damn. Lady Burlington stood at the top of the staircase smiling down at them. She wore a demure wrap, but he did not for one minute misconstrue her intent as anything innocent.

"What a surprise, Lady Burlington," he said, wishing it were true.

"That is all, Tom," she said to the footman. "I'll look after Lord Harry now. You may retire."

"But his lordship said I was to—"

"That is all, Tom," she repeated in a firm voice that bordered on frightening.

The footman gave one questioning look at Harris, who shrugged. Apparently the footman knew better than to argue with his mistress, so he made a quick bow then took his leave. Harris wished he could do the same.

"You were being so quiet, I hardly knew you had arrived," Lady Burlington said, her voice sweet as treacle but no less frightening.

"We have business, I believe?" Harris said.

She nodded, and indicated that if he wished their conversation to continue, he would have to meet her upstairs. Unenticing as that was, he acquiesced and ascended the stairway. She smiled a predatory smile and took his arm. He allowed himself to be ushered into an intimate sitting room that was lit by two flickering tapers and doused with enough perfume to make the air nearly unbreathable.

So much for hoping the woman had purely business on her mind.

"I'm here as requested," Harris said when the door shut behind him, leaving them conspicuously alone.

"Yes, and prompt, I see. Rather eager to meet me, Lord Harry?"

"You indicated it would be worth my while."

"Indeed. Brandy?"

She made a fuss over the decanter that waited nearby on a low table, making sure to bend over and give him full display of her décolletage. He pretended to observe with pleasure, but in truth he'd seen better. On Miss Rastmoor, for instance.

"I notice you've removed your jewelry," he commented.

Actually, she'd removed most of her clothing, as well, leaving the demure wrapper she'd been in draped over a chair as she swayed about in nothing more than a diaphanous dressing gown. Ordinarily he would have found the effect quite enjoyable, an attractive female making herself so available to him. She was a woman who knew what she was about and was accustomed to making men comfortable with her. Very comfortable. Since it was obvious what she intended to charge him in payment for whatever information she might offer, it seemed a shame that he could not dredge up any interest.

This had never before been a problem for him. Certainly he'd had interest aplenty when he'd relieved Miss Rastmoor of her scarab. Hell, he'd been a little too interested, in fact. Just now, however, he found the very notion of engaging in anything remotely intimate with his hostess to be exceedingly distasteful.

"There's no need to stand on formality here, Lord Harry," she purred, sliding up to hand him a glass. "Why not take off your coat and make yourself at ease."

"Why don't you first tell me why I've been invited up here, Lady Burlington?"

"I should think that much would be obvious," she said.

"Indeed. What is obvious is that you have a house full of Egyptian antiquities."

"My husband is a collector," she said.

"Well, someone here is a collector. And what of that lovely bauble you were wearing at the ball? Oddly enough, it bore a strong resemblance to a piece I happen to know was stolen not too very long ago."

"You don't say? How very fascinating. But let's discuss it later. Right now there is so much else we could be doing."

"We'll discuss it now, if you don't mind. Where is the rest of the jewelry? In your possession?"

She sighed as if this were a huge imposition. "No, I don't have it. I only received a few pieces."

"A few? Who has the rest?"

"How do I know? Gone to whomever would pay for them, I suppose. Come, my lord, surely you can think of something other than thousand-year-old trinkets just now."

"I can indeed. I'm thinking of a certain friend who is in need of my help just now. What do you know of that, my lady?"

"Honestly, Lord Harry! You act as if he did not deserve what's become of him."

"He's being held prisoner by ruthless people! What can you mean, he deserves such a thing? What do you know of any of this?"

"Perhaps I should ask just what do *you* truly know of it," she said, running her fingers up his arm and over his shoulder to play with the hair at the back of his neck. "Just how well do you really know this Professor Oldham, exactly?"

"Well enough." By God, he knew the man a damn sight better than she did, if she could think for one moment he was deserving of the treatment he'd received.

"Yet you still persist he had nothing to do with the disappearance of those artifacts?"

"I do, and again I'll ask what you know of it all."

"Only as much as I've been told by an interested party. Come, make yourself comfortable and perhaps we can discuss this at length. Afterward."

She was pulling at his coat, brushing her body up against his as if he'd asked her to. It should have been provocative; instead it was infuriating. Clearly she had the artifacts, but very little idea what was truly at stake. Where had she been getting her information? And what, exactly, did she plan to do with it?

"There will be no afterward," he said. "Tell me now: what do you know of my . . . of Professor Oldham's situation and the theft of those artifacts?"

"Perhaps you should ask Oldham, my dear."

"Well, that's a bit difficult, as he's being held captive in Egypt."

"Oh? So that's what you think?"

Now she had the nerve to laugh at him. This was too much. He'd never been one to manhandle a woman—unless she asked nicely, of course—but tonight his patience had been overtried. He took her by the shoulders and held her out where she had no choice but to face him.

"Tell me what you know, damn it!"

A shadow of fear swept across her face. "He's in England. They've brought him here."

"I don't believe you."

"It's true."

"How do you know?"

"That doesn't matter! The man stole from them. You're right, they are ruthless people and they will do what they can to see their treasure is returned to their land."

So she did understand at least that much of the threat. Professor Oldham's captors were a band of Egyptians, men they had worked peacefully with to help conserve the antiquities, to try and halt the wholesale thievery of artifacts. It was Oldham's greatest wish to see his work revered by the people of that nation. He wanted to preserve and protect their rich history, not pillage it as so many of their countrymen did.

Yet when a whole year's worth of excavating turned up missing, suspicion fell on Professor Oldham. The Egyptians feared he had betrayed them, using their labor and their resources to find the treasure, then stealing it out from under their noses for his own greed. They held him, ordering Harris to find and return the treasure. If he failed, Professor Oldham would suffer. Their deadline was nearly up and Harris had pitiful little to show for his efforts.

He could, however, vouch for the older man's character. "Professor Oldham is an honest man. He would never betray his Egyptian friends! Someone else orchestrated that theft and implicated him."

He knew it was true. Of course he'd found very little to prove it, though. So far it was as if those artifacts had magically brought themselves to England. As of yet he could find no connection between the original thieves—whoever they were—and any of the persons who appeared to be in possession now. Without that proof, Professor Oldham's captors would never absolve him, and without the return of the artifacts—or the exorbitant ransom they demanded—they would never release him. It all hung on Harris's shoulders, and so far he'd failed miserably.

"Silly boy, you think you understand him? Charles Oldham is not the selfless scholar you seem to think him. Trust me, if he felt there was more profit to be made by bringing those treasures here to England, then that is likely what he did. His friends in the desert are fully justified not to trust him."

"You don't have the slightest idea what you're talking about. He loves Egypt; he's dedicated himself to preserving those artifacts."

"Oh? Perhaps you never heard of a certain correspondent of his, one P. Anthonys, right here in London."

"Of course I know of this P. Anthonys," he said sharply.

Yes, he knew of this person. Professor Oldham had been corresponding for nearly two years, answering endless questions from the man, sending detailed descriptions of every article they unearthed. Of course Harris knew of him; he'd been the first person he tried to locate when all this insanity began and he came rushing back to England.

"Then you realize no P. Anthonys really exists?" Lady Burlington said with a condescending sneer.

Yes, that thought had crossed Harris's mind when his search for the fellow turned up nothing.

"Clearly he is just a ruse, a false name used by Professor Oldham's collaborator. Together they plotted to get the artifacts out of Egypt and bring them here to be sold for profit."

"There you are wrong, my lady," he was pleased to inform her. "I have seen several of Professor Oldham's letters to and from this Anthonys person, and there was nothing in them to suggest any plot or conspiracy."

There was nothing to suggest they were completely harmless, either. He made no mention of that fact.

"And if I could produce evidence to the contrary?" she said carefully.

"Are you indicating that you can?"

"Perhaps you ought to find out."

He thought about it; he truly did. In the end, he simply had no stomach for it.

"I won't play your game, Lady Burlington. If you have information that will help me rescue Professor Oldham, then share it. Otherwise, I'm afraid it's time for me to take my leave."

She pouted. "I'm disappointed, Chesterton. You've not yet bothered to ask how any of this might actually benefit you."

"It's clear what you think will be a benefit, my lady. Sorry to say, you are wrong."

"Your uncle may think otherwise."

What the devil did his uncle have to do with any of this?

"As you must be aware, my uncle and I are somewhat estranged."

"Indeed. But he and I are not."

Hellfire. He should have known. Nedley Chesterton was involved in this. Why had he not seen his uncle's hand from the beginning? Who else had such reason to hate Oldham? Indeed, everyone knew of Markland's resentment toward the man, but why had Harris not for one moment suspected his uncle? Damn, but he'd been a shortsighted fool.

"Now, Lady Burlington, you have my full attention. What interest does my uncle have in this matter?"

"Let's see, to which matter do you refer? The matter concerning Professor Oldham's shameful larceny, or the matter concerning your rather scandalous involvement here with me?"

Damn the scheming bitch. "All of it."

"Well, then. Your uncle has graciously sent ransom to retrieve Professor Oldham, at your expense, of course."

"At my expense? Good God, the ransom they demanded was far beyond anything I can afford."

"True, but as your uncle firmly believes you are one of Professor Oldham's conspirators, then surely you could easily repay him. In artifacts."

"What? Hell no. Even if I were in possession of any artifacts, I'd never give them over to my uncle. Those artifacts rightfully belong to the people of Egypt. It was Professor Oldham's intent all along, and I'll not have his reputation besmirched by even so much as a hint that he would ever condone what has occurred."

"I'm afraid you have no choice, Chesterton," she said, toying with his lapels. "The ransom has already been paid, and the Egyptian faction believes what they believe. Professor Oldham has been sent back here, and his days among the pyramids are finished. He will never be allowed to dig there again."

"So this is my uncle's revenge? He fabricated lies, then paid the ransom, condemning Professor Oldham to assumed guilt and public humiliation, did he?"

"You should be grateful. He saved the man's life."

"He destroyed the man's life. That hateful old bastard."

"You should speak more kindly of your dear uncle, Chesterton."

"When he has reason to deserve it, I would be most happy to."

She'd been working at his cravat and now pulled it slowly

away from his neck. Fine. Let the scheming slut have it. That would be all she was getting from him tonight.

"Such broad shoulders, sir," she cooed at him, running her hands over him. "It seems all that digging in the sand has agreed with you."

"Well, you do not agree with me, my lady."

"On the contrary, sir. I can be most agreeable."

"Not to me. Not when you are on friendly terms with my uncle."

"Now now. You never know who might be listening in on our private conversation."

Her hands were working at his trousers now. The cravat was one thing, but this was entirely another. He took her by the shoulders again to push her away from him. Odd, he'd meant to be firm, but not cruel. However, she cried out as if he were harming her.

"You are too bold, sir!" she practically shouted. "Take me if you must, as I'm hardly a match for your force."

With that, she tumbled affectedly into a silk-draped settee. Her dressing gown was quite miraculously askew, and she threw one hand up to her forehead and another to give show of covering her bosom. Harris was left to stand over her and wonder what the devil she was about.

It was then, of course, that the door was flung open and noisy, male footsteps pounded toward him. He had just enough time to steel himself for the attack.

Lord Burlington. Of course. He should have seen this disaster coming a mile away. By God, he'd been an absolute idiot.

"Unhand my wife!" Burlington stormed.

Harris was grabbed by the collar and whirled around to face his accuser.

"You again!" the man sputtered. "I knew there was something amiss! I should have called you out that first time I found you in my house. You've had your eye on my wife ever since."

"No, I assure you neither of my eyes nor my hands have come close to your wife for any of the purposes you assume."

"Liar! You cannot deny what I see right before me. Blackguard, I will kill you for this!"

"Yes, yes, I'm sure you would, but . . ."

He didn't exactly get around to finishing that sentiment,

however. Another set of heavy footsteps entered through the doorway, and Harris realized the full extent of this snare when he glanced up and recognized the hefty figure. He supposed he should have expected this, too.

"Hello, Uncle. I did not realize you were in Town."

Nedley Chesterton simply harrumphed. Harris was actually impressed that he got even that much from him. It had been years since the old man had so much as looked his way.

He certainly was glaring now, though.

"Damn it, boy, do you think to cuckold a man in his own home and get away with it?"

"And it's very lovely to see you, too, sir."

"Don't think you can lickspittle your way into my favor now, you dissolute pup."

"I wouldn't dream of it. How fortunate that you happen to be here just now, though."

His uncle merely frowned at him.

"Yes, fortunate indeed!" Lady Burlington declared, pulling herself together and rushing to cling to her husband's side. "I can't imagine what he would have done with me had you not arrived just now!"

"I can," Lord Burlington snarled.

"Indeed you probably can," Harris agreed. "You've had to live with her all these years."

It appeared her chaste and delicate ladyship was just about to swoon again. Right after she disemboweled Harris for inferring an insult.

"You have brought shame and dishonor to our family," Uncle Nedley grumbled. "If it were in my power, I would disinherit you."

"So you may have mentioned once or twice," Harris acknowledged.

"He won't live long enough to inherit anything, Nedley," Burlington said. "I'm calling him out. Harris Chesterton, choose your second and make amends with your maker."

"Second? I'd rather not even have a first. Can't we simply discuss this as rational men, Burlington? Surely you don't really believe that I would—"

"I believe a scoundrel like you would be capable of any crime. It's pistols at dawn, Chesterton!"

"Oh, good Lord." *Must the man turn this into a cliché?*

"I will attend you, Burlington," Nedley offered.

And wouldn't the old man just love that? He'd been wishing for years that Harris would cock up his toes. Now he would have an unobstructed view of the event.

An event he was obviously a very large part of orchestrating. Harris had been such a fool to be lured in this way; he almost deserved to die. Of course he had no intentions of doing so.

The easiest thing, naturally, would be to avoid the stigma and give Burlington the satisfaction he demanded. After all, Harris was a good shot. He could give a convincing show to stave off any cries of cowardice, yet he could trust himself to aim carefully and not end up with any uncomfortable murder charges. A flesh wound would suffice.

Unfortunately, there was always the chance that Burlington might get lucky and wing him. Or worse. Or that Uncle Nedley had planned for this all along and would seize the opportunity to step in, ridding himself forever of his hated nephew and then claiming Burlington had done the deed in a fair duel. It was certainly not at all beneath his uncle to let some unwitting partner take the blame for his own actions.

No, Harris corrected himself. It would appear Burlington was less a partner and more a pawn. Harris would be willing to bet he had no idea this was all staged for his benefit. To judge by the smug expression on Lady Burlington's face, she was looking forward to this turn of events just as much as Nedley. Likely she was hoping Harris might conveniently rid her of Burlington, while Nedley was hoping Burlington might rid him of Harris. Either way, someone would end up well pleased, and it would not be Harris.

"Oh, very well," he said at last, determining that going along with them was the only way out. For now.

"Good. If you are not a coward, you will meet me in two days. I'll have my man send directions around to your address. You must learn, young man, that fiends like you do not rule the day in England."

Odd, it certainly seemed as if they did.

Chapter Fourteen

It was morning and Penelope's eyes were still red and unattractively swollen. Drat that Lord Harry! He should not be allowed to do this to her, ruin her sleep and ruin her day. Her meals, too, it would seem.

She was dreading breakfast. Surely after last night's, er, occurrence Mamma was not going to let them eat in peace. She'd have plenty more to say on the subject, Penelope was certain. Indeed, so would Anthony.

A wedding in one week? No, that would never happen. And she had not only lost her scarab, but her one hope to convince Anthony to let her travel. He would never let her go now. The Tollersons would be leaving soon, and she would be left behind. She suspected Lord Harry was already gone, wherever he might be going. Anthony had neatly supplied the conveyance, she'd supplied the financing, and a wedding date had certainly given the man ample motive to leave and never look back.

It was a horrible start to her day.

And now, as she moved listlessly through the house, it seemed things were getting even more horrible. She heard angry male voices coming from Anthony's study. At first her heart fluttered, hoping—like an idiot—that Lord Harry had come, but she frowned in confusion when she heard her brother call the other man by name.

"These are grave accusations against my future brother-in-law, Mr. Chesterton."

The other man, older and more gruff than Anthony, swore. "And they're bloody well true, Rastmoor. I saw them with my own eyes. Your so-called future brother-in-law was having his way with Lady Burlington right there in her husband's home. Disgusting. I tell you, the man is not fit for anyone's sister."

Lord Harry's uncle was here? And he was claiming that Lord Harry had . . . Good heavens, but what she'd seen pass between Lord Harry and that scantily dressed banshee at the ball last night truly had been the arranging of an assignation! And right before he'd helped himself to whatever Penelope had to offer, too.

Infuriating! The man was disgusting. She'd been correct all along—Harris Chesterton truly was the most horrible fiancé imaginable.

Good God, and she'd almost fancied herself in love with him! The thought made her nearly sick, especially since she detected a tiny part of her still was. All morning she'd been fighting to ignore a desperate little voice inside, calling out and begging her not to believe such things and to give Lord Harry a chance to explain himself. Merciful gracious, but she would have to silence that voice immediately.

It turned out to be rather easily done. All she needed was to continue eavesdropping.

"Burlington called him out, of course, but we've yet to see if the craven will show up tomorrow."

"You believe he won't?"

"He's a poltroon, a dastard. Very likely left Town already."

"So he acknowledged that Burlington's claims against him were true?"

"Of course he did. How could he not? We both found him there, in a state of undress very much misusing the poor woman. I assure you, it gives me no pleasure to admit what an abomination my own nephew has become, but I feel it is my duty to inform you of his true nature. I beg you to spare yourself and your sister the indignation of connection to such a vile mongrel."

Anthony did not reply immediately. She knew he was taking it all in, determining whether or not to believe the man. Yet how could he not? As the earl had said, it could certainly give him no pleasure to announce such things about his own nephew. There was no reason for Anthony not to believe him.

For Penelope's part, she had more than enough reason to believe every word of it, despite that annoying little internal voice. Just now it was actively sighing in relief that Lord Harry might have chosen the craven's way out rather than getting himself shot to death by a vengeful husband. Oh, but she really could not be at all happy with this dratted voice.

"Thank you for your time, and for your concern," Anthony finally said. "I will certainly take it into consideration."

"A marriage between your delicate sister and my degenerate nephew would be a most disastrous thing, I'm afraid," the uncle declared. "I only pray it is not too late to save her virtue."

Penelope winced. Anthony, however, surprised her by his indignation.

"My sister is a lady, sir. Rest assured she has behaved like one."

Drat. She almost wished she'd not heard that. Now she was in Anthony's debt.

"I'm certain she has. It's my devilish nephew I worry about, Rastmoor. Trust me, if you care for the well-being of your sister, do all in your power to keep her far away from Chesterton. He's no good."

"I'll certainly consider what's to be done, sir. Thank you."

The men were ending their conversation, so Penelope quickly ducked into the next room. She needed a moment or two to run through all this new information. Had Lord Harry truly been found with Lady Burlington? She had no reason whatsoever to disbelieve his uncle's claim, yet it did not sound entirely right. Lady Burlington was too willing to be "misused." Who on earth could ever accuse Lord Harry of such a thing? True, he might be unscrupulous, but he would never do anything to a lady without her consent. That was not like him at all. Why, he was . . .

For heaven's sake. What was she doing? Lord Harry was a

bounder of the worst kind, and she could only be a fool if she ever thought to make excuses for him.

Why, next time she saw him she would tell him that . . . Oh, but it was unlikely there would ever be a next time. He'd gotten what he needed and even run away from an honest duel. Clearly the man was miles from here by now, just as she'd expected. Maria had been right all along. This truly did end badly. She began to wonder if she should ever trust herself again after such monumental failure in judgment.

"Penelope?"

Anthony stood in the doorway. She glanced up at him, and past him, but there was no sign of the elder Mr. Chesterton.

"He's gone," Anthony answered for her. "You heard him?"

"I did."

He took a step into the room. To gloat, she expected. He'd always thought her capable of so much idiocy, he must be simply bursting with pride over his prophetic abilities.

"Perhaps he is mistaken," he said at last.

She almost laughed at that. "No, that's highly doubtful. Perhaps you'd like to know that I saw Lord Harry in a rather intimate tête-à-tête with the lady just last night, while he thought I was distracted by dancing."

"You made no mention of that!"

"No, I suppose I didn't."

Perhaps she should have. Now it was too late. She'd ruined herself and ruined her chance of ever being allowed to travel. Worse, she'd broken her own heart in the process.

"You should have told me about him, Penelope."

"I know. It was wrong, but I just couldn't . . ."

Couldn't what? Couldn't admit she'd intentionally tried to deceive her brother, or that Lord Harry had never felt anything for her? She refused to answer herself.

"There, there," he said softly. "I suppose you wouldn't have wanted to acknowledge it. I understand."

"You do?"

"Of course. Come here, little sister."

To her absolute shock and amazement he stepped toward her and actually embraced her. Tenderly! It was almost as if he weren't angry at all that, once again, she had thrown them into scandal.

"I can guess how you must feel."

"You can?"

"You trusted the man and he turned out to be a scoundrel."

"Really he—"

"No, don't bother to defend him. He blinded me to his flaws, too. You can hardly be blamed for it. You did nothing wrong."

Nothing wrong? Did he really believe this? If she were a decent sister, she would confess the truth, confide in him that . . . *No, just keep quiet. Don't say anything.*

"Trust me to handle this for you, Penelope. I'll take care of everything. I'll see that you're left quite undamaged from this debacle."

"Er, how?"

He patted her on the head and stepped away to smile down at her. "Don't you worry. I'll take care of Lord Harry."

"You will? But how . . ."

"Don't fret yourself over that. You just take care of mending your heartbreak. And I think I know just what might help."

"Might help?"

"How would you like to take a little trip?"

He was still smiling the sweetest brotherly smile. Was he this happy to finally banish her to the country?

Then he tapped her on the nose as if she were a child. "I believe you should go to Egypt, after all."

"I should *what*?"

"Of course. That's the perfect thing to take your mind off this. I'm sure the Tollersons would love to take you along when they go. They're fine, honest people; they would be excellent companions for you. And how about if we ask your friend Maria if she'd like to go along? Would that be acceptable?"

Acceptable? Good heavens! It would be marvelous! But what about his belief that she would destroy the Sphinx, or that the Tollersons were too old to even keep track of their own teeth, let alone look after her?

"Are you toying with me, Anthony?" she asked. "Because if you are, it's a very cruel joke."

"No, Penelope. I'm not toying with you. If you can recall, I had my heart broken once. I know how it feels and, believe it or not, I honestly want to help you."

"So you would send me to Egypt?"

"I thought that was what you wanted?"

Indeed, it was. Most earnestly! But . . . what about Lord Harry? Not that she cared, of course, but surely his uncle would be even more ungracious toward him now. And had Lord Burlington truly called him out? What if he were shot? And now Anthony was furious with him, too. What did he have planned for the man? True, Lord Harry had used her badly, but she'd been the one to facilitate it.

"What do you mean," she asked carefully, "that you'll take care of Lord Harry?"

"Never you mind. I'll simply see to it that he does nothing further to malign your character or play fast and loose with your reputation."

"Oh," she murmured, as if his answer had been any sort of real explanation.

"Now you go up to your room and give yourself time to recover. I'll have some breakfast sent up to you. And I'm sure you would not mind if I were the one to break this distressing news to our mother? Or would you prefer to do that yourself?"

"Er, no, you're welcome to do that." *Goodness, by all means that was a conversation she'd very much rather avoid.*

"Fine," he said, that still-sweet smile just as unfamiliar to her. "Go rest. I'll take care of everything."

She was so off-balance by his unexpected attitude that she couldn't think of anything to say but a weak little "thank you." She was already in her room, taking her first bites of the breakfast he did, indeed, have sent up for her, before she thought to wonder just exactly what he truly meant by "I'll take care of everything." Since she'd been very careful to keep her brother in the dark about "everything," she found it quite difficult to comprehend just how he would be taking care of it.

Still, he'd offered her Egypt! She found herself quite torn between a feeling of triumph and a rather nagging little feeling that things were not about to be resolved so easily. She decided to focus on the first.

HARRIS GRUMBLED AS HE READ THROUGH LORD BURlington's latest note. The man was not going to make this easy, was he? Messages had been sent back and forth, with the nobleman calling Harris every scathing insult available to him, coward being his favorite. Nothing Lord Harry said could placate the man or dissuade him from his desire to meet on a field of honor.

Damn the idiot. As if the man hadn't been cuckolded often enough, why should he suddenly feel the need to avenge himself where Harris was concerned? Didn't he see he'd been offered an easy way out? Surely he couldn't really believe he stood so much as a thin chance of surviving a fair duel with the nefarious Harris Chesterton? Apparently he did.

It was lunacy. Harris had no intentions of meeting the man, but if he was pushed into it he was for damn sure not about to devolve. If he had to face Burlington over this ridiculous issue, he was tempted to do so with lethal accuracy. No way he would stand there and let Burlington—or Nedley, his unsurprising second—plug him with holes. He had no doubt that was dear Uncle Nedley's intent. If Burlington didn't kill him straight out, he was certain his scheming uncle would. This was all very convenient for the old man.

He had no time for this, though. Professor Oldham was in danger. Indeed, Harris had not slept last night but had left Burlington's home to investigate Lady Burlington's claim that the scholar had been ransomed and brought back to London. It seemed this was, indeed, the case, but Harris had not managed to get information to indicate the man's whereabouts. His uncle sent word that if Harris wanted to find Oldham, he would have to meet Burlington. Supposedly, if he survived the duel, he would be given the man's location.

Harris assumed that "if" was the very operative word. It was clearly his uncle's intent that he not survive. Yet he could not very well abandon Oldham at this point, could he? Of course not. He returned the note to Burlington with assurance that he would meet him. The next morning.

That would give him eighteen hours to find Oldham on his own. A pounding at his door, however, told him finding time to do that might be a bit difficult.

He went to the door, expecting yet another round of insults from Burlington. It was, however, a far more personal insult. From Lord Rastmoor.

No sooner had Harris opened the door to him than the man planted a powerful fist into his face. It was merely reflex action that caused Harris to turn his head just in time to avoid having his nose obliterated. Hell. Apparently word of last night's trouble had reached Penelope's brother.

"Bastard! You treated my sister like a whore and now you've broken her heart!"

"Hello, Rastmoor," Harris said, adjusting his jaw and rather surprised to find it was not broken.

"Don't ignore the facts, Chesterton. She trusted you! Damn it, but this morning your uncle dropped by to tell me how he'd discovered you last night in flagrante delicto with Lady Burlington—just hours after I'd found you with Penelope. I did not thrash you then because you led me to believe your actions were simply those of a man in love. I could overlook that, Chesterton, but not this. Penelope is not some little plaything you can treat this way!"

"So, do I take it you're calling off the wedding, then?"

"Calling off the wedding? Hell, I'm calling you out!"

"Well, then you'll have to stand in line, Rastmoor. I'm afraid Burlington has beat you to it." He dabbed at his bottom lip, which was swelling quite rapidly and beginning to bleed.

"Your uncle seems to doubt you've got bollocks enough to meet him."

"I have no desire to murder that windbag, and even less inclination to murder you."

"Then you are a coward."

"No, I simply have too many other things to do this week."

"You are worse than a blackguard," Rastmoor grumbled. "What, are there still wives in Town you've not dallied with?"

"Look, there are things you know nothing about. Your sister is fine; I've not ruined her, I assure you. I've left her no worse than I found her."

"Are you suggesting she was already damaged goods? It's true she may have had several fiancés already, but—"

"And you insinuate she may have allowed them certain liberties? Now who is insulting her? Damn you, Rastmoor, if you've so much as raised your voice at her or accused her of—"

"I accused her of nothing more than trusting you, sir. And look what she gets for that. Her heart is broken!"

"She is fine; better off without me, as a matter of fact."

"I won't argue with you there. She will be fine, and she *is* better off without you. In fact, I'm making very certain she will be safely out of your reach while she recovers. I'm sending her to Egypt."

"Egypt? Good God, don't you think that's a little drastic?"

"She's begged me for years to let her go there. If you cared anything for her you might have paid attention to her interest in the subject."

"She never mentioned it. Egypt? Are you certain?"

"Of course I'm certain! She's my own sister, damn it. I've never let her go, but now I realize I should have. I should have let her pursue that passion, rather than letting her be victimized by yours."

"Penelope Rastmoor has never been victimized by anyone," Harris said.

He was beginning to wonder if, in fact, they'd all been victimized by her. So she was interested in Egypt, was she? He should have realized it. She'd had the scarab, after all. And he'd found her in that room in Burlington's house, hadn't he? He should have paid attention. She'd known what that phallus was all along. What else did she know about his missing artifacts?

Hellfire. The girl was the key to all of this.

"I'll see that she never has to lay eyes on you again, Chesterton."

Damn. She'd wanted to go to Egypt all along, hadn't she? This was the very thing she'd been negotiating with her brother. And now they'd all played into her hands and she was getting exactly what she wanted. But why? What would she get out of this journey to Egypt? Would she, perhaps, be bringing additional artifacts back to be sold off to the highest bidder? Who was she in league with?

"As I said, Rastmoor, there are things you don't know."

"I know enough to keep you away from my sister."

"I can most readily assure you," Harris said, eager to get rid of this man and get busy making sense of this whole mess, "I would never dream of damaging an innocent." Which clearly left her out.

"And you'll not go around town spreading vile rumors about her?"

"I will not. You may choose not to believe it, but I bear a great deal of respect for your sister, Rastmoor."

This was even more true now that he realized how brilliantly she'd played her game. And won.

Rastmoor studied him, apparently considering whether or not to believe Harris's declaration. In the end, he appeared to believe.

"Very well. I suppose we don't have to come to meeting on a field."

"A relief, indeed."

"But I'm warning you . . ."

"Yes, yes. I'm to have no further contact with Penelope."

"Damn it, don't speak her name!"

Harris nodded an apology. "I meant, I will have no further contact with Miss Rastmoor."

"You're damn right, you won't."

With that, Rastmoor scowled at him again, then marched to the front door. He let himself out with one last, meaningful glare. Indeed, there was no denying that man intended to hold Harris to his word. Pity. Things were bound to be tense between them when Harris completely broke his word and found a way to question the girl.

He waited long enough, at least, for Rastmoor to be out of sight before he collected his gloves and his hat to go out and do just that. The knock at the door that interrupted him was softer than the others he'd answered today. Bother, what new trouble would this visitor bring?

He opened the door almost tentatively, then nearly jumped out of his skin when he found Miss Rastmoor staring back nervously at him.

"Good God! What are you doing here?"

"I've come to warn you!" she declared. "Anthony is very upset."

"So I'm aware. You just missed him."

"Oh no. I'd hoped I would beat him."

He peered around her to confirm that the little idiot was, indeed, alone.

"Good God, Penelope. Did you come on your own? This is far from the fashionable area."

"Then it's less likely I should run into anyone I know, isn't it?"

"That's hardly the point. You can't possibly think it's a good idea for a young lady to be marching about town all alone!"

"Well, you might at least be a bit grateful that I thought to come warn you, despite how you treated me."

"Warn me of what?"

"That my brother is an excellent shot. If he called you out, I think it is a good idea for you to avoid meeting him."

"Oh, you would have me show myself a coward?"

"I heard your uncle telling Anthony that he seems to believe you've already done that."

"Your brother allowed you to be present for that conversation?"

"Of course not. I was eavesdropping."

"Naturally. I swear, Penelope, you go hunting trouble, don't you?"

"Apparently I do. I certainly found enough of it when I found you, didn't I?"

"It was never my intent to compromise you."

"No, it was merely your intent to steal from me."

"I can explain that."

"Oh, truly, I'd love to hear it!"

"Look, I don't have time for this. Tell me why you are so eager to go to Egypt?"

"How did you know about that?"

"Your brother. Now tell me what you know about those antiquities."

"Do you mean my scarab? I know you stole it from me. Do you still have it or have you already been to the pawnbroker?"

"Pawnbroker? You believe *that* is what I'd do with such an extraordinary piece?"

"It's common knowledge you have no money, Lord Harry. I assumed you'd sell that, then take yourself out of London in that shiny phaeton my brother so generously provided you."

It was actually quite painful, for some reason, to realize this was how she thought of him.

"I no longer have that shiny phaeton."

"You sold it, too? Well that was rather foolish. Lord Burlington might be able to trail you if you leave London by coach."

"Burlington will have no need to trail me. If I cannot get the information I need in order to save my . . . Well, I've agreed to meet the man in the morning."

"But that's ridiculous! What if he kills you?"

"Then that will save your brother the trouble, won't it? I should think that might please you."

"Unlike you, I do not take pleasure in others' misery. I would, in fact, be just the slightest bit distressed should some jealous husband or vengeful brother actually kill you."

"Miss Rastmoor, that is quite by far the sweetest thing you've ever said to me."

"Don't make too much of it. I'm still quite angry over my scarab. Tell me where it is so I may at least go and buy it back."

He couldn't help but smile at her attitude. She was a lying little schemer, of course, but he did appreciate her spunk.

"The scarab is here. It is not destined for the pawnshop, I assure you. As for your brother's carriage, I have returned it. It should be waiting for him when he arrives home."

She seemed quite perplexed by this news. It was a good look on her, he had to admit. However, he was determined not to become distracted. Penelope knew more than she was showing. He'd answered her questions; now it was time for her to answer some of his.

"So you see? I'm not a complete villain. Now tell me, Penelope—"

"I don't believe I've given you leave to call me by my name."

Now he couldn't help but laugh.

"You very much did, my dear. Last night, in that dark room. If what passed between us there did not grant me the right to call you by name, I don't know what would."

She blushed. That, also, was a very good look on her.

"If you truly were a gentleman, sir, you'd kindly forget that event."

"Impossible, Penelope. I will remember that quite fondly for the rest of my life."

And this was no lie. He wasn't exactly pleased to realize it, but the young woman had proven to be unforgettable.

"I hope you will, too," he added, taking advantage of her awkward silence and reaching out to touch her face.

She jolted away from him, but her face went even deeper pink. He knew there was no doubt that the brief taste of intimacy they'd shared would always remain in her memory. That, indeed, was a satisfying thought.

"I've already forgotten most of it," she lied, trying to sound smug.

He was not deceived.

"Then perhaps you need a reminder," he suggested, stepping closer and reaching for her again.

She dodged him. "Once was more than enough, sir."

"It was not, and you know it. However, I will acknowledge that pursuing this aspect of our relationship in greater depth is probably unwise."

"Yes, considering my brother already wants to kill you. He did call you out, didn't he?"

"He thought about it, but we settled our differences like civilized gentlemen."

"Oh? What did he make you agree to?"

He cleared his throat, realizing the irony of things. "Er, I had to agree never to see you again."

She laughed. "Well, I'm happy to see you are keeping your word."

"I did not invite you to come pounding at my door."

"I only came because I was worried about you."

This time when he took a step closer to her she could not back away. He had already chased her back against the wall. All she could do was blink her huge eyes at him like a frightened rabbit. He never realized how attractive a rabbit could be.

"I believe I like having you worry for me, Penelope."

"It is purely selfish," she said. "If something should happen, I'd likely feel guilt for pulling you into this silly arrangement we had."

"You mean our engagement?"

"Our *false* engagement."

"It doesn't seem to be so very silly after all. I hear you will be getting a trip to Egypt."

"Er, yes. Anthony seems to think that will soothe my broken heart."

"You are quite the actress," he said, stroking a lock of her hair. "I take it Egypt is what you were after all along?"

"It is."

"Why?"

"Why? Why not? It seems an utterly fascinating place, so rich with human history and all manner of strange, exotic things."

"It can be rather hot. And dusty. And life there is hardly what you are used to here."

"I know! That's what makes it so compelling. It seems so very . . . Wait, have you been there?"

"I have."

Now her eyes went even more huge. She suddenly seemed to forget her fear of him looming over her, and she leaned toward him as she fired off questions faster than he could answer.

"Have you been to the pyramids? Have you traveled along the Nile? Have you ridden a camel? Have you seen the ancient treasures? Is it all every bit as fantastic as it seems?"

"Yes, and more so. Now you tell me, my dear, where exactly did you come by your scarab?"

"Don't you mean *your* scarab, since obviously you have no intention of returning it to me?"

"No, I won't return it to you. Tell me who you got it from."

"Why?"

"Because it is stolen."

"Stolen? No, surely not!"

"Surely so. Shall I take it that you are personally acquainted with these thieves? Working with them, perhaps?"

"No! That's ridiculous."

"Is it? Are you certain you're not planning your journey around procuring another shipment of stolen artifacts?"

"Of course not! I'm no thief, Lord Harry."

"You're quite an accomplished liar, my dear. Why on earth should I believe you are not a thief, as well?"

"I'm not! I purchased that scarab, just as I told you."

"Conveniently, though, you never quite got around to telling me who you purchased it from."

"Because she asked me not to tell anyone."

"Obviously, then, she knew it was stolen. Who was it? Lady Burlington, perhaps?"

"Of course not. I would certainly never buy jewelry from her."

"Then who?"

It was clear she did not wish to divulge her source. He couldn't blame her, of course. It would surely indict the party. Perhaps even endanger her, as clearly the thieves trusted her to keep their identities secret. Harris moved closer to her, touching her neck now, tracing his fingertips along the delicate line of her jaw.

Oh yes, he would get the information out of her. She'd already demonstrated to him she was not proof against his seduction.

"Very well," she said, trying to shake him off. "I'll tell you."

"Yes, you will." *Wise girl, to give in before he took things any further.*

"I got the scarab from Maria."

Chapter Fifteen

Penelope was having an awful time breathing. It wasn't that Lord Harry was crushing her; no, he was barely touching her, as a matter of fact. It was just that he was so close, so attentive. She could feel heat radiating off his solid body, and it was impossible to escape his icy eyes. His beautiful, icy eyes.

That he could have such an effect on her without even trying did not make her feel particularly safe. Not that he would hurt her; not physically, at least. But she was beginning to sense that physical injury was the least of her worry where he was concerned. It was all those other things he could do to her that had her worried. And oh my! What he could do to her.

"The scarab came from your friend, Maria? Miss Bradley?"

"Yes."

"And how did she come by it?"

His touch bewitched her. She could not step away from him even if she tried. Not that she wanted to try, of course. She wanted to melt into him, let her body linger here in this half haze of sensation for the rest of eternity. Or at least another half hour, or so.

"It was given to her by an admirer," she replied, obediently answering his questions.

"Who?"

"I don't know. She indicated the gift was not invited. I believe she was a bit insulted by this gentleman, in fact, and threatened to throw it away. I offered to buy it from her. She would not take what it was worth, so I bought her the bonnet she'd been admiring, instead. With my pin money."

"You paid for it with a bonnet?"

"It was all she would accept. I'm *not* a thief, you know."

"And you have no idea who the admirer was?"

He was pulling away from her, letting unfeeling air drift between them. Perhaps if she answered him more specifically he'd go back to touching her again.

"No, if I had any idea I'd tell you," she said. "And I don't know why she couldn't simply return the scarab to him, either. I am rather happy she couldn't, though."

"I'm sure you are. Do you have any idea of its true value?"

"Of course. I've been studying antiquities for some time now."

"Then you surely would have been a bit suspicious about your friend suddenly coming into possession of it."

Wait, did that sound just a bit as if he were accusing Maria of something unpleasant? Or was he questioning her honesty? She was suddenly glad for the momentary air between them. Perhaps it was helping to clear her brain.

"She said it was a gift from an admirer, and I have no reason to doubt her."

"And it never dawned on you this secret admirer might have come by the scarab through illicit means?"

"No, it never dawned on me. I've told you all I know about it. Now if you'd be so kind, please step aside, sir."

"Oh? Is my presence bothering you, Miss Rastmoor?"

Perhaps she should not have said anything about it. It seemed he rather enjoyed knowing he bothered her. He was looming even closer now, his fingers trailing over the skin at her neck and down toward the fichu she had tucked carefully into the front of her gown. She had a feeling the gauzy material would provide little barrier should the man decide to investigate what lay beyond that flimsy fabric.

Not that he hadn't done ample exploring last night. The vivid recollection brought a heated flush racing to her cheeks.

Yes, the man's presence was most certainly bothering her, in the most pleasant way possible. Which was very, very bothersome.

"Perhaps I should be going now," she said.

He did nothing to facilitate this. Instead, he merely leaned in closer.

"Are you certain that is what you want?"

No, she was actually trying desperately to ignore what she wanted.

"I've done what I came for," she said. "I should be off."

"I agree," he said, predictably going for the fichu. "This most certainly should be off."

Drat. She should have pinned it in place. Before she had time to react, he whipped the fichu out and traced his finger over the expanse of skin that was now exposed. She drew in a quick breath and struggled not to let him see just how much she liked what he was doing.

"Please, sir..."

"Please? You'd like more?"

"I believe I've already had more."

"And as I recall, I believe you liked it," he said.

She was about to protest, but her legs went weak and she was unable to form words. Lord Harry had once again pushed her gown aside and was stooping to pay homage to her breasts. Indeed his memory was impeccable. She *did* rather like this.

"And you are certain there is nothing more you'd like to tell me regarding how that scarab came to be in your possession?" he was asking.

Apparently now she could not comprehend words, either.

"Er... the *what* came to be in my *what*?"

He chuckled, a warm, animal sound. "What indeed, Penelope."

Now he was giving her full attention. He kissed one breast, then moved on to the other. His tongue flicked over her nipples, sending sparks of electricity through her body. Thank heavens his arms had gone around her to hold her upright, else she'd likely have dissolved into a boneless pile at his feet.

She allowed her arms to circle him, her hands to roam over his muscular back and his broad shoulders. The feel of his lips against her sensitive skin was almost overwhelming, and the pressure of his body against hers was delightful. When he left off luxuriating over her breasts, his mouth came up to capture her own. He was delicious.

His tongue played at her lips, parting them and surprising her by slipping in to do battle with her own tongue. She would have expected such a thing to be somewhat unpleasant, but it was far from that. It was remarkable, a model for other body parts and a reminder of what he would be capable of doing to her, if she would only let him.

Indeed, she *would* let him. She'd be helpless to refuse, after all. Somehow he had a power over her she could not deny. She had no wish to deny it.

"You're even more lovely in the daylight," he said, pushing himself away from her so he could gaze down on her exposed breasts.

She was giddy with his praise. It crossed her mind that he could merely be using empty flattery to manipulate her into a greater willingness, but she hardly cared. He said the right words and she'd understood them. All that mattered was that he was holding her, touching her, and wanting her. It was the same sort of wanting she felt for him. It was virtually impossible for her to be *more* willing.

"Perhaps we should go up to your room?" she asked, her voice wavering just a bit.

His reply was a deeper kiss along with a rumbling growl. She assumed that was another compliment. She pulled herself closer to him, arching into him and feeling him pressing against her. Oh, but how lovely if her gown were to accidentally fall off of her and his trousers should suddenly come open.

"Penelope," he murmured as his lips and hands left fiery trails over her body.

"Lord Harry," she murmured in response.

"We need to stop."

His words confused her. *Stop?* What on earth did that mean?

"No," she argued. "It feels decidedly as if we ought to continue."

"Which is exactly why we should stop."

He took his own advice and let go of her, reaching out only to pull her gown back into place. Drat! Apparently this is what *stop* meant.

"I promised your brother I would not treat you this way," he said.

"You promised my brother you would not see me again," she reminded. "Obviously you haven't adhered to that."

"All the more reason I should get you home. Now."

"You don't want me to stay a bit longer?"

He drew a deep breath and took another step away from her.

"I want you to stay a great deal longer," he said, to her relief. "But you would only regret it and hate me for it."

Hate him? Even after he'd lied to her, spent an evening with Lady Burlington, cowarded his way out of a duel, seduced her in a very public place, and stolen from her, here she was back in his arms and begging for more. No, if she did not hate him by now—and she had tried desperately to convince herself that she did—it hardly seemed likely that she ever would.

"Don't look at me like that," he said.

"Like what?"

"Like you don't care what could happen, about the consequences should I not usher you out the door right this very second."

"Well, I don't care. I'll be leaving for Egypt soon."

Now it appeared he was angry. He grabbed up her fichu and haphazardly stuffed it where it had been. Well! That was certainly taking liberties. Besides, the man had no skill for such things as arranging fichus. She did her best to right it. It was not a very successful effort, given that the man seemed far from done manhandling her.

Taking her by the arm, he practically dragged her toward the door. How insulting, to say the least. Here she had practically thrown herself at him and now he was rejecting her. Dramatically. Oh, but it was embarrassing.

"Very well," she said, sounding just as angry as he looked. "You don't need to be so gruff about it. If you don't want me, just say so."

He paused and turned back to her.

"If you think I don't want you, then you're an ever bigger fool than you appear. Of course I want you. Lately it seems that's the only thing I do want. Damn it, Penelope, I can't think straight when I'm with you. And right now, that's a very dangerous thing. For all of us."

She had no idea what he could possibly mean by "all of us," but she completely understood his actions. He was, once again, tugging her arm. He led her to the front door of the building and flung it open.

A desperate sort of panic settled on her. Lord Harry was getting rid of her, and she had every reason to believe it was the last time she might ever see him. Surely if someone didn't shoot him on a field of honor, he would leave Town. Obviously his desire for her, was not nearly as strong as he claimed. If he felt half the way she felt, how could he possibly walk away without much more than a few kisses? Indeed, he'd soon be rid of her and out of her life.

She was searching for just the right argument that might change his mind as they stepped out into the late morning sunlight. Her feet froze in their tracks when she spotted Anthony jumping from his carriage and stalking their way. She was simply not having a good day so far.

"Rastmoor," Lord Harry said as a curt greeting.

"Damn you, Chesterton!" was her brother's curt greeting. "I got home only to find my sister was gone. On a hunch I came back here."

"Yes, I found her at my door so now I am returning her to you."

She could not at all like the way he spoke of her as something like a lost puppy. It got worse. When Anthony approached, Lord Harry lifted up her hand and ceremoniously passed her off to her brother.

"I suggest you keep better track of her," Lord Harry warned.

"I'm not the one who lured the silly chit away," Anthony replied, holding her arm tightly and glaring daggers at Lord Harry.

Now Lord Harry was glaring daggers. "Good God, man. No one has to lure Penelope to do anything. You would seriously let her go off to Egypt on her own? Considering what she's capable of, empty head and all? Damn it, Rastmoor, if you were any decent sort of brother you'd keep her under lock and key!"

"Excuse me, but I can hear you both," she inserted.

"Hush," they said in unison.

Brutes.

"I will not lock up my sister," Anthony said.

He would, however, bruise her arm, he was holding it so tightly. She squirmed, but he ignored her.

"Perhaps you've not noticed," Lord Harry said, "but she cannot be at all trusted."

"Neither can you, Chesterton."

"That's exactly my point, Rastmoor."

Anthony seemed about to reply, then frowned and glanced her way.

"Why did you come here?" he asked her.

She bit her lip. This was not a very comfortable question to answer.

"I was afraid you'd come to challenge Lord Harry to a duel. I had to warn him."

"Warn him?"

"That you are an excellent shot, Anthony."

"I've no doubt Chesterton could hold his own," Anthony said. "Provided he'd bother to show up."

"I told you, I am not much inclined to kill you, sir," Lord Harry said.

Penelope gave him a frown. "So you'd just stand there and let my brother murder you?"

What a horrifying thought.

"You'd rather I shoot him?" Lord Harry asked.

"No, of course not, but . . ."

"Fortunately it seems neither of us will come to that," Anthony interrupted. "Thank you for returning my sister, Chesterton."

"My pleasure."

Really, did he have to sound so sincerely glad to be rid of her?

"Good day to you," Anthony said, nodding toward the other man.

Penelope wished she could think of something witty to say, but the thought of letting her brother drag her home without hope of seeing Lord Harry again was enough to wipe all wit away. She could merely glance up at him and mutter a weak good-bye.

"Take care of yourself, Miss Rastmoor," he said simply.

There was not any emotion or hint that their parting might be the least bit distressful for him. Indeed, they were both right about her. She was silly and empty-headed, wasn't she? What a fool to let herself care, and to hope that perhaps Lord Harry might care just a bit in return.

Anthony led her to his carriage and helped her in. She managed to refrain from looking over her shoulder at Lord Harry as they pulled away, leaving his drab little apartment behind. No doubt he did not linger on the street watching after her.

"He's a far nobler man than I esteemed him," Anthony said after a minute of silence.

"He was eager to be rid of me."

Her brother gave her a sad smile. "Indeed, that's how it appeared."

"Well, no matter. I'm well rid of him. Thank you for taking me home, Anthony. It seems I have a good many things to do to be ready for my trip."

"Apparently so do I."

HARRIS WATCHED THE CARRIAGE UNTIL IT WAS OUT OF sight. Damn, but refusing that woman was the hardest thing he'd ever done in his life. The most honorable, too. So why didn't he feel better about it?

Because he was a selfish bastard, that was why. He wanted her in his bed and that's all there was to it. He wanted to take advantage of her, ruin her, and make her forget every other man on the planet. He doubted he'd even feel remorseful afterward. Hell no. He'd simply want to do it all over again.

But for once he'd taken the high road. He'd put her needs ahead of his wants. Now she was gone and he doubted Rastmoor would be foolish enough to let her out of his sight for a good long while. Harris was free to put his focus into what he should have been doing all along. He needed to find Oldham and locate those artifacts. Perhaps it was still not too late to salvage the man's lifework.

But where to start? Lady Burlington claimed they'd brought Oldham to London. But why? Uncle Nedley hated him. Would he go to the trouble of destroying his career, then actually bring him home? Still, by paying that ransom he'd convinced the Egyptians that Oldham had betrayed them. This was an even worse fate than to have waited for Harris to reattain the artifacts and return them with proof of Oldham's innocence. Indeed, it did sound the sort of convoluted cruelty his uncle was capable of.

But London was a big city. If Oldham were here, how was Harris to discover where they had stashed him? He had so little to go on.

The scarab. That was the clue. Where had it come from? If Penelope's story was to be believed—and there was no way of knowing when the girl was honest or when she was not—some mysterious gentleman had given it to Miss Bradley. On the off chance this was, indeed, the case, who was that man? And where did he get it?

The logical summation was that he must have been involved in the theft. If Harris could find that man, he would likely find all the answers he needed. Lady Burlington had insinuated that one of Penelope's own admirers was involved. That seemed to lead him back to Markland. Very well, he would investigate the man.

Indeed, there was also a second man he could not discount. *Mr. P. Anthonys.* Harris had simply assumed this person was just another scholar, but since Lady Burlington indicated suspicion, perhaps Harris had been too quick to abandon his search for this nonexistent person. Whoever he was.

He'd seen the letters; he'd actually brought them from Egypt with him in hopes of finding the author. Unfortunately, he'd not paid attention to the direction when Oldham had been writing to the fellow. All he had were the letters with their Egypt address; there was no record of P. Anthonys' location. Apparently Oldham knew the address by heart and had not needed to record it somewhere. All Harris had been able to deduct was that this Anthonys person lived in London.

Which put him right back where he had been, which was, basically, doubting that he even existed. P. Anthonys must have written those letters anonymously. But then who was the man in truth? Did this send him back to Lady Burlington's clue, Markland? Perhaps. That, unfortunately, sent him back to recalling Penelope's gushing praise over the man last night.

Unsurprisingly, this reminded him of how lovely she'd looked and how sweet she had tasted when he'd maneuvered her into that back room. And that, even more unfortunately, reminded him of what he had just refused. Damn.

He had to find some way to forget her. Well, no better way than to immerse himself in his investigation. Since he had no real new information, and since he was not up to a visit to Markland this early in the day, he'd have to go backward. He'd go over Professor Oldham's letters one more time. Perhaps there would be something he'd overlooked.

An hour later he was willing to admit he'd not overlooked a thing. All his latest perusal of the stack of letters managed to turn up was a reference to the British Museum and a splitting headache. He assumed the headache was from all the rereading he had to do since his rebellious brain kept losing track and he'd have to go back to the top of a page. It seemed his mind would far rather dwell on Penelope's soft skin and her tempting curves than to focus on someone else's letters he'd already read several times.

But what of Mr. Anthonys' reference to his time at the museum? Could it possibly be relevant? Did the man work there? At the very least it appeared he frequented the place. Perhaps someone there might know the name. He supposed he ought to at least investigate. Besides, being busy would keep his mind off Penelope. He hoped.

Surprisingly, the rest of Penelope's morning had not been as disagreeable as expected. Anthony had been oddly kind toward her. He'd brought her home without lecture, and he'd even managed to distract Mamma from delivering any unwanted sermons. He sent Penelope off to her room and advised her to rest and do what she could to take her mind off Lord Harry. Unfamiliar with how to handle such a situation, she thanked him, then took his advice.

He and Mamma politely left her alone. It was quite nice, actually. It did allow her time to sort through some of her feelings where Lord Harry was concerned, in fact. Unfortunately, that led to some rather troubling introspection. It was distressing to realize her heart might just possibly have been a bit more invested than she'd ever wish to admit. The more she thought on it, in fact, the more she decided she did not much enjoy introspection. That could certainly explain why she'd done frightfully little of it over the years.

It seemed the parts of her that professed to have good sense were quite miffed at the other parts of her. Those other parts, unfortunately, were quite determined to continue in their foolishness, and after an hour of such introspection, she found herself very much agitated by the war that raged between her sensible parts and, er, those other parts. Fortunately there was little chance she'd ever be in company with Lord Harry again, because it was clear which parts would win the day if she ever was.

Clearly she needed to find something to keep her various parts occupied. Prudently, she began hunting for something to do. Needlework? Reading? Counting dust motes as they drifted through the air? None of that seemed the least bit distracting to any of her parts.

It was a pity her letter to Professor Oldham had only been posted yesterday. She could use a word from him just now. How very curious she was to see what he might say about those antiquities she'd described for him. Sadly, though, Egypt was far away and it would likely be months before she could reasonably expect a response. It seemed that was the only subject she might care about enough to get caught up in and forget about Lord Harry.

Thinking of him just now, though, triggered a new wave of blushing and remembering. Drat, but perhaps not even a letter from Professor Oldham would be enough to rescue her from her memories. Lord Harry had definitely left his mark on her. *All* of her.

Well, then, what she needed was fresh, distracting conversation. She needed her best friend. Indeed, Maria would know how to turn her mind to other avenues of thought.

She sat at her desk and dashed off a note inviting Maria to visit, then hurried downstairs to have a servant carry it to Maria's house. She was surprised to discover they already had a visitor. He must have been here for some time already, because she found Anthony at the front door, bidding good-bye to Mr. Ferrel Chesterton.

"Good day, Miss Rastmoor," he said upon seeing her.

"Mr. Chesterton," she replied.

She really could not fathom what business her brother had with the man, but decided it really didn't matter. His presence, however, was just one more reminder of his handsome cousin, which did make her wish she hadn't seen him.

"Do you need something, Penelope?" Anthony asked.

"I was coming to find someone to carry a note for me," she replied. "I wanted to send an invitation to Miss Bradley."

"Miss Bradley?" Mr. Chesterton said. "I happen to be going by that way. Would you like me to carry that for you?"

"I'm sure there's no need to trouble you, sir," she replied, feeling just a bit awkward that the man would involve himself in her personal affairs. "I'll have one of the footmen take it."

But he assured her. "It would be no trouble at all. I'd be happy to make your delivery."

Oh bother. Why was the man so eager to be of service to her? Hadn't Anthony mentioned to him that she and Lord Harry were no longer engaged? Was this fellow somehow trying to make peace between their two families, or something? Oh well. Perhaps she should not condemn the man for simply being helpful.

"Thank you, Mr. Chesterton. That would be fine, if you are certain it is not putting you out."

"No, indeed not."

Not wanting to be rude, or give Anthony any reason to wonder at her hesitation to allow him, she smiled and handed over the note. She'd not expected anyone other than a servant to see it, so she'd covered the note on the outside with a cleverly exaggerated plea for Maria to make haste to visit, as if there were some great emergency. She did not indicate anything of her current dilemma, but surely it would be enough to make Mr. Chesterton wonder at her desperation. Hopefully, though, he might not mention to his cousin just how distraught all these recent events had made her.

"It is a pleasure to be of use to you, Miss Rastmoor," he said, clutching the note to him as if it were a royal summons.

She smiled and nodded, but was careful not to be too gracious.

Anthony, however, was practically gushing over the man.

"That's very generous of you, Ferrel," he said. "And thank you for coming over on such short notice."

"Anything for friends," the gentleman said with an overstated bow.

Anthony slapped him on the shoulder, thanked him again, then sent him on his way. Mr. Chesterton seemed quite in a good mood as he trotted down the steps to the sidewalk out front. Penelope offered him one gratuitous wave, then was happy to let Anthony shut the door.

"Interesting young man," he said. "I like him. Odd considering his father is a bore and his cousin is . . . Well, it's surprising at any rate."

"You like him? I was unaware you even knew him."

"Only casually. But I'm looking forward to knowing him better."

Knowing him better? Whatever could Anthony mean by that? Good heavens, but she certainly hoped she might not interpret that as anything other than idle conversation. It would be unendurable if her brother should view this Chesterton as someone who might consider taking Lord Harry's place!

It hardly took introspection to realize that all of her parts were in full unison on one thing: there would never be anyone to take Lord Harry's place.

IT WAS JUST BEFORE NOON AS HARRIS STROLLED ALONG Oxford Street on his way to the British Museum. He should have kept the phaeton for a day or two, at least. Why he felt the need for a clear conscience on that matter when it was so littered with guilt on so many others he couldn't quite say. He decided not to ponder the question.

Right now, he needed to keep his focus on his search for the elusive P. Anthonys. It seemed unlikely he'd find any sort of connection to Oldham or the stolen artifacts simply by taking a walk to the museum, but as he had nothing else to do, he might as well know for certain. For all the good it would do.

"Chesterton!"

He turned as his name was called. It was, of all people, Ferrel, hailing him from just around the corner. Harris tried to appear pleased to run across his younger cousin.

"How nice to run into you, Ferrel."

"I'm glad to see you walking about," Ferrel said. "Word is Lord Burlington called you out. Surely you didn't do away with the fellow already!"

"No, sorry to say, I've not committed murder yet today. That's scheduled for tomorrow."

"Well, that's happy news indeed," Ferrel said. "Tell me, whatever did you do to the man?"

"It's not what I did to him, but supposedly what I did to his wife."

"You, too?"

"What's that?"

"I'm sure you heard the rumors regarding me and that certain lady in question. But I swear, cousin, I never did. It was a dreadful misunderstanding!"

Good Lord. So Ferrel had had a run-in with the Burlingtons, too? Had that woman chased after every man in London?

"I'm afraid I'd not heard those rumors. When on earth did that all happen?"

"Oh, some weeks ago, I suppose."

Ah, no wonder he'd heard nothing of it. Likely he was traveling from Egypt at that time. He'd have to ask around, gather the particulars. That would surely prove amusing.

"And did Burlington call you out, as well?"

"No," Ferrel replied. "I rather thought he might, though, the way the man went on. He walked in on us discussing a simple business matter and gravely misunderstood."

"How unpleasant for you."

"Very! As if I would ever . . . er, I mean, I suppose some might find her dashed attractive . . ."

"I don't."

"Nor I. Some do, apparently. Her husband seemed convinced she'd been playing him false and assumed it was with me. But father was there and helped explain the situation."

"Your father was there?"

"Yes, he'd arrived with Burlington just as I was conducting my business with the lady. Pity you didn't have him there when you were in the hot water, eh?"

"Indeed. Such a pity."

Damn Uncle Nedley. He'd help his own son, but crucify his nephew.

"Well, no doubt you are a far better shot than that doddering old fool," Ferrel said, clearly not about to let Harris's impending doom ruin his day. "You'll make quick work of it, I don't doubt."

"It might be difficult for you to imagine, Ferrel, but I have no wish to meet him or anyone else on a field of honor. Even if we were both to devolve, I still find no amusement in the thought of grown men playing at murder."

"My, how very modern of you, cousin."

Clearly this was an excellent joke to the man. He laughed quite freely. Harris chose to let the subject drop.

"Tell me, though. What brings you to this part of town?"

At this question he detected a sudden nervousness in the man. Well, how very odd. What could possibly make the young man so uneasy? So uneasy, in fact, that his hands fumbled and he dropped the paper he'd been holding. A letter, it appeared. Harris stooped to pick it up for him.

He could not fail to notice that words had been jotted on the outside. It seemed whatever this letter was, the recipient was urgently requested to pay a call on the sender. That in itself was not overly interesting, except Harris noticed one important detail. He recognized the handwriting.

P. Anthonys. Good God, but this letter was written by the very same hand that was attached to his sole suspect!

"Thank you, sir," Ferrel said, practically ripping the letter out of Harris's hand.

Harris decided to let it go. He would, however, do what he could to gather information. Ferrel was somehow involved with P. Anthonys? Astonishing, to say the least.

"Well, cousin, don't tell me this is a love letter," he said, grinning innocently. "I've not heard you had set your sights that way."

"No, no it isn't a love letter!" he denied fervently. "I'm merely delivering it for a friend."

"Ah, I see." No, he really didn't, but he was determined to find out more.

"In fact, I must be going along now," Ferrel said. "I'm expected somewhere."

"Of course. I wouldn't want to make you late."
"Thank you."

They exchanged hasty good-byes and Ferrel was off. Harris pretended to head in the other direction. However, as soon as he felt it was safe, he backtracked to follow the young man. By Jupiter, it seemed he would find this P. Anthonys, after all. Who would have ever suspected mild, unassuming Ferrel Chesterton?

He trailed the man through a residential area. After some few minutes, Ferrel knocked at a door and was easily given entrance. Harris did not recognize the address, so he snagged a boy passing by and asked if the lad might know who lived there. For a mere tuppence he gained his answer.

Miss Maria Bradley. Ferrel had taken that note directly over to Miss Bradley's house. An interesting development, to be sure. How on earth was she involved? Could it be P. Anthonys was one of her admirers? And just how did Ferrel fit in? Harris would lurk about and watch.

Eventually, he knew, it would all lead back to Penelope. But how?

Chapter Sixteen

Penelope began to doubt Mr. Ferrel's ability to deliver a letter. Surely if Maria had gotten the missive she would not wait a whole hour before rushing to visit, would she? No, of course not. Mr. Ferrel must have shirked his duty. She'd have to send off another note. Very frustrating.

Before she'd do that, though, she'd best take a minute or two to calm herself. It would do no good to write a note in her current irritable state. Better to take herself for a brisk walk first.

She'd walk in the direction of Maria's house. That way, if her friend was already on her way, she'd be unlikely to miss her. She did so long for Maria's insight on things. Maria was an intelligent, sensible person. If Penelope had but listened to her in the first place, much of this could have been avoided.

Still, she realized that no amount of misery now could make her truly regret introducing herself to Lord Harry at that ball those few days ago. She was glad she'd done it. How vibrant and alive that man made her feel! Then again, how very much the opposite she felt now, knowing she'd never see him again. Oh, but what a ninny she was! Surely Maria could talk sense into her.

Or maybe not. As she drooped along the sidewalk, Penelope happened to notice her friend walking toward her. But Maria was not alone.

Aside from her dutiful maid, walking three steps behind, Maria was accompanied by Lord Harry himself. What on earth could this be about? What was her best friend doing with *her* fiancé?

Very well, it was her former pretend-fiancé, but still. There was the principle of the thing. Maria was out walking with him and Penelope was not.

Maria's eyes caught sight of her and went large.

"How wonderful!" she exclaimed, but Penelope had to wonder if this was her friend's true sentiment. "Why, I was just on my way to your house."

"Were you?" Penelope replied. "How thoughtful. And look, you've brought along a friend."

"I met him along the way and he rather invited himself, I'm afraid," Maria said. "He assured me you wouldn't mind, but I somewhat doubted that."

Penelope glared at Lord Harry. He simply shrugged at her.

"Apparently Miss Bradley heard some ridiculous rumor that you and I have become enemies now, Miss Rastmoor," he said, as if that were the farthest thing from the truth.

"What a ridiculous rumor, indeed," she said sweetly. "How could anyone think we might be enemies? After all, you merely ravished another woman, agreed to fight a duel, insulted me to my brother, and stole jewelry from me. Of course we are but the best of friends."

"Exactly," he said, then turned his most enchanting smile on Maria. "You see, Miss Bradley? There is no bad air between us."

"Oh yes, I can see that perfectly," Maria said with a dramatic roll of her eyes. "Now if you'll excuse me, I'd like to walk the rest of the way with Miss Rastmoor."

Penelope stepped past Lord Harry to loop her arm with Maria's. "Indeed. Neither of us have any further need of you, sir."

She pretended to miss the knowing little smirk he gave her.

"Thank you for accompanying me," Maria said, but she had the good sense to sound suitably insincere.

"Yes, good-bye, Lord Harry," Penelope agreed. "You are quite free to go about your business. You know, seducing someone's wife, polishing your dueling pistols, breaking in through windows . . ."

"Thank you, Miss Rastmoor," he said with an overdone flourish. "I strive to live up to expectations."

Ooo, but the scoundrel had the nerve to grin.

"Come along, Miss Bradley," she said, turning her back on him and leading Maria back down Oxford Street. Maria mumbled an obligatory good-bye, which Lord Harry returned with a most courtly bow. The dratted man appeared much amused by all of this.

"Insufferable man."

If only she did not suffer whatever it was her heart was doing with every step she took in a direction away from him.

HARRIS LEFT PENELOPE TO GO ON HER TITTERING WAY with Miss Bradley. Damn them both. Penelope had no right whatsoever to be so blatantly rude to him, especially after he'd made such a painful sacrifice in returning her—mostly unmolested—to Rastmoor. And Miss Bradley had been no help whatsoever. She'd received that letter from Ferrel, then proceeded to receive Ferrel for practically a full hour! What on earth could the man have been doing in the girl's sitting room so long while Harris was left cooling his heels on the street, hoping no one realized he was watching the house?

When at last Ferrel left, Harris had decided not to follow him but to see what the Bradley chit would do next. He'd thought perhaps he'd chosen wisely when she appeared, bonneted and wrapped for walking. He trailed her for a while, then when she happened to catch sight of him was forced to make it appear pure happenstance he was nearby.

Hell, he'd learned nothing at all about the girl's intended destination. Had she been rushing off to meet this P. Anthonys? He assumed so, but the girl claimed she was off to visit Penelope. She claimed she was in a hurry, too. Harris could not sway her from her story, although he tried all manner of subtle conversation. In the end, all he'd learned from his little walk with Maria Bradley was that she disliked him and was fiercely loyal to Penelope. Oddly enough, he had to mark those things in her favor.

It did nothing, however, to further his cause. He needed to find P. Anthonys and he needed to find him now. There was no telling where Oldham was, or what condition his captors had left him in. Even after all this time and effort, Harris was still floundering with very little information.

Perhaps he'd have been further ahead to have followed Ferrel. He could still hardly believe it, but his mild-mannered cousin was somehow involved in this. At least this gave Harris one slight advantage. Ferrel was forever incapable of keeping secrets. Harris had failed at getting them out of Miss Rastmoor or her duplicitous friend, but he could hope for better luck with Ferrel.

All he had to do was find the young idiot.

That, actually, turned out to be easier than expected. He'd only needed to wander the way of Markland's lodgings and there they were, both young men casually meeting up on the street. They seemed to pass some quiet information between themselves, and at one point it appeared as if Markland might wish to argue with something Ferrel said to him.

Damn, but Harris wished he dared move closer to them, yet surely if they noticed him loitering about here they'd never continue their private conversation. There was nothing he could do but follow at a safe distance as the two disputing gentleman made their way into the park. They found an out-of-the-way place and, fortunately, continued discussing.

Harris was practically overjoyed. The men seemed to think continuing their discourse beside a low brick wall offered them privacy. Instead, it offered Harris a place to eavesdrop. Perhaps the heavens were showing some mercy on him today, after all.

"But can you be certain now is the best time for it?" Markland was asking.

"It should have been done already," Ferrel replied. "I will not wait longer; it has to be tonight."

They had Harris's complete attention, of course. Tonight? What could they be planning that had to be done tonight? He strained his ears and held his breath, inching along the backside of the low brick wall, as close to them as he dared.

"But do you know what you're getting yourself into?" Markland asked.

"Of course I do! I've been planning this for nearly a year. I thought you were my friend, that I could trust you in this."

"It's your life we're talking about, though," Markland went on. "You cannot just impulsively break into—"

"Shush! No one can know about this."

So Ferrel was breaking into something, was he? Perhaps Harris had underestimated his cousin all along.

"Tonight, when everyone is asleep. I'll have the carriage in waiting. All I need you to do is to meet the man at the ship. Pay him for his trouble, and I swear I'll make it up to you."

Pay a man at a ship? So they were taking something abroad. Harris had a fair idea what it was, too: stolen Egyptian treasure.

"I can't believe I've agreed to help you with this," Markland said with a heavy sigh.

"But I have no one else to turn to," Ferrel said, with just a hint of desperation in his voice.

"Yes, I know. It's for a noble cause, and all. Still, I say you should have considered Chesterton."

"My cousin? Damn it, but of course I considered him. He's the reason it has to be now. The man's too involved already. You know what he's about. If I wait another day there's a chance he'll swoop in and . . . Well, I don't trust him."

"I doubt he'll be any threat," Markland said. "Seems to me he's rather preoccupied with his new fiancée."

But Ferrel merely scoffed at that. Harris was duly offended.

"I happen to know on good authority that my cousin has no plan whatsoever of actually taking Miss Rastmoor to the altar. It's all for show."

"Well then, it is quite a show at that!" Markland laughed.

Insensitive lobcock.

"He thinks an engagement will get him in my father's good graces while he continues his usual schemes. No, he is too close to this. I need to act now before he ruins it all. Please, Markland, you must help me with this."

"Oh, very well. I see you have your heart set. Yes, I'll meet your man at the wharf tonight while you do your dark deeds."

"Thank you! I promise to repay you every bit."

"Yes, yes. Just promise me in days to come I will not be forced to hold your drunken head while you rail on and on about what a fool thing you did here, acting on impulse and forced to live in regret all the rest of your days."

"That will not happen! I assure you, sir."

"Very well, I will believe you. It seems there is nothing to dissuade you, so I might as well help out. But come, I'm feeling as if I could use a bit of luncheon."

Ferrel heartily agreed with the notion of food, and without another mention of the crime they were plotting, the men headed off. Unless he wished to be seen, Harris could do little but hide behind the wall and wait until they were a good distance away before he could set after them. At that point, however, they were lost. Foot traffic around the park area had picked up, and Harris cursed under his breath when several minutes of searching proved he was not going to find them again.

Damn and damn! All he was doing was finding pieces to this puzzle, not coming any closer to solving it. And now it appeared things were even more complicated than he'd known: Ferrel was willing to commit criminal activities that would jeopardize Professor Oldham, and somehow he'd gotten Markland to agree to help. Markland's animosity must be greater than Harris ever imagined.

He allowed a moment for cursing the man. Damn him! Could Markland possibly be so unaware of what was at stake? No, certainly he could not. He knew how things were, the danger Oldham was in. Apparently, though, he simply did not care. Good God, but if the old man ever learned of Markland's insensitivity, it would break his heart.

Professor Oldham may have developed a great rapport with Harris over the years, but always his heart had longed for a deeper connection with Markland. Ferrel's selfish conspirator may have been raised by his grandfather and taken the family name of that pretentious patriarch, but he would always be something Harris was not. Markland was Professor Oldham's firstborn son. His *legitimate* son.

Despite Harris's love and devotion for the scholar all these years, despite what he had become to him and how they shared their passion for Egyptology as well as a deep disdain for

Nedley and his ilk, those prized positions would always be held by Markland. Oldham fairly worshipped the proper, priggish Markland. His callously infrequent letters were like gold to the older man; the mere mention of his name brought raptures of joy, and every word of Markland's mildest success sent him over the moon. No matter how many artifacts Harris dug up or how many of Oldham's writings he had gotten into scholarly publications, Harris was only ever second best. Markland was the first, and always would be.

Yet when his father—kidnapped, maligned, abandoned—needed him most, this was how Markland responded? He helped a useless pup like Ferrel actually steal the very treasure that could have been used to save the man. At least, it could have been used if Harris had gotten to it soon enough.

But he hadn't. Instead, his uncle had been able to gather it together and go about plotting his revenge. Even if Oldham truly was back safely on English soil, he'd be ruined. Outside of his blind worship for Markland, the only thing Charles Oldham cared about was his work. Now that Nedley had carefully destroyed his credibility with the Egyptian people, that would be over. Damn! And all because Harris had gotten too caught up with a beautiful woman and failed to act in time.

Well, perhaps he had not failed yet. Ferrel was going to get that treasure tonight, was he? Not if Harris managed to get to it first. Fortunately, he'd already found his way into Burlington's home once. He could easily do it again. Just as soon as it got dark.

"I TAKE IT YOU HAVE HAD YOUR FILL OF LORD HARRY," Maria said when they were alone together in Penelope's private room.

"Most definitely," she vowed. If one could lie in a vow.

"Then you have mended your heart?" Maria asked.

"I told you, my heart was very slightly involved. No mending was needed."

"And what of your plans for traveling to Egypt? Have you given up that, as well?"

"I do not have to. Can you believe it? Anthony will let me go after all!"

"He will? He has agreed?"

"He has! I could scarce believe it myself."

"But . . . how on earth did you sway him?"

"I didn't; it was his idea. He's convinced my heart is broken and he suggested I travel."

"He suggested it?"

"He thinks a journey to Egypt will help me recover."

Maria sighed and shook her head. "Only you, Penelope Rastmoor. No one else could have possibly made this work in her favor."

Penelope wasn't entirely certain Maria meant it as a compliment. She also wasn't entirely certain any of this really *was* going in her favor. Somehow Egypt without Lord Harry didn't seem quite so very enticing as it once had. She must have been making a face as she contemplated this unusual change in attitude, because Maria commented on it.

"You think perhaps this won't work out, after all? Are you concerned your brother will change his mind and not allow you to go?"

"Oh no, he seems quite content to send me off."

"Then why are you not singing and dancing in the street?"

"It's just that . . . well, things may have worked out for me, but I'm concerned that Lord Harry is getting the bad end of the bargain."

"Lord Harry again? I thought you did not care what happened to him."

"I don't, of course, but it just seems rather unfair for him."

"Unfair? For *him*? But he's an unscrupulous bounder!"

"I know, I know. But it would be a shame for him to die in a duel, and I did promise to help him gain his uncle's approval, and—"

"Good gracious! You're completely in love with him!"

"Honestly, Maria. Don't be mad."

"Unfortunately, I'm not. But I fear you are, Penelope. Oh, but you simply cannot be in love with that . . . that person."

Somehow Maria made *person* sound like a bad word.

"Of course I'm not in love with him," she reassured. "Oh, perhaps for one or two minutes I fancied I might be, a bit, but that faded quickly."

"It doesn't seem that way."

"Well, it is."

Maria was quiet. Penelope chewed her lip. The silence between them felt a bit uncomfortable. Not quite honest, either.

"Very well . . . perhaps there is still some lingering shadow of sentiment, but nothing more," Penelope admitted.

"How much is still lingering?"

"A mere drop. I'm not mutton-headed enough to fall very much in love with a man like that. The tiniest bit, that's all."

"Are you certain?"

"Of course."

"Good. Because he's completely dreadful and not at all for you."

"Yes, I know. He's terrible, really. And certainly if I did happen to love him—which I'm almost sure I don't—"

"Almost?"

"Almost positively. Besides, I know he does not at all feel the same toward me."

"That's a surprise."

"Why, just this morning when I went to his house—"

Maria screeched and clutched at her arm again. "You went to his house?"

"It's more just a couple of rooms, actually. And not at all in a fashionable area."

"You went *inside*?"

"I thought it more prudent than being seen on the street with him."

"Heavens! And you went there alone, I expect?"

"Of course! I could hardly ask Mamma or Anthony to accompany me, could I?"

"But how did he treat you?"

"Wonderfully. Well, that is, until he grabbed my arm and dragged me out of there."

"He dragged you? Oh no! Where did he take you?"

"Back to Anthony, of course. And you can imagine he was not pleased."

"I should think not. Yet he still is going to let you go to Egypt?"

"He's convinced I'm in love."

Maria frowned. "I wonder where on earth he could have gotten that notion."

"I suppose I did rather lead him to think it."

"As long as you're not foolish enough to think it yourself."

"Must we go on about this? Please, I would much rather leave it. Tell me, instead, about the ball. What did you do after I left last night? Did you dance again with anyone?"

Maria's expression lightened. She blushed, too. "Indeed I did! I stood up with Mr. Markland. I have to say, I thought him a bit cool at first, but later on he seemed very charming indeed."

"How lovely for you."

Aha, so there was something there already. Penelope knew it. She'd seen right from the start that Markland showed an interest in her friend. Not that she'd gloat that she'd been the one responsible for piquing the man's interest in her. No, indeed. Far better to let Maria think she'd captured him all on her own.

"And he had many questions about you," Maria said with a smile. "I think perhaps you have an admirer."

"What? Oh no, Maria. I assure you when I spoke to Mr. Markland last night it was all about you."

Now Maria frowned. Heavens, but that was an odd response. Well, she supposed Maria always had been far too humble for her own good. She'd best set her right immediately.

"Surely if Mr. Markland asked about me it was simply as a way to learn more about you."

"Can you believe such a thing?" Maria asked.

"Of course. Truly, he has given me every reason to believe he holds you in quite high esteem."

Maria laughed at her. "Indeed, no need to flatter. He is quite the catch, you know. And I believe he wouldn't at all mind being caught by you, Penelope. You should be glad to have attracted a gentleman such as he. What a difference from Lord Harry. And so handsome."

"Yes, he is. But really, you can't say that he is any better proportioned than Lord Harry."

"I suppose they are similar in some way, but Mr. Markland must be thought superior."

"I'm glad you appreciate Mr. Markland's fine qualities—indeed it seems he has many—but I'd be amiss if I didn't point out that Lord Harry is very fine in some ways, as well."

"And what ways would those be?" Maria asked.

Instantly Penelope felt her face go warm. Drat. Maria noticed.

"I daresay I can guess what you prefer most about Lord Harry. You've crept off into corners with him enough."

And obviously Maria did not approve.

"Well, you'll be relieved to hear that Lord Harry's interest in me has been rather limited."

"You mean once he got what he wanted he lost interest?"

"I assure you, the gentleman most certainly did not get everything he wanted." *Drat.*

"I'm so happy to hear it! I must confess, I feared perhaps he'd taken advantage of you, that things had gone to the point of worrying for consequences."

Well! Shame on Maria for even suggesting such a thing. Never mind that Penelope had very nearly begged him to do such things . . .

"I'm quite pleased to assure you they have not," Penelope said. "Lord Harry was only too eager to return me to Anthony even when . . ."

Oh, but she very nearly said too much. No way would she ever want to actually admit to that she'd thrown herself at that man and been flatly rejected. Some things a lady should simply not discuss.

"You mean it was his idea to take you back to your brother when you'd have been willing to stay with him? Why, Penelope!"

"Don't look at me as if I've suddenly become a monster."

Maria's expression softened. "So you really *are* in love with him."

Well now, that was the worst possible thing Maria could have said. Not only was it insulting, but Penelope hated the feeling of hopelessness that welled up inside her at such a simple phrase. Indeed, she'd been fervently denying the possibility of such a thing, but suddenly she could not. Her own heart confirmed her worst fear.

Maria placed a hand on her shoulder. "I'm sure it will all work out. You do have rather good luck in that area, after all. Suitors come and go and you seem to be no worse for it."

"Of course I'll be fine," Penelope said, sliding away from

her friend and suddenly needing to rearrange the jumble of knickknacks and lotions on her dressing table. "After all, he doesn't love me and I certainly don't wish to love him. In just a matter of time I'm sure I'll forget him altogether."

"That's the spirit. You'll be over Lord Harry just as quickly as the others."

"Of course. I have no doubt."

Well, that was a lie, but it seemed to give Maria a good deal of peace.

"Then there is no harm done. You will have your trip to Egypt, then return and marry someone appropriate someday."

"I suppose so."

They were both silent for some moments. Penelope was trying desperately to picture herself blissfully wed to someone appropriate but was coming up empty. Apparently she was simply not that imaginative. Her fantasies had room for just one gentleman, apparently, and he was far from appropriate. Thankfully, Maria changed the subject before she could become very morose.

"I have to say, everything I've heard about Mr. Markland makes him out to be quite the proper gentleman."

Ah, good. Once again they were back on Mr. Markland. It seemed Maria's imagination was returning to one specific person, too. Heavens, perhaps she would make it all the way to the altar before Penelope would!

"Indeed, I have heard nothing to the contrary. He seems a very decent sort of gentleman."

"And you did note how handsome he is, did you not?"

"Most certainly! There's no one who could deny he's quite dashing."

"And he rescued you from that carriage, of course."

"Quite true. He seems a most remarkable gentleman."

"Then certainly you should fall in love with him," Maria said.

"Yes, I should . . . er, what?"

"You must be half in love already."

"With Mr. Markland?!" Penelope wasn't positive she'd heard correctly.

But Maria clasped her hands in something like glee. "Yes,

yes . . . you only just met, and you've still got that silly Lord Harry to get out of your system, but I can see the attraction is already there. On both sides, I daresay."

Goodness, but she must set her friend straight at once. "Not on mine, indeed. Have no fear. All his attraction is focused on you."

Odd, but Maria looked quite terrified at the thought. "On me? Oh my! Whatever should give you that idea?"

For heaven's sake. Was the girl so very rattled at the thought of it? How lucky she had Penelope to help her through this grand emotion.

"Of course you're anxious at the thought of it all," Penelope said. "But you have no need. I can see clearly how you feel about him."

"And just how do I feel about him?"

"You're the one in love, of course. I knew as much when you asked me to help with your appearance last night."

"But I certainly never said I was in love with Mr. Markland!"

"Do you think you had to?" Penelope asked, not quite able to keep from grinning at her friend's obvious awe of the man. "You've certainly not ceased praising Mr. Markland since the moment I mentioned him after that little incident with the carriage."

"Little incident! You very nearly died, Penelope," Maria declared. "And I have only ever praised the man for *your* sake. I thought surely Mr. Markland would rate far higher in your esteem than Lord Harry. At least, he ought to."

"And why on earth would you think that? Mr. Markland is a mere mister, while Lord Harry could very well be a duke himself one day. And true, Mr. Markland has fine enough features and he is undeniably tall and elegant, but surely you've noticed what a remarkable figure Lord Harry cuts without even trying!"

"What? Even after all he's done you still find Lord Harry more attractive than Mr. Markland?"

This was too much. Why, how dare Maria insinuate that Lord Harry was not absolutely the most attractive man in all of London! Clearly there was something wrong with her eyes.

"I did not see you offended by his looks as you strolled

casually along with him," she noted, probably with slightly more spite than the situation merited.

"I was being polite."

"Yes, I noticed. And you weren't particularly racing to arrive at my house where you must have known you would no longer have him to yourself."

"Penelope! Gracious, as if I could ever . . . Why, he's not at all my type!"

"And you claim Mr. Markland isn't, either."

"No, he isn't."

"Then who, I'm left to wonder, were you so eager to impress at the ball last night?"

Maria opened her mouth as if to answer, then quickly shut it again.

"So there is someone?" Penelope asked. "And he is neither Mr. Markland nor Lord Harry?"

Maria seemed to think long and hard before finally replying. Penelope leaned in eagerly to listen. Unfortunately her eager listening was cut off. Mamma came through the door just at that moment, and she was not smiling. It was not as if Penelope would have expected her to smile, of course, considering. But drat her inconvenient timing!

"What is this, Penelope?"

The offensive object in Mamma's hand was immediately recognizable. As was the young maid who sheepishly trailed her into the room.

"It is a shawl, Mamma," Penelope answered.

"Well, obviously I know that. What I'm asking is why did you give specific instructions to throw it out to the rag-and-bone man? Honestly, Penelope, you cannot be discarding your purchases just as fast as you make them."

"But Mamma, I didn't purchase that. It was bought for me."

"Well I certainly don't recall buying this, and I'm very sure I would remember such a—"

"It was a gift from Lord Harry," Penelope informed her.

Mamma paused in midrant. "Oh. Well then. Carry on, Milly."

She shoved the ugly article toward the sheepish maid and marched out without further word. Milly seemed slightly confused, but balled up the shawl and glanced at Penelope for confirmation. Indeed, it had been a stroke of genius to bring the girl here. There was no better place in London for her to be safe from Lord Harry. And Penelope was quite determined to keep her clear of the man.

"Thank you, Milly," she said to her. "Discard that and I never want to see it again."

Milly nodded, curtsied, and left. Unfortunately, Maria seemed to decide it was time for her to do the same. Penelope was unable to reengage her friend in the enthralling discussion of Maria's tender emotions. With little more than a hasty farewell, the woman dismissed herself and Penelope was left alone.

Drat. She'd been certain her friend had nearly been about to confirm suspicion; there was some particular man who'd captured her eye. But who the devil was he? The question was almost—but not quite—enough to distract Penelope from her own romantic dilemmas.

Chapter Seventeen

Penelope was very nearly asleep when someone rapped at her door. Her first thought, oddly enough, was for Lord Harry, but that was just silly. Of course he wouldn't stroll through her house and rap at her bedroom door this late at night. No, indeed. He'd be far more likely to try to climb in through her window.

Except that he probably couldn't be bothered. He'd made it plain earlier he'd had more than his fill of her. Perhaps he was off trying to climb into Maria's window—he had seemed to enjoy her company rather much. Not that it mattered one way or the other, of course. Maria claimed she did not care for Lord Harry, and Penelope reminded herself that neither did she.

She was angry and done with him. Her silly brain had no reason at all to continually conjure his image, the warmth of his touch, the sweetness of his kiss . . .

Oh, so infuriating! Now, even gone from her life, he was robbing her of sleep. Indeed, she had every reason to be angry with him.

Not to mention whomever was still rapping at her door.

"Yes, yes. Come in," she called, tucking the blanket around her and expecting her maid.

It was not the maid. It was Anthony. What could bring him here at this hour? Had something happened?

"What is it?" she asked quickly.

"This arrived for you, just now," he said, handing her a letter.

A letter? Goodness, but who would send a letter in the middle of the night? It could only mean something dreadful!

"Who sent it? Where is it from?" she asked, not reaching for it even though Anthony stood just feet away, holding it out to her.

"I cannot guess," he replied. "But since it arrived by some anonymous boy who would not give it to a servant but insisted on waiting for you, I'm assuming it must be important. I had to become rather firm to get it from him."

"What does it say?"

"It says it is only to be opened by you."

"But what can it be about?"

"Perhaps if you would open it you might get some of your answers," he said, practically shoving it at her.

Clearly there was no way to avoid it. She snatched the letter from his hand. If Lord Harry had been brutally shot, then she might as well know of it.

"Well?" he asked. "If it is some vulgar thing from your former fiancé, I assure you I'll—"

"No, it is not," she said, suddenly full of relief on that count but at the same time, dark confusion on another. "It is from Maria."

"Miss Bradley? At this hour?"

Indeed, that concerned her, as well. She scanned through the letter rapidly.

Dearest P.

When you receive this, I will be gone. I am eloping! All is planned to prevent our discovery until we have made good our scheme. I know this must seem very shocking and sudden, but I hope that you—above all people— might see to forgive me and perhaps even wish me happy. I simply could not leave without giving you a word, my dearest friend.

The gentleman is good and worthy, though you have made your differing opinion clear. I dare not write his name here, but you will, no doubt, guess. You are aware he visited me today, and I only wish our need for secrecy did not prevent me from telling you more.

I love him, and pray someday to have your blessing.

It was not signed, but of course she knew her friend's handwriting on sight. She did not, however, know how to make sense of the letter. Could it be true? Maria was eloping? Good heavens!

"What is it?" Anthony asked.

"It is Maria," she replied, not quite sure what else to say. "She has run off."

"Run off?"

"With a man, apparently."

"What!?"

"I've read through it twice, yet I can scarce believe it."

"I can *not* believe it," Anthony said. "Miss Bradley has run away with a *man*?"

"She is female, you know. There's no need to gape as if such a thing were an assault on nature."

"Yes, but . . . what is she doing running off with a man?"

"They are eloping, of course."

"Impossible! Miss Bradley has been nothing but a wallflower all these years. Who on earth could she possibly find to elope with?"

Penelope had to swallow a few times before she found her voice to answer.

"I'm afraid it might be Lord Harry."

It was a ridiculous notion, of course. Why on earth should Lord Harry run away with Maria? More importantly, why should Maria run away with him? She claimed she did not very much like the man. Still, Penelope had seen the two of them together. Indeed, there was no one else Penelope could think of who had paid a visit on Maria during the day. Who else could it be but Lord Harry?

Heavens, but she suddenly found it difficult to breathe.

"Chesterton? Are you certain?"

She nodded. "I saw them together today. He has made it a point to befriend Maria at every possible opportunity. It must be him."

"She names him?" he asked, leaning in to view the letter.

At this point, there was little reason to hide it. She handed the letter up to him.

"She indicates that it is him," she explained. "See? She knows I will guess it, then begs my forgiveness. It can only be him; I know he visited her today. I saw them walking, deep in conversation. Planning this . . . this travesty, no doubt."

"You are not in favor of it?"

"Certainly not! He's not fit for someone so true and gentle as Maria Bradley."

"How true can she be if she elopes with her best friend's fiancé?"

"Former fiancé, may I remind you."

"Indeed, yet I thought I clearly detected a bit of attachment between the two of you."

"Of course Maria and I are attached. We've been friends for years, since—"

"Not you and Maria, you and Chesterton."

"As you can see, any attachment you thought you detected was clearly imagined."

"Clearly. And these are tears of joy for your friend you're shedding now?"

"I am not shedding tears!"

"Something in your eye, perhaps?"

"You know, a dear friend of mine could be making the worst mistake of her life. It might be nice if you were to think of ways to help her rather than stand here in my chamber and accuse me of sentiment that I assure you I do not feel."

"You want me to help? How, exactly?"

"We've got to stop them from running away, of course!"

"So you do want Chesterton for yourself."

"No, I want to save my friend!"

"Which would leave Chesterton for you."

"No! I don't want him. I want you to save Maria from him!"

He seemed to miss the point completely. Unconcerned, he simply shrugged. "And why is this suddenly my responsibility?"

"Because you care about Miss Bradley and don't want to see her victimized by this blackguard."

"You mean the blackguard you were desperate to save from Burlington just earlier today?"

"That was before I realized just how much of a blackguard he was. Honestly, Anthony, stop trying to change the subject. We must think of a way to help Maria."

"And just what would you have me do, Penelope?"

"Well, go after her!"

"Go where?"

"Scotland, probably. Please, Anthony. It's the only way to save her; find them and bring her home. Surely they haven't gotten far yet. Find her, bring her home, and then no one will ever need to know about this!"

"You cannot be serious."

"Of course I'm serious. Hurry! Get going! They must be headed north. We know Lord Harry has little money, but perhaps he sold that lovely carriage you gave him . . ."

"No, actually. He sent it back to me."

"He did? He told me that, but I didn't know if I could believe him."

"Apparently you can. Penelope, what is really going on here? I don't see how—"

Before she could interrupt him to beg him to hurry, he was instead interrupted by the sound of someone pounding at the front door below.

"What the devil could that be?" he asked.

She could only shrug and admit that she truly had no idea. Surely Maria's aging auntie could never pound so hard. Grumbling, Anthony marched out of her room and she heard his boots echoing down the stairway. Whoever was pounding below would certainly be in for a treat, disrupting Anthony while so much chaos was already going on around them.

With luck it might be positive information from Maria. Perhaps the couple had not gone off as planned, after all. Penelope dashed over to her window and looked down into the street to find out for herself.

She could tell nothing. No carriage was visible, and whoever was still beating the door was far too near the house for her to see from her vantage point directly above. She carefully opened her window just a crack in hopes of recognizing voices.

The pounding ceased as she heard the front door creak open.

"Well, this is a surprise," Anthony's voice boomed out.

"No doubt. Is your sister here? Is she well?"

It was Lord Harry. Thank heavens! He was not gone with Maria, after all. Even better, he was here, asking after her!

"Of course she is here, not that I have any intention of letting you see her, though."

"Is she well? Has there been any trouble?" Lord Harry went on.

"What the devil are you ranting about? Yes, she's well."

"Are you certain? Is she in her bed?"

"I hardly think that's any business of yours, Chesterton."

"Have you looked in on her? Is she truly there?"

"Of course she is. Where else would she be at this hour? And what in St. Peter's name have you been about with Miss Bradley? That letter arrived and got Penelope all in a lather."

"Letter? What letter? Have you already heard something from the kidnappers?"

Anthony was understandably perplexed. "Kidnappers? What kidnappers?"

Good heavens! *Kidnappers?* Perhaps Maria hadn't run off at all. Perhaps she'd been kidnapped and that letter she'd received had been simply to throw them off the track. Oh, but thank God Lord Harry had shown up to inform them. Something must be done!

Pulling the window shut, she grabbed up her wrapper and ran to the corridor. She had to get downstairs and make sure Anthony was going to act. His tone of voice had sounded like he'd very much rather just slam the door in Lord Harry's face and forget he'd heard anything of this. She could not let that happen. Poor Maria! What on earth could be happening to her?

She was several paces away from her bedroom and just about to put her foot down onto the first step heading toward the lower floor when someone grabbed her from behind. She was pulled up so sharply all the air pressed out of her lungs. A heavy cloth was suddenly rammed over her mouth, muffling any sound she tried to make. These actions were so sudden, so unexpected, that for half a heartbeat she was simply stunned, unable to react in any sensible manner.

When at last her instinct kicked up and she realized her urgent need to struggle, arms were holding her tightly, that cloth being stuffed mercilessly into her mouth as she vainly thrust her head back and forth trying to dislodge it and break free. It was no good. Panic took over and she staggered, flailing and kicking. Her assailant was strong, though, and nothing she did seemed to have any effect. Good heavens! She was being dragged away from the stairway, down the corridor and back into the shadows.

Nothing made sense. Who held her? She could not turn her head and see. Perhaps more than one set of arms pressed against her, keeping her from escape and holding her upright, though her thrashing legs surely were not making their job easy. She choked and gagged on that horrible cloth. She couldn't seem to catch her breath; her chest was tight from restraint and another cloth was held tightly over her nose. It smelled dreadful when she could drag in a short draft of air.

But not enough. She could feel her struggles becoming weaker as the shadows around her played frightfully over the walls. She was being taken into the narrow servants' passage—felt herself being pulled down the confining staircase there.

Clearly she detected hushed voices. Course, unrefined tones muttered curses at her struggles, and she had the impression of two people working together at the task of hauling her against her will down to the servants' rooms. It was impossible to fathom; who on earth could think they might treat her this way and not face serious consequences? Surely Anthony would hear her struggles. And Lord Harry was nearby, too. No doubt he would never allow such a thing.

But the shadows grew darker and the voices more unintelligible. She staggered, her legs crumbling beneath her. She needed air . . . needed to breathe . . .

"I'M ASKING IF YOU'RE ABSOLUTELY POSITIVE THAT PEnelope is safely upstairs in her room?" Harris repeated himself, as patiently as possible.

Rastmoor's condescension was wearing thin.

"Yes, of course she is," the man replied, obviously not hearing what Harris was trying to convey. "Where else would she be?"

"Damn it, that's what I'm trying to tell you," Harris went on. "Someone is planning to kidnap her!"

"You're mad. Who on earth would want Penelope?"

"Any number of people for any number of unpleasant purposes, I'm afraid."

"And just which people and what unpleasant purposes are you concerned about at the present time?"

"I'm not certain. I was—"

"Not certain? You've come pounding on my door claiming she is in danger and you haven't any idea from whom?"

"What the hell difference does it make? I was making my way into Burlington's back hallway when I overheard—"

"You were what? Breaking into Burlington's house?"

"That's not the point here!"

"It's likely a point for Burlington."

"The man is involved in some rather unsavory things, and—"

"And what does that have to do with my sister? What have you gotten her into, Chesterton?"

"I'm attempting to tell you if you'd kindly stop interrupting me at every turn! I was just now at Lord Burlington's house, where I overheard some disreputable men plotting to get her. They plan to take her tonight!"

"Whatever for?"

"For ransom; for anger toward me; for outright spite; who knows! The important thing is that you are aware of the threat and can make absolutely certain she will not be harmed."

"Of course she will not be harmed."

"Good. I'm going to try to find out what—"

Yet again, he was interrupted. This time from above as Lady Rastmoor called out from the nearby stairs. Her descending footsteps were sounding nearer.

"Anthony? What's all the hubble-bubble? Was someone pounding at this hour?"

"It was Chesterton, Mother," Rastmoor called.

The woman appeared around the corner. "Ah. So I see. What does he want?"

"Nothing, Mother. He is just leaving."

Harris nodded at the lady. She merely sneered in reply.

"So where is Penelope?" she asked after glancing around

the entrance hall to ascertain that Harris had not—this time, at least—been in the process of seducing the girl.

"Upstairs in her bed," Rastmoor replied. "As she should be."

"No she isn't," the woman said.

"Of course she is," Rastmoor declared. "I was just speaking with her moments ago."

"Well she isn't there now. I heard some fuss, but when I went to look for her, she wasn't there. I thought she must be down here with you."

Harris felt an icy dread grip him inside. "We have to find her!"

"But I was just with her," Rastmoor repeated. "She must be there."

"Her room is empty," Lady Rastmoor repeated, eyeing Harris suspiciously. "What is going on tonight?"

Rastmoor seemed to wholeheartedly agree with his mother's suspicions. He glared at Harris with clenched fists as if he would love nothing better than to come to blows.

"Where is she, Chesterton?"

"I tell you I don't know, but if she isn't—"

Once again he was cut off. This time from below. A woman's scream echoed up from some lower portion of the house.

Harris was already pushing Rastmoor aside and running after it before Lady Rastmoor uttered her own worried yelp. Or perhaps that was due to the fact that Harris trampled her foot in his haste. Either way, he did not pause to attend her. Damn it all, Penelope was in danger and it was his own bloody fault!

"The kitchen," Rastmoor declared. "This way!"

Now it was Harris's turn to be shoved aside as Rastmoor barreled by. Actually, Harris could not entirely mind being overtaken in such rude fashion. Rastmoor was the one carrying a light. Plus, Harris had to admit that even with a lamp, he had no idea how to get to the kitchen, or wherever else that scream might have come from. At least for the time being, he was dependent on Rastmoor to lead the way.

He followed the man through darkened passages clearly set apart for servants. They came to a doorway that appeared to lead toward a staircase, but as the dim light of Rastmoor's lamp fell on it, they paused for the ashen-faced figure who appeared there, climbing unsteadily up the stairs. Harris recognized her immediately.

The little giggling maid from Burlington's house. She was most definitely not giggling now. Good heavens, was her lip bloodied?

She cowered in terror as they approached.

"I swear, sir, it weren't my idea! Honest, I'd have never helped them do something like this!"

Harris spared a quick glance at Rastmoor then looked back at that girl. "What did they do? Who was it?"

"My Tom thought they was just wanting to pinch a bit, you know, take a little something that his lordship might never even miss. He told me to let them in, so I did. I shouldn't have, but I did. Then they was asking who was in the house, was everybody asleep, and all!"

She was talking, but she wasn't making much sense. Harris had to hold back the urge to shake her. Tom was that stocky footman he'd encountered at Burlington's, as best he could remember. No wonder the thug hadn't been at his post there tonight, allowing Harris to creep into the home and overhear the brutish whispers of a plan to kidnap Penelope. But where was she now? He would beat the answers from this chit if he had to.

Fortunately, she went on before he had to resort to that.

"I thought they was after the silverware, you know, but instead they went upstairs and took *her*!"

Lady Rastmoor had come up behind them and gasped out loud at that.

"Where did they take her? Which way did they go?" Harris asked.

"I don't know," she said, shaking her head and putting her fingers to her swollen lip. "I tried to stop them, but one of them hit me and threw me down the stairs! They threatened Tom and said if he didn't do what they wanted, they'd make sure he got the sack . . . and me worse!"

Harris wasn't quite sure that was adequate motivation to make up for this Tom fellow's involvement in the matter at hand, but he hardly had time to discuss that now. He needed to find Penelope and get her back from these men before it was too late.

"They can't be far," Rastmoor said. "I just left her."

His mother was understandably shaken. "Someone has taken Penelope? Is that what this is about?"

"We'll find her, Mother," Rastmoor assured.

Harris was determined to make that prophetic.

"You check the house," he directed Rastmoor. "I'll see if I can find anything outside."

Rastmoor grunted something like approval, so Harris left them. That witless servant girl must know something more about this, but damned if he had the time to drag it out of her. Perhaps Rastmoor would have better luck. In the meantime, Harris was not about to sit around idle. He found the servants' entrance and bolted out through it.

The street outside was quiet. One lone carriage rattled in the near distance, just out of sight. Penelope! They must have had a carriage waiting and thrown her into it. He was only moments behind them.

Running, he turned the nearby corner onto the next street, following the sound. He didn't get far before two unpleasantly large men stepped out from the shadows. Damn. One had a pistol, the other had a knife. Harris had a headache.

One man he recognized; the infamous Tom. Damn it. Dear Tom had taken advantage of his little maid's presence in Rastmoor's house. He must have used her to get access to Penelope.

"Looking for something, milord?" the unpleasantly larger of the two men said.

"Where is she?" Harris demanded. "Where are you taking her?"

The man didn't even pretend to wonder what Harris had meant. The brute just looked him up and down—clearly detecting his foolishly weaponless condition—then laughed. Harris could smell his whiskeyed breath even from this distance. Indeed, the man appeared as dangerous as he was foul.

"If you'd like to find out, then all you need to do is follow us this way." He motioned with his pistol toward a small, rattle-clap gig parked just up the street.

It was clear he expected no argument. Well, Harris had never been very good at blindly following directions. He did his best to ignore the pistol and dug in his heels. Crossing his arms and glaring, he offered a simple, "No."

The younger and slightly smaller footman shifted nervously. The odiferous man with the pistol did not. He simply grinned and kept his gaze firmly on Harris.

"They're taking your ladylove the same place we's supposed to be hauling you." He snorted. "Didn't figure you'd be so easy to find, though. Thanks for saving us some trouble."

"I try to be accommodating."

"Good. Then get yer sorry fine arse into the carriage, milord, before I have to go wasting a bullet on you."

He didn't know if he could believe the man about the intended destination, but he did believe his threats about shooting him. The lout looked all too eager for that, as a matter of fact. Well, considering he had few options, Harris decided to acquiesce. Besides, that carriage with Penelope in it was getting farther and farther away with every heartbeat. At least if he pretended to go quietly he'd be in a better position to find her than if he rebelled and got shot in the chest.

"Very well. Take me to her."

The nervous Tom seemed relieved, though the man with the pistol showed no emotion either way. Harris interpreted this as a good omen. If his abductors were not in perfect unison, there was a chance—slim, perhaps—that he could use that for his advantage. He hung his head and let the men lead him across the street toward a dusty gig that seemed more a pile of refuse than a carriage.

It was unattended and he could easily see why. The geriatric horse harnessed there seemed to have barely enough life in it to stay on its feet, let alone wander off voluntarily. The decaying gig was in equally unimpressive condition. In fact . . . was this the same pitiful conveyance Harris had just sold not two days ago? Hell. Fate was too cruel.

"Get in," his host demanded.

Harris complied. Yes, it was the same carriage. It smelled worse now, however.

The man with the pistol handed him a length of black cloth.

"Blindfold yourself," he barked, then climbed inside with Harris.

Surprisingly, the footman did, too, and took up the reigns. Harris knew it would be asking for trouble to argue, so he simply did as ordered and pulled the cloth around his head.

Well, he was rather familiar with London. He'd have a fair idea which way the carriage was going, even if he couldn't see.

They were rather tight together in there, and Harris found himself more than a bit uncomfortable as the carriage rattled and clanked into motion. Every slight imperfection—not to mention the rather large ones—was painfully noticeable as Harris was first jabbed in the arm by the pistol and then poked by the footman's pointed elbow as he slapped the reigns in a vain attempt to encourage the feeble horse to take on something approaching a trot.

Dear God in heaven, he could only pray they'd get there in time to save Penelope. Hell, he prayed they might get there at all.

Chapter Eighteen

The light finally broke through to her consciousness and Penelope cracked open one lazy eyelid. Heavens, but she was sleepy. What on earth had she been doing to make her sleep in so? The day must be half over, the way the sun was nearly blinding her.

But it was the oddest sun she had ever seen. What was going on? She blinked and tried desperately to figure out why she was lying on her floor instead of in her nice, comfortable bed. Slowly, she recalled.

She was not in her bedroom at all! It was not even morning. Darkness still hovered around her, temporarily blocked from view simply because someone waved a lamp in her face.

"Oh, wonderful. It appears they've not quite dispatched you altogether."

A voice? Indeed, a man's voice, but one she did not at all recognize.

The lamplight shifted away from her face, and at last she was able to make out her surroundings. She struggled to sit up, but two gentle hands pressed her back.

"No, just give it a moment or two, my dear. That draught they gave you will take time to wear off," the voice continued.

"Draught?" she asked, although it came out more as a muddled grunt.

"You're safe. I don't believe anyone harmed you in any way, but clearly you've been drugged with something."

Yes, it appeared the voice was correct. She felt as if her arms were a hundred miles long, though she was in no actual pain. Standing up would be quite problematic, though, but surely she could not simply lie here on the floor with a strange man looming nearby. Concentrating, she pushed up into a sitting position.

The lamp was off to the side now and she could make him out. He was older, yet not at all ancient. His dark hair was well on its way to being gray, and it seemed to have lacked for a comb. For just a moment she found his eyes and felt an odd sense of familiarity. *Lord Harry!* But no, of course Lord Harry was not here and she did not know this man. It was just the drug still lingering in her body. Clearly when she'd been accosted in the assumed safety of her own home, her attackers had made her senseless. What a dreadful feeling.

So just how long had she been incoherent with this stranger? And where were her attackers? What did they plan to do to her? She struggled to get her legs to cooperate and to drag herself up off the floor.

The man merely smiled at her and patted her hand. "Now, now. Rest easy, my dear. I doubt anyone has intention of hurting you."

Well, that seemed a ridiculous thing to say. She'd been drugged, abducted, and dumped on a floor! Why on earth would he assume these brutes would have any intention other than hurting her? Oh, but her memory was becoming clearer. She'd been in the corridor outside her bedroom, listening to Anthony when . . . Gracious! She was in her nightgown!

It was no use trying to make herself more modest. She was sitting here on a dusty floor with a strange man and wearing nothing more than her nightgown and a thin wrapper. Well, she supposed as she tugged it closer around her, at least she was still wearing it. Thankfully those thugs who grabbed her hadn't divested her of it.

"It is a bit chilly, I'm afraid," the man said, apparently misinterpreting her nervous attention to her attire.

His own clothing was hopelessly crumpled, and he seemed

completely oblivious to that fact. As he moved in the lamplight, she could notice the threadbare condition of his coat, not to mention its outdated styling. She almost smiled, being suddenly reminded of her first glimpse of Lord Harry. This gentleman, however, was not nearly so disheveled. It was obvious, though, he was not one who placed high priority on his appearance. Perhaps he had hardly taken note of hers. She hoped.

But what were they doing here? Who had taken her? And how was this kindly, rumpled man involved? Surely he was not an enemy, but then what possible other reason could he have for being here with her?

He was moving around in the shadows, and she fought to make her eyes adjust. What was he doing? Dust and damp swirled in the air as he poked about, making Penelope choke.

"Here, you may use this to keep warm," he said, returning with some large bulk of oily cloth.

It smelled of dead fish. Still, it would at least cover her. This man might not be an immediate threat to her, but at some point she could expect her abductors to return. Who knew what they had in mind, what they might do to a passably attractive—and basically helpless—young woman in a nightgown. Perhaps smelling like refuse and decay was not a bad idea. She pulled the cloth around her and wrinkled her nose.

"I'm afraid there is a dearth of sweet-scented air here on the docks," the man said. "But at least you won't be shivering."

"The docks? Is that where we are?"

"I believe so, although they had me rather in the same condition as you when they brought me here."

"And why in heaven's name have they done that? What do they want us for?"

He shrugged, causing his ill-fitted coat to rumple even more. "Ransom, I suppose."

"Ransom?" That certainly sounded sinister, and perhaps it was a bit optimistic to hope that, after all she'd put him through, Anthony would spend actual money to get her back.

"That's why they took me, although the first group to have me were Egyptian loyalists and I really have no idea who this last set were."

"Egyptian loyalists?"

"Yes, it's a long story, I'm afraid, and one I'd come to believe had been resolved when they gave me up and let me be brought back here, but apparently—"

"Wait, wait . . . what are you talking about? *Who* kidnapped us?"

"Well, I don't quite know who is ultimately responsible for bringing you here, but I was initially nabbed in Cairo and held there. You are not from Egypt, I take it?"

"Heavens, no! I'm from London. We are still in London, aren't we?"

"Yes, this is London, although presumably they've got us here on the docks so we can be more easily sent elsewhere."

"Elsewhere? Gracious! Where else would they send us? Egypt?"

"Oh, I doubt that. I fear I'm no longer welcome there."

Could it be the drug was still affecting her brain? Nothing was making sense. Was this man really talking about Egypt? It must be a dream, although she could certainly never recall a dream smelling quite this bad. But how surprising that the man claimed to come from Egypt, of all places. Surely this could not be mere coincidence. This had to have something to do with the antiquities she'd seen at Lord Burlington's, with the scarab that Lord Harry had taken from her and . . .

Lord Harry. Indeed, he must have a part in this! After all, she'd never met any other criminal, so he could be the only possible link to this sort of thing. And he'd been there, at her house, hadn't he? Indeed, yes, she knew he had. She could distinctly recall his voice, hearing him downstairs talking with Anthony about . . . kidnappers.

Oh! And there had been that letter from Maria . . . she'd nearly forgotten. Maria had eloped with Lord Harry, but then he'd arrived and begun talking about kidnappers and she'd been so worried that something dreadful had happened to Maria and . . .

But apparently the kidnapping discussion had not been about Maria. Drat! Lord Harry had been talking about kidnapping *her.* Yet why would he have discussed it with Anthony if he hoped to get away with it? Perhaps he'd been trying to distract Anthony while his hired henchmen carted her away. Yes, that seemed logical. But then what had happened to Maria? And where was poor Anthony?

She was breathing rapidly the more she thought of it all. Lord Harry had done this—there could be no other explanation. He stole her heart, he stole her necklace, and now he'd gone and stolen her. For ransom, this gentleman had said. Yes, that sounded like something Lord Harry would do.

She wished to heaven that she'd been born a man so she might be able to use a few of the choice words she'd heard Anthony employ a time or two when he'd been angry and thought gentle ears were not around. *Drat!* and *Botheration!* hardly seemed adequate to sum up her emotions just now. Indeed, she was furious. A bit frightened, too. And undeniably heartbroken. Yes, she could indeed wish she'd been born male. She'd have never even noticed that handsome blackguard in the first place.

Instead, all she seemed able to do in her female state was pull her knees up toward her chest, hug them tightly, and cry. It was most cowardly and surely most annoying. She did not wish to cry, but her eyes blurred and her nose got all itchy just the same.

"There, there, little miss," the gentleman said, crouching down beside her. "All will be well. I'm certain of it. Surely they would not have taken you if they did not know you had a well-to-do family who wanted you back. Think of it, your father will surely send the money right away and you will be home before noon."

"My father has been dead for years," she announced.

Her face was going puffy, she could just feel it. Botheration, indeed! She smelled of fish, her nose was runny, and her complexion was gone. What more could happen to ruin her day?

"Then you must have a brother, or an uncle . . ." the man was saying, sounding very much like a patronizing old uncle himself.

"My brother," she replied, wiping her nose with the unpleasant fabric. "But he'll probably argue for days before agreeing to pay two shillings for my return. That is . . . provided he will pay anything at all."

"Now now, this is not the time to be feeling sorry for yourself."

Was he serious? This was *precisely* the time to be feeling sorry for herself! She'd been kidnapped by thugs, abandoned by her brother, and cruelly betrayed by the heartless rogue she accidentally let herself fall in love with, for heaven's sake. What other reasons could she possibly need to feel sorry for herself?

"Put your mind onto more pleasant things," the man pattered on. "I'll bet a pretty girl like you has a handsome young suitor out there waiting for her, eh?"

Her voice cracked when she replied. "He's the one that likely formulated my abduction! I'd rather not think of him just now, if you don't mind."

"What? But a moment ago you seemed as if you had no idea who—"

"It *has* to be him. Who else could it be? There's no one else so devious, so greedy, so callous . . . I should have known he'd never really help me get away from my brother."

"Away from your brother? I thought you just said it was one of your admirers who orchestrated this?"

"Oh no, he's not an admirer. We were simply engaged."

"Your fiancé is responsible for this?"

"It would appear so. I would think you must know him, too, if he's got you kidnapped, as well."

The man seemed confused by all this, which was odd given he had such an intelligent-looking face. His forehead wrinkled as he contemplated her words.

"Your fiancé is Egyptian?"

Well, clearly her estimation of the man's face was way off.

"No, he's from England. What on earth is all this about Egypt? Everything seems to be about Egypt lately. You come from there, Lord Burlington has a whole collection of artifacts, I lost my precious sca—"

"Lord Burlington? Surely he is not your fiancé!"

"No, of course not!"

She nearly gagged at the thought. As if she could have possibly done half the things she'd done with Lord Harry with some ogre like Lord Burlington! It was too horrible to imagine.

"Lord Burlington already has a wife," she replied, thankful she could do so. "I was simply referring to the mysterious collection of Egyptian artifacts that seemed to show up in his house one day."

"I didn't know Burlington collected."

"I didn't either. Still, there it was. Lovely items, too. I saw the most unique little alabaster cosmetics jar and . . . well, it seems I was not the only one fascinated by them. My stupid fiancé also had an eye for that collection. I thought he was simply trysting with a servant girl, but now I'm convinced he was breaking in to steal them."

"Steal the artifacts?"

"Yes. I told you he is a horrible person. He stole my lovely scarab necklace; yes he did."

"You have a scarab necklace?"

"Not anymore; he stole it from me! That's why I'm certain he's involved in this. How odd, though, that everything he steals seems to have some connection to Egypt. Except for me, of course, although Anthony did finally say he'd allow me to go there . . ."

"Anthony is your fiancé?"

"Anthony is my brother. But if he does pay that ransom and buy me back, I doubt he'll ever let me out of his sight again! Oh, but this is just dreadful."

The poor man was still as confused as ever. He shook his graying head and seemed to think long and hard before coming up with another question for her.

"So just who is your fiancé? If he has such an interest in Egyptian artifacts, it's very possible that I might have met him at some point."

"Oh, you'd never be the sort to make friends with a despicable, thieving, deceitful person like him. I can tell you are nothing at all like him."

"I must say, miss, that you don't seem to be someone like that, either, yet you are the one engaged to marry him. Who is this paragon of human depravity you intend to spend your life with?"

"He's terrible. You'd hate him," she said.

She would have very happily gone on to give him further detail of Lord Harry's uselessness, along with the man's full name and address, even, but sudden noises just outside the door to their little cell interrupted. She clutched the dreadful blanket closer and tried to scramble up to her feet. The older man bent to help her. He seemed to realize, too, that they'd been far better off alone than they were likely to be with the arrival of whoever this might turn out to be.

Huddling next to her newest best friend, Penelope managed to get to her feet. The man put his arm around her and she gladly let him. Any illusion of safety and protection was most welcome just now.

Something rattled at the door; a key in a lock. She could make out men's voices, orders being barked back and forth, and clearly the men were not cheerful. She glanced up at her companion and he gave her shoulder a fatherly squeeze. It might have helped ease her nerves if she were simply concerned about singing at a house party or meeting the queen, but given the circumstances here, she still wanted to cry. Or to vomit. Neither would be at all helpful.

Finally the door swung open. Light from a lantern spilled in, showing even more filth surrounding them but completely obscuring the identity of the new arrivals. She held up one hand to block out the glaring light, but all she could make out behind it were three shadows. Three unnervingly large shadows.

Unexpectedly, one of the shadows came charging toward her.

"Penelope! Thank God."

Lord Harry! Of course she knew his voice. Now that he was nearer she recognized his shadow, too—solid, broad, perfectly proportioned, and strong. She didn't even recall she hated him until it was too late.

He grabbed her elbow and pulled her away from the older man, encircling her with his arms and holding her tightly to his chest. Oh, but he was so warm and smelled so much better than the vile blanket she'd been using! She wanted nothing more than to wrap herself into Lord Harry's warmth and let him carry her someplace safe.

He wouldn't, of course. She came to her senses and remembered that as soon as he spoke again, his voice harsh and angry.

"What the hell are you doing to her! Keep your bloody hands off . . ."

She realized his anger had not been directed at her. No, indeed, he was glaring at the older man. Now, however, his words had ceased and he seemed to be frozen in place.

"You're safe!" he said with a completely different tone of voice.

Again, his words were not for her. He didn't exactly shove her out of the way, but he did rather shift her over to one side as he stepped forward and threw an arm around the other man's neck. How odd! Somehow she'd been very nearly dragged into a rather heated embrace between the two men. She wasn't altogether comfortable with that.

Fortunately, it did not last long. The men stepped apart again to observe one another.

"I'd heard you'd been brought to London," Lord Harry said.

"Here I am," the other man replied.

"And you are well?"

"I was a bit more well before you ripped that attractive young lady away from me. I take it you know each other?"

Good heavens, so her cell mate truly was acquainted with Lord Harry! Clearly he'd not paid much attention to what she'd said about him, either. He was smiling and chatting as if Lord Harry's presence was the most wonderful thing imaginable. Surely he must have realized by now this was the very man she'd been warning him about!

Then again, it would appear her own body was not heeding that warning, either. It seemed quite content to lean against him and draw from his warmth and his self-assurance. He clearly was not afraid, not the least bit concerned about being here in this foul little room with no window. He showed no fear of the two hulking shadows that still lurked in the doorway. Oh, she wished she could feel more like him.

Then again, why should he be concerned? He was the one who brokered all this, after all! Wasn't he? Perhaps not.

"How sweet," one of the hulks scoffed loudly. "Looky at the little reunion."

"Ain't that making me all teary-eyed," the other responded with buffoonish laughter.

"You'll be teary-eyed when this is all over," Lord Harry said, turning sharply and taking a step toward the doorway.

The dark hint of a pistol aimed in their direction was unmistakable. Penelope gulped back an anxious cry. Those horrible men had weapons! And just now they were pointing them at Lord Harry!

Thank heavens he had the good sense to stop moving toward them.

"You just mind yourself there, lordship," the pistol man snarled. "If ye keep quiet and don't give us no trouble, we won't need to shoot none of ye. Start acting up, though, and we might get a little upset. You might not like what we do to yer little lady there."

"Touch her and it will be the very last thing you do on this earth," Lord Harry snarled right back.

A fiery hot chill raced up Penelope's back. It was not from the dampness of the night air, nor was it a chill of terror, either. Quite shockingly the opposite, actually. Heavens, but she was glad Lord Harry did not use that tone of voice around her very often. The things it did to her!

The thugs merely laughed at Lord Harry's inspiring show of defiance. They shut the door loudly, taking their lantern and its light with them. The sounds of the lock rattled at the door again, and Penelope remembered to hug her blanket once more.

Now she was alone in the semidark with two men, one whom she knew and one whom she didn't and neither of whom she had any reason whatsoever to trust. For Lord Harry's part, in fact, she had every reason *not* to trust him. Mostly, though, it seemed it would be her own dratted emotions where he was concerned that she ought to worry about. Heaven help her, but she loved him whether she could trust him or not.

DAMN IT, BUT THIS WAS UNCOMFORTABLE. HE WANTED to hold Penelope so badly that every nerve in his body threatened mutiny. He half feared at any moment his reasonable self would be put on notice and the body would simply stalk over to her and do as it pleased. And it would be pleased, he had no doubt of that.

But of course he couldn't let that happen. This was hardly the time or place for such things. She would never let him, not considering how they had parted company last. And besides, they were not alone.

"What the devil have they got you here for?" Oldham asked.

"I expect we'll soon find out. Those two gits that dragged

me here said they expect whomever they are working for to show up here anytime now and give further instructions."

"Who do you suppose it is?" Oldham asked.

Lord, but it was good to see him again. For over a month now he'd fretted over the man, worried that his captors had got tired of waiting and had simply rid themselves of their prisoner. It was horribly unfair how Nedley had worked things all out, but by God he was glad to have the man back on friendly soil.

At least, it would be friendly once they found their way out of this mess.

"No idea," Harris replied.

He did have an idea, but the last thing Oldham needed right now was to discover his own favored son was the prime suspect. Markland's discussion with Ferrel regarding meeting a man at a ship tonight seemed to confirm his involvement in this. Damn, but it would be a shock to poor Oldham.

And what did Markland have in store for Penelope? Harris gave another long glance her way. She stood apart from them now, watching back and forth as if she were trying to make her mind up over whether to stay here with them or go pound on the door and beg for release. Indeed, he could hardly blame her for mistrusting him.

"Patience, my dear," he said to her. "You are far safer here on this side of that door than you would be on the other."

"I'm not so certain," she said.

"She fears her fiancé is the one who has conspired against us," Oldham explained in complete seriousness.

Harris couldn't help but laugh. "Oh, does she?"

"She says he's a horrible person and capable of much criminal activity."

He couldn't tell for sure, but in the dim light he thought he detected the faintest hint of blush creep over Penelope's pale cheeks. Good. She needed some color after a night like this.

"I don't doubt that he is," he agreed. "From what I know of him, he's the sort to do all manner of wicked, shocking things."

Ah, she blushed a little more deeply at that.

"Doesn't sound like a good match at all," Oldham said with a perplexed frown Harris had come to know well. "Miss, surely you have recourse? I should think it ill-advised to continue an engagement with such a man as that."

"Now now, I must beg you not to go putting such notions into her head," Harris said.

He made his way to Penelope and slipped his arm around her. She pretended to ignore him, but at least she didn't pull away or kick him in anyplace valuable. Poor thing, this whole situation must be most taxing for her. She looked so adorably forlorn.

"Perhaps introductions are in order," he said, taking a deep breath and diving in. "Miss Penelope Rastmoor, may I please present my father, Charles Harris Oldham? Father, Miss Rastmoor is my fiancée."

He wasn't sure whose expression seemed more amazed. Certainly Oldham's went from mildly to intensely perplexed, but Penelope was equally unable to hide her bewilderment. He would have loved to have drawn out the moment, toyed a bit with it to drain every bit of amusement that he could; however, as this was not a drawing room but a makeshift prison chamber, he decided he'd do well to just get on with things.

"Although, as you might have surmised, as of late things have not been on the best of terms."

His father stared, incredulous, at Penelope. When he spoke, he directed his conversation to her.

"My *son* is the terrible criminal you suggest has put this nightmare together?"

She, however, directed her words to Harris. "Your *father*? He cannot be! Everyone knows your father is dead."

Ah, sensitive, sweet Penelope. He took a deep breath to prepare for the inevitable explanations. He wondered if her eyes could, in fact, go any rounder.

"The previous Marquis of Hepton is dead, that is true, but he was not my actual father. My mother—rest her soul—confessed it on her deathbed in my fourteenth year. I, Miss Rastmoor, am in fact a bastard."

"But your father . . . the marquis, that is, he claimed you. How can you be a . . . what you say?"

He loved the way she stammered and struggled to grasp the situation. Indeed, he supposed it must be awkward for her, realizing she'd been locked up here with the very bounder who'd left his by-blow to be raised by another man. For Harris, it was worse than awkward. It was the final mark against him in this foolish game of hearts he'd unwittingly allowed himself to play.

Penelope took one step back from him as if he were a leper. It was small, but he knew what it meant. If she hadn't already believed when she arrived here that he was a hopeless miscreant—and apparently, according to his father, she did—this last bit of information regarding his parentage would surely seal it for her. He *was* a hopeless miscreant.

He'd simply never regretted it until now.

"As far as the law of the land is concerned, I am Lord Harris Chesterton," he declared. "In reality, though, my name should have been nothing so grand. I should be Harry Oldham, after my true father."

Now she shifted her gaze back to Oldham. "And this is your father? A simple *mister*?"

Fortunately, his father was not easily insulted. He merely smiled patronizingly.

"I hope I'm not so very simple, and in fact it is professor."

"Professor?" Why yes, her eyes *could* go even rounder. "Professor *Oldham*?"

"Yes . . ."

"Oh, but I've followed your work!" she squealed, suddenly forgetting about Harris's leprosy and stepping toward them. "I read every article you publish, and I keep your *Guide to Digging along the Nile* beside my bed always! I can't believe it's truly *you*!"

"It is me," Oldham said.

The older man shuffled his feet. Clearly now he was the one feeling awkward. Harris, on the other hand, was the one feeling left out. Penelope gushed on and on about the many wonderful things she'd read about the famous Professor Oldham and his various adventures in faraway Egypt. Damn it, but did the girl have no idea at all that her own bloody fiancé had been along for most of those adventures? Hell, he'd been the one to write half those damn articles while his father was too busy trying to convince the locals that they weren't digging up some ancient curse to bring famine or plagues down on them all.

But what was a gently bred female like Penelope doing reading their articles? They were not published in *Lady's Monthly Museum* or *La Belle Assemblée*, after all. Perhaps her brother had kept more scholarly journals lying about, but Harris hadn't gotten the idea the man was particularly interested in such things. Could it honestly be that Penelope's interest in Egyptian antiquities went somewhat beyond just the obvious gilt and glitter?

It seemed so. She was just now describing some of the treasures piled up at Burlington's in a manner far too detailed to come from someone with merely a passing interest. By God, the girl actually knew what she was talking about! Harris found himself oddly short of breath. To think, she wasn't only beautiful and tempting and delicious, but she had a brain, too.

And damned if he hadn't filled that brain with ample reason to despise him.

He thought to join in their conversation, to explain to her that he was every bit as knowledgeable and adventurous as his renowned parent, but noises outside the door put an end to casual discussion. Penelope clutched at that ragged blanket again, and Harris felt the hair at the back of his neck rise in anticipation. Their captors had returned. Very likely they would soon learn what this was all about and who, exactly, had brought them here. And what would happen next.

He moved closer to Penelope, positioning himself between her and the door. Oldham was at his side. Still, he knew they would be no match for hired thugs with weapons.

As the added light spilled into the room, he quickly took stock of his surroundings. He was by no means an expert at dealing with this sort of situation, but he had enough sense to know it was a good idea to be prepared. He made mental inventory of the various bits of rubbish heaped around them.

It seemed the room they were in had been used for storage; no windows, high ceiling, and only the one door. It was damp and drafty and smelled of fish and rot. What one might expect at the docks. He had assumed as much from the sounds and smells along the route as he tried to envision it while his abductors had carted him—blindfolded—here.

Very likely they were to be transported somewhere via water, and that could be bad. Their best bet for escape would be before they were trussed up and tossed onto a boat. Surrounded by water and at the mercy of God knew how many captors, they would have little hope of getting away. He needed to take stock of their resources and think up a way out of here *now*.

A man entered their room. He was well dressed and followed by the usual thugs, so Harris realized their true abductor had arrived. With the lantern light behind him, though, the man's face was in shadow. Damn. Harris needed to know for certain what—whom—they were up against.

"Hello, Harry," he spoke after a suitable pause to build the tension.

Harris knew the voice immediately.

Chapter Nineteen

He called him Harry. Penelope shuddered. Whoever this gentleman was, Lord Harry knew him well. She could see his face in the yellow light. Lord Harry's eyes were cold and a muscle ticked in his jaw. Oh yes, he knew this man. And he didn't much care for him.

"Good evening, Uncle," he said.

Oh. So this was his uncle. Now it made a bit more sense why Nedley Chesterton might be so very hateful toward his nephew. The man was not truly his nephew at all.

"So here is Kingsdere's favorite heir," the man said with unpleasant scorn. "To think my father's title could end up going to a shiftless bastard like you. It makes me sick at my stomach."

Indeed, if Lord Harry's sickly elder brother died without heir—as seemed very likely—all the family titles would go to him. No wonder this uncle seemed so unhappy. He was cut from inheriting by a bastard that his cuckolded brother had chosen to claim. This, she was horrified to realize, might give the uncle good reason to wish Lord Harry at the bottom of the Thames. Coincidentally, the Thames was very nearby.

But why was Professor Oldham here? Oh, certainly she was

thrilled beyond measure for a chance to finally meet the man, but truly she had always hoped for a more suitable venue. Conversation under their current circumstances would be strained at best.

"Oldham, I need you," the angry uncle announced suddenly. "Come with me. Now."

It seemed Professor Oldham was going to obey, but Lord Harry laid his hand on his arm to stay him.

"What on earth can you possibly need him for? Your grievance is with me, Uncle."

"If not for him there would be no you," the uncle replied. "And I'll deal with you later. For now, I need your, er, father's expertise on a little shipment I must go to prepare."

"Shipment of what?" Professor Oldham asked.

"Those lovely little rarities you so graciously dug up in Egypt, of course. My good friend Burlington was kind enough to keep them at his house—for a fee that included payment of some rather embarrassing gambling debts—but now that we've found a buyer, it's time to box them up and ship them out. Since I can't make heads or tails of half of it, I need Oldham here to make sure all is in order for the voyage to France."

"Your buyer is in France?" Lord Harry asked.

His uncle sneered at him. "And soon all your pretty knickknacks will be, too. Doesn't that just drive you mad?"

Then he laughed. It was such an unpleasant laugh that Penelope couldn't help but cringe. Poor Lord Harry, to have such a relative as this! No wonder he'd not turned out well.

"They belong in Egypt," Lord Harry said. "We had an agreement with the people there. You had no right to steal those antiquities—there's been too much of that already."

"Yes, yes, I know all about that. Lord Elgin and his marbles upset the people of Greece; your silly Egyptian friends think they have some claim to this . . . It's an old story, I'm afraid, and one that I really don't care to hear again. Fortunately, I don't have to. Come along, Oldham. You've already been ruined as far as your career is concerned. Don't make matters worse by giving me reason to start shooting your loved ones."

Professor Oldham lowered his head and did as he was told. How awful to see such a great man treated this way! Then again, Penelope was rather grateful that he didn't argue. The two thugs at the door both held pistols this time, and they seemed rather eager to use them.

She inched closer to Lord Harry, and he put an arm around her. She enjoyed it more than she should have, especially given the circumstances.

"At least if I'm involved in their shipping, I can assure the antiquities are kept safe," the professor said, turning to give his son a rather forlorn smile. "Pity our friends from Egypt aren't here. They could have followed me home and stayed in the old house where we used to meet them."

What was that? The professor's eyes seemed to hold a secret message as they met Lord Harry's. He nodded. It was an almost imperceptible nod, but as Penelope was as close to him as she could make herself, she noticed it. Clearly something unspoken passed between the two men. What was it she saw on Lord Harry's face? His arm tightened around her.

"When I've got this taken care of, I'll be back for you, Harry," the unpleasant man said. "And your pretty little miss. Let's just hope no one does anything to upset me in the meantime."

Clearly that last part was a warning. Oldham nodded. He understood. If he did not cooperate fully, something dreadful would happen to his son. Penelope felt it safe to assume that would include her, as well. So they were to be held here as assurance that things went as planned. But then what? She did not want to consider what might happen when they were no longer needed.

The way those two thugs were eyeing her, though, indicated that they were considering, too. They seemed rather pleased with their mental efforts. Ugh. How revolting! She pressed yet closer to Lord Harry.

Uncle Chesterton shoved Professor Oldham through the doorway, but motioned to one of his brutes on the way out. "You stay here. Keep an eye on them."

The man smiled an all-too-willing smile. Penelope shuddered. It was disgustingly obvious that he'd be only too happy to keep much more than an eye on them. On *her*, at least.

If she could have inched herself closer to Lord Harry, she would have.

The door shut and the room was dim again. They were alone with their shifty-eyed keeper. Not at all a comfortable position.

"I suppose when this is all over my uncle will have you kill us," Lord Harry said to the man, not making her the least bit more at ease.

The man shrugged. "If I'm lucky. Then again, he might be going to do you in hisself."

"He might. Either way, we all realize he can't very well let us go free after this."

"So I guess you and yer lady here don't have much to look forward to, do ye?"

"I don't suppose you'd be interested in some sort of bargain, would you?"

The foul man cocked an eyebrow at Lord Harry. He was curious. Ah, Lord Harry must have something planned! For a moment or two she had hope, but that faded as the man's expression changed.

"From what I hear, you ain't in no position to make no bargains," the thug grumbled. "I hear you got nothing but what yer uncle thinks to give ye, and beyond that some bloody lord wants to put a bullet in ye for dallying with his wife. Don't sound like you're in much place for making deals, if you don't mind me saying."

"I've had dozens of angry husbands want to put any number of bullets in me," Lord Harry said. "And I've got nothing from my damned uncle all these years and still I manage to get on fairly well. Now I've no intention of dying here tonight, so if you'd be so kind as to let me walk out that door I'm ready to make it worth your while."

"Yer uncle pays me a pretty penny to do as he says. Just what have you got that might possibly interest me to go against him?"

Penelope was more than eager to hear the answer. Did he have resources she was unaware of? Had he tucked some priceless treasure in his pocket before they dragged him here? Had he a pistol? What could he possibly produce that might save them?

"Her."

What was that?

"If you let me go," he explained. "I'll leave *her* behind for you."

Being the only female in the room, she could do nothing but assume he referred to her. Good heavens, he couldn't, could he? He'd honestly barter her person for his own escape? Well, then he was an even greater scoundrel than she'd already thought him, and she'd thought some very unpleasant things about him!

To prove his point, he grabbed her by the arm and pulled her to stand in front of him. By gracious, he was presenting her for inspection! She tried to be invisible, but of course she couldn't. The thug was able to run his disgusting gaze all over her in the flickering light from the lamp.

"Easy on the eyes, isn't she?" Lord Harry asked.

She craned her neck to glare at him, but his eyes evaded her scathing look.

"And I can vouch for what's underneath, too," he went on.

Oh! The horrible creature.

"So ye'd give her over to me, eh?" the thug questioned.

"Just as soon as you let me walk through that door," Lord Harry agreed.

"And what's to stop me from takin' her now?" the thug asked. "Seems I'm the one with the pistol here."

"You'd be able to make full use of her and keep that pistol on me? I think not," Lord Harry said.

As if to make his suggestion even more alluring, Lord Harry reached up to run his fingers over a loose strand of hair that fell against her neck. Her skin prickled at his touch and she felt warm. Drat, she should most certainly not feel that little thrill in the pit of her stomach. He was merely using her to barter! Her stupid body had no right to respond the way it did.

But then he leaned in and she felt his soft breath against her ear.

"Trust me."

She could barely make out the words, but heard them all the same. What could he mean? Could he honestly expect her to trust him after all he'd done? Of course she wouldn't. Then again, she had little else to hope in just now. Did she dare trust him? Could he have some sort of plan to save them despite his cruel bargain with the leering brute? She didn't know which would be more foolish, to trust him now or not to.

The thug seemed blissfully unaware that any communication had passed between them. He was still shamelessly scrutinizing her, his eyes flicking up and down. She hated it, but was not so nauseated that she didn't realize that as long as he was in this manner distracted, Lord Harry might stand a better chance of overtaking him. If indeed that was something near to his plan. If indeed he truly had a plan.

Hoping she'd chosen wisely, she drew a long, deep breath and let her wrapper fall slightly open. The thug's eyes grew wider and darker. Wretched man.

"So," Lord Harry asked the man after a pause long enough for her to breathe a few more times, "do we have a bargain?"

The thug put his tongue back into his mouth to answer. "She ain't likely going to cooperate."

"Hmm, no that's true. Very well, I'll tell you what. I'll help you bind her before I leave."

"Bind her?" the man questioned.

"Yes, bind her?" Penelope repeated.

Lord Harry nodded toward a pile of something in the corner. "I noticed a rope. If you agree to let me go, I'll help you bind her."

This seemed an intriguing notion to their captor. His lip twitched. "Bind her, eh?"

"She likes it," Lord Harry added, which really was going a bit further than necessary.

"Very well," the thug said. "Get the rope."

"I'll need some light," Lord Harry said, picking up the small oil lamp and moving toward the corner.

"Don't be trying nothing tricky, though," the man said, apparently not as entirely brainless as he seemed.

"It was just over here," Lord Harry said, ignoring the man's warning and poking at some of the formless refuse piled in the corner. "I saw it when my uncle came in here with that lantern."

Penelope stayed where she was, now in shadow. This seemed to confuse the thug. He glanced rapidly back and forth between her and Lord Harry, not quite able to decide who to train the pistol on. Perhaps this was what Lord Harry was hoping for, a moment of distraction where he could overpower the man, or make a dash for the door. Yet he did nothing. He was still in the corner poking through debris. Was he, perhaps, waiting for her?

But what could she do? She felt so helpless, and she hated it. Never before had her wits abandoned her like this. Should she attack the man? Or should she simply wait for Lord Harry to act? She didn't much like that option. What if he truly had no intention of saving her? Or worse, what if he did and he got himself killed in the process?

Well, she simply could not have that. If the man did have any intention of saving her—and she wished to give him every opportunity to do just that—then he would no doubt appreciate a distraction. She would have to create one for him.

Grabbing at her skirt, she suddenly hoisted it up to her knees and began screaming.

"A mouse! Oh heavens, a mouse ran over my foot!"

She danced around frantically, putting herself farther and farther away from Lord Harry and pulling her skirt up higher and higher to give the thug the best view possible in the muted lamplight. His eyes followed her intently. The pistol was now not precisely aimed at either one of them.

"Help! I think it ran up into my underthings!" she cried, tugging at her clothing in the most provocative ways she could think of. "Get it out! Oh, get it out of there!"

Dancing her way toward the thug she leaned forward, jiggling her body with all her might as she pretended to dig for a wayward mouse down the front of her nightgown. She felt like an idiot, but it was clear that she had the thug's complete attention at this point. The pistol practically hung limp in his hand as he watched her every move, transfixed. She heard her gown tear and could only wonder just how much of a show she was giving him, but it was all for a worthy cause. She hoped.

From the corner of her eye she could see Lord Harry moving toward them. She barely had a moment to realize what he was doing, and then it was done. He had launched himself at the thug and the two of them toppled over, clattering to the floor in a heap.

She had to jump out of the way as the two men wrestled, arms and fists flailing in the dim light. The pistol hit the floor with a thud, then skittered just out of reach of either of them. Drat, but it seemed the hired brute had not been as completely caught off guard as she had hoped. He still had ample energy to battle Lord Harry.

Well, she could put an end to that. She scooped up the gun and yelled at them.

"Stop it, or I'll shoot!"

They didn't stop. This was not good. If she did fire the weapon, there was a chance she might hit Lord Harry. Plus, then the weapon would be useless—she had no clue how to go about reloading it. What on earth could she do to put an end to their vicious pummeling and give Lord Harry a chance to take the upper hand?

Very well, she had distracted the thug once. She could surely do it again, couldn't she? It would simply require a bit more drastic measures.

Tucking the pistol between her legs, she reached to her neckline and began working at the fastenings of her nightgown. Her fingers were cold and clumsy, so she ended up ripping at the fabric. By God, she'd find a way to get that man's attention.

She felt her clothes begin to sag, so she slid the thin gown off her shoulders and over her arms. Heavens, but it was chilly in this damp room. Her thin shift remained intact to barely cover her, but it did little to dispel the cold. Or the fear.

Retrieving the pistol, she allowed the nightgown to slide down, past her waist and over her hips. It fell into a heap on the floor. Such a pretty garment of very fine linen; she hated to sacrifice it this way, but this was a desperate maneuver for a desperate situation.

"Oh help, my nightgown fell off!" she cried out.

No reaction from the two men pounding at each other on the floor. How insulting! She'd best try again.

"I said, help! My clothing fell off!"

This time she was heard. The frantic forms on the floor slowed just a bit. She took a deep breath, praying this would work.

"Oh dear. What if my shift should fall off next? I would be left completely naked!"

Aha, she caught a set of eyes. Yes, the wrestlers were faltering. Any second now Lord Harry would take his opportunity and . . . But wait, those weren't enemy eyes fixed on her. They were Lord Harry's! Oh, for pity's sake, she'd distracted the wrong man.

The thug flopped Lord Harry onto his back and raised up a fist, aiming to obliterate his beautiful face. She was too far away to do anything but give out a worried shriek, almost feeling the force of the man's blow herself. It did not land in Lord Harry's face, however.

Her cry had been just enough to warn him of the impending strike, and he turned his head just at the last moment. The thug plunged his fist hard into the floor. Boards cracked—or perhaps it was bone—and the man let out a pained screech. In a split second Lord Harry had regained his focus and took full advantage of the man's injury.

He thrust the thug off, rolling onto his feet and stomping hard onto the man's wounded hand. The thug cried out. Penelope cringed as more cracking was heard. Most unpleasant business!

"Give me the pistol, Penelope," Lord Harry ordered.

She'd forgotten she had it. Gladly, she handed it over. Lord Harry stood over his victim, holding the pistol directly over his face.

"Now tell me what my uncle plans to do," he said.

The man groaned, so Lord Harry lowered the pistol an inch and repeated his question.

"What are my uncle's plans?"

"He's already done most of it," the man snarled. "He's sent word to yer Egyptian friends that you turned on them, that you and the other fellow took all that stuff and sold it."

"I know about all that. Why did he bring Miss Rastmoor here? What are his plans for her?"

The man merely shrugged. Lord Harry applied more pressure onto his hand and jammed the gun into his cheek.

"Why is she here? Tell me or your next of kin will be digging teeth out of your brains."

Penelope swallowed back something she'd already swallowed once today. Most unpleasant business, indeed!

"She's here 'cause your uncle likes the looks of her, that's why. He says you ain't worthy of something like that so he figures he'll take her for himself then do away with her and say you done it."

"What? That's insane. I'm engaged to be married to her! No one will believe I'd do anything to harm her."

"Won't matter much when you're dead, will it? Oh yes, he's planning on getting rid of you, too. Tells me you've got some half-wit brother who ain't fit for the title. With you—and your little missy here—out of the way, I guess he thinks it might be time for your brother to finally succumb to his weak constitution."

"He wouldn't dare!"

Lord Harry's face had gone red, and for a heartbeat or two Penelope thought he might actually pull the trigger and scatter the man's facial features all over. He didn't, though. He simply growled once, then stepped away, still keeping his lethal aim.

"Penelope, get the rope," he said.

She didn't dare disobey. Hurrying, she ran to the corner where the oil lamp still glowed and where a length of rope could be seen among the refuse. So he'd been truthful about that. She only hoped he hadn't been quite honest about his intended use for it.

"Tie him up," he said.

Ah, good. He'd been planning to use the rope on their attacker all along. At least, she was content to believe that.

She retrieved the rope and quickly did as Lord Harry asked. She made sure the knots were tight, and only half apologized when she had to secure the man's damaged hand. He hadn't been particularly kindhearted toward them, after all. Lord Harry balled up a nearby rag and stuffed it into the man's mouth.

Then he rummaged the man's clothing and eventually produced a large, lethal knife that had been hidden in his boot.

"Ah, now this is rather nice," Lord Harry said with a smile.

The thug tried to kick him, but the ropes held him helpless. Perhaps he might have cursed, but that rag in his mouth prevented that, too. Penelope rather liked this arrangement.

"Let's go," Lord Harry said, finishing his task and tucking the knife in his own boot. He jammed the pistol into his trousers at his waist.

He took her arm and led her to the door. One turn of the knob and they were free; their captor had not locked them in, relying on his thug to keep them there. The night air around them was silent and dark. A large wall surrounded the docks area, but that only added to the shadow and mystery of the place. It was easy enough to slink along it and keep out of view from anyone who might have been prowling about.

"My uncle's carriage is gone," Lord Harry whispered. "So is the one they brought me in. They must have gone to collect the treasures. We'll have to find a way out of here. Just keep quiet, and stay with me."

She nodded, not exactly certain where else he'd think she might go just now. She was hardly dressed for a ball. She was hardly dressed for anything, as a matter of fact. That might present a problem.

HE COULD FEEL HER SHIVER AS THEY MADE THEIR WAY along a darkened alley. So far they'd seen no one, but he'd heard the voices. The night watch was patrolling the docks, and of course this part of town was never fully asleep. He knew if there was any hope of rescuing his father and getting those artifacts back, they'd have to hurry, but in Penelope's condition . . .

Well, he couldn't very well drag a nearly naked woman all through London while her teeth chattered and she died of the cold, could he? No, somehow he'd have to tend to her needs before he could take care of the rest. Somehow.

God, but he'd nearly lost his mind when they'd found she'd been taken. To see her then, huddled in that filthy room . . . He'd been overwhelmed with relief, yet at the same time ready to commit murder. To think that someone could have hurt her—and that it would have been his own damn fault for dragging her into this mess—had been more than he could bear.

Whatever he did now, he would see that she was safe first.

"Here, put this on," he said, sliding out of his coat.

She didn't argue. Her slender arms slipped easily into his sleeves, and he could tell she appreciated the warmth. He appreciated the sight of her in his clothing.

Damn, but what had she been thinking, stripping off her nightclothes back there? Yes, he supposed she'd hoped to create a diversion, but did she honestly think he'd be able to think straight with her nightgown dropping down to the floor like that? Didn't she know what that would do to him?

Apparently not. Even now, with their lives in peril and danger just footsteps away, she glanced up at him with an innocent smile. Even after all this she trusted him to keep her safe. Hell. He wanted to keep her, true, but *safe* was not the first word that came to mind at the thought.

Naked. Sated. Begging for more. Yes, those were all the ways he'd like to keep her. *Safe* didn't exactly enter the picture until much farther down on the list.

Not that he would ever let damn Nedley anywhere near her again. Nor any of these hired thugs, either, nor any other unsavory type who might seek to use her for some nefarious purpose. Unfortunately, he was afraid he'd have to include himself among that number.

Damn it, but he needed to get her back to Rastmoor. Quickly.

He found an old door in the high wall around the docks. It was locked up tight, but when he tried it the hinges groaned and then broke. He slid the door out of the way and peered out. The city streets were dark and quiet. Perfect.

"Let's go," he said, taking her hand and leading her through. "Let's go find you some clothes."

She frowned at him. "Clothes? But we need to rescue Professor Oldham!"

"I'll handle that. First I need to get you safely home, and it will be a lot easier to do that if you aren't displaying yourself all over town in your underclothes."

She was, apparently, clever enough not to argue. If she were seen out here with him like this, her reputation would be ruined. Even more than he'd already ruined it. Yes, Oldham needed rescue, but Penelope would come first.

They stayed in the shadows, leaving the docks behind. It was necessary to travel a bit before they came to anything resembling a decent shop, but eventually Harris spotted something promising. A tiny shop selling an assortment of used items, including clothing. Broken windows in the upstairs apartments indicated they were abandoned. Good. No one around to hear them break in.

He took Penelope around to the rear of the shop where he motioned for her to be silent as he pried at the lock at the shabby door. She seemed appalled.

"We can't simply break in!" she hissed.

He shushed her and simply broke in. Drawing the pistol and

keeping her behind him, he led them inside. The place was small, but thankfully empty of any shopkeeper. Shutting the door behind them, he guided her toward the front of the shop where some of the more enticing items were located. She followed hesitantly.

"Here," he said, leaving the pistol at the ready on a nearby table so he could grab up an attractive muslin that hung on a rack with several others. "Try this."

"But it isn't mine!"

"Of course it isn't yours. I cannot get you all the way back to Mayfair without someone seeing you, and they cannot see you dressed in . . . well, in nothing."

"I have your coat over me. It covers."

"Not enough."

Indeed, not nearly enough. Even now, he could see more than enough of her to want her. Badly. She was safe and alive and warm, and he ached to get her into his arms again. Only a true blackguard would think these things about her after the way she'd already been treated tonight. And he thought them repeatedly.

"Very well," she said with a dramatic sigh.

She began shrugging out of his coat, and he found himself helping her. By God, he should probably not stand this close as he helped the woman disrobe. Still, he could not find it in himself to move farther away. He watched, enthralled, as the coat slid off to reveal her feminine form displayed plainly through the thin fabric of her night-damp shift. Breathtaking.

The coat fell away and she stepped closer, reaching to take the muslin gown from him. He found that his hand would not release it to her. Finally her gaze came up to meet his. He knew exactly what he wanted to say to her, what he ought to say to her, but words would not come. He could do nothing but stare into those huge, trusting eyes.

"Please don't take me back to Anthony just yet," she said. "You'll need help to rescue the prof—er, your father."

"I will find help. You need to be safely home, where you belong."

"I don't want to go home. I want to go with you."

Damn it, but he didn't want to argue with her now. There

were a good number of things he did want to do with her, but arguing was not one.

"You can't. You need to be safe."

She was so close he could feel the heat from her body, see the little bumps on her skin where the night air touched her with a chill. Her eyes were so deep he felt himself falling in and drowning.

"I don't want to be safe," she said.

Oh hell. He responded the only way he could. He pulled her to him and tilted her face up toward him so he could kiss her senseless.

God, but she tasted good. His lips took hers and he wondered if she realized she was anything but safe now. The pounding in his veins supplanted any voice of reason that might have reminded him who he was and what he was about. Apparently he was senseless, too.

His hands roamed over her body, the shift being brushed aside so he could feel the satin warmth of her skin. He cupped her breast. The breathy gasp she gave only made him want more, so his thumb found her nipple and stroked over it until he was rewarded by a hardened little peak. She returned his kiss with the same desperation he felt inside himself.

She pressed herself against him, her tongue playing with his and her fingers digging into the damp linen of his shirt. The fact that she seemed to want him every bit as badly as he wanted her did nothing to promote gentlemanly behavior. He kissed her ruthlessly as his body strained against his trousers.

Hell and damnation, the girl strained right back against him. By God, she was arching herself into him, rubbing her soft, warm curves over his most sensitive area. If she wasn't careful, she'd end up getting much more than a few stolen kisses. He was on fire for her, and it wouldn't take much to fan that flame into an inferno. They'd both be lost forever.

Her family had saved her before, at Lady Burlington's ball. Tonight she was alone, completely at his mercy. If he didn't get control of himself, no one would.

HOW COULD HE POSSIBLY BE IN SUCH PERFECT CONTROL of himself? After all they'd been through, seeing him nearly beat to death by that horrible thug, Penelope could scarcely keep her hands off him. The thought of losing him forever made her all the more hungry to keep him with her now.

Yet he was pushing her away, babbling something about needing to keep her safe, take her back to Anthony. She did not want to go to Anthony. She did not want to go anywhere. She wanted to be with Lord Harry.

"I thought I was lost, waking up in that smelly little storeroom with some strange man," she said when he pulled back and tried to take her hands off his neck. "Then you showed up and I knew I'd be safe."

"You won't be if you don't put this dress on and let me take you back to your brother," he said.

"I don't want my brother," she said, realizing she was going to have to be painfully honest with the man. "I want *you*."

He paused for a moment before he replied. "No you don't, Penelope. You've been through a lot . . . a terrifying ordeal, I'm sure. Perhaps you feel something for me right now, but it's nothing more than gratitude."

Gratitude? The man was very much mistaken.

"I do feel something, Lord Harry," she said, bold enough to reach right out and grab the man's trousers where they fastened at the front flap. "But it is hardly mere gratitude, I assure you. Can you possibly not feel something of it, too? When you had me alone at Lady Burlington's ball I thought perhaps you did. Was that purely for show, or did you enjoy more than simply stealing my scarab that night?"

"My behavior that night was reprehensible. I should never have taken such liberties."

"Then why did you?"

"Because I wanted you, damn it! And I want you now, but I need to take you home."

"So my brother can ship me off to spend the rest of my life in exile? You know as well as I do that's what will happen to me now."

"But you'll be safe."

Safe. The word sounded like profanity. All her life everyone wanted her to be safe. She'd been so safe she'd never even learned what to do in a moment like this, when her insides were on fire and she'd have been willing to do or say anything just to get this man to kiss her again.

"And what of you?" she asked. "Will you be safe?"

"You know I have to rescue my father, and get those artifacts back, if I can."

He wouldn't be safe. And then he'd be gone. If he didn't simply get himself killed, he'd likely head back to Egypt. She would grow old and die without him. She'd be safe, but she'd be alone.

But she was not alone now. Indeed, as long as Lord Harry was here with her, she was safe. And she was determined not to miss her one last chance to find out what might have been, if the man she loved had turned out to be the right fiancé and not the very wrong one. She moved closer, working at the fastenings on his trousers.

"I don't want to be safe," she whispered, feeling her cheeks go warm at her own brazenness. "I want you."

"Penelope," he said, placing his hands over hers and meeting her gaze steadily. "Don't. I'm not the sort of tame little pup that you're used to."

"And thank God for that. I never wanted any of them before."

He leaned in to kiss her. She was almost afraid to give in to it, worried that just as soon as she did he'd pull away again and start trying to be noble and gentlemanly. But he didn't. His chaste, tentative kiss grew in heat and intensity.

His arms went around her and he pulled her to him. She willingly melted into him and gave her lips up for his full use. He took them greedily, his wonderful hands skimming over her back, touching her and igniting her.

He was holding her so tightly her fingers had to abandon their efforts at his trousers, so she contented herself by pulling up his rumpled shirt and sliding her hands up underneath. His skin was as hot as hers felt now. The light hairs running in a teasing line up from his waist to his chest delighted her fingertips. She played at studying him, enjoying him.

Thankfully he released her mouth so she could draw a long, needed breath. His kisses did not end, though. They followed the line of her jaw and her neck and her shoulders. It was heavenly, waves of scorching sensation following everywhere he touched her with his lips or his hands. She pressed closer in to him, breathing in his scent.

Indeed, she'd never wanted any of this with any other man before. It was impossible to imagine ever wanting it with another. Apparently for her it was Lord Harry or no one. He was more than enough. She would simply have to drink her fill of him tonight and savor it in her memories once he was gone.

Now he was working at her shift, pushing it aside and finding access to what was beneath. She sighed as his fingers brushed her nipples, his hands coming over her breasts to hold them, cup them, tilt them toward him as his kisses came down to worship them. She raked her fingers through his thick dark hair, praying he would never stop as he took first one, then the other hardened peak, into his mouth.

She slid her arms around him again, clawing at his shirt and gathering it into her fists. With one easy tug, she pulled it from him and over his head. He seemed surprised and pulled back from her, but only to look down and smile. She realized she was smiling, too. Ah, but the man's chest was a wonder to behold.

He was solid and well sculpted, like the marbles she'd visited time and again at the British Museum. Only better. He was warm and living. And hers for the taking.

"You play unfairly, Miss Rastmoor," he said. "I am shirtless, but yet I must still battle the fabric of your annoying shift."

Well, that was easily remedied. She bunched it up in her fists, too, and yanked it over her head. The cold air washed over her, but it only served to make her skin all the more sensitive to his nearness, the heat radiating from him.

"Now who is unfair, sir?" she asked, cocking one eyebrow at his trousers.

He didn't reply. He seemed temporarily incapable of it. Instead, his mouth merely froze in a half-open state and his eyes shifted to search her body, from head to toe. She stood motionless, willing herself not to flee such careful scrutiny.

Never had any man seen her this way, in the very state God and nature had created her. Rarely had she seen her own self, dashing quickly between changes as the bathwater cooled and she slipped into fresh attire. Did he like what he was seeing now? Was he pleased with all she had to offer him? It was everything she could do not to beg him to speak.

Finally he did. "Good God, Penelope. You're beautiful."

Ah, that was a most excellent reply. The fact that the truth of it was evident in his expression made her go warm all over. She didn't have to move back to him because in an instant he had reached for her and pulled her into another embrace. She soaked up his warmth.

"I want you so badly," he murmured.

The truth of that was evident as well, although not so much in his face as in his trousers. She tried to slide her hands to his waist again, working at the fastenings. He was kissing her neck and then her earlobe, which seemed to do something to affect her balance. The fastenings were not unfastening. The sensations of his kisses and his skin pressed against hers were nearly too much to bear.

She wobbled a bit. His eyes met hers and she saw the question in them. She knew what he asked.

"Yes," was all she managed to say.

He didn't wait for more. In an instant, he scooped her into his arms and was kissing her lips. Something brushed against her arm and she realized in her wobbling state she had leaned a bit too far in one direction and thrown him off-balance. They listed into a rack of clothing. It tumbled to the floor, spreading an assortment of dresses, coats, wrappers, and other soft sundries into a careless pile.

She glanced down at the pile, then back up at Lord Harry. He was holding her tightly and let out his breath in a ragged sigh.

"Are you certain this is what you want?"

"I am," she assured him, knowing exactly what he meant.

Carefully, he stooped to lower her into the scattered pile. It was remarkably comfortable. Probably, she decided, that was because Lord Harry was there with her. She pulled his face toward hers for another kiss. Or two.

She was touching him all over, running her hands over his muscular back, the sturdy form of his arms, across his very firm backside. Ah, but she did like that part of him. How much nicer, though, if she could finally get rid of those trousers. She went back to work on the fastenings.

He chuckled at her fumbling, then finally took pity and helped her. As he moved slightly away to lean on one elbow beside her, the placket finally fell open. She was presented with the vision of a lifetime.

"Oh! My!"

He was going to speak, but she decided she did not really wish for conversation just now. She pressed her fingertips to his lips and went on with her investigation of the magnificent object below. *My my my my my.*

He seemed content to allow her perusal. Would he permit her to do more? She dared to find out. Carefully, not wishing to cause any discomfort, she reached out and touched him. There.

He drew a sharp breath the moment she made contact. She pulled her hand back and glanced up at his face. He was smirking.

"Frightened?" he asked.

"I don't want to hurt you."

At that he laughed. "I assure you, that is not very likely."

"Are you certain? It seems rather . . . sensitive."

"Oh, it is. Just as I know for a fact you yourself have one or two very sensitive areas."

She was blushing again, wasn't she? To make matters worse, he was just now touching her in one of her very sensitive areas. His hand slid along her thigh and came closer, closer to that part of her he'd been introduced to at the ball. Oh, but she did hope they furthered their acquaintance!

Trying to ignore the dizzying waves of pleasure his touch brought her, she reached to touch him in a similar manner. As his fingers danced around her delicate cleft, hers glided over the velvet softness of his rock-hard member. Did this cause the same wonderful sensations for him that it did for her? Oh, but she hoped so.

Still not certain just what she was allowed, she let her fingers circle him. Goodness, but the girth of the thing was remarkable. At least, she assumed that it was. The man seemed so extraordinary in every other way, she could only expect that this was no different. She realized his breathing altered a bit as she stroked him up and down.

"This is good?" she asked.

He had to swallow before answering. "Yes. This is good."

Well then, it seemed she had puzzled out what to do already. She tightened her grip on him ever so slightly and increased the speed of her gentle stroking. He seemed pleased, but then he did a similar thing to her—increasing the fervor of his attentions—and she found it suddenly difficult to concentrate.

The same overwhelming feelings that had nearly sent her out of her own body when he was doing these things to her at Lady Burlington's ball began to swirl and gather inside her core. She felt her body becoming not her own, but a separate entity that responded purely on instinct, rocking against him, pressing into his hand as it explored her and caressed her most intimate area.

She tightened her grip on him, hoping this would anchor her, but somehow that seemed to only make the sensations within her grow stronger. It was building rapidly, her breathing coming now in short gasps and muffled moans. It was terrifying and heavenly all at the same time.

Just as she was about to cry out, overcome by it all, he stopped. He moved away from her, putting his hand over hers where she still held him in a fist. She blinked, suddenly worried she'd hurt him after all.

"Wait," he said. "I cannot take it if you keep doing that, and I insist that you at least let me be a gentleman in this one area, my dear."

"What?" He was not making sense and she was desperate for him to get back to what he'd been doing.

"Ladies first," he said.

That didn't make any sense, either, but then it hardly mattered as he shifted position, kissing her between the breasts, across the belly, around her naval, and at last dropping a long, heated kiss onto her aching, desperate need. She fell back into the clothing around her and tried to gulp back another moan.

Heavens! He was kissing her there, and then some. He was not only kissing, but exploring, nibbling, and suckling. His tongue was tasting her, invading her. She could barely breathe from the sensations this new method produced. Oh, but the man was ingenious!

Again, she was rocking with him, letting him do as he pleased and discovering that with every move he made, every subtle touch, she was falling deeper into his trance. It was as if the room around them whirled with color and the blood pounded inside her head. He was carrying her to a place she'd never been, could have never even imagined. She dug her fingers into his arms, his back, his shoulders. Any part of him she could grasp, frantic for salvation.

Just when she felt as if she could take no more, her body rocked with the ecstasy his actions had brought. Far more intense than anything she'd experienced before, she fell into his care and let the waves wash over her. Nothing around her existed, only his body and hers.

Just as she was beginning to think perhaps she would not die from pleasure, he was shifting again. This time, he was over her, his eyes meeting hers. He was questioning her again.

Since she knew she'd never be able to speak coherently, all she could do was smile and wrap her arms around him, bringing him closer. He understood. Whatever he was willing to take from her tonight, she was willing to give.

His kisses were warm and sweet over her lips, her throat, her shoulders. She held him, her nipples tingling from the brush of his skin. She felt him, his most fascinating part, pressing against her. His movement caused another wave of wonderful sensation, then suddenly he was entering her.

It was a bit shocking at first, not quite what she'd been feeling thus far, but certainly not painful. He pressed into her, filling her and causing a moment's panic as she instantly worried that she'd made the wrong choice here. What was she doing? How could she actually accommodate such a... well, he'd seemed fairly large and she doubted she was...

Oh! Indeed, she could accommodate! Very well, apparently. Good heavens, but he was completely inside and her body was involuntarily clenching around him, enjoying the feel of this new experience. The raging ocean that had begun to calm inside her roared to storming tumult again and she was once more feeling a bit wobbly.

"Penelope..." he said, breathing her name into her ear.

"It's wonderful!" she said, arching her body toward his.

The movement seemed to encourage him. Slowly he shifted and for a heartbeat it seemed as if he would leave her body too soon, but then he was thrusting, entering her again, even more fully than before. She moaned in response. How could he possibly be bringing her to yet a higher plane of such indefinable pleasure?

He was, though. It seemed as if he were as lost as she was in this new world of wonderful. His motions increased in power, in urgency as he thrust again and again, his body nearly crushing her and the waves of pleasure rocking her again and again. She drew whatever breath she could, and cried out when the delight of it all became too much. His own passion seemed to be growing, too, and just as she was swept away by completion, she felt him reaching his own.

Her body welcomed his climax, and she clung tightly as they both spiraled back to reality. It was not a rapid descent. When he finally moved to the side, freeing her to fill her lungs at last, she realized he glistened from perspiration. Indeed, she was burning with heat herself, even in the cold night air.

It had been wonderful. Unimaginable. Everything she could have wished for. She snuggled against him and allowed herself to simply breathe, to feel the various muscles in her body tingle and settle into this new state of being. Indeed, everything about her seemed to have been changed.

Did he know? Was he possibly aware of all this had meant to her? She doubted it. She hoped not. It had been selfish on her part to demand this from him when, truly, there were so many other things he needed to deal with. But she would never regret her demands.

He would leave her soon, but she would always have this night.

"You must be cold," he said after some minutes of holding her closely in the darkness and silence.

"You've kept me quite warm," she replied, carefully keeping any awkward sentiment from showing in her voice.

"Are you . . . well?"

"Yes, thank you. That was very nicely done."

"Er, I'm happy to hear it. You don't feel any . . . that is . . ."

"I feel fine, thank you. You have no need to worry that I am in any way disappointed."

"Indeed, I'm relieved to hear it, but—"

"Was it adequate for you?"

"Adequate?"

She thought he might actually be about to laugh at her, but she didn't look up into his face to find out. Better that she didn't see if he felt he might need to lie and tell her it was more enjoyable for him than it truly was. After all, he was an expert at this. No doubt her efforts had been somewhat rudimentary as far as his own pleasure was concerned. She had no wish to hear him confess it, though.

"Did you enjoy yourself, sir?"

"Hell, Penelope, you were amazing."

Well, if the man were lying, he did it well. She was pleased with his estimation and decided not to consider the likelihood of him simply being polite. She wanted so badly to believe she'd been amazing for him.

"And of course I understand the responsibility that accompanies such actions and I want you to rest assured that—"

She stopped him. "No, there is no need for that. I was quite aware of what I was doing, and I thank you. Please don't spoil it now by pretending it was anything more than it was."

She was quite proud of herself. Her voice sounded perfectly sensible and relaxed, as if she did this sort of thing with gentlemen all the time and never gave it another thought. She forced a smile and settled into a comfortable snuggle again.

Indeed, he claimed she had been amazing and that was all there was to this. They both enjoyed the encounter and soon it would be ended. She would let him go and simply be grateful for the memories she would carry forever.

She refused to waste her final moments with him in silly, obligatory rhetoric. She did not need him to take any responsibility for anything. That would be supremely unfair of her, given the circumstances. As much as she ached to hear him lie and tell her he cared or had any hope of a future with her, she could not allow him to be so noble.

He would only come to resent her for it, and she would hate herself for that.

Chapter Twenty

He hated himself. What sort of man would take advantage of a woman this way? Especially a woman he fancied himself in love with. By God, how had he let it come to this? He truly was in love with her and this is how he'd treated her. Indeed, what sort of man did that? The very worst sort of man, and that was what he was.

How could he have done this, taken her here, in this anonymous little shop like some cheap whore? She should have had a wedding night with satin pillows and scented rose water. What had he given her? Memories of a frenzied coupling on a pile of old clothes. That was no way to start out their life together—if in fact he could hold any hope they might indeed have a life together.

Of course he couldn't. He'd caught her in a moment of weakness here; he'd never get her to agree to marriage in the clear light of day and the security of her home. Once she was safe and back where she belonged, she'd realize how he'd pounced on her in a vulnerable moment and she'd have nothing but regret for what passed between them here tonight. It was inevitable. She'd despise him.

How could she not? She was an intelligent woman, after all.

She knew he had nothing to recommend him; no money, no future, no honorable family, no good name . . . Indeed, he was the very last man a woman like Penelope Rastmoor deserved. Come morning, she would certainly realize this.

What a fool he was. If he tried to tell her how he felt, she would laugh in his face. This was not love. To call it that was an insult. But, by God, he had no idea what else to call it. Certainly lust could never rip his heart out and shred it this way.

Perhaps it was insanity. Indeed, that seemed likely. Only an insane person would lie here with a woman he'd so greatly wronged snuggled tightly against him while his own father was nearby in grave danger. He must be insane to be wishing for wedding bells when he knew full well his own uncle was planning his funeral. As was Burlington. And now, after this, Rastmoor would, too.

Bloody hell. Why did insanity have to feel so damn good?

Penelope snuggled in closer, nuzzling and kissing his neck. He closed his eyes to commit the feeling to memory. One that would have to get him through whatever life he had left, he supposed.

"Perhaps we should be on our way," she whispered.

He didn't comprehend her words at first. "What?"

"To find your father," she said.

Damn. The spell was broken. Already reality was seeping in, and any moment now she'd realize what he'd done and how much she hated him.

He'd best cut his losses and get moving. At least he could still save his father, even if his own life was in tatters. Oldham had hinted that their Egyptian friends might not have completely given up on them. Perhaps at least one of them still had something worth living for.

"Come then," he said, stirring and pulling his arm out from under her head. "The city will be waking soon. We should hurry."

He could not decide what her mood was now. She simply nodded and went about re-dressing herself. Was she hurt by his abruptness? Pleased that soon she'd be rid of him forever? Had she simply used him to soothe her nerves after a harrowing ordeal? Damn, but he hoped it was more than that.

She retrieved her shift and pulled on the stolen muslin, tugging at it where it clung to her delicious form and smoothing out the wrinkles. Even in someone else's dress with her hair disheveled she looked like a goddess. He'd give anything for the freedom to worship at her altar for the rest of his life. Or at least for the rest of this night.

But he had no such freedom, and no such right. All he could do was get her home safely, then bid farewell. That would be the best thing for her.

"Where do you suppose your uncle was taking Professor Oldham?" she asked as she tidied her hair, calm and collected as if she'd merely stepped in from the wind rather than been ravished by a scoundrel.

"I don't know," he replied, moving nearer and helping to do up the back of her gown.

"Lord Burlington's, perhaps?"

"Perhaps."

"Is that where we'll go, then?"

"No, first we'll take you home."

"There's no time for that! I can help you."

Hell. She was going to be difficult about this, wasn't she? He took her by the shoulders and turned her around to face him. It was a risky maneuver, considering how easy it would be to kiss her this way.

"No, you can't, Penelope," he said, and would have continued except that she interrupted.

"So you're going to charge in there all alone? And not expect to get yourself killed?"

He hoped this meant she was concerned for his well-being. More likely, though, she was questioning his effectiveness. Not that he could blame her; he was questioning it, himself.

"Hopefully I won't be alone," he replied.

"Because you'll have me with you."

"No, because my father told me where to go to find help. Armed, masculine help."

She frowned at him. "I didn't hear him mention anything about that."

"Well, he did. When he mentioned our Egyptian friends. They are here, in London."

"I believe he was lamenting the fact that they *aren't* here, actually."

"That's what it sounded like, but I believe he spoke in code."

"In *code*?"

She didn't believe him in the least. He had to agree, it did sound a bit far-fetched.

"He didn't want my uncle to know, but I'm certain he was saying that our friends from Egypt are here, in London."

"He was saying that?"

"Yes. He was."

"I didn't hear it."

"But it's what he meant."

"You're certain of this?"

"Yes." *Mostly.*

"Did he happen to tell you where in London we might find them?"

"In the same house where I've met with them before." *Hopefully.*

"And where is that?"

"Beyond Russell Square."

"And where are we now?"

"Well . . . I believe this would be Whitechapel."

"Oh," she replied, glancing toward the storefront window with new interest. "I've never been in this part of town before."

"I don't doubt it. And I fully intend to get you out of it as quickly as possible."

She smiled up at him as if they had simply been taking a stroll through the park. Damn it, but the girl was being intentionally thickheaded. When was she going to realize that her life was in danger and he'd been the one to cause it? Instead of rushing her back to safety, he'd tossed her on the floor and shagged her until they'd both lost track of time and reality. She truly ought to hate him—for everything.

"Then we should be off for Russell Square," she said. "How are you planning to go? Shall we walk?"

As if there were any other means. By God, her confounded optimism was grating. Especially when he knew how dramatically it would turn once the glow of lovemaking faded and she understood just what he'd done to her. And how he'd do it again in a heartbeat.

He was about to reiterate the importance of her not accompanying him to meet the Egyptians and the necessity for her to quietly allow him to take her directly home—at least as directly as they could make it with the darkened streets and who knew what manner of dangers between here and there—when a sound in the street caught his attention. A carriage! This could be a good thing, or it could be a bad thing.

He pushed her behind the one rack of clothing they did not topple in their heated passion.

"Hide yourself," he whispered, slinking into shadows and moving closer to peer out the front window.

She harrumphed at his precaution, but she stayed behind the rack. He glanced out into the street. The sound of a carriage rumbling toward them, with the clop of one set of hooves, echoed in the narrow space between buildings. He moved closer to the window, risking the moonlight filtering in.

There it was, just coming into view. Fortunately, it did not appear to be Uncle Nedley or any of his hirelings come to search for them. Nor did it appear to be some hapless hackney he might jog out and hire to carry them swiftly to Mayfair.

It was a rag-and-bone man.

Damn. The lone mule plodded listlessly, and the cart—not carriage—behind it wobbled to the left and to the right. The various items piled into the cart jostled about, too, clattering and clanking. Somehow, the driver seemed to be able to sleep through it all.

No one stirred at his approach. A dog barked from an alleyway, but the mule ignored it and lumbered along. Somehow the piles of rubbish and secondhand wares managed not to tumble out onto the street while the driver hunched over and snored. The cart drew no attention and left no trail. Aside from the clopping, the rattling, and the snoring, it was almost as if it were not really there at all.

Ah, but that gave him an idea.

"Hurry! Come on!" he called, moving swiftly to retrieve his nearly forgotten pistol.

Penelope stuck her head out from behind the clothes. He could see her gaze catch on the cart rolling by, and she seemed to gather what he had planned. She smiled at him.

"That's perfect! No one would think to look for us on that cart. You're brilliant, sir."

Trying not to swell too much with pride—or anything else—

he unlocked the front door and led her quickly out into the street. He called to wake the rag-and-bone man.

"We need conveyance," he said.

The man eyed him, then eyed Penelope. Then eyed her again. If the man hadn't been nearly ancient Harris might have knocked him off his rackety perch. As it was, he simply gave him a warning glare.

"What have ye got for me?" the old man asked after a moment or two.

Damn. He was penniless.

"I have a ring!" Penelope said.

She held up her hand to display a demure little band. Of course Harris was loath to let her part with it, but they needed to be on that cart quickly. Besides, he was taking the girl home. Once there, no doubt Rastmoor could purchase her ring back for her.

The savvy man was pleased to receive her ring in exchange for delivering them across town. Harris helped her into the cart then went to give the man directions, careful not to let her hear. If she realized he had no intention of taking her to find his Egyptian friends with him she'd likely begin arguing all over again. Best let her settle in quietly.

The old man agreed to convey them, polishing his new acquisition and placing it in his pocket. Harris was congratulating himself on such a smooth transaction when Penelope let out a startling squeal. He whirled, looking for danger yet finding merely Penelope digging through some of the items collected in the old man's cart.

"What is it?" he asked.

She pulled out a length of brightly colored fabric. No, it was more than that. It was trimmed and finished—a shawl. Dear God, it was identical to the hideous item he'd purchased for her at that shop several days ago. What horror would allow two of these to exist?

Judging by Penelope's reaction to it, though, the world could not hold enough of these monstrosities.

"How much for this?" she called to the old man, hugging the shawl like a precious thing.

"What else have ye got?" the man asked.

"Penelope, you've already got one just like it," Harris

reminded her, wondering if the night's events hadn't finally taken their toll.

But she shook her head. "No, I don't. I was angry with you so I threw it out."

And now she regretted it. Ah, but the sentiment was so dear Harris practically rejoiced aloud. She cherished the ugly thing he had given her!

"It's mine now," the old man reminded. "Ye want it back, ye'll be payin' for it."

Her expression fell and she looked as if she might suddenly cry. Oh God, Harris would give anything to prevent that. He rummaged his pockets, desperate for something of value. Ah! Yes, he did have something.

"No, not the knife!" Penelope said when he pulled it from his boot.

The old man paled. "Now, I don't want no trouble, here . . ."

"Take it," he said, handing it to the man. "The lady needs her shawl."

Penelope tried to protest, but he would have none of it. The old man seemed pleased with his haul, and at last their bartering was done. Harris climbed up into the cart and settled himself beside Penelope.

"What if you need that?" she asked quietly when they were hidden among the contents of the cart and clattering along the road.

He patted his side where the pistol still rested. "I have the other."

She shuddered at the thought, but said nothing more about it. He pulled her tight up against him. There'd be hell to pay once he got her home to Rastmoor, but for now she was content to rest against him, yawning. He tucked the shawl around her and really did not mind that he'd had to buy the dreadful thing twice.

SHE MUST HAVE DRIFTED TO SLEEP, BECAUSE SHE'D BEEN blissfully unaware of her uncomfortable surroundings until a pot from the rag-and-bone man's pile dropped onto her lap and startled her. She roused quickly, glancing at the darkened houses around them and eventually recognizing them. Mayfair! Heavens, they'd come all the way to Mayfair already.

"Shh, don't worry. You're safe now."

Lord Harry was beside her, his arm wrapped snugly around her in the most caring manner. She liked that, but not that he'd brought her here. She'd not heard Lord Harry give the old man directions or she'd surely have argued.

"You need to go find your friends, not bring me home!" she protested now.

"After I know you are safe, then I'll go find them."

So it had been his intent all along to leave her. She should have known. So far he'd found her useful for just one thing, hadn't he?

Not that she was complaining about that. Good gracious, no! That had been wonderful, heavenly. She only wished she'd been able to prove to him that she had other good qualities, as well. That there were other things about her that might interest him, might be of use to him. She wanted him to want her near him, and obviously he did not. This should come as no surprise.

"But when will . . ." she began to ask, wishing he might give her some hope that he'd find a way to be with her again, but her words trailed off as she became aware of a great commotion ahead.

She craned her neck to see around the masses of rags and dishes and broken chairs that surrounded them. Indeed, there were carriages and torches up ahead, just around the bend on Regent Street, just beyond the next . . . Why, it was just in front of her own home!

What was happening? She strained for a better look.

"Got us a ruction, we do," the rag-and-bone man said, his raspy voice making Penelope jump again. "Want I should go around it?"

Lord Harry had peered around the piles on his own side of the cart, and now he glanced back at Penelope, his brow furrowed.

"I hope it's nothing that—"

But he stopped. They could hear shouting ahead. It was Anthony! His voice rang out, the words reaching them quite clearly through the empty street.

"It's Chesterton!" he was declaring loudly. "I don't know where he's taken her or how he thinks I'll let him get away with this, but we will find him. I'll see my sister safe, and I'll see him hanged!"

There were other voices, too, but they were just a muddle of noise. Not that they mattered. It was clear what was happening. Anthony thought Lord Harry had kidnapped her, and now he was rousing a party to go after him! Well, how fortunate that soon she and Lord Harry would be there to tell them the truth of the matter.

But Lord Harry called up to the driver. "Stop! Don't go any farther."

She looked at him, perplexed. "But that's my brother! He's looking for us."

"Indeed he is, and it appears he's enlisted the night watch and a pack of bloody constables."

"Oh my, has he?" she peered around, trying to get as good a view as Lord Harry seemed to have.

The driver did as commanded and pulled his tired mule to a halt. Indeed, she could make out several large men collecting in the roadway ahead. Rather sweet of Anthony, it was, to go to so much trouble to find her. She hoped everyone wouldn't be too very upset when they arrived to prove all this clamor to be unnecessary.

If, of course, they did arrive. Why had Lord Harry ordered the man to stop the cart? She turned to him, questioning.

"I can't go with you," he said before she had a chance to ask.

"What do you mean?"

"Your brother is looking to have me hanged!"

"But once I tell him you had nothing to do with those awful men taking me, then—"

"Then he will still hate me and I'll have to answer a thousand questions and the constables will haul me in and it will be tomorrow afternoon before I can convince anyone to let me go."

And by then something dreadful could have happened to his father. Oh, but she understood his quandary immediately. He did not have to say any more.

"You *cannot* come with me!" she agreed.

"I'm sorry," he said, taking one of her hands in his and raising it to his lips. "I'm truly, truly sorry. For all of it."

"I'm not," she said, realizing what he planned to do. "But please don't simply—"

He did. He shoved the piles aside and slid out of the cart. She had to fight back the urge to grab at him and make him stay.

"Tell your brother whatever you have to, just don't tell him where I'm going."

"Where *are* you going?"

"To save my father."

And without another word or a backward glance he was gone. He ran off, backtracking and disappearing around the bend in the road where they had just come from. His footsteps faded a few seconds after he was gone.

"Yer young fellow run off, did he?" the rag-and-bone man asked.

She shifted to sit on her knees, facing forward.

"There was no young fellow. I've been alone all night."

The old man gave a knowing—and degrading—laugh. She half expected him to argue with her, so she supposed she ought to be happy with nothing more than insulting laughter.

"Go ahead," she commanded, or at least she tried to sound commanding. "You may move on now. Take me to that house, the one with the lights burning. My brother is there."

He just gave a knowing smile and slapped the mule back into motion.

She had no doubt what he must be thinking, but tried to ignore it. "If you have no story to tell my brother that differs from mine, then I'll see you get rewarded well."

He chuckled. "I was young once meself, you know. You ain't done nothin' tonight hundreds o' other young people ain't doin' . . . or wish they could be doin'. Don't worry, fancy miss, I'll tell yer story. Course, a little some'ing extra to take home for me wife wouldn't be bad of ye . . . maybe something from your brother, or what."

"I promise, your wife will be more than happy to see you when you get home."

* * *

Damn, he'd wasted too much time! He couldn't afford to slow down. Unfortunately, though, he couldn't for the life of him run another step. He had to pause, to lean against a post and catch his breath.

He'd been all over London tonight and was no further ahead than he'd been an hour ago. Thank God he'd gotten Penelope home safely, at least. He could only imagine what things her brother had said to her. Hell, he should have been there with her to take the force of Anthony's anger. She shouldn't have had to face it alone.

Knowing her, though, she'd not quite told her brother all of what had happened tonight. He rather hoped she would not tell him; not tonight, at least. She deserved some time to think through what had happened, to know for certain how she felt about it. By God, he hoped she might not hate him once she'd had time to contemplate. It would be dashed difficult to convince her to marry him if she did.

It would also be dashed difficult to rescue his father without help from their Egyptian friends. Unfortunately, it seemed he would have to. He'd gone to the house—the small house his father kept in London—but when he'd finally roused the housekeeper he'd been told the Egyptians had indeed sent word they were in Town, but they'd never arrived at the house.

Something must have happened to them. He had an idea what: Uncle Nedley.

So, here he was now, running—literally—across town again. He was back in Mayfair, on his way to Burlington's. Damn, but he hoped he'd be in time.

He no longer had hopes of getting any of the treasure back. No, if he'd had his friends perhaps that would have been possible, but not alone. Alone he'd be doing well to simply rescue his father. There was no telling what they'd face; Uncle Nedley might have hired himself a virtual army to get those treasures packed up and taken to the docks. Hell, he might have already completed the job and made Harris's rescue attempts unnecessary.

While he'd been off ruining poor Penelope, his uncle could have been pocketing French payment and doing away with Oldham. He needed to keep moving. There was too much at stake to waste any more time.

Taking a deep, burning breath and wincing at the shooting pain in his side, he took up his pace again, passing rows of stately homes and finally turning onto the street that would lead him to Burlington's house. There he could see evidence of his uncle's activities.

Two wagons waited in front of the house. One was already full of an assortment of crates and carefully wrapped items. The second was very nearly full. Two men worked to load that wagon—one was another hired thug, one was his father. Thank God!

He ducked into the shadows to catch his breath and formulate a plan. Where was his uncle? Was anyone armed? What was to keep his father from simply walking away?

True, running away might be more effective, and perhaps the older man could accomplish such a thing right now, but Harris was fairly certain he himself could not. If they escaped, it would be by walking. Slowly.

"Hurry!" someone called.

Harris took care to keep hidden. There, in the doorway of Burlington's house, he could see his uncle, pointing and directing as forcefully and quietly as he could. He appeared to be unarmed. Could it be this easy? Could Harris simply wait for Nedley to turn his back then waltz in and tap his father on the shoulder? Things never quite seemed to work out that way for him, so he was understandably skeptical.

But if his damn uncle thought he was still miles away, under guard, why should he be on full alert here? He'd already bullied Oldham into believing if he didn't do as told things would go badly. Hell, his father likely thought by cooperating he was assuring their well-being when Nedley returned to the docks. He may not have figured out that Nedley's intentions were exactly the opposite.

Well, he'd lost the upper hand when Harris and Penelope tied up his thug and left that rotting storeroom. He'd better let his father in on the secret now, before someone might learn the truth and inform Uncle Nedley. If he knew his prisoners were no longer there to be used as leverage, things might get ugly here.

Carefully, he skulked along the walkway, keeping out of sight but inching closer to the wagons and his unwary father.

He watched carefully for his chance. Any minute now Nedley was bound to glance away, or step back indoors, and he would . . .

"Ah, here's the very devil," a voice growled in his ear.

The cold sting of metal pressed into the back of his neck. Damn. Someone had discovered him, and this someone had a gun.

"We've been a waiting for ye," the someone said in a familiar voice.

It was the bloody thug they'd left tied up at the docks. How the hell had the man undone himself then made it here before . . . Well, he supposed it really wasn't so difficult to believe. Harris had hardly come straight here, had he? No, he'd certainly allowed plenty of time for the rogue to loose his binds and arrive to warn his master. Damn, damn, and damn.

"Here he is, sir!" the mongrel called out.

Nedley glanced their way, holding up one hand to block out the light from the nearby street lamp so he could make them out in the shadows. He smiled.

"Ah, Lord Harry. At last. So good to see you. I've been expecting you, ever since Bert here had the good sense to come tell me you'd managed an escape."

Harris could only glare as the thug—Bert, he supposed—shoved him out into the light and forced him to move toward the grand stairs at Burlington's front door. Uncle Nedley watched with a smug smile. Damn it some more.

"So what has taken you so long?" he asked, then grinned even broader. "Oh, I think I can guess. Where is your lady fair, anyway? You didn't lose her, I hope?"

"She's someplace where you can never reach her," Harris answered.

"How noble. You saw to her safety before you came to look after your father. Touching. Don't you find that touching, Professor?"

"Leave him be, Nedley," Oldham called out from where he stood near the wagon. "You've got what you wanted. I'm ruined, my life's work is destroyed, you've made your profit . . . What do you need with my son?"

"Your son?" Nedley left his place at the door and made his

way to stand near them on the street. "You think I did all this to hurt you?"

Oldham was glaring at Nedley. There was real hatred in his voice when he spoke. "His mother told me how you'd leered after her, tried to comfort her as her husband languished in his sickbed. You've always hated it that she turned to me all those years ago instead of you."

Harris cringed. He knew the story. The former marquis—the man everyone assumed was his father—had suffered from some of the same weakness that plagued his older brother. His mother was young, lonely, and caring for a sickly child as well as a dying husband. She'd rejected the unwanted attentions of her brother-in-law, yet fell in love with a lowly tutor, a lonely man who was grieving the recent loss of his wife. For years, Oldham had not been told of the product of that brief union. The marquis had forgiven his wife and raised Harris as his own, until his death when Harris was just a child.

Nedley had known, though. He'd guessed it. Harris was nothing like his supposed father or his weak, incapacitated brother. Nedley had known and had made life hell for them once the marquis died. He'd taken over as trustee and punished Harris's mother for her refusal. He'd punished Harris for his mere existence. Now, apparently, he was punishing Oldham, as well.

"Oh, but you are mistaken, Professor," Nedley grumbled. "True, I have heartily enjoyed engineering your downfall, but that was merely a side effect of my real goal. Come indoors and we'll discuss this like gentlemen."

It was spoken as a suggestion, but the gun jammed into his skin assured Harris that there would be no quibbling on the matter. The thug brushed his hands over him, discovering his pistol, and disarmed him. Damn. He'd carried the heavy thing all over London for nothing! Uncle Nedley laughed.

"You are completely out of your element here, Harry. Do stop sulking and cooperate."

The whole group of them traipsed indoors, with one hired thug left outside to guard the wagons. Harris slid an apologetic glance toward his father, who simply shrugged. Whatever Uncle Nedley had planned, they would soon be finding out all about it.

He ushered them into the room that had been used for housing the artifacts. There was no sign of Lord Burlington, but there was ample sign of his lady. She sat quite contentedly in one of the comfortable chairs. She seemed rather pleased to see Harris, too.

"Lady Burlington," Harris said, nodding toward her. "I see you are keeping excellent company again."

"And I see you are, once again, in quite a load of trouble," she replied.

"So what do you plan to do now, Nedley?" Oldham asked their host. "Have your brutes drag us out to Burlington's garden and garrote us quietly?"

Harris could have chosen a much less gruesome way of phrasing things, but he did admit he was rather interested in hearing his uncle's answer to the question.

"Of course not," Nedley said. "We'll stay right here and your son will shoot you in the heart. I will be forced to kill him, of course. Purely in self-defense, you see."

"What?" Harris exclaimed. "I won't shoot him!"

"No, of course you won't," Nedley said with a weary sigh. "Which is why I'll have to do it myself and then simply tell everyone that you did it. We had planned to carry things out a bit differently, but now that you've left the docks and come here, we'll simply have to improvise."

"No one will believe it," Harris declared. "Why on earth would I shoot my own father?"

"Because he discovered that you were double-crossing him. He was planning to sell the antiquities back to the Egyptians, but you sold them to the French. He confronted you, so you killed him. Poor, poor Lady Burlington was caught in the middle of this, seduced by your smooth words and your charming ways. You used her to get to the treasures, you vile snake, and then you murdered her husband."

"I used her to . . . wait, where *is* her husband? You lunatics haven't already done anything to him, have you?"

"Sadly, the lout hasn't yet returned from tonight's debauchery," Lady Burlington said, brushing lint from the fabric of her chair. "But as soon as he does, you will end his life in a fit of jealous rage."

"In our grief at such tragedy, her ladyship and I will comfort one another," Nedley said, smirking. "And you will have all that blood on your hands."

This was beyond ridiculous. Just how many people did they think Harris could murder in one night? First they planned to claim he'd killed Penelope, now his own father and even poor Burlington. What next? Wait, he truly did not want to know that. The way his day had been, he could expect something even worse to come barging through the door.

And here it was now. Footsteps pounded and voices called out from the entrance hall. Harris was almost afraid to wonder who this might turn out to be.

Chapter Twenty-one

"There he is!" Penelope shouted, peeking around Anthony as he flung open the door to Lady Burlington's favorite drawing room.

Nedley Chesterton was there, holding a pistol aimed at Lord Harry. His thug was holding one, too. Heavens, but Nedley's pistol seemed oddly familiar. Had it been Lord Harry's? Well, that was rather careless of him.

"What the hell is going on here?" Anthony demanded.

Nedley glanced back and forth between her, Anthony, the local magistrate, and the three constables he'd brought with them. It was obvious the villain was formulating another plan. Thank heavens they'd gotten here before he'd been able to carry out whatever had been his last plan.

"I'm glad you're here!" the villain cried out. "This man was trying to murder me!"

He pointed at Lord Harry. His rather strong accusation was somewhat diluted by the fact that Lord Harry was standing all the way across the room and completely weaponless. And was ragingly attractive in his disheveled attire. Well, she supposed that part may have been having more effect on her than it did on Anthony and the constables, but still . . . she was awfully glad to see him breathing.

But now Lady Burlington spoke up, jumping to her feet and rushing to Nedley's side.

"Yes, it's true," she agreed, in a great flurry of sudden nervousness. "He burst in here, threatening to take horrible liberties with my person if I didn't allow him access to my husband's collection."

"So he could abscond with it, selling it for filthy profit," Nedley added, then pointed a hateful finger at Professor Oldham. "Aided, no doubt, by the man who cuckolded my poor dead brother!"

"Don't be ridiculous," Professor Oldham said. "I would never sell these precious items for mere profit. They belong to the people of Egypt!"

Arguing erupted. Nedley accused everyone of all sorts of things, Lady Burlington moaned about how poorly used she'd been, Lord Harry defended his father, Professor Oldham rattled on with something about how a certain pasha named Ali was eager to have the treasures returned, and the magistrate called for everyone to calm down. Anthony appeared to be suffering some digestive ailment. Penelope merely wanted it all to be over so she could throw herself into Lord Harry's arms again.

The pandemonium was only silenced when the front door behind them opened and someone else came charging into the house. Nedley turned his gun in that direction, and two constables lunged out to grab the arms of this latest arrival. Everyone grew silent and craned their various necks to see who it was.

"Markland," Lord Harry said. "I should have known you'd be involved in this."

"What the hell is going on here?" Mr. Markland—somewhat out of breath and clearly as confused as any of them—asked as the constables dragged him into the room. His gaze paused over Professor Oldham.

"Father, are you unharmed?"

Father? Did Penelope hear that correctly? Mr. Markland called the man *father*? But she thought the professor was Lord Harry's father. How could Mr. Markland be so confused?

Professor Oldham seemed confused as well. He smiled at Markland and nodded. "I'm fine, my boy, just fine. Had a bit of an ordeal, but it appears the worst of it is over now, thank heavens."

"No, no," Nedley cried out, now turning his gun toward the magistrate. "Nothing is over! These men were trying to kill us, I say! Take them into custody, man."

The magistrate seemed unsure what to believe at this point. Fortunately, Lord Harry seemed to know exactly what was needed. He leapt toward his threatening uncle, hitting the man with force enough to knock him backward and off his feet. The hired thug noticed, too late, and fired off his pistol.

Penelope cried out—as did Lady Burlington—but a constable grabbed the thug and held him. It seemed the brute was a dreadful shot and no one was hit. The gun in Nedley's hand was now safely in Lord Harry's hand as the older man hit the carpet with a house-shaking thud.

The magistrate was taking no chances, though, and pulled the gun from Lord Harry's hand. Penelope fumed with anger to see him treated so roughly, but Anthony spoke up before she gathered her breath to do so.

"Have a care," he called out to the magistrate. "This man is not the villain here. He's been one of the victims, kidnapped by his own uncle. That man."

Now it was Anthony's turn to point, and he did, directly at Nedley Chesterton. One of the constables trotted over to him and helped him up, keeping a firm hand on his arm, however.

"What's your part in this, Markland?" Lord Harry asked. "Are you in league with my uncle, trying to make a profit off your own father's hard work?"

Mr. Markland gave a condescending sneer. "Ah, my dear brother. Such a joy, as usual. How does our father tolerate your company for such extended periods?"

"He seems to tolerate that every bit as well as he does such prolonged separation from you," Lord Harry replied with a smirk to make Mr. Markland's sneer look amiable.

"Now, boys," Professor Oldham said with no smirk or sneer at all. He seemed rather uncomfortable, which, she figured, was to be expected. "I know you have unresolved issues between you, but—"

Once again, the tension in the room was enhanced by the sound of the front door opening and footsteps entering. Who on earth could this be? Penelope could scarcely guess. She couldn't imagine it might be anyone particularly helpful, though.

At first glance, it seemed she was right. Two men appeared in the doorway. They were tall, and made to look even taller by the elaborate turbans they wore on their heads. They were bearded, and their baggy, flowing apparel was accentuated by richly stitched sashes cinched tightly at their waists. Lethal swords hung at their sides, and their dark eyes seemed to miss nothing as they peered at the frozen assembly.

"Khalil! Ibrahim!" Professor Oldham suddenly called out.

"You are acquainted with these, er, gentlemen?" the magistrate asked. It seemed a very good question.

"But of course," the professor replied. "They are our dear friends."

Dear friends? Heavens! Penelope had met Lord Harry's murderous family members and now these sword-bearing dear friends . . . She would hate to imagine what an actual enemy might look like.

"It's good to see you both," Lord Harry said to the slightly terrifying men. "Although I went by the house and was told you had not arrived."

"We could not go there," one of the men replied in remarkably excellent English. "Someone was following us and we knew there was danger."

"So they came to me," Mr. Markland explained, seemingly quite proud of this fact. "And told me their concerns. They were fortunate they found me at home. When they arrived, I was right in the middle of assisting a friend who, I'm sorry to say, is quite vexed with me now for forcing this change in his plans."

At that very moment, the voice of someone quite vexed indeed could be heard in the entryway. Footsteps sounded with it. Two sets, if Penelope was not mistaken. And oddly enough, the footsteps seemed to be accompanied by domestic bickering.

"But my dearest, I'm determined to press Markland into taking us straightaway, just as he promised," a male voice was saying.

His companion appeared to be female. And familiar.

"But perhaps this isn't such a grand idea for us anyway," she said.

Penelope was still in the midst of trying to convince herself she'd misguessed the owner of this voice when these two latest arrivals came into view through the doorway. Footsteps and bickering ceased immediately and their eyes got large. The masculine half of the pair took his partner's hand and pulled her closer to him.

"By the devil, what's all this?" he asked.

"Good evening, Cousin," Lord Harry called to him.

Indeed, it was quite a shock to find Mr. Ferrel marching in this way, but what Penelope found even more amazing was his companion. *Maria!* And good heavens, why was she clinging to Mr. Ferrel as if she honestly enjoyed clinging to him?

Could it be that perhaps she did? Oh my, things began to dawn.

Judging by Mr. Ferrel's protective stance and Maria's fearful clinging, Penelope began to realize just exactly what her friend had been trying to tell her in that letter earlier. Maria had not been confessing her love for Lord Harry, but by some odd twist she'd been talking about Mr. Ferrel! But of course it all began to make sense now.

"Maria!" she exclaimed, rushing to her friend. "You and Mr. Ferrel are eloping!"

"Penelope!" her friend exclaimed in return, letting go of Mr. Ferrel only to latch onto her. "Please say you do not hate me for it."

"No, of course not," Penelope assured her. "You are free to marry Mr. Ferrel anytime you like, but I cannot help wonder at your sudden arrival. How on earth did you know to come here?"

"We didn't," Maria said. "Mr. Markland was being so kind as to help us run away. We were going to go by boat so it would be difficult to find us, but then his, er, friends showed up. We were already inside the carriage on our way to the river and Mr. Markland said there was no time to rig up another. He made the driver come here straightaway."

"And I'm glad we did," Mr. Ferrel said, glaring at Nedley. "Father? What is all this? What is going on?"

"I'll be the one asking questions, my boy!" Nedley declared. He appeared even more unpleasant than usual, and the way he was glaring at Maria was simply uncalled for. "What do you mean, running off in the night with this . . . this . . ."

"This beautiful young woman?" Mr. Ferrel finished for him. "I love her, Father, and I will marry her, with or without your blessing."

"But I expressly forbade it! You'll be a duke someday. You can do far better than this . . . this . . ."

"No, Father," Mr. Ferrel said, enunciating carefully. "I will be husband to Miss Bradley someday. Lord Harry will be the duke."

"Not if I can help it, he won't!" the angry parent said.

Without warning, he broke free from the constable and lunged. Not at Lord Harry, as Penelope might have expected, but at her. She was too stunned to move. He held her firmly, pinning her arms to her side. Shockingly, the man produced a knife from just inside his coat. It glinted briefly in the flickering lamplight, then he was pressing it tightly against her throat.

How in mercy's name did this come about? She shifted as much as she dared, angling her head just enough so that she could find Lord Harry. He met her eyes. His expression assured her that he had no intention of letting this horrible man damage her. Indeed, she knew he would not allow it. Despite the warm metal of Nedley's knife, she willed herself to relax.

"Release her or I'll shoot!" the magistrate called out.

Nedley ignored him. His hold on Penelope seemed to only get tighter.

"You'll have to shoot through her, then," he said. "Now get out! Everyone but my nephew, get out!"

No one moved. She felt the knife press harder into her skin.

"Let her go, for God's sake," Anthony said. His voice cracked just the slightest bit. How very sweet! Her brother actually worried for her.

"Uncle," Lord Harry said. His voice did not crack. It was deadly calm and remarkably controlled. "Let her go. It's me you want. She's nothing to you."

"Ah, but she is something to you, isn't she?" his uncle said. "You've got plans to marry her and get yourself a fat little heir or two, don't you? Well, my doddering father might not recognize what you are, filthy bastard, but I do. I'll be dead before I see any of my family's rightful titles fall onto your worthless head!"

"I don't care about your damn titles!" Lord Harry said. "I care about her. Let her go. You can do whatever you want with me."

Oh, but that was even sweeter than Anthony's crackling voice! If it wasn't for the horrible knife cutting into her skin just where it could potentially do some serious damage, she would have swooned away. Lord Harry cared about her! He admitted it right here, in front of all these people! Oh, but she truly hoped she lived long enough to tell him just how much she returned the sentiment.

"Tell your friends here to leave," Nedley said. "Unless this room starts to empty out now, this chit is going to be bleeding."

To emphasize his point, he jabbed the knife harder. She couldn't help but let out a sharp squeak. Drat it all, but this man was hurting her! She did not care for this one bit.

Lord Harry made a noise something like a growl and moved another two steps closer. Nedley snarled back at him.

"I don't see anyone leaving. I thought you said you cared about her. Tell them to leave!"

"I'm not leaving," Anthony said. "Put the knife down now, Lord Nedley."

Nedley just ignored him and growled at Lord Harry. "Call off your exotic watchdogs. Now."

From the corner of her eye, Penelope could see that Lord Harry wasn't the only one who'd been inching his way toward her. The frightening men in turbans had been coming this way, as well. Their movement was almost undetectable, but somehow Lord Nedley must have detected it. Likely he detected the gentlemen's hands resting on those bright, curving swords they wore, too. What Penelope wouldn't give for one of those right now!

She glanced back at Lord Harry, wondering how he'd react. That dratted knife was pressing pretty sharply into her skin. Would Harry beg everyone to leave them? Did he have some sort of plan? She rather hoped so!

His eyes met hers and then flicked to look down toward the table directly next to her. Did that mean something? She thought perhaps it did. Lord Nedley was making it rather difficult for her to turn her head and follow Harry's glance, but she managed to twist just enough that she caught sight of an object. It was there, resting in its customary upright position, just on the table.

The funerary phallus. Ah, she knew quite well that implement could make a suitable weapon. True, it was not quite as lethal as those Egyptian scimitars, but it might do to subdue Nedley long enough for a sword to become useful. She darted her glance back to Lord Harry to let him know she understood. She also hoped he recognized the question behind her understanding. How on earth was she to get that phallus in her hands?

She blushed at the mere thought of it, recalling her first encounter with that phallus, which, oddly enough, made her think of a certain other first encounter with something vaguely similar. In truth, standing here with Nedley's knife at her throat was probably not the most appropriate time for her to be recalling what had passed earlier in that darkened shop room, yet how could her thoughts not wander there? If she was to die tonight at this madman's hand, at least she'd had that one hour of bliss.

"What do you want, Uncle?" Lord Harry asked, clearly stalling for time as he looked for an opportunity. "What can you possibly hope to gain now, after all this?"

"I'll be rid of you!"

"You don't really think they'd let you murder me in cold blood."

"Don't I? They're letting me murder her now."

He grabbed her by the hair and pulled her head back, exposing more of her neck. She gasped before the awkward position cut off her air. The knife grazed across her skin. Had it cut her? She thought so, though the pain was only slight. Was that a good sign, or a bad sign? Had he done as he'd been threatening and caused her serious injury, or was this just another warning? She could only judge by the reactions of those around her.

She heard Maria screech and Anthony swear. Lord Harry swore twice. The magistrate off to her left cocked the pistol he'd taken from Lord Nedley earlier.

"It's now or never, Harry," the man spat. "You do exactly as I say, or she dies."

"Very well. What would you have me do? Just don't hurt her any more."

It was difficult to breath and impossible to swallow. With her head tilted back this way, all she could see was the side of Nedley's horrible face and the ceiling. It appeared Lady Burlington's bathtub had leaked at some point. It seemed a real shame that her last vision in this life would be of a moldy stain in someone else's ceiling.

"Here's what you'll do for me," Lord Nedley announced. "All of you. First, my dear magistrate, if you'd be so kind as to unload that pistol, please."

That seemed a rather silly command, she had to admit. Of course he'd want to disarm the man, but why not just take the pistol from him? Surely even a fool like Nedley could see that a pistol might be a far more useful weapon than this knife. Although, she wasn't at all certain she'd rather be shot than slashed.

The magistrate made some pretense of disagreeing, but all it took was for Lord Nedley to press that knife more sharply against her throat and suddenly the man capitulated. She took that to mean whatever this horrible villain had done to her, it certainly must look dreadful to the bystanders. But she was too busy trying to focus on what was happening to allow herself time to worry more about it.

She could hear the mechanical sounds of the pistol being unloaded. No one was speaking. Nedley was breathing heavily; she could hear it and smell it, unfortunately. Finally the magistrate's feet sounded on the floor as he moved toward them.

"Here. It's unloaded."

"Give it to my nephew there," was the response.

This surprised her. Why on earth should he want Lord Harry to have that unloaded pistol? Perhaps simply so he could keep an eye on it. Indeed, he would not want to risk it falling into someone else's hands where he might not see them reload, she supposed.

Now the footsteps moved in Lord Harry's direction. It sounded as if he passed the pistol over. Well, this was no help.

Now she couldn't even see Lord Harry or that nearby phallus. How would she ever know if there was a chance to use it?

"Now get out," Nedley ordered. "Everyone but my nephew."

"I'm not leaving," Anthony repeated.

It seemed the others felt the same way. Penelope could feel the knife. The tension was beginning to show in Lord Nedley's grip. The knife dug at her, but it was not steady. It had begun to shake just slightly.

"Very well," he said. "Stay. And watch your bastard friend blow his brains out."

More gasping. Penelope choked. What was this crazy person ranting about? Watch *who* do *what*? He couldn't possibly mean . . .

"That's right," he went on. "Load it, Harry. Yes, load it, hold it to your temple, and pull the trigger."

"You're insane!" Lord Harry said.

"Do it! Or stand there and watch her die in your place."

Silence all around. The water stain on the ceiling was beginning to take on macabre shapes in her mind. How many ages had it been since this ordeal began? She squirmed, trying to find a more comfortable position, but Lord Nedley jerked ruthlessly at her hair and kept that knife pressed against her. Still all she could see was that dratted ceiling.

"What's the matter, Harry?" he asked, taunting. "I was hoping you might love her enough to die for her. Don't you?"

What a horrible man! That was hardly a fair question. Oh, she longed to hear Lord Harry announce that he did indeed love her enough to die for her, but for heaven's sake, she really didn't want him to actually prove it! But just how awful would it be if he did *not* declare his love and instead simply let his foul uncle do away with her? Gracious, but there was simply no suitable solution here.

She heard the click of metal.

"You'll let her go?" Lord Harry asked.

Now what was that sound? Tamping? Good Lord, he was loading the pistol. Was he actually going to do this thing? Lord Nedley laughed.

"I have no use for her, Harry. Besides, I have a feeling the good magistrate and all your little friends here will have some sort of arrangements for me when all this is over."

More clicking and tamping. "Then why not let her go now? Why end this with blood on your hands?"

"Because it will be your blood! Now go on, load it."

"It is loaded," Lord Harry replied, his voice terse and angry.

"Hold it to your head. Do it!"

Penelope tried squirming again, but it was no use. The knife bit into her and she let out a cowardly little whimper. No! This was unconscionable; it couldn't be happening.

"Let me look at her," Lord Harry demanded.

"Keep that pistol pointed at your head."

"Let me see her."

"Oh, very well. She ought to be allowed to watch you put a bullet in your brain on her behalf, I suppose."

He jerked her head again, this time shoving it downward so that the muscles in her neck twinged and she found herself dizzy. She gasped in a deep, welcome breath and waited for her vision to clear. Lord Harry was watching her. She met his eyes, hoping he didn't see the despair she felt. It would not do at all for the man to know just how miserable she was now, not when he was doing something so very noble to save her.

Sure enough, he held that horrible pistol pointed directly at his temple. It was the most distressing sight. Wasn't anyone going to do anything? Couldn't any of these people help him?

"There, now you can see her. Say your good-byes, but don't try anything. The second that pistol moves or anyone even thinks about being a hero, she dies."

"Harry, no! You don't have to do this!" she managed to choke out.

"I have to do whatever I can," he replied, still keeping that gun in its deadly position. His eyes, however, darted from hers to that looming phallus.

Yes, yes... she knew it was still there. But how did he expect her to use it just now? She could barely breathe, let alone turn around and grab it. Oh heavens, please don't let the stupid man be relying on her to save him! Not when he was the one with the pistol pointed to his own head.

"I have to end this, Penelope," he went on, his eyes still speaking something she could not quite understand. "He's not making empty threats. Take things into your own hands; it's not as hopeless as it seems. I know you can handle it."

Gracious, could the man say nothing meaningful? She hardly wished to stand here with a knife at her throat listening to him spout dreary platitudes!

"Oh shut up," Lord Nedley growled. "Just tell the baggage you love her and get on with it."

"Very well," Lord Harry said with a sorrowing sigh. He abandoned his platitudes and simply spoke the words. "I do love you, Penelope."

Oh how wonderful! He said it! He did love her! A wonderful warmth and lightness came over her, and she was almost able to forget all about the painful knife and the horror of their situation. Harry Chesterton told the world that he loved her!

Then he had to go and ruin it by firing that dreadful weapon.

The sound reverberated throughout the room. It was loud, jarring, and final. Her ears were ringing, drowning out the cries of the people around her, but not the terrible thud as Lord Harry dropped the gun and slumped to the floor. Dear God, but he'd done it! She wished she could have died on that floor with him, too.

She could not, though. His murderer had left her alive. Lord Nedley had jolted at the initial, horrible sound of that pistol, but now his body relaxed, and his breath came out in a long, even stream. The knife fell slack.

"Ha!" he gloated. "The bastard solved my problems!"

He would hardly be problem free for long. Penelope ripped his distracted hands from her, whirling to grab up the waiting phallus and swinging it with the full force of her anger. He staggered back, but didn't fall. She swung again, connecting nicely with the side of his head. His eyes rolled, but he still remained upright. So, she hit him again.

This time he went down. Right onto the spot where Lord Harry had fallen. Oddly enough, though, the spot was empty.

Empty? But how . . .

Then she saw him. Lord Harry was not a lifeless form occupying some other part of the floor; he was in the process of rising to his feet, rubbing at the side of his face and smiling at her. *Smiling!* And breathing as he did it!

She pitched the phallus and threw herself at him.

"You're alive!"

He swooped her into his arms, and she held on to him as

tightly as she could. He was alive! It was impossible, but it was true. A quick glance up into his face assured her his head was still intact, although there were a few angry marks from the exploding powder. Still, how could this possibly be? Perhaps she was dreaming. She gingerly reached up to touch those beautiful, lively powder marks.

"Only slightly singed, my dear," he said. "I'm afraid my uncle's hopes have been dashed."

"But . . . how?" she asked. "Surely you cannot be that dreadful of a shot!"

She did not get an explanation. The room was in turmoil. Lord Nedley lay moaning on the floor next to the phallus while the magistrate, constables, and furious Egyptians swarmed over him. Lady Burlington was screeching at him and calling him the most shocking things and berating him for failure. Indeed, it would seem the man's problems were only just beginning.

Anthony came rushing to Penelope's side and practically tore her from Lord Harry. Maria and Ferrel were with him. Professor Oldham, too. There was fussing and flustering all about her before she could finally assure them that she was fine. The knife had merely nicked her.

"That was quite a parlor trick, my boy," Professor Oldham said when things were finally somewhat settled. "How on earth did you manage it?"

Lord Harry simply grinned at them all and opened up his hand. There—a bit sweaty, perhaps—was the wadding and the ball Penelope could have sworn she heard him place into the barrel of that gun. So he had never loaded it! They had all watched him, had all been fooled, yet he had never been in any danger at all. And to think, she'd suffered great agonies seeing him hold that pistol to his head and pull the trigger. She'd nearly died of the horror!

"That was cruel," she said, unable to refrain from smacking him sharply. "I thought . . . but it appeared as if . . . Oh, but you should have said something to let us know you'd be safe!"

"I did, of course," he said.

"You did not!"

"But I did. I used words like *empty*, and *not hopeless*, and I thought you understood."

"How on earth could I understand what you were doing from that? That was hardly an explanation."

"It was code."

"I don't speak code."

"Well, I couldn't very well just come out and tell my bloody uncle that the gun wasn't actually loaded, could I?"

"You could have said *something*! I thought you were dead."

"But I'm not, am I?"

No, thank the gracious Lord he was not. He appeared quite fine. Quite fine indeed.

But Anthony would not let her go back to him. He declared that she must give her story to the magistrate and then be rushed home. Their mother must be worried sick, waiting there in hopes of Penelope's safe return. Yes, she supposed she should not prolong her mother's agony. She ought to let Anthony speed things along and get her back quickly.

Yet how could she simply leave Lord Harry, not knowing if she'd ever see him again? She tried to catch his eye, to communicate through more of his "code" and let him know the truth of how she felt about him. She could not. He was fully occupied with the barrage of questions the magistrate was hurling at him.

"So you are brother to the Marquis of Hepton?" the magistrate was asking, among other things.

"I am," Lord Harry replied. "Although I have not seen him in almost three years. Sadly, he is not very well. My uncle is his trustee and keeps me from him."

The magistrate seemed to make note of this. "I would be prepared to assist in making other arrangements for your brother, sir. Chances are your uncle will be unavailable to continue looking after him."

Well, Penelope could only imagine that was good news for Lord Harry's incapacitated older brother. But what of his poor cousin? She glanced off to where Ferrel Chesterton hovered over Maria.

"I'm so sorry," he was telling her softly. "Can you possibly still wish to marry me now, with my father on his way to prison and my future so very uncertain?"

"Of course I do!" Maria said. "So long as you are not on your way there to join him."

"No, I'm happy to say I was completely unaware of any of his recent schemes. Although I begin to see now why my father was so unhappy when I took that scarab and gave it to you as a gift."

"That scarab was part of your father's stolen collection?" Maria asked, aghast.

"It seems so. At the time, though, I swear I thought it was a part of my mother's jewels—she had so many, God rest her. My father enlisted Lady Burlington to try to get it back from me."

"So that is why you were found with her and accused of..."

"I was a fool to put myself in that position, my dearest."

"And I was a fool not to trust you," Maria declared. "I should have believed you about that actress, too, shouldn't I?"

"I will never give you another reason to doubt me, my love."

They fell into each other's arms, professing undying devotion and being altogether disgusting about it. Honestly, it was almost enough to turn one's stomach. Penelope was certain she would never be such a sap if she were fortunate enough to ever end up in Lord Harry's arms again. Truly, they would have far better things to do than talk such treacle.

Still, she was happy for Maria. It seemed she and Mr. Chesterton were quite devoted. True, her own happy ending was far from assured, but she should in no way begrudge Maria. Despite the cow eyes and mooning, Penelope smiled along with them.

"But what of all the artifacts?" Professor Oldham asked, drawing her attention back to the more pressing matters. "Certainly they can be returned now to their rightful owners?"

The magistrate frowned. "Can anyone verify who that would be, sir? These gentlemen are claiming the items for themselves." He pointed to Lord Harry's Egyptian friends who were carefully examining the few pieces still left in the room and remarking softly to one another in their own language.

"But of course these items belong to them!" Professor Oldham exclaimed. "Can there be any doubt of it? I have all the documentation in my records you need to identify each and every one of these pieces and determine that they should never have been brought to England in the first place. They were stolen, pure and simple."

"And Lord Harry was merely trying to steal them back, that's all," Penelope added for Anthony's benefit, then wondered if perhaps she might have done better to keep her mouth shut. The magistrate gave her a rather curious look that said he was interested in more information regarding Lord Harry's efforts at stealing things.

"Lord Harry is our friend," one of the Egyptians said, thankfully. "Anything he did was with our complete agreement, and the Egyptian people owe him a debt of gratitude. It seemed we would never see any of these again, and yet here they are."

"I tried to keep Nedley's bumbling thugs from breaking anything as we packed them up," Professor Oldham said. "Instead of boarding a ship for France, we should be able to simply send them on with you, back where they belong. Unless you think you need to unpack everything to get a look at it first."

The Egyptians mumbled to themselves again, then the second one spoke. "We trust you, Professor. We are content that our items have been treated with care. Well, all of them, perhaps, but this one."

He plucked the phallus up off the floor and examined it. For dents, probably. He glanced at Penelope with raised eyebrows then looked over at Lord Harry. Penelope's face went warm.

"You should be very nice to her, my friend," the Egyptian said as he broke into a knowing smile.

Penelope's face began to sizzle.

"I intend to," Lord Harry replied.

Ah, but what an excellent reply it was, too. She wanted to run to him with assurances that she was only too eager to be nice in return, but Anthony kept her pinned to his side. And drat, but now Mr. Markland crowded in, slapping Lord Harry on the back and putting just one more huge body between her and the man she loved.

"For a moment there I thought perhaps you really were fatskulled enough to put a bloody bullet in your brain," he said.

"Sorry to disappoint you," Lord Harry responded, clearly still bristling at his estranged brother.

"You're a sad excuse for a gentleman, dragging our father and Miss Rastmoor into this, Harris," Mr. Markland said. "But I have to admit I'm not eager to see you dead."

"Perhaps I'll live long enough to atone for my many transgressions, then," Lord Harry said.

"Let us hope so," his brother replied.

The men didn't exactly fall into one another's arms, but Penelope could tell this was a major step forward for them. Clearly they still begrudged each other for whatever lay in their past, but just for now the two brothers were not feuding. Penelope was not prepared to hold her breath for warm reconciliation, but it was good to see them in some measure of agreement.

"Come," Anthony said, reminding her that he was still at her side and still in charge of her person. "We should be going now."

Sadly, she had no reason to argue. They really *should* be going now. She'd already told the magistrate all she knew about things when she first arrived home in the rag-and-bone cart. The rest of things he'd seen for himself. If there were more questions to be answered, surely the magistrate could call on them at home tomorrow. There was no reason to keep Mamma waiting—and worrying—any longer.

"Very well," she said, allowing Anthony to guide her from the room.

"Wait!" Lord Harry called behind them.

She turned. He was watching them; watching her. She wasn't sure what to make of his expression. Worried, perhaps? What could he possibly be worried about now, though? His father was safe, they'd made things right with their Egyptian friends, and even Mr. Markland was at peace with him. Had something been missed? Was there still some grave matter left untended?

"I meant what I said, Penelope," he said softly, meeting her questioning gaze directly.

For only a heartbeat she was confused by his meaning. Then she understood.

"I *do* love you," he went on.

Oh! The dear, darling man. Indeed, she did love him in return, and he needed to know that. Without any doubt or impossible-to-comprehend code words. She broke from Anthony and shoved through the other bystanders, virtually throwing herself into Lord Harry's arms. He was ready to receive her.

"I love you, too!" she said, burying her face against his warm chest and holding him so tightly that it would take Anthony and both the Egyptians to pry them apart.

None of them bothered to try, though. Lord Harry held her tightly and pressed kisses into her hair. Anthony merely cleared his throat. Loudly.

Considering that was the only sound audible in the room just now, Penelope realized everyone must be staring. She peeked up to see that, sure enough, they were. Maria looked slightly uncomfortable around such a display, but her pursed lips were indeed hinting at a smile.

"Rastmoor, I suppose I might as well let you know," Lord Harry said after clearing his own throat. "I never truly intended to marry your sister."

"Oh?"

"I lied to you. Repeatedly."

"I'm sorry to hear that."

"And I need to inform you that my pedigree is not entirely in order."

"That's startling news, of course."

"And it's quite likely that I am, in fact, the very worst fiancé to be had in all of London."

"I don't doubt it, sir."

"But if Penelope is willing to have me, I must beg you to give us your blessing."

She watched Anthony's face. What would he say? Lord Harry had not done a very pretty job of pleading his case. She might have to produce tears in a moment or two to soften her brother's heart. Not that tears would be difficult to come by if, indeed, he tried to give a rejection.

"You've put my whole family through quite a lot, Chesterton," Anthony said. "A sensible man would keep his sister as far away from you as possible after all this."

"I understand your concern," Lord Harry said. "I would likely do the same, had I a sister."

"But you don't, and now you are asking for mine."

"Begging, I believe, was the word I used," Lord Harry corrected.

"Yes, so it was. And you think you can look after her? Love her and cherish her and all that?"

"I can, sir, and I will. All my life."

"Which, judging by how you've lived it thus far, might prove to be remarkably short," Anthony noted. "Are you quite certain all this rubbish with kidnappings and robberies and international intrigue is over?"

"I'm hoping that it is, yes."

"As am I. Well, I suppose I might consider you for her."

Her heart nearly leapt out of her chest. Anthony was willing to consider! They might have his blessing after all! True, she had no intention of *not* ending up married to Lord Harry at this point, but she did rather hope they wouldn't have to run away and live forever estranged from her family to do it.

"But, you understand, I have one condition," Anthony added.

"What? Anything!" Lord Harry said.

She believed he meant it, too. She could feel his heart inside his chest, pounding as frantically as hers.

"Will you, for God's sake, take this woman to Egypt so she'll leave me bloody in peace about it?"

Epilogue

The air was hot; it was a heat she'd come to love. The sun burned down with a golden intensity she knew words could never describe. The sounds of foreign voices and exotic animals were nearly commonplace to her now. The scent of the marshy Nile was almost unnoticeable anymore. Indeed, she'd come to feel perfectly at home here among the sand and the pyramids that had once existed only on the pages of books for her.

"Are you bored with it yet?"

Lord Harry stood at her side, his coat long since discarded, shirtsleeves rolled up and the white linen clinging to his glistening body. Good heavens, was the man serious? Was she *bored*?

"No," she assured him. "Not even close."

"Even though it's been nearly a week since we've dug up anything of any interest?" he asked, reaching out to finger the warmed scarab—*her* scarab—that hung at her neck. His Egyptian friends had returned it to her in gratitude for her help in retrieving their stolen artifacts.

"Perhaps it's been a week since *you've* dug up anything of interest," she said, smiling up at him and letting her eyes convey more than just her innocent words. "*I* find hidden treasure in my very own tent every night."

He chuckled, and squeezed her tight. For nearly two months they'd been here, living blissfully like nomads, some days in Cairo, meeting with scholars and cataloguing their finds, other days returning to sleep in their tent at the foot of the most magnificent constructions on earth. She was hard-pressed to say what inspired her most, the sight of the pyramids rising over the endless dunes, or the bronzed form of the remarkable man beside her.

She moved to lean into him, to press her lips to his salty skin.

"This has been far more exciting than I could have possibly ever imagined. No one could have convinced me I would ever end up with such a honeymoon, or such a husband."

"You do not regret it yet?"

"Never! Do I need to worry that perhaps you've begun to?"

"Not in a century, my dear. I only hope I can keep you this happy once we've returned home."

"It's hard to believe our time has gone already."

"I know. But it will be the wet season here soon, and I've word that my brother needs me."

She did not like the serious tone in his voice. "Mr. Markland?"

"No, my other brother. The marquis. Ferrel writes that he's not responding to the new treatment the physician recommended."

"Oh dear! You had such hopes for that."

"He's not at death's door, but I wanted to do more for him than my uncle has done."

"You've done well as his trustee," she assured him. "You've done well with *all* your new responsibilities."

"I've been absent. At least my cousin is doing a fine job of overseeing things."

She rested her face against his chest. "That was kind of you to arrange for that."

"Well, with my uncle in prison and a good bit of his fortune forfeit, Ferrel needed some way to provide for his new wife. Still, it is my responsibility to look after my brother and I have not been there."

"Of course you feel that way; he's your brother and you want to be with him. It's time for us to go back home."

"You truly aren't disappointed? You won't find life with me in England to be deadly dull and tedious?"

"Dull and tedious? With *you*? Oh, but I'm certain you'll find a way to make genteel domestication very entertaining."

"I will certainly try to find *something* to do with you to while away the hours."

"Oh?" she said, looking up into his tanned face and matching the suggestive tone in his voice. "Can you think of an engaging activity to pass the chilly nights back in our homeland?"

"The nights?" he asked and brushed a teasing kiss across her lips. "I was thinking mostly of the days."

"My, but you are a bit naughty, sir."

"Thankfully, so are you, my love. I'm only worried for how best to explain things to my father."

"Er, I'm quite certain he already has some idea what goes on between us at this point . . ."

He laughed at her. "I'm afraid there are times anyone within half a mile of our tent might have some idea what goes on between us, my dear."

She felt herself blushing, but he continued.

"Actually, I'm referring to a project of a more scholarly nature that my father wishes to undertake."

"Oh?" Indeed, this sounded quite interesting, too.

"My father has been corresponding with a gentleman in London and is most impressed with the young man's ability for concise description and vivid imagery. His hope is that we can secure the man to collaborate with us on a book covering the subject of our most recent discoveries."

"How wonderful. I'm sure the book will be a huge success."

"Trouble is, I'm not quite sure how to inform my father that working with his esteemed correspondent might be a bit of a distraction for me," he said, giving her a sizzling smile. "After all, I've been sharing my bed with this person for over two months now and am woefully under-rested."

She wrinkled her brow, confused for a moment, then suddenly it became clear. Heavens! Somehow he knew about P.

Anthonys! Gracious, but he'd found out her last remaining secret!

"You didn't think I knew about that, did you?" he asked, still smiling as if he were very proud of himself.

"But how could you possibly find out?"

"Your handwriting," he explained. "I've known since the day you signed the marriage register."

"Yet you said nothing?"

"If you'll recall, we've been rather preoccupied with other, er, topics."

Drat, but he was bringing her to blushes again. Indeed, they had been preoccupied. Still, she should have told him that she'd been misrepresenting herself. Professor Oldham might be very offended now to discover the truth.

"What will your father think of me?" she asked.

"He thinks you are a brilliant young woman, of course." He chuckled and pushed her slightly away from him as if to study her. "Once I explain the situation, he will realize you are a brilliant young man, as well."

"So I am brilliant, am I?" she questioned, smiling up at him and quite pleased with this estimation.

"Well, perhaps not as brilliant as you could be. After all, you did choose a very unsuitable fiancé."

She made a pretense of slapping his arm. "An unsuitable fiancé, indeed! Several, in fact. However, in the end I've been quite a genius at choosing a husband, and there has only been one of those."

He snuggled her up against him again. "Quite true. I will never argue against your wisdom, my dear."

"Then that makes you a bit of a genius, too, sir."

The man was so very clever, in fact, that he knew enough to cease this silly conversation and drag her back into their tent for some far less intellectual discourse. Indeed, he'd been a dreadful fiancé. As for his performance as husband, however, Lord Harry had turned out to be entirely perfect.

Turn the page for a preview
of a new historical romance
by Kate Noble

If I Fall

Coming April 2012 from
Berkley Sensation!

APRIL 1823

It was over.

Everything was all right again.

Sarah closed the door to her bedroom, sinking back against it with an audible sigh of relief. Finally, the horrendous night had ended, and she was safe again.

It wasn't meant to be a particularly taxing evening. After all, it had only been a card party, with supper and some light amusements thereafter, Bridget on the pianoforte. Just close friends, her mother had said. No one there would dare mention . . .

The Event.

And to their credit, no one did. No one would think to do so in the Forresters' own home. But that didn't stop them from staring. And whispering.

Sarah pushed herself off of the door, giving herself the smallest of shakes. "Close friends." What a laughable conceit. When your father is consumed by antiquities, and your mother has one daughter entering her third Season and another daughter her first, the term "close friend" becomes muddied. What Lady Forrester considered a close friend was, apparently, the wife of the man whose personal collection of Roman statuary Lord Forrester was trying to acquire. And said Lady's sons—who happened to have been among the men who danced with Sarah more than once last Season.

Although, that had been before.

She pulled her weary body over to her silly little scrolled dressing table, and sat on the small velvet stool that had always reminded Sarah of nothing so much as a tuffet. Which, of course, was why Sarah had picked it out when she was twelve.

No one should be held accountable for his or her adolescent tastes.

The dressing table was fluffy, if a wooden object could be described as such. There were cherubs, and clouds, and other white-painted rococo touches that made the twenty-one-year-old Sarah certain she had been a slightly ridiculous child.

She took off the pearl drop earrings, the pearl pendant at her throat, placed them aside.

She glanced at her left hand. Now naked. She quickly looked up, moved her gaze back to the fat woodwork of the silly dressing table.

Somehow, today, the silliness was a comfort. Because she could recognize it. It reminded her of herself . . . before. Though as she turned her face to the dressing table's mirror, she could not recognize the face that stared back at her.

It was not twelve.

It was not one-and-twenty.

It was ancient.

The face did not smile. The eyes were hollows of exposure in the moonlight. If she went so far as to light a candle in the dark room, she would see herself, true. She would see the pearl pins in her golden hair; she would see the light green eyes that bespoke her Anglo-Saxon ancestry, and her pale unlined skin that attested to her youth. But the old woman with hollow eyes would still be underneath. Because . . .

Because that's who she truly was now.

A swift knock at the door, and the curt entry of Molly, her maid, snapped Sarah to attention.

"Ah, miss, quite the party tonight!" Molly said, efficiently straightening her cuffs before she approached Sarah and struck a flint to light the candles at the mirror.

"Yes," Sarah said, again painting her face with the serene

smile she had tried to adopt all night. She was certain it had only fallen a few times over the course of the evening, and that she had quickly recovered. "My mother does love to have her *friends* over."

Molly, whose professionalism belied her youth—she couldn't have more than a few years on Sarah herself—hummed a non-committal reply, as she began pulling the pins from Sarah's hair.

But the sweet relief of having her thick straight hair give in to gravity's pull was negated by the truth Sarah knew, and Molly was too smart to say.

"Be honest, Molly." Sarah finally broke the silence that had been filled only by the brush being pulled through her hair. "Tonight was a disaster."

"It was no such thing, miss!" Molly declared, the brush never stopping. "The courses were all served on time. None of the china was cracked. And we could all hear her Ladyship's laughter all the way in the kitchens."

It was true. Her mother's laugh did carry—especially when it was forced.

"I suppose your definition of success differs from mine." Sarah sighed.

"It might at that"—Molly shrugged—"but don't think we didn't see you standing up to dance with that Lord Seton. He seemed a jolly sort."

He seemed the sort to report back the answers to any and all of his probing questions to the nearest gossip columnist, Sarah thought wearily, recalling his pointed questions and his short breath, due to too-tight stays. Worse still, he was the only one to have asked her to dance. Maybe she no longer looked the type to wish for a dance.

Maybe that was one of the times the ancient woman who lived beneath her skin had slipped through the surface.

"Now, would you like to dress for bed, miss?" Molly asked, taking the pearl-headed pins and placing them precisely, in the case next to the matching jewelry. "Your parents are still in the drawing room, having a bit of cold cheese before retiring. Perhaps you'd wish to join them first?"

Sarah saw herself blanche in the mirror. But while the

thought of rehashing the evening with her parents was bad, the idea of lying in bed with nothing to do but rehash the evening to herself was even worse. She needed a distraction.

A warm glass of milk. A lurid novel. Anything that could remove her from herself.

From what they called her in whispers.

"Thank you, Molly, I can see to my dress. The kitchens must need an extra hand this evening."

"You have the right of it, miss." Molly smiled kindly as she curtsied. "Good evening, miss."

"Good night, Molly," Sarah replied distractedly.

A novel. From the library. She could slip down the servants' staircase, and avoid the possibility of her parents hearing her on the main stairs. On the way back up, she could retrieve a glass of warm milk from the kitchens while enjoying the distracting comfort of their bustle and hum.

A novel. That should do the trick.

UNFORTUNATELY, WHILE ONE COULD IN THEORY AVOID the drawing room doors if one were, say, leaving the house, it was impossible to cross to the library without passing said doors.

It was luck that had them closed.

It was bad luck that they were thin enough to hear through.

"It could have gone worse." Sarah heard her father's gruff voice as she tiptoed across the foyer. His usual booming jubilance was countered by a certain reserve. As if he were asking a question instead of knowing his own opinion.

"Not much worse," Sarah heard in a feminine grumble of reply. She would have continued on past the drawing room doors, she would have nodded and smiled curtly to the servants bent over pails to clean as she headed briskly to the library, shutting the door behind her.

She would have done so—except for one thing. The voice that responded to her father had not belonged to her mother. It instead belonged to her sister, Bridget.

"Come now, my dear," Lady Forrester replied this time, the weariness apparent in her voice. "I thought the evening went . . . as smoothly as we could expect."

"Smoothly?" her sister scoffed. Sarah, via some previously unknown gift for subterfuge, silently went to the door and knelt at the jamb, half concealing herself behind a potted plant. She briefly locked eyes with a footman, who was busy dusting footprints from the marble tiles in the foyer. He looked back down again, and quickly resumed his work.

"*Smoothly* would have been if Sarah hadn't looked like she was about to faint the entire time," her sister replied in that lecturing tone she took on when she thought she knew better than everyone else. "*Smoothly* would have been if Rayne's wedding announcement hadn't been printed just yesterday."

Sarah could feel the blood rising to her face. It was silent beyond the doors, Bridget's pronouncement simply hanging in midair for the barest, longest of seconds.

The announcement. God, what horrific timing.

It had been almost four months since that terrible night, when Jason Cummings, the Duke of Rayne, had dashed everyone's hopes and called off their engagement. Shortly thereafter, Lord and Lady Forrester had retired with their daughters for the spare remainder of the Little Season to Primrose Manor, the family seat near Portsmouth. Four months should have been plenty of time for people to forget. For Sarah to forget.

It had been peaceful at Primrose. Comfortable. There, Sarah had room to breathe.

But it was also quiet. And the quiet only let the memories slip in.

As such, she had been determined to return to London for the Season proper. New gowns, new plays, new people. It would be, in her estimation, a fresh start.

She had expected some questions. Some whispers.

But not like this.

It hadn't helped that Jason had been so bloody *good* about the matter! Once the engagement was called off, he told everyone who would listen that absolutely no fault lay at Sarah's door, that she was nothing if not a kind and deserving young lady. And then, blessedly, he left town for an extended stay on the Continent.

But when Jason left London, he left the gossipmongers behind.

The day after they first arrived back, the gossip columns

noted their arrival. Strange, as no one really noted the comings and goings of the Forresters before. They were proper young ladies of good family, of course, but not high ranking enough or scandalous enough to pique a newspaperman's interest. For heaven's sake, her father was president of the boring, stuffy, academic Historical Society. The Forresters could not have been less salacious if they tried.

But there it was. In bold print.

"The Girl Who Lost a Duke Returns to Town."

After that, Sarah avoided the papers.

So she hadn't known about the announcement. Until yesterday, when one of her mother's "friends" told her.

"Oh my dear," Lady Whitford said, coming over to clasp her hands in a show of sympathy early in the morning. Too early, really, to be paying calls. And far too early to be wearing such a ridiculous silk costume of patriotic ribbons across her bodice. But there she was, her round face shining with predatory concern, the feathers from her striped turban flopping into her earnest eyes. "How can you stand it? How can you go on?"

And then she told her. The Duke of Rayne had been married last week in Provence, to noted historian Winnifred Crane. Sarah tried to feel something. Anything. Other than a wistful sort of dread.

Because, while Sarah had been certain that she would be quite able to go on, contrary to Lady Whitford's opinion, it seemed more and more people were just as certain that she wouldn't. She couldn't, they'd said. Enough people repeated the same thing to her with wide, sad eyes, and thus she began to question herself.

Would she be able to go on? Should she even try?

She held out a small hope that something, anything would happen to distract the population. A global catastrophe, a declaration of war, anything. But sadly, the only bit of gossip involved some gentleman who got caught in, and then managed to escape from, Burma—and since most people could not locate Burma on a map, it was not of nearly enough interest to waylay the ogling of the "Girl Who Lost a Duke."

Therefore, the dinner party that Lady Forrester had planned

for weeks, as a casual reintroduction of herself as a hostess, while also easing her daughters into society again, had been a clamorous game of expectations. People had been expecting her to break. To make some sort of comment about the situation.

And the whispers and stares had made her want to do nothing more than oblige them.

To give in to gravity's pull.

Bridget's imperious voice broke the silence from within the drawing room, and broke through Sarah's racing thoughts. "And *smoothly* would have been if anyone had bothered to remember that they were there to meet me, too."

"Bridget!" her mother admonished, shocked.

"It's true, Mother!" Bridget replied, adamant. "Any woman that spoke to me made sure to ask, 'Oh, and how is your sister?'" Bridget's voice took on a quality of mock concern, her pitch eerily like that of Lady Whitford. "And any man who thought to talk to me could barely put two words together, as if they were afraid that I was tainted with the same man-repelling stain!"

"For heaven's sake, Bridget—" her mother tried, but Bridget would not be stopped.

"This was to be *my* Season. How am *I* supposed to catch a husband when Sarah looks like she's going to break into pieces at the idea of a dance?"

"Bridget, that's enough!" her father interrupted. "Such petulance is ugly."

Sarah could have heard a pin drop. Their father usually left the set downs to their mother. If such words from him landed heavily on Sarah all the way through the door, she could only imagine her sister's expression.

"Ugly it may be," Sarah finally heard Bridget say shakily, "but it is the truth. And if you don't do something, we may as well all dye our clothes black to join Sarah in mourning her lack of husband!"

Sarah barely scooted back behind the potted palm in time to avoid the swinging door as her sister made a dramatic exit, unknowingly marching past the object of her fury and up the stairs without a backward glance.

The door slowly creaked closed, a million years passing

before the latch caught. Sarah caught the eye of the scrubbing footman again, but this time, before he looked away, Sarah knew the blush that crept up over his face was a mirror to hers.

The young footman might feel for her, but Sarah was alone in her humiliation. Of all people, Bridget! Of her whole family, Bridget had been the most supportive, the one who had propped her up the most through the winter months in Portsmouth with little to do but watch the ships sail in and out of the harbor. The one who had immediately sworn a lifelong vendetta of hatred against the Duke of Rayne, as all good sisters do. The one who had their trunks packed to come back to London before the decision had even been made.

Foolishly, Sarah had thought she was doing so in support of her. The fact that it was to be Bridget's debut Season had completely slipped her admittedly preoccupied mind. But obviously, it had not slipped Bridget's.

So now, not only was Sarah miserable and wretched, but her mere presence was destroying her sister's Season, too.

Brilliant.

Sarah was so caught up in her own burning frustration, she almost missed her father's voice when it rumbled forth again.

"I received a letter from the Portsmouth steward," he began, his voice hesitant and careful. "He has asked that I return to oversee the installation of the new well. It shouldn't take me more than a few days."

"Darling, I really would prefer if you didn't leave just now." Her mother's voice was honey and lemon—soothing but stern, the way it always sounded when she negotiated for what she wanted. "Or if you must, make it as short as possible. The Season has only just begun, and if Sarah is to endure, she needs the support of the family behind her."

"I was thinking I would take Sarah with me," her father replied, much to Sarah's own surprise. And her mother's, apparently.

"What on earth for?" Lady Forrester asked.

Her father paused a moment before answering.

"I didn't think it would be this bad."

There was a pause, heavy in the air.

"Neither did I," her mother finally said softly. "But we'd hoped . . ."

"Hoped, but not prepared," her father countered.

In her mind's eye, Sarah could see her father. He was likely sitting on the edge of her mother's favorite stuffed settee, looking down at his interlaced fingers, twiddling his thumbs the way he always did when he was thinking.

"I don't know if she's ready for this. I don't know that I am."

Sarah's heart, dampened under layers of her own effort, went out to her father. Outside of herself, he had been the one most hurt by the Event.

Her father had loved Jason. They became acquainted as members of the Historical Society, and Lord Forrester (father of three daughters) had been practically giddy at the idea of not only a son-in-law but also one with whom he could converse for hours and hours about antique pediments and arcane painting techniques.

"Oh my darling." Her mother's voice came through the thin door, placating her husband. "Maybe we can find a way to take Sarah's—and your—mind off the troubles."

"I would have him removed from the Historical Society if I could," her father stated, his voice muffled by what Sarah had to assume was her mother's shoulder. "But I cannot allow personal feeling to belie—"

"I know, I know," she soothed. "But for now, let us be thankful that Rayne had the good grace to remove himself to the Continent. And let us hope he—"

And that was the point that Sarah decided she had heard enough.

Because as hard as it was to think and hear about her parents' disappointments in her—it was infinitely more difficult to dwell on the Duke of Rayne, where he was, and what he was doing.

She stood up abruptly, and crossed the foyer as fast as her feet would carry her to the library, without concern that her footfalls were too loud or rapid to be mistaken for a servant's. Without care for the eyes of the footman following her. And without any idea for whom she would meet inside the library's doors.

"Oh my God!" Sarah cried, coming to a sudden halt.

"I'm afraid not, Miss Forrester," the elegant figure that lounged with a volume of poetry in her hand said. "It's just me."

"L-Lady Worth," Sarah breathed, as breeding won out over shock and she curtsied. Phillippa, Lady Worth, the unofficial but undeniable reigning leader of the ton, did not smile and stand in return. Instead, she flipped the book shut and regarded Sarah with a bemused expression.

"Oh, so you do know who I am. I was beginning to wonder if you remembered me at all from last Season."

"Lady Worth, of course I remember you," Sarah replied, blushing to the roots of her hair. "I attended your garden party last year, and of course you were at . . ." *my engagement party*, she stopped herself from staying. Instead she shook herself. "I apologize, let me fetch my parents. It is quite odd hours for calling, but—"

"Yes, I am aware it is quite odd hours for calling," Lady Worth replied as she stood to her full height. She was dressed in easily the most beautiful evening gown Sarah had ever seen, but to Lady Worth, it was likely just her Tuesday ensemble. "Your butler may seem stern, but entry was fairly simple. I just told him I had been here for your supper party, and had left a reticule behind. He allowed me to search on my own." Lady Worth suddenly frowned. "I am going to recommend to your mother that you reinforce the need for security with your staff. After all, I could have been a thief—or worse yet, a reporter."

"My mother," Sarah repeated, latching onto a solid form throughout Lady Worth's bewildering speech. "Yes, allow me to fetch her, she's just across the hall . . ."

"Never mind that." Lady Worth waved her hand in dismissal of the idea. "I have come here to see you."

"Me?" Sarah squeaked.

"Yes, child. For heaven's sake, when did you become such a mimic? Last Season you seemed to have more brains that that."

Sarah, not having an answer to that, prudently remained silent.

"How long have you been in town, Miss Forrester?" Lady Worth asked, as nonchalant as if she had asked the question in full daylight in a room full of society ladies.

"A fortnight, ma'am," Sarah answered, her eyes following Lady Worth as she gently paced the carpet.

"And in that fortnight, how many invitations have you received from me?"

"Ah . . . I am uncertain . . ." Sarah hedged.

"Lucky for you, I am entirely certain. Two. You have received two invitations from me to come to tea. I know this because I rarely ask anything of anyone more than once."

"Oh," she replied, knowing she sounded stupid and out of her depth . . . because in truth, she was. "I think, ma'am"—she tried valiantly—"that my mother thought—that is, she didn't want us to accept any invitations until after we had settled . . ."

But at that, Lady Worth stopped pacing, and simply stood with her hands on her hips. "I have always preferred the truth to pretty lies, my dear. But if you insist upon continuing with that sentence at least speak it with conviction."

Sarah's head came up sharply. She met the challenge in the taller lady's eyes. And decided to rise to it.

"How could I visit with you, Lady Worth, when your family is connected to Jason's?"

Sarah had thought to shock Phillippa Worth. And she had. But not for the reasons she had imagined. Because while she read surprise in that lady's eyes, she also recognized not horror, but applause.

"Yes, my husband's brother is married to the Duke of Rayne's sister." Lady Worth waved her hand in the air again, seemingly waving away anything that she did not consider important. "But that is exactly why you *should* have accepted my invitation."

"Lady Worth, I . . ." Sarah tried, but suddenly, she felt very tired. The weight of the party, overhearing her parents and sister's conversation, and now the mad assault on logic and propriety that was Lady Worth being in her library, settled over Sarah and she could no longer stop her shoulders from slumping.

"Do you mind if I sit down?" she asked, already half seated on the settee.

Lady Worth, to her credit, immediately sat down with Sarah, and in what she must have thought was a sympathetic gesture, patted Sarah's hand.

"Would you like me to call for some tea? Or perhaps sherry?" Lady Worth inquired kindly.

Sarah let out a small, exhausted laugh. "Lady Worth, we are in my house. I should be offering tea to you."

"Oh," she replied, with a smile. "I nearly forgot. And I think this will be simpler if you take to calling me Phillippa, and I, you, Sarah."

"What will be simpler?" Sarah asked, hoping to finally understand . . . anything.

Lady Worth—Phillippa—regarded her quietly for a moment.

"It's too early in the Season for you to be this tired," she finally observed.

Sarah thought about denying it, thought about making excuses . . . but somehow, she couldn't fight it any longer. She couldn't pretend to be even and fine. The only thing left to do was admit her failings.

To give in to gravity's pull.

"I don't know what to do," Sarah admitted. "Tonight, we had our first party—my mother was so excited to be a hostess again, and it's my sister's first Season, and it was just—"

"Terrible," Phillippa supplied. At Sarah's questioning look, Phillippa smiled in bemusement. "Really, you should simply assume that I know everything already. It saves time."

"Yes, but how—"

"At least three of your evening's attendees were at the Newlins' ball after your fete. Interestingly, no fewer than five people fought through the crush to rush to my side and let me know—as the only connection to the Duke of Rayne in town—just how unfortunate your supper party was."

Sarah started rubbing one of her temples. "Wonderful. Everyone will know."

"Oh, I'd expect that it will be in the papers tomorrow."

"So all of London thinks I'm a fragile mourner for a missing Duke."

"Where did you find that description?" Phillippa peered at her intensely.

"My . . ." Not wanting to implicate her sister, Sarah changed tack. "I feel like I'm disappointing my family, most of all. And I don't know what I could do differently. I smile, and everyone thinks I'm covering my feelings. I frown, and everyone thinks I'm about to break down and cry. I don't know how to act under such scrutiny. I wish I could just go back to being one of a thousand girls. And not—"

" 'The Girl Who Lost a Duke'?" Phillippa finished for her.

Sarah nodded, then turned her gaze to her hands. "My father . . . I think he's planning to go back to Portsmouth soon, and perhaps it would be easier—"

"Don't you dare," Phillippa intoned severely, her expression suddenly focused and serious. "Now you listen to me—first of all, do not concern yourself with how your family feels right now. I know it is curious advice, but you have been a dutiful daughter for your entire life. You have never given them reason to be disappointed in you, so do not let them make you feel as such now. Nor should you let the world make you feel as if you are somehow damaged goods. You are no such thing. In fact, when one takes a thorough accounting of your actions, one can only conclude that you have not only done no wrong, you have, in fact, done everything right."

"Exactly!" Sarah cried. "I did everything right. *Everything.* I got top marks from every teacher I had, I learned to play the pianoforte—a little—to sew, to speak French and Latin. I came to London, and only accepted dances from men my mother approved of. And then I met a man who was supposed to be the one I would spend the rest of my life with and I . . ." Her voice broke, an echo of the seam that still sat along her heart. "I did everything right. And somehow, I still lost."

"You lost a battle," Phillippa agreed. "But the war is long. And the enemy . . . changeable."

"What do you mean?" Sarah asked.

"Public perception," she said with a smile, "is a tricky thing. The world looks at you now as 'The Girl Who Lost a Duke.' You have to change that. Else, no amount of time spent in Portsmouth is going to kill that idea here. In fact, as more time passes, it will be cemented as such. *You* have to make the world stop looking at you with pity."

"How?"

"First of all, stop looking at yourself with pity. Tell yourself a hundred times a day that it was Jason's loss, not yours, in ending the engagement. Even if you don't believe it." Phillippa gripped Sarah's hand. "Then, you take London by storm. Be charming, vivacious. Just this side of outrageous. Flirt with appropriate men and dance with inappropriate ones. Be the person every hostess absolutely must have at her party. Put on a mask and save your true feelings for when you are in private. Soon enough, all of London will have forgotten the 'Girl Who Lost a Duke,' and instead think the Duke of Rayne utterly mad for having let you escape."

"I . . . I don't know if I can do all that," Sarah replied breathlessly.

"*You have to.* It is how you survive." Phillippa's face suddenly shuttered with old memories. "It is how I did."

Sarah looked at the hand gripping hers. Then, she ran her gaze up the elegant dress and stature of the queen of society sitting in her library. But for once, it was not the extravagant dress or the beautiful jewels at her throat that Sarah envied. It was her posture. Her conviction. Her strength. Phillippa Worth was everything a young lady aspired to be. And she knew it.

"How do I begin?" Sarah asked.

Phillippa's eyes lit with anticipation. "We already have."